Westburn Blues

Westburn Blues

Jim Ellis

Copyright (C) 2018 Jim Ellis
Layout design and Copyright (C) 2018 Creativia
Published 2018 by Creativia
Cover art by Cover Mint
This book is a work of fiction. Names, characters, places, and incidents are the product of the author's imagination or are used fictitiously. Any resemblance to actual events, locales, or persons, living or dead, is purely coincidental.
All rights reserved. No part of this book may be reproduced or transmitted in any form or by any means, electronic or mechanical, including photocopying, recording, or by any information storage and retrieval system, without the author's permission.

Acknowledgements

Thanks to Cynthia Weiner, for her support and encouragement; and a warm thank you to Heidi Smith and Ethan James Clarke, Silver Jay Editing for their editing guidance and proofreading. A special thank you to my Good Lady, Jeannette.

Thanks to John Curran, Duncan Cameron and Teddy Hunter who put me in touch with local Scots-Italians. To Captain Roy Smith, formerly of Clan Line for seaboard life. And to Clive Service for restaurant and kitchen lore.

I'd like to thank the Scots-Italians who shared their family stories: Elsa Acerini; Mario Bacchi; Dante Biogoni; Vincent Caira; Luigi Guisti; Tony Matteo; Ciano Rebecchi; Aldo Spella; Roland Toma; Doris and Sandro Vanni.

For my friends Cello Toma, Joe Rossi and Hugh Church.

Chapter One

"Dante, go to soldier. In dugout behind cow shed," Old Mario said.

"A soldier?"

"Talk. He is British, from Scotland."

Mario gave Dante food wrapped in a clean dish towel, a jug of milk. "Agate milked the cow," he said, and handed Dante a flask of his own red wine. "Feed him."

Sergeant Alfred Forte, Seaforth Highlanders, came from Kempock, the small town next to Westburn. In July, Germans had captured Fred in Sicily and transferred him to Italian custody to a POW camp near Rome.

Italy signed an armistice with the Allies in September 1943, taking her forces out of the war. The guards had vanished, and Fred had walked out of the camp. He'd no desire to be taken again by German forces occupying Italy and sent to a POW camp in Germany.

Dante and Fred weighed each other up. Fred wore ancient countryman's work clothes, a stout navy cotton jacket and grey cotton trousers, a black beret placed straight on his head—kit given him by friendly Italians when he went on the run and passed from hand to hand, sending him on to Liguira and Garbugliago. His broken footwear, with a dirty sock protruding from the cracked upper of the left boot and a gap between the sole and the upper of the right, told of his long hike, two hundred miles through the Apennines to his father's village.

The time in captivity had affected Fred, sapping his self-confidence, making him wary, afraid of recapture. The long walk up the Italian Peninsula, often navigating by night, had reduced him to skin and bone, draining the fighting spirit right out of him. In the flickering light of a candle made by Old Mario from sheep fat, a dishevelled, gaunt man, not yet twenty-five, stared at Dante. Fred cowered at the back of the dugout, holding a thick wooden shaft, trying to merge with the bales of straw, rough wooden plough, firewood pollarded from olive and chestnut trees, scythes, spades, hoes, a thresher, flails, rakes.

Dante, sixteen, was dressed in the torn remains of a velvet suit jacket bought by his grandmother before wartime rationing bit, the sleeves finishing above his wrists, over a soiled blue shirt. Ragged velvet trousers hung at half-mast above rough-worn peasant's boots, repaired more than once by Old Mario, and now finally with wooden soles, shoe leather being impossible to find at this stage in the war. He shuffled under Fred's vacant gaze, glad that the foreigner couldn't see the holes in his socks.

"That stick in your hand," Dante said. "Put it down."

He said it again in English.

"Sorry," Fred said.

Dante laid the food and drink on a roughhewn table. He pulled a stool and a bucket to the table.

"Sit down," Dante said, pointing to the stool, and sat on the upturned bucket. Dung smell wafted in from the byre, but Fred was too hungry to notice.

Fred drank the milk in two gulps straight from the jug. He wiped his mouth with a soiled handkerchief, then rubbed his hands, took the clasp knife from Dante's hand, cut two thick slices from Agate's round loaf, piled hard cheese shavings on the bread, laid translucent wafers of cured ham over the cheese, and wolfed it down. He cut a slice of polenta into squares and popped them into his mouth, one after the other.

"Delicious," Fred said. He took a long pull from the flask of Mario's sour red wine, then swallowed more. "Been a while since I had wine."

"The ham," Dante said, "is from wild boar. My grandfather shot one a while back; cured it himself in the stagionatura. He kept quiet about it. If the Fascists knew, they'd stop our meat ration."

They spoke Italian. Dante held out his hand.

"I'm Dante Rinaldi. I'm from Westburn." They shook hands.

"Alfredo Forte, from Kempock; call me Fred. My dad's Italian, and my mum's Scots; born in Kempock. But he's British; had a passport since they married."

"How long have you been on the run?"

"About six weeks."

He told Dante about his escape and the Italians who'd helped him along the way. "I'd never have made it without them. Makes me proud to be a Scots-Italian. I came here; it's where my family came from. I might try to get to Switzerland."

When the Italian soldiers abandoned Passo Corese near Rome, there were 4,000 POWs; too many for a successful escape. With his Italian looks and fluent Italian, Fred reckoned he'd a better chance of getting away. He approached his C.O.; told him he had relatives in Liguria, living in Garbugliago, a village in the hills behind La Spezia and the Cinque Terra, who were bound to assist him to the Swiss border. The C.O. gave permission.

A friendly Italian soldier, a camp guard heading for home, gave Fred a school atlas.

"Leave before Germans come," he said.

Fred exited the camp wearing his shabby battle dress that identified him as an escaped POW. He'd have to get rid of it. Navigating the Apennines running the length of the peninsula would be hard, but safer. He carried his few belongings in a sack with cloth shoulder straps cut from an abandoned shirt and sewn on with his service housewiff. Peasants who saw Fred, a soldier hiding from Germans and Fascists, pass while working their small holdings, fed and sheltered him. One family—the father had worked in Scotland—gave him work clothes, and he got rid of his British Army battle dress. Fred passed for Italian. A family of charcoal burners advised him to watch out for the hard fit men of the Guarde Forestale who might take him prisoner. Fred, ever on the alert, ignored the natural beauty of the mountains travelling northwest to Garbugliago.

"You look Italian; speak good Italian," Dante said. "That must have helped."

"It did. What about you? How did you end up here?"

"My grandparents had come back to Italy by the time I was born," Dante said.

Old Mario and Agate had sold up in Westburn in 1925 and returned to Garbugliago. Agate melded with her village and never returned to Scotland, though she wrote often to her son, Luigi.

Dante's grandfather came back from Italy to Westburn in December 1938; his first visit since he had returned to Garbugliago. Old Mario intended taking his only grandson to Italy for several months to attend school, to spend the summer on the family small holding, and to become Italian.

Going back to Italy returned Mario Rinaldi to his peasant roots: his pale Westburn face retreated, and the Ligurian sun transformed his complexion to the colour of the family's polished mahogany table. Like the treasured, well-used furniture, his face showed signs of wear: the lined forehead; deep gashes on either side of his mouth that vanished into a full and luxuriant moustache with waxed, pointed ends. A sombre countenance under his habitual flat cap, a meagre dewlap, a thin fold of skin on his jaw, mouth working in small movements chewing and smoking twisted black stogies, thumbs hooked in waistcoat pockets, he might have passed for a rural Mafioso. Past seventy,

Old Mario, a lean, muscular countryman, was strong as the mature chestnut trees bordering his small farm.

"I thought my grandfather was wonderful when I met him. He had a silver tongue."

The twelve-year-old Dante had loved the stories about life on the farm: hunting wild boar, rabbit and hare; shooting birds; harvesting olives; picking grapes; milking the family's only cow; moving the handful of goats to fresh pastures; and Old Mario making and drinking grappa and wine.

Dante's parents did not want him marooned in Italy if war broke out. But Dante, full of boyish enthusiasm, pleaded, begged his parents to let him go.

"Only for summer holidays, Celestina," Luigi said, always deferential to his father. So Dante went to Italy, but on condition that he return in August to Westburn for the new school term.

"My first time away from home and I never slept the night before we left," Dante said. "In the mornin' I was goin' crazy wi' excitement."

Dante and his grandfather left Westburn for Italy in January 1939. They spent four days on the train, crossing into Italy from France. Old Mario waved his passport.

"British and Germans, go to war," he said. "Mussolini strong. Il Duce is clever, he join Germany. British lose war."

Dante kept his British passport hidden in a linen pouch under his shirt.

"Old Mario, back then before the war, he was dead keen on Mussolini," Dante said. "The war and the German Army cured him. I had no idea how much my life would change, an' no' for the better."

Depressed and hungry from the wartime rationing, missing his family, Dante dwelt on the happy times in Westburn before the war.

"I never realised how much I liked Westburn. Someday, Ah hope I'll get home to my mum an' Graziella, my big sister."

"What stopped you going home?" Fred asked.

In 1939, the British and French armies faced the German Army on the Siegfried Line. Skirmishes along the front and dogfights above the lines disturbed the calm of the "Phoney War." By sea, the U-Boats attacked Allied ships: at the beginning of September, the U-30 torpedoed and sank SS Athenia with the loss of 98 lives. Two weeks later, the U-29 torpedoed and sank the carrier HMS Courageous. The family refused to risk Dante's life bringing him home by ship. Obtaining permission to leave Italy and travel overland into a war zone was not easy.

"Safer to stay here," Dante said. "Then Italy declared war, and it was too late."

"Bad, that was bad," Fred said.

Poor grieving Dante could not understand why his country had made his father a prisoner for being an Italian. A man who'd fought on the Allied side against the Germans and Austrians in the Great War, surviving the horrors of the White War on the Dolomites, was wounded on the Piave. Dribs and drabs of worrisome news reached Garbugliago. Then, late in 1940, the letter from the Red Cross arrived telling him that his father had drowned when the Arandora Star went down a hundred and twenty-five miles west of Ireland. Old Mario and Agate mourned for their son, and they wept for their distraught grandson. Dante felt the British and the Germans murdered his dad. He raged for months afterwards, and he cursed the war, the British, the Germans, and Mussolini.

"My dad's dead; killed on that boat, the Arandora Star." He wiped his eyes with his sleeve. Fred laid a hand on Dante's shoulder. He had much to tell Dante about the sinking of the ship, but not yet.

"God forgive me," Dante said, "but when I thought about my dad, an' the disaster at Dunkirk, the Germans thumpin' us, the British an' the last of the French taken off the beaches on boats, I said the British had it comin'."

"It's all right, son. I understand. Mum and Dad know your family," Fred said. "Funny we never met; but then I'm older." He wanted to cheer Dante up. "My dad used to take me to the Italian grocers in West Stewart Street. Did you ever go there?"

"Sometimes, for a treat," Dante said. "I loved it."

The Italian grocery in West Stewart Street, owned by a man from Garbugliago, had always been packed with a bounty of Italian delights: pasta, cured hams, rich-smelling cheeses, and the wine that the men drank when they played cards in the back shop reserved for the men. They played Scopa, a Neapolitan card game. Luigi took Dante among the men for almond biscuits, a cup of drinking chocolate, a spoonful of sweet jam or a dainty glazed fruit.

"I was there when the cops raided the shop," Dante said. "They scared me. There was a right commotion."

"That was in 1938," Fred said.

"Yes."

The police entered the shop looking for Fascists and Italian propaganda. All they found were old editions of Italian newspapers: Il Secolo, published in Genoa; La Nazione, the La Spezia daily. Near the wine racks they found bottles of Val Polcevera, Colli di Luni del Tugullio, and Riviera Ligure di Ponenti Golfo wrapped in ancient broadsheets of La Stampa and Corriera della Sera. They left the wine and removed the newsprint.

Most Italians in Scotland took little interest in politics in the homeland; they were glad to have done well and planned to stay in Scotland. But the British popular press described them as traitors. Some families recently arrived, sent wives and children back to Italy. The men stayed working. Italians worried more but carried on.

Fred handed the flask to Dante, who swallowed a mouthful or two of the red wine. He thought the boy might benefit from talking about his Westburn memories; and he could do with cheering up himself.

"Your grandfather told me he'd lived and worked in Westburn for many years."

"That's right. My grandparents came over in the 1890s, but they came back here to Garbugliago before I was born. I first met Old Mario in 1938."

* * *

In 1895 Dante's grandfather, and his new wife, Agate, six months pregnant, took to the road, leaving Italy to escape poverty and make a better life through hard work and thrift. The idea of Scotland, a faraway land of sea lochs and mountains on the West Coast, drew them. They came from Garbugliago. Mario and his wife walked most of the way, he taking casual work on farms and building sites, she seeking domestic work, cleaning, washing and ironing clothes to earn enough for the next stage of the journey north.

Three months after setting out, Mario and Agate arrived in Ostend. Luigi, their only son, was born, and they stayed several weeks.

"My dad was born in Belgium," Dante said. "Old Mario made sure he was an Italian citizen." Mario registered Luigi's birth with the Italian Consul in Brussels.

They took ship across the English Channel from Ostend to Dover. A moderate roughness of funds allowed them to travel third class by train from Dover to Carlisle where the surplus cash ran out. With enough money left to feed themselves, the Rinaldis walked across the border to Scotland. They liked the shore and the sea views as they travelled north along the West Coast. From the day they arrived on the outskirts, having passed through Kempock, Mario felt the tug of Westburn. Its natural beauty, the blue skies, the sweeping panorama of mountains and the river, delighted him. Mario decided to establish roots. Agate, weary and footsore, offered prayers of thanks for deliverance to San Giuseppe, Patron Saint of La Spezia.

A handful of Italian families had settled in Westburn. There was room for the Rinaldis, and Mario found employment.

The Rinaldis saved hard. In 1897, Mario rented premises near Cappelow park, home of Morton, football club. He opened Rinaldi's Café in Wee Dublin, the Irish quarter.

Mario, established in business, wrote to his relatives and friends telling them of his success. They followed him: a trickle of close-knit families bound by blood and hardship, settling among the Scots and the Irish, a connection between Westburn and Garbugliago that flourished into the twentieth century.

The café prospered, and in 1904 Mario sold the business in the East End to a distant cousin from Garbugliago. He moved to the edge of the West End, buying a tenement flat in Campbell Street, entered through a tiled close. He opened a posh café in Grey Place a few minutes' walk from his new house. By 1910, Rinaldi's Café had become a Westburn institution, popular with the genteel citizens.

"My family found Scotland strange when they arrived," Fred said.

"So did my grandparents," Dante said.

The Westburn Scots accepted the Italians as shopmen, recent arrivals, peasants who minded their own business, but they did not love them. They remained Italians with strange ways: talking foreign, reeking of garlic, eating outlandish food like fidelini and trenette, noodle lasagna made from chestnut flour, everything smothered in olive oil and funny-looking sauces.

"White worms and wee beasties covered wi' the boak," one citizen of Westburn said.

Dante's father, Luigi, had a happy childhood in Westburn. He spent the last year of school at St Mary's, opened in 1909, built with monies donated by Scots-Irish Catholics. Mario Rinaldi gave what he could afford.

Luigi Rinaldi was proud of his fluent Italian, but thought that he belonged to Scotland; he spoke English with a Westburn accent.

"They had some terrible barneys wi' the Irish," Dante said.

Fred nodded. "I heard about that."

To the impoverished Irish, recent arrivals shunned by Presbyterians, the Italians were outsiders lower than themselves in the pecking order.

Agate clad Luigi for the winter, a self-conscious adolescent attending St Mary's in his Italian clothes: sturdy warm coat; long, woollen socks below his Nicky Tams and ankle boots; woollen scarf; and a large, flat, worsted cap.

"That's some fuckin' bunnet," a bareheaded and threadbare Scots-Irish boy from the Vennel said one chilly morning.

Two Scots-Irish attacked Luigi, a better dressed and better off, but just Eyetie shite.

Luigi fought back, hammering one of his attackers. Brother Michael, the Irish assistant headmaster, pulled the boys apart, boxing ears, cuffing them. He lined them up and gave each of them six of the best with his well-used Loch Gelly tawse. Luigi and his tormentors nursed aching palms and blood-blistered wrists as they sat in class.

When Luigi got home, his mother's fingers fluttered above his injured eye, touched his split lip. She swallowed her tears as she applied a cold compress to Luigi's bruised face and swollen eye; dabbed iodine on his split lip. Agate held her son's battered hands. Her intake of breath whistled in Luigi's ears when she looked at the clusters of blood blisters and red lines erupting on the inside of Luigi's wrists.

"Mario look. This Brother Michael is barbaro. Insult family."

"Si," Luigi said. "Egli è merda."

Agate told Mario to go to Brother Michael and tell him he must never beat their son again. Mario said no; he did not want a reputation as a troublesome foreigner. Agate defied her husband, and next day kept Luigi from school. Dressed in her Sunday clothes with hat and gloves, Agate slipped through the staff entrance of St Mary's and knocked on the door of the Brother's office.

The Brother, a haughty man, sat back in his chair and glowered across his desk at the Italian woman. Sure, hadn't he studied the Faith and been educated for teaching at the Irish College in Rome? He would deal with her.

"And who might you be?" he demanded.

"Mrs Rinaldi. Yesterday boys attack Luigi. You beat my son like animal. I keep him home. Never you do again."

Brother Michael paused, sipped tea from the cup resting in the saucer on his desk, then raised weary eyes to the ceiling. His long sigh fractured the silence.

"I punished Rinaldi for fighting. If he misbehaves, I'll thrash him again."

Agate pulled off her shoe, and balanced on tip-toe and shod foot, waved the sharp heel in his face.

"Stronzo!"

Brother Michael's jaw dropped. She had called him an arsehole.

"Get out of my office and don't come back."

"Vaffanculo!"

Sweet Jesus; now she'd told him to fuck off.

Agate drove the heel of her shoe into the cup and saucer. Tea spilled on the desk and splashed onto the Brother's trousers; shards of broken china crashed to the floor.

"Luigi no come back. I take him to Protestant school. Husband, he go to Bishop; make troubles. Then he come for you."

Brother Michael's superior would ream him out if he heard of the incident. The Brother's stomach heaved, terrified that Mario Rinaldi would black his eye; or worse, knock out his front teeth.

"Now, now, Mrs Rinaldi, we can't have that. Sure it'll do Luigi no good at all putting him among Protestants. If Luigi promises to behave, everything will be all right."

"Luigi is good boy. No need promise." Agate placed her shoe on the floor and slipped it on. She fixed Brother Michael with an icy stare, turned and left the office.

"He was a right bastard that Brother Michael," Fred said. "An Irish nutter. He was headmaster in St Mary's when I was there; beat the Hell out of me a couple of times. The boys'll thank God he's retired and gone back to Ireland."

Dante handed the flask to Fred.

"There's wine left. Finish it."

"Thanks, son. Are you not tired?"

"Not me; I'd like to speak English now. It's been a long time."

Fred said Okay. He liked Dante; a level-headed youth.

"Have you any idea how long I might be here?"

"Maybe a few days. When it's safe Ah'll be takin' you further up the mountain to Decimo, a hamlet, to hand you on to the Widow Murro. She'll hide you. There's Catholic partisans up there. After that, Ah don't know, an' it's better Ah don't know."

Fred shook his head. Dante laughed.

"Don't worry, Fred. Ah've taken a couple of shot-down pilots up the mountain; one American and one British. Ah didn't need any help. Ah heard they got away."

"Good, son. I'm in your hands. Tell your grandparents thanks for the food and wine. You'll come tomorrow?"

"Ah'll come in the evening with food and wine. You'll have to make what's left of the bread and cheese last until then. You've got water?"

"I've enough. I'll see you tomorrow. Good night, Dante."

"Good night, Fred. Give me your boots. Ah'll ask ma grandfather to repair them. Ah enjoyed talkin' to you."

The next evening, Dante came to the dugout.

"Only chestnuts, a handful of mushrooms and stale bread," he said. "The ham's finished. Plenty of wine. Ma grandfather likes his wine." He handed the food and the wine flask to Fred. Dante dug into the pocket of his ragged velvet jacket and produced a small bottle. "Grappa, made by ma grandfather."

"That's good, son, thanks." Fred drank the grappa. "Ah, strong stuff." Fred wiped his lips with the back of his hand. "What was it like when you came here?"

"The first few months," Dante said, "Ah loved hunting, helping on the farm. Ah could speak Italian like as if Ah was born here. Ah went to school; like primary school. It got iffy after the war started."

The late winter and spring of 1939 in Garbugliago made Dante proud of his Italian heritage, but Old Mario flirted with Fascism; he enrolled Dante in the Avanguardista. The Fascists in Garbugliago had the people worked up when Mussolini declared war on the 10th of June 1940.

"Wear uniform today," he said.

"Ah don't want to," Dante said. "Ah hate it."

Mario raised his hand to the boy, threatening to cuff him, and with Agate nodding approval, Dante changed into the black shirt, grey-green knee-length trousers and long socks. Mario completed his grandson's humiliation by placing a tasseled black fez at a jaunty angle on Dante's head.

"Arditi cap, worn by Italian storm troops," he said. "When you are fourteen you join Figli Della Lupa; Sons of the She Wolf."

They walked to the village, and Dante joined the detachment of Avanguardista marching in the square. Villagers, encouraged by local Fascists, cheered them.

Later, Mario took Dante, still wearing the Avanguardista uniform, to a place in the hills. Through binoculars they watched troops moving west along minor roads. Back in Garbugliago, rumours had spread of armoured cars on the streets of La Spezia.

Dante did not share his grandfather's excitement.

"Ah want to go home to ma Mum and Dad, and Graziella," he told Old Mario, who just shook his head. Dante cried himself to sleep.

"For a while the war unsettled me," Dante told Fred in the dugout.

Refugees from towns and villages near the front came to Garbugliago and nearby villages looking for a place to stay. Some people let rooms to these poor souls at exorbitant rents.

Dante asked Mario if they'd be having lodgers. Mario shook his head.

"No, but we help when we can. What they do to the refugees is wrong."

The uncertainty hanging over Garbugliago during the early months of the war perplexed Dante. It was far from clear how the war would turn out; no one knew how it might end. Dante felt loyal to Italy. But he was a patriotic Scots-Italian true to Great Britain, and a frightened wee boy worried about his family back in Westburn.

He loathed the blackout. The laughter of young men and girls of the village hiding in the shadows scared him. Rumours swept through the mountains. Peasants who'd never been farther than La Spezia or Genoa terrified themselves, spreading stories of saboteurs guiding enemy bombers to targets.

Late in 1940, Italian forces suffered reverses in the Mediterranean, Ethiopia, the western desert, the Battle of Britain. But village families, decent folk, sympathised with Dante's plight, and were kind to him. He made friends at school.

Hardship crept in as the war went on. Schoolchildren gathered waste newsprint and paper to send to the Italian Army fighting with the German Army in Russia. The soldiers stuffed the paper inside their uniforms. Paper insulation was feeble protection against the Russian winter.

One morning in class, the teacher, a Fascist, pointed to Dante, "Inglesaccio; you are English bastard."

"Ah'm no' English," Dante said. "Ah'm British, and Ah'm a Scots-Italian."

The teacher boxed Dante's ears for impertinence. He went home for the midday meal, and refused to go back to school. Old Mario examined Dante's bruised ears, took off his neckerchief and wiped away the tear stains on his grandson's face. His belief in Fascism had taken a knock. Later, three years of war and an occupying German Army killed off any lingering enthusiasm for Mussolini and his German allies.

Mario decided to act, unlike the time in Scotland when the assistant headmaster beat his son Luigi and he'd wanted to avoid trouble. Now he was home, in Italy.

"Come," he said, and took Dante's hand. At the school gate, Mario watched a teacher supervise the assembly of pupils. "Is that him?"

"Yes," Dante said.

Old Mario strode into the schoolyard, Dante trailing behind. He grabbed the teacher by the lapels and pulled him up on to his toes.

"Apologise, or I'll break your bones." He waved a finger at the teacher. "Be quiet. Get the police or your Fascist friends, and I'll come for you. Now apologise to my grandson." Mario pushed the teacher's face down, level with Dante's head.

"I'm sorry," the teacher said.

"Now, Dante," Old Mario said. "You go to class."

After he turned thirteen, Dante left school to work on the farm, helping Mario and Agate live off the land as shortages spread. And with the war going against Italy, he didn't join Figli Della Lupa, Sons of the She Wolf. Day by day, the war affected Garbugliago. Eleven local men died in Russia; another was killed at El Alamein. A survivor said of the battle that the Germans deserted the Italians, leaving them to the mercy of the British Army.

"At times Ah didn't know whether Ah was comin' or goin'. One minute Ah was loyal to Italy; five minutes later I wanted to cheer the British. Ma friends here grieved for the dead, the wounded, and for the thousands of Italian prisoners of war."

Dante grieved with them. He'd cheered when the Italians sank the old battleship, HMS Barham. And he celebrated the successes of the Decima Flottiglia attacking Allied shipping in the Mediterranean.

"Ah'm tellin' you, Fred; now Ah'm glad the British are winning."

An awkward silence after the talk about life in Italy, and the war. A marching song popular with the Avanguardista celebrating the conquest of Abyssinia filled Dante's head; he hummed the tune as Fred devoured the last of the food.

"The tune," Fred said, "I heard it back when I was on holiday in La Spezia before the war."

"Fachetto Nero Del Abbesine," Dante said. "A boy from Westburn, just back from Italy before war broke out, sang it one Saturday in the Italian school."

Later that day, Dante sang it, and quite out of character, his father erupted.

"Be quiet," he said, and cuffed Dante hard, boxing his ears and pushing his frightened son into a chair. Graziella, terrified, collapsed in tears.

"Shut up," Luigi said. "Shame on you, singing of a bad war. What the Fascists do in Africa is terrible; a stain on Italy."

Luigi pushed Celestina aside as she came into the living room, drawn by the commotion. In the hall he dried his eyes, then bolted the bathroom door, horrified at what he'd done. He washed his face, composed himself, and disgusted, left early for the shop.

Celestina sat on the settee.

"Come," she said to her children, opening her arms, and they sat on either side of her. "Your singing, Dante; the song upset your father. He is a good man, and he loves you both with all his heart. In the White War, terrible things happened; your father suffered. That's why he doesn't go back to Italy, and he worries about us."

Luigi walked to the shop, head down, ashamed of himself and concerned about Il Duce and the creeping influence of Fascism on the Scots-Italians. He worried about their vulnerability since the 1920 Aliens Order, placing his people under police surveillance, punished by deportation if they broke the law.

Long before Italy invaded Abyssinia, the Italian government spent money on Italians abroad: dining clubs for Scots-Italians, sporting events, Italian holidays for children. Luigi suspected that these stratagems legitimised the regime and indoctrinated children.

"No good will come of Mussolini's meddling," Luigi muttered as he walked.

He would have nothing to do with events organised by Fascists—the fools who called Il Duce "the Messiah" who'd saved Italia from civil war.

Proud to be Scots and Italian, a volunteer for the Alpini, fighting by the side of the British and the French, Luigi had no desire to relive the fighting on the Izsonso. When Luigi heard of former Italian soldiers parading in uniform with Scots ex-servicemen, having foregone the regular olive green shirts of combat veterans for the black shirts of Fascism, he shook his head in disgust.

Some Scots-Italians yearned for their home villages and relatives. Luigi, proud of his Italian heritage but born in Belgium, and grown to manhood in Scotland, resisted the emotional pull of Italia. True, he had extended family in Liguria, and had spent brief furloughs from the front with them.

Luigi did not know the sunny uplands of Italy: the rhythms of the seasons, of sowing and harvesting, the beauty and vibrancy of the cities. He soldiered; an Alpini, for three years at the hell of the front.

After the war, married and settled down with Celestina in Westburn, Luigi often attended the Armistice Day service at Westburn Cenotaph, mourning alone for all the young men who had suffered and died in those terrible years.

He had to tell someone about the war; someone he trusted. When Luigi chose her, Celestina knew that he loved her.

In 1915 when Italy entered the Great War on the Allied side, Luigi, an Italian citizen, went to Italy and volunteered for the Alpini, elite mountain troops. By 1918, Luigi wanted an end to the fighting and the killing. Across No Man's Land, Austrians, Hungarians and Germans felt the same. One day, while attacking the Austrian lines, the machine guns and the rifles stopped. The silence halted the charging, scrambling Alpini line. Fifty yards to the front a helmeted head appeared above the rim of the Austrian trench; an officer yelled through a speaking trumpet, "Italians, go back; go back. You don't want to die." Then, in a gesture of good faith, his machine gunners and riflemen shot high, and the Alpini returned to their lines.

Austrians and Italians worked against the killing: staging fake raids; observing informal truces to recover dead and wounded. Visits to the other side took place and gifts were exchanged.

"The white silk blouse I wear in the summer," Celestina said, "I made it from an Austrian parachute flare. About Christmas time, a patrol came over to the Italian lines. An Austrian soldier gave the silk to your father, who gave him pipe tobacco and they drank grappa. Young men who'd rather have been home."

Celestina left the room and came back with a brown leather photograph album.

"Your father's pictures from the war." She withdrew a postcard-sized sepia print, and handed Dante a picture of his father. "Pietro, the mule, was his friend at the front, carrying food, water, weapons, ammunition. Your father grieved when a shell killed Pietro. Keep the picture."

Dante saw his own likeness in his father's younger, smiling face, eyes shaded by the brim of his Alpini hat.

Celestina told Graziella and Dante that, in quiet moments on clear days, Luigi liked to borrow binoculars to look across sixty miles to Venice. Magnifying the beautiful skyline of the city let Luigi mull over four days on leave spent there, lifting him out of the squalor and brutality of the front.

September 1918, on the Piave River, a round from an Austrian trench mortar hit the position, blowing his comrade to bits; nothing left of him but shards of flesh and bone, tatters of uniform. The explosion hurled Luigi out of the trench. He was in shock, his right arm and leg lacerated by shrapnel. He spent four months in a military hospital. Released from the Italian Army, Luigi came home to Westburn in March 1919.

Home six weeks, often sunk in lethargy, Luigi refused to work in the family business, irritating his parents by sleeping late, walking around the town he loved, glad to be home, and in the evening drinking wine.

But the torment didn't stop; Luigi's parents, puffed up that their son had been a soldier of Italy, wouldn't let him forget the war.

"Italy give you medals," Old Mario said. "You are hero."

Luigi downed a tumblerful of wine, refilled the glass and drank it off.

"You have no fucking idea what you're talking about. If you mention the bloody war again, I'm leaving. I'll find work elsewhere."

Although proud to have served in the Alpini, and to have fought elite German Alpenkorps and Austrian Kaiserjager, Luigi regretted what he'd had to do. The front terrified him, but to avoid death, he got a grip on himself.

"Let me tell you what it was like," Luigi said.

He told them about the death of his friend Salvatore Giannini.

"He was a great chap; handsome. I spent a leave with him in the Cinque Terra. I wrote to his intended."

August 1918, out on patrol, a barrage of daisy cutters bracketed the squad. Luigi made it back to the Italian lines. Salvatore, hit in the buttocks, did not. Luigi went out and carried him back to the trench. His shattered hips revealed exposed bone, joints and shredded flesh. Blood pumped out of him, staining the trench. Luigi knew that Salvatore would die in agony, but said he'd take him to a dressing station; it was hopeless.

"I'm done for, end it now," Salvatore had said.

"I shot him. I killed my friend, then I tied his body to a mule and sent it to the rear for burial."

Luigi refilled the tumbler with wine, and gulped it down.

"The wounds to my arm and leg got me out of the line; saved my life. Twenty-three when I got out of the hospital, and fucking ruined by the war. I'll never leave Westburn, and I won't go back to Italy."

Agate sobbed; Mario blew his nose.

"I'll start work in the café tomorrow morning," Luigi said.

"Graziella, Dante, after your father told me what happened to him in Italy and when he came home, he never again spoke to anyone about it," Celestina said.

Dante knew that these were his father's last words on the war.

Luigi went to work again for his father in the posh café. The mood of the café and the daily routine helped him bury the war deep in his memory. The brilliant jars of boiled sweets lining glass shelves, the display of assorted chocolate and macaroons. The presentation of cakes and sweetmeats, the posters of the Ligurian Riviera. The comfortable basket chairs and tables. In the mornings, the soothing, rhythmic thump of the ice cream machine. Luigi smiled at Westburn's taste for weak coffee and milky tea; appetites for a dish of hot peas, Ninety-Nines and fruity drinks.

And here in the café, in the summer of 1919, he met Celestina Belando, from Martinello, a village near Garbugliago. She was an orphan who'd lived with an uncle, her father's brother, a poor man who sent her to Scotland in 1913 when she was thirteen.

Celestina had become a petite young woman, the respected and loved nanny to the children of a prosperous Italian family in Kempock, a small coastal town on the West Side next to Westburn. She visited the Rinaldi Café on her day off, and liked it when Luigi spoke to her in Italian.

Luigi became determined to woo Celestina, and one day asked her to walk with him. The next Sunday, he waited for her outside St. Ninian's and after Mass walked with her to Ashton to the house where she was nanny. He walked with her for many Sundays that summer. Celestina's employers thought that Luigi should have asked their permission. Old Mario heard about it.

"Forget this orphan. I find you a wife, from Garbugliago, not Martinello," he said.

"Yes, good Italian girl from Garbugliago," his mother said.

Luigi said nothing, and the next Sunday after Mass, by the new war memorial for the dead, the sun shining over the panorama of the river, Loch Long, the Holy Loch, and Loch Goil before them, Luigi asked Celestina to marry him. She smiled and said yes.

Luigi's parents protested, having assumed the right to arrange his marriage. Celestina's employers regarding her as family, wished that their permission had been sought. Celestina and Luigi married in September 1919; the families rallied, celebrating in style. Following Nuptial Mass in St. Ninian's, a hired coach took the bridal party and thirty guests to Casa Italia in Glasgow.

That first year of marriage, the young couple lived with Old Mario and Agate. A surface calm kept hidden the tensions that festered between the new bride and her mother-in-law sharing the same house. Agate's love for her son led to a veiled jealousy of Celestina. Old Mario kept out of the domestic tensions of the young couple living in the family home. And Luigi, while giving Celestina support in private, before and after he made love to her in their bedroom, would not take on his mother. Respect and love for her and a horror of rows held him back.

He'd had enough of quarrels in the Alpini, chafing under the petty tyranny of NCOs and the insane orders of officers. Agate's barbed remarks, her severe face, wounded Celestina; Luigi simmered with fury. They had to find their own place or risk a permanent breach with his mother. Luigi and Celestina resolved to open a new business, leaving the posh Rinaldi's Café in Grey Place, and be free from Old Mario's influence.

When Luigi broached the subject, his father, driven by Agate's shrill remarks, dismissed him. It vexed Celestina and drove Luigi to frenzy; he'd lie awake next to a slumbering Celestina, fantasising about putting down Old Mario and Agate.

Luigi and Celestina made love often: the sublime comfort and joy of each other's arms in the small hours when passion wakened them. And one morning as they dressed, she said, "I'm going to have a child." Luigi, overcome with happiness, covered her in kisses, and tears.

"Celestina, you make me so happy," he said.

Luigi and Celestina had their due: Old Mario augmented their savings, helping them to establish a new fish-and-chips shop. The couple rented a tenement apartment without bathroom, but with a WC. A kitchen cum living room, with black-leaded coal-fired range, a black cast iron sink with brass swan neck cold water tap.

Luigi and Celestina slept in the kitchen in a set-in bed hidden by a door. The bedroom had a set-in bed. The good room too, over-furnished and seldom used, had a set-in bed.

Graziella Rinaldi was born 20 August 1920, delivered by the midwife at the apartment above the fish-and-chip shop in Holmscroft Street. She was the first child and a much-loved daughter.

The Rinaldis lived beside their working-class customers in a grid of cobblestone streets packed with nineteenth century sandstone tenements. To the east lay the badlands of the Avenues, and to the west, a row of tenements with tiled closes occupied by respectable Presbyterians. In the heart of the grid stood the Clachan Bar where men drowned their sorrows.

The douce Scots and Scots-Irish neighbours were private folk who kept to themselves. In the maze of tenement closes, tramped earth drying greens, a builder's yard and several family shops, children capered. Girls played peever and beds, skipped with the rope; boys frolicked as soldiers and cowhands. The Tims and Blue Noses rubbed along, but sometimes the peace would fail. Then men, mad with drink, resumed the wars of religion.

Luigi and Celestina worked hard, starting the business with a coal-fired fryer, and when they could afford it, installing a three-pan, gas-fired fryer. Dante's father made aprons from potato sacks for the heavy work in the back shop, away from customers' eyes, preparing to open for business. Luigi Rinaldi respected his customers. In the front shop he dressed in a white apron, white shirt and black tie, standing behind the counter for frying and serving. He made excellent fish and chips: buying haddock, the finest cold-water fish, cooking the batter golden and crisp, the white flesh tender and moist, and Maris Pipers, the best potato for making perfect chips: crisp to bite on, hot and tasty on the inside.

The people of the neighbourhood flocked to Luigi's fish-and-chip shop. After a year or two, as they got to know and like the family, they asked for things, and Luigi responded. He stocked lemonade, cream soda, Irn Bru, dandelion and burdock; snacks made from sliced potatoes dipped in batter and deep fried, jars of pickled onions, mutton pies, and black pudding suppers. His ambition rose to opening a proper fish restaurant with dining booths and tables, but the Great Depression, the Hungry Thirties, and the war shattered his dreams.

Graziella adored Dante from the day of his birth on 12 November 1926. The big sister, six years older, took care of him as they grew up together. And Dante loved Graziella, looked up to her. Dante and Graziella made Catholic friends at school, and with Protestant children in the quadrant, when together they sang Christmas carols in the Salvation Army Hall opposite the chip shop.

The good years before the war: the happy time for Graziella and Dante, of parties in the Casa Italia where they met Italian children from all over the West Coast.

Families with a roughness sent their children to Italy each summer for a couple of months, but Luigi and Celestina kept Dante and Graziella in Westburn, instilling an Italian identity by sending them to the Italian School held each Saturday in the Westburn Hall that became a jazz club after the war. There, Graziella and Dante practised their Italian vocabulary.

Luigi prospered; he joined with a partner, Jimmy Adams, expanding his business to include importing and processing the finest beef dripping from Argentina, which they sold and distributed to fish restaurants throughout the West Coast. By 1936, Luigi and his partner had a hand in the distribution of fresh fish to the fish-and-chips shops south of Glasgow. Luigi wanted better accommodation for his family, but near to the chipper and the folk who made the business a quadrant institution. He moved the family west on Holmscroft Street, buying a three-bedroom apartment with a bathroom. The Rinaldis lived among the respectable Protestants of the tiled closes.

At seventeen, Graziella's father introduced Graziella to a Westburn Italian boy, Tony Rebecchi, like herself born in Scotland to Italian parents who came from Garbugliago. Within months they were in love. When Graziella turned eighteen and Tony twenty-one in the spring of 1938, they became engaged. Both families were happy. That autumn they married.

"It was a great wedding. Ah liked Tony," Dante said. "Ma dad pushed the boat out; he hired the Casa Italia in Glasgow. Ah remember it well."

Luigi Rinaldi and Tony's father provided cash for the young couple to open a café looking onto the river at Cardwell Bay. A year after it opened, Rebecchi's Café had become a popular gathering place for young people.

Britain declared war on Germany on 3 September 1939. Tony volunteered, finishing up in the Seaforth Highlanders, an infantry regiment.

"What happened in Scotland," Dante asked, "when Italy declared war on Britain?"

"Turned real nasty for a while," Fred said.

In 1940, twenty thousand Italians in the UK attended Fascist clubs for fellowship and friendship. The British knew the few Fascist leaders, but the Secret Service, MI5, considered all Italians a threat.

" 'Collar the lot,' Churchill said. The police had taken your dad away, and the mob wrecked the family chipper in Holmscroft Street, terrifying your Mum," Fred said. "The police didn't try to stop them, and a neighbour took her in."

Fred's parents ran a popular family café; that his father was a British subject married to one, and Fred had volunteered for a Scots Infantry Regiment, didn't inhibit the miscreants.

"The bastards looted and wrecked our cafe."

Stationed up north in Fort George, he asked for compassionate leave, but his commanding officer refused. 'We are at war,' the C.O. said. "I felt like telling him to fuck off, and I wanted to desert, but that would have made things worse."

Fred finally got leave. The scale of attacks on the Italians in and around Westburn shocked him.

"Folk we knew broke in to the shop, stole stock and wrecked the café," Fred said.

The police baton-charged mobs of young and not so young men as they were looting Italian-owned shops and houses. Fred's younger sister had clothes stolen. At school she challenged the child of Irish immigrants wearing her coat.

"Aye, an' so what?" the Irish girl said. "Yer nuthin but a Tally bastard. Ah hope they take yer dad away tae a concentration camp."

Her watching classmates jeered.

"Yer jist a fuckin' wog," one brazen hooligan said, and punched Graziella in the face.

"Your sister had a hard time," Fred said.

12 June 1940, two days after Italy declared war, bands of rough young men from Westburn flocked to Kempock. They came by bus and bicycle, others arrived by foot until they numbered several hundred. A loose band, a hundred strong, broke away to attack Graziella's cafe, and the police struggled to hold off the mob. Graziella stood her ground. She told the ringleaders to go to hell, and offered the stock to the police.

"Give it to the soldiers stationed in Westburn. My husband is in the Seaforths. Better the troops have it than this rabble," she said.

Graziella had made a futile gesture; the mob looted and wrecked the shop.

A few months after the riots, Italians returned order to their lives and reopened for business. The Scots returned, hiding their shame, denying the crimes some of them had committed. People rubbed along again, though tensions within the Italian community simmered for several weeks. Some cafes and chippers in the town centre had not been touched by the rioters. Italians born in Argentina, who'd settled in Westburn, hung signs outside their shops saying that they were Argentineans, not Italians, hoping to spare their businesses from the rage of looters.

"Ah understand," Dante said. "But Ah don't like it."

"Then it got worse when we heard about the Arandora Star," Fred said.

"Tell me," Dante said.

"You're sure, Dante?" Fred asked. "You're ready for what happened?"

"Ah'm sure."

The Arandora, a fine ship built in 1927, was refitted in 1929 and re-named Arandora Star, to carry 354 first class passengers cruising worldwide. The government requisitioned the vessel when war broke out and converted her for transport duties. Arandora Star evacuated troops from Norway and France in June 1940. When Italy declared war on Britain, the government chose the ship for grim work.

On 11 June 1940, the day after Italy declared war on Britain, police swept suspect Italian men into custody and internment. Dante, exiled in Italy for the duration of the war, did not witness the indignities suffered by his father when the police came for him, nor did he share the anguish of his mother and Graziella when they arrested Luigi.

The police took Italian internees to Princes Pier Station to begin the train journey that would end in Liverpool for embarkation on the Arandora Star and internment in Canada. The police inspector in charge told Graziella to wait on the pier, but permitted Celestina to see Luigi in the holding area and give him a parcel of food for the journey.

"How is my dad?" Graziella asked, when her mother came back from the holding area. Celestina just shook her head, sobbing into her handkerchief.

Graziella approached the police inspector at the station entrance facing the pier.

"Can I see my father before he leaves?"

"No; there's a war on. He's an enemy alien."

Graziella's face turned white under her smooth, sallow complexion. She weighed up this cop, a fixture of thirty years in the Westburn Constabulary.

"My father is an Italian. He's lived here all his life. While you sat on your fat bottom in Westburn in 1916, he fought Austrians and Germans in the Alps."

"Get her out of here before I lift her."

Graziella shook off the restraining hand of an embarrassed Sergeant Lachlan Ponsonby, a well-liked regular in the family chip shop. She thrust her head forward.

"Go on, I dare you; arrest me. We're Scots-Italians, and my husband volunteered for the Seaforths. You know the Fascists; why not take them? You persecute innocent men, and harass women. That's all you're good for. You're a bloody disgrace."

Graziella turned on her heel, anticipating a heavy police hand on her shoulder. She took Celestina's arm.

"Come on, Mum, let's get away from here."

Commanded by Captain Edgar Wallace Moulton, Arandora Star left Liverpool on 1 July 1940 bound for St. John's, Newfoundland, and her passengers to Canadian internment. Aboard she carried three hundred and seventy-four crew and military guards, and about one thousand two hundred German and Italian internees, including eighty-six German POWs. The Italians numbered seven hundred and twelve men of all ages. Arandora Star, a grey fugitive painted in her wartime livery without the Red Cross on her hull showing that she carried Axis prisoners and civilian nationals.

At 6:58 on the morning of 2 July, U-47, commanded by Lieutenant Commander Gunther Prein, spotted Arandora Star. Perhaps Prein mistook the grey vessel for an armed merchant cruiser. He had one torpedo left and fired it. The missile struck the ship, and the explosion destroyed power onboard. Overhead, a Sunderland flying boat came, responding to Arandora Star's S.O.S.

Thirty-five minutes later she sank.

Horror and terror ran wild on the stricken vessel as she settled in the freezing North Atlantic. She carried fourteen lifeboats: the torpedo explosion had destroyed one; another lifeboat stuck in its winches; two launched damaged, rendered useless.

Men in their hundreds clung to the ship, others jumped into the sea, crashing into wreckage and debris, floating in life jackets and struggling in the freezing water. Waves swamped a lifeboat. The death-gurgle of seawater flooding into the ship's stacks, and the men aboard and in the sea fighting for their lives as she went down, struggling free of her suction as it threatened to draw them with her beneath the waves.

And the sea gave up the dead, to the Scots on Colonsay; the Atlantic Ocean delivered two hundred and thirty-one to the Irish. The first corpse came ashore at Burtonport, Donegal. In the cemetery of Terrmoncarragh, the Irish buried an Italian beside a Lovat Scout. Another drowned Italian floated ashore at Inishowen, and the Irish buried him in the Sacred Heart graveyard, Carndonagh. The wreck of a lifeboat on the shore of Ross of Mull Peninsula reminded the islanders of the loss and killing. The tides drove ashore ninety-two unidentified corpses from the Arandora Star. More than eight hundred men died.

Italy mourned: the people of Bardi wept for forty-eight drowned men, and the townsmen of Lucca for thirty-one dead.

Later, HMCS St. Laurent, a Canadian destroyer, rescued five hundred and eighty-six survivors. The sick went to Mearnskirk

Hospital near Glasgow. The authorities cited her commanding officer, Lt. Commander Harry DeWolf, for heroism.

Fred's father had a cousin, Aldo Forte, who survived the ordeal of the Arandora Star. Aboard HMCS St. Laurent, when she docked at Glasgow, he asked a sympathetic Canadian sailor to call his family and say that he was alive.

"Aldo knew your dad," Fred said, "and while he struggled to get on a life raft, saw your dad high up on the boat deck, and waved at him to jump. Your dad just smiled and waved back. He must have known he was going to die."

Tears filled Dante's eyes and spilled onto his cheeks. He sobbed, and then got a grip of himself.

"Ma dad was a strong man; a good swimmer. Why didn't he jump?"

It was worse than Dante had ever imagined. He cursed and swore, but finished up crying again for his father and all the poor drowned men.

"It's the forgotten tragedy," Fred said.

"All Ah can say is it's grim," Dante said. "The day God blinked."

"The Navy sunk Prein," Fred said.

Lieutenant Commander Prein, his boat, U-47, her officers and men, vanished on 7 March 1941 after an attack by the destroyers HMS Wolverine and Verity. Wolverine got the credit for the kill.

"Good," Dante said.

"What about ma sister, and ma mum?" Dante said. "How are they gettin' on?"

"Yer mum's doin' fine, but she said to ma mum 'No get a totty.' " Fred laughed.

Dante smiled. Just like his mum to mention a shortage of potatoes.

"My mother wrote, 'Graziella's working with your mum in the chipper, keeping everything right,'" Fred said. "Her cafe's shut; can't get the stuff for repairs. She waited for Tony to come home, so they could fix up the café together."

Fred rubbed his hands, sliced some cheese, and made another sandwich with the stale bread Dante had brought. Dante handed him the small flask, and Fred sipped the sour red wine.

"You've no' heard about Tony?"

"Ah think he's in the army," Dante said.

"Seaforths," Fred said. "After Dunkirk, we were in North Africa and Sicily. Tony's dead, son. German paratroops killed him in Sicily earlier this year at a place called Francofonte. Ah'm so sorry. The Germans captured me a couple of days later."

Dante had liked Tony Rebecchi, and wanted to be with his mum and adored big sister, to comfort them; to mourn with Graziella.

"Jesus, Ah wonder how she's doin'."

"My dad wrote to say Graziella wears black. Whispered hello to him in the street."

Dante swallowed tears for his big sister, imagining her clad in the black, shabby widow's weeds of wartime Scotland.

"She visits Tony's mum and dad, and all they talk about is Tony; then they start greetin'."

An ancient, angry word that he'd forgotten came to Dante.

"Fuck this war; it's ruined Graziella's life. Ma dad said war meant misery. This one has wrecked ma family. Ah'll fix everything when Ah get back home."

Dante was past sixteen. When the war was over and he'd done with it, he'd get back to Westburn.

Italy was in the war on the side of the Allies, and Dante behind the German lines, distant from the Italian Co-Belligerent forces, too young to enlist, wanted to do right in the struggle. He'd speak to his grandfather.

Early next morning, Dante shook Fred awake. "There are Germans and Black Brigade down in the valley. Maybe they're comin' up to the village. Here's your boots."

Fred ran his fingers along the welt where the sole, cut and shaped from an old tyre, attached to the upper by close driven nails. A stitched patch of old leather covered the crack on the left boot.

"Great job," Fred said.

"You look Italian, so if we get stopped on the way to the Widow Murro, answer the questions. We'll tell the Germans and the Milizia we're out harvesting fungi. Ah hope you make it to Switzerland."

"Why the rucksacks and the sticks?" Fred said.

"You'll need a stick going up the mountain. There's some spare kit in the old rucksack. After Ah pass you to the Widow Murro, Ah'm joining the Catholic Partisans up there. Maybe they're Fiamme Verdi; the Green Flames. Old Mario said Ah could go."

Fred weighed up his chances. He was behind German lines. If he was lucky and got away, he'd finish up interned in Switzerland. Bad luck meant recapture and being sent to Germany, a POW for the duration of the war; or perhaps shot as a spy if taken by Fascist militia. On the run, he'd thought about a risky crossing of the German lines, finding a way back to the British lines and the Seaforths, but gave it up.

Now Dante had shown him a way to be a soldier again and recover his fighting spirit. Fred was a trained infantryman, skilled with small arms, a seasoned campaigner, a Scots-Italian, and a Catholic; Fred would fit in. And he'd watch out for Dante.

"I'm staying. I'll come with you."

Old Mario came to the dugout.

"Time to go up the mountain to the Widow Murro, Fred."

"I'm staying. I'm going with Dante to join the partisans."

"You are a brave man. Hurry and get away. But first, come with me."

They walked to the village church.

"I take you to the knight, Nicolo the Lombard, who went on the Small Crusade. He fought on God's side. We believe that on his way home to Lombardy from the Holy Land he died here from old wounds."

The bones of the Lombard knight interred in the wall of the church behind a rude bas relief; a simple, primitive rendering of a soldier wearing chain mail under a surplice adorned with the Crusader Cross, a helmet with nose piece, carved by a twelfth-century country stone mason. Nicolo the Lombard held his sword in both hands, hard against the pommel, point down, the hilt resting on his breast, cross-guard forming an approximate crucifix. The knight's features were worn smooth by the searching fingers of Carbugliagians seeking his blessing before departing on perilous journeys.

"Touch his sword," Old Mario said, "for you two will fight on the right side against evil." Mario took Dante and Fred's right arm and placed their hands on the hilt of that ancient weapon. "Bless my grandson, Dante Rinaldi, and Alfredo Forte, Italians from Scotland. They go to fight Fascists and Germans." The three men bowed their heads a moment. "Nicolo of Lombardy will keep you both safe."

At the stoup by the door of the church, they dipped the fingers of their right hand in the Holy Water, and made the sign of the cross.

"Wait," Mario said. "Open your collars." He placed fine silver chains over their heads, and gazed at the medals adorned with the head of Mithras in profile—souvenirs from Rome from when he'd visited with Agate before the war. Old Mario had a deep sensitivity for the holiness of the past.

"I believe in God the Father, His Son, Jesus Christ, and the Holy Ghost. I pray to the Holy Virgin; but I want to know the old gods are around you. Mithras, god of Roman soldiers, will keep you safe."

Dante and Fred tucked the medals below their shirt collars. Mario kissed his grandson on both cheeks, and shook Fred's hand. "I want to see both of you when this war is over."

Chapter Two

They ascended the mountains behind La Spezia above five thousand feet, about ten miles from Garbugliago, a long hike through green sward, a mass of grass and roots, hellish to walk through when wet, and it took a good part of the day. The Widow Murro had given them directions and sent word to the commandant of the band that they were coming, and she had vouched for them.

On an easy stretch, Fred said to Dante it would be a difficult time. "There's hard fighting coming."

Fred had lived through the horrors of the BEF evacuation from Dunkirk, and gone up against the Germans and Italians in North Africa, and he knew how well German soldiers fought.

After the armistice, the Italian Army had fractured. Men scattered across the country. Soldiers vanished as snow from a pitched roof bathed in winter sun, before the Germans completed their occupation of territory not yet in Allied hands. Friendly guards at the POW camp had told Fred. He'd heard more from peasants who'd given him shelter. Thousands of Italian soldiers just went home. Some of them, southerners far from home behind German lines, and northerners determined to oppose Germany, joined the partisans. Men prepared to fight, and carrying what arms and munitions they could lay hands on, gathered in the mountains and remote places.

One family who'd taken Fred in, whose son had made it home, told him, "I didn't want captured by those swine. Rounded up to work like a slave in Germany, treated like merde by Nazis."

Bolstering his own confidence, and concerned that Dante might have the jitters as the hike to the band neared its end, Fred said, "The Americans and the British fight their way up Italy. They'll push the Germans out, but it'll take a while."

They faced a stiff climb over rocky ways, scrambling through a bleak mass of loose rocks and stones shifting underfoot. As they entered a chestnut forest, they heard voices carried by the wind.

"That must be the camp," Dante said.

A curtain of delicate snowflakes fell in the chilling air as Dante and Fred emerged from the trees and walked between rocky buttresses forming a gateway to the camp. A sentry lounging against a tree, torso crossed by bandoliers, wearing a sidearm, captured German potato-masher grenades thrust into his belt, rifle resting against the tree, waved them into the band's winter hideout.

"He's easygoing," Dante said. "He should've challenged us."

Armed strutting men draped in bandoliers, grenades, daggers and bayonets hanging from belts moved about the camp, ignoring Fred and Dante.

"Amateurs," Fred said.

Dante shrugged. "They carry a lot of kit."

"Can they use it?" Fred said, thinking of the disciplined enemy: the Fallschirmjäger, the Waffen-SS, the Wehrmacht and the Italian fanatics of the Fascist Militia and Black Brigades.

Fred placed a restraining hand on Dante's shoulder. "Look at this place. Bloody freezing shelters." He shivered and jerked his head.

Fred shook his head, the infantry sergeant again. "They should be dug in; this camp is wide open; this mob couldn't box eggs."

"You're from the Widow Murro. I've been expecting you. Major Sandro Giuntoli, 3rd Alpini Division Julia, 9th Alpini Regiment, L'Aquila Battalion."

"Sergeant Alfredo Forte, Seaforth Highlanders; captured in Sicily by the Germans; escaped from an Italian POW camp north of Rome when Italy signed the armistice."

"You've travelled far; and your young friend?"

"Dante Rinaldi from Scotland; staying with my grandparents in Garbugliago when the war started. My father fought in the Alpini; the White War and on the River Piave."

"Excellent," the major said. He waved the steel pincers. "I got this in Russia, before Stalingrad." He drew the points of the pincers, tracing a proud scar from below his black eye patch ending at the edge of his mouth.

Fred's breath whistled through pursed lips. "That's bad luck, sir. What happened?"

"A Russian mortar blew in the dugout; hot metal flying everywhere. I got hit in the eye and torso. The eye's gone." He lifted the eye patch to reveal a staring artificial eye, unmoving, stark white sclera surrounding a dark pupil. "The German surgeon said he couldn't save the eye, and I agreed to have it removed. I hate this damned glass eye. I leave it in the socket, but I cover the eye. Scars on my chest and back cover mortar fragments still in there."

The major briefed Fred and Dante. "Over six weeks, men came here to join. A few soldiers, new recruits to the Italian Army; no experience, only basic training. And a handful of experienced soldiers joined. Some of them fought in Abyssinia."

"How many exactly?" Fred said.

"Ten recruits and eight veterans," the major said. "And the majority are townsmen and peasants; eager enough, but inexperienced."

"Fanatics?" Fred said.

"None; the band is Catholic, and has contact with the Catholics of the Green Flames, the Brigatte Fiamme Verde. We are the 1st Independent Company, Fiamme Verde. We keep back from the Communists and the People's Catholic Brigades."

"Suits me; we're here to fight. I'll look after Dante."

Giuntoli eyed Fred again. "So you're a sergeant, but tell me, where have you served?"

"BEF, Dunkirk, North Africa. I fought Italians at El Alamein."

The major nodded. "What else?"

"I landed in Sicily. I fought Germans until they captured me. Listen, mister, I've been in the army since 1939. I volunteered for the infantry. I'm a platoon sergeant; I've trained infantry, and I've led them in the field."

The major held up a placatory hand and smiled. "Now we're on the same side."

"My men dress like brigante," the major said. "Some of them have cavalier notions of guerrilla fighting. Malmavivente: the mountain people take them for criminals." He waved his steel prosthetic and shrugged. "Some of them are peacocks. They've shot at Germans and Fascists from far away, but damaged nothing, and they are proud of it. They are not ready."

The former soldiers prepared to fight on against the Germans had brought weapons, good ordinance from the Italian Royal Army: mortars, rifles, pistols, revolvers, grenades. Everyone had a weapon, a rifle or a sub-machine gun. Pistols, too, and bayonets, daggers, ammunition.

In October 1943, workers in the German-run Beretta factory started smuggling Beretta submachine guns out of the factory, and a number had come up the mountain to the band. Eager hands assembled these excellent weapons.

"What about mortars," Fred asked, "and machine guns?"

"Two Brixia mortars, and rounds. I'd like more. A Breda light machine gun, but little ammunition."

"The Brixia, the Red Devil, a nasty little weapon," Fred said. "It'd be good to get a couple of German MP 34s, or MP 42s. They're bloody great machine guns."

"We thought about weapons and didn't give enough thought to tools. We're short of tools. I didn't look far enough ahead," the major said. "I should've thought of it and issued orders."

Fred shook his head. "What do you have?"

"A couple of hand axes, knives. Some trenching tools, a few spades."

The band needed more winter clothing, and a food supply identified. Warm dugouts to prepare. The band had to gather axes, wood saws, picks, spades. Major Giuntoli planned to send out patrols, and gather detailed knowledge of the area.

Fred rubbed his hands and muttered to Dante, "Jesus Christ, an armed Fred Karno's Army!"

He asked Dante to return to the farm, telling him to scrounge what he could from Old Mario.

"Take him with you," Fred said, pointing to a youth lounging against a tree in a thick, greasy, soiled sheepskin jacket, hide on the outside, a soldier's bustina resting on his ears, baggy dark rough woolen trousers tucked in at the knee to coarse, thick woolen socks. Fred's eyes widened when he looked at the youth's footwear. Criss-crossed broad, dirty yellow leather straps wound down the lower legs, fastening thick-soled moccasins to his feet.

"That boy is right out of the past; he's from another age," Fred said. "Dante, he'll help you carry whatever your grandfather can spare. Get back here by tomorrow; early as you can."

"Wait; that boy is a girl," the major said. "She escaped when Germans and Fascists burned the farm on the far side of the mountain. They shot her parents, stole the animals and food."

"What happened?" Fred said.

"Her name is Chiarina Inserti; she's sixteen. She doesn't like anyone to talk about what happened to her family. She's a brave young woman, and under my protection."

"Dante is about her age," Fred said. "It will be good for both of them to meet another young person."

The major beckoned Chiarina closer. "Do you want to go down the mountain with this boy?"

"Yes, yes, I do," she said.

"If anything happens to her, I'll hold both of you responsible," the major huffed.

"Dante, you heard what the major said?"

"I heard," Dante said.

"On your honour?" Fred said, taking a chance, for he'd only known Dante a few days.

"I swear, on my honour," Dante said.

The major rose and went into the hut. He came back and handed Chiarina a Beretta semi-automatic pistol and a spare clip of ammunition. "You know how to use this?" She nodded. "Take food and water," the major added almost as an afterthought as he dismissed them.

* * *

Dante, a natural navigator, knew the mountainous terrain surrounding Garbugliago. Young and fit, he revelled in punishing ascents of steep slopes, showing off to this girl—what was her name?—making a dashing descent, risking injury, leaping across gaps and hurtling down boulder-strewn slopes, the nails on his boots scraping and screeching over rocks. But she came right behind him, drawing level, laughing, eyes flashing, joyous at her prowess, matching the ferocious pace he'd set. Dante blinked when she passed him, stepping on the path ahead, jumping over gaps, the thick goatskin soles of her moccasins gripping slippery surfaces as she made a swift descent. Halfway down the mountain in a shaded glade, they stopped.

Chiarina removed her thick off-white, oiled woollen mittens, and offered Dante her leather water flask.

"After you," Dante said.

When they'd slaked their thirst, Chiarina unwrapped a clean cloth, spread it on her knee, and broke off a piece of stale chestnut bread. She withdrew a clasp knife from inside her sheepskin coat and cut thin slices from a small hard cheese, laid them on the bread, and handed it to Dante.

"Eat," she said.

She removed the soldier's bustina, shook out her hair, and looked at him.

"I am Chiarina Inserti, from the other high side of the mountain. My name means clear and bright." A friendly smile lit her face. "I herded our sheep and goats," she said, by way explaining her fleetness of foot descending the mountain. "You can call me Chiarina." She extended her arm.

Chiarina's outlandish clothes vanished from Dante's vision. He saw only her abundant dark brown hair, the depth of her brown eyes, the sallow ivory complexion. They shook hands.

"I'm Dante Rinaldi, from Scotland."

"Yes, you are from far away."

Chairina smiled and was even lovelier. He released her hand, and for the first time in his young life, Dante felt the sweet agony of love.

Dante surprised Old Mario and Agate by returning so soon, and they did not approve of this yokel shepherd girl. However, when she'd removed the sheepskin jacket and the bustina, they recognised her for what she was: a decent, attractive country girl. They fed Dante and Chiarina cheese, bread, and polenta garnished with fragments of thrush, small birds trapped with nets.

Old Mario gave them both a shot of his homemade grappa, a strong fortifier against the cold. Old Mario dozed in the chair by a small fire; Agate fussed, making up a bed.

Chiarina and Dante sat back from the fire, taking tiny sips of grappa, stretching the moment. Dante had never met a girl like her and didn't want her to leave.

Chiarina smiled. "It's the first time I've sat with a boy drinking grappa. My father used to give me a drop on cold nights when I'd brought the animals home."

Large families were common among the locals and Dante assumed that Chiarina belonged to one.

"What about your brothers and sisters?" Dante said.

"Just an older brother, Franco. He died in Cephalonia fighting the Germans. All brave men." She turned away stifling a sob. "We heard rumours. What the Germans did was evil."

Twelve thousand Italian soldiers fought the Germans for ten days. More than a thousand died fighting. Then the Germans executed five thousand Italian soldiers. Four thousand soldiers surrendered, to embark on three ships for Germany. The ships struck mines. The Germans machine-gunned Italian soldiers jumping into the sea.

"My parents were heartbroken; so was I. I miss him. He was handsome and so kind."

"I'm so sorry," Dante said.

Chiarina turned to Dante and forced a smile. "Grazie."

She was close to tears. Dante didn't want her upset; it would be difficult for her to talk. But in the fine heat of the fire, and with the grappa warm and bracing, he felt that it would be good for her to open up.

"Would you like to tell me what happened to your mother and father?"

"All right; it's the first time I've spoken about it since I told Major Giuntoli when I joined the band. Fascists and Germans killed my mother and father. They aided the band, but they would not help our enemies."

German troops and the Black Brigade came to the family's small holding, the officers demanding food for their men and information about partisans. Chiarina's father and mother said they had nothing to give and had no knowledge of partisans. Black Brigade soldiers executed them. In the confusion of destroying the property and killing the animals scattering in panic, Chiarina had run for safety with Major Giuntoli's band of partisans.

"Oh, Chiarina," Dante said, moved by her suffering. He leaned over and touched her hand. "This cursed war."

"I know," she said. "And you Dante; what brought you to Italy?"

Dante told her his plight began as a holiday. Then Italy declared war on Britain and he became an exile.

"The British interned my father, an Italian citizen, but he was no Fascist. He fought the Germans and the Austrians on the Isonzo in the last war. My dad was Alpini. They sent him to Canada on the Arandora Star. Hundreds of Italians drowned when a German submarine torpedoed her. My dad was one of them."

"That is bad," Chiarina said.

"Yes," Dante said. "My big sister, Graziella, lost her husband, Tony Rebecchi, a Scots-Italian. He was in the Seaforths, like Fred, but was killed fighting Germans. Fred had a letter from home, and Graziella's in a bad way. She's only twenty-three, already a widow. Rioters wrecked the family businesses when the war started. I want to get home to help my mum, and Graziella."

"You have suffered too, Dante," Chiarina said. "I am so sorry." Now Chiarina touched Dante's hand.

"Thank you," Dante said.

Chairina sat well back in her chair, her face relaxed.

Jesus, but Chiarina is just adorable, Dante thought. Chiarina yawned, and Dante covered his mouth, screening a sympathetic yawn.

"We have a long day on the mountain tomorrow," Dante said. "Time to turn in."

Upstairs, Chiarina removed her fighting garb and wrapped herself in one of Agate's nightgowns, relishing the luxury of soft pillows and feather mattress of Dante's bed, the rough clean sheets, and heavy quilt. She fell at once into deep, untroubled slumber.

Dante lay up in the barn, snug in his mountain wear, cradled in soft hay, lulled to sleep by thoughts of Chiarina and the familiar, earthy smells of the barn.

Next morning at sunup, after a meagre breakfast of ersatz coffee and hard chestnut bread, Dante and Chiarina began the hike back to the camp. They carried tools given by Old Mario: a couple of spades, an ancient but sharp saw, and an old axe. They fastened a couple of worn but whole blankets over their shoulders, and in a sack carried precious food given by Agate: sausage, polenta, mushrooms, and a loaf of chestnut bread.

* * *

Major Giuntoli had the band assemble in the clearing between the accommodation.

"This is Sergeant Alfredo Forte, Seaforth Highlanders, a crack infantry regiment of the British Army. He fought the Germans and escaped from a POW camp north of Rome."

The men waited, staring at Fred.

"Britain and Italy are allies," the major said. "Sergeant Forte and his friend, Dante Rinaldi, are Scots-Italians. They will join us. The sergeant will help me train you to become fighting men. When he implements my orders, you must obey."

Meaning to impress on his first formal encounter with the band, Fred borrowed the major's swagger stick and ordered the men to muster in two ranks. He nodded to Dante, who joined the end of the front rank. Fred grabbed a slow city boy and pushed him into the front rank.

"Scozzese bastardo," a smirking soldier, a veteran in the rear rank, said to the man on his right, with a slight jerk of his head toward Fred.

Fred pushed through the front rank and grabbed the soldier by the front of his soiled shirt.

"What's your name?"

"I am Sergeant Paulo Roncelli, once a Bersaglieri. Get your hands off me."

"Right now, you're just Roncelli."

Fred tightened his grip and drove his left fist into Roncelli's stomach. He sagged, but Fred held him up, slapped him about the face.

"Io sono Scozzese-Italiano; Sergente Forte. Stand up straight. You two, support him." The soldiers on either side propped the wheezing man up.

Stepping back, facing the two untidy ranks of would-be partisans, Fred called them to order.

"Attenzione!"

The men shuffled their feet, but the lines stayed ragged. Fred paced along the front rank and turned in to the rear rank, pushing men into position with the swagger stick, yelling in their faces to stand up straight.

"Dress your lines," Fred said.

The soldiers understood, and the civilians, following their example, obeyed too: heads turned right, right arms stretched to the next man's shoulder, and they shuffled and dressed the lines.

"Attenzione!" Fred yelled, and the fifty men stood erect. Fred paced the line again, moving men an inch or two until satisfied that the ranks were as they should be. He turned to the major.

"They're ready for you, sir. Soldiers, salute your officer when he speaks to you."

The major inspected the band.

"Already they look better," he said when he'd finished. Then he ordered four veterans to direct the men in cleaning up the camp. "When it's done, report to me."

"The enemy don't know we're up here. We haven't done anything to attract their attention."

"Then let's send men out to forage, while we can," Fred said.

Fred and the major selected four men from the surrounding area, two of them former soldiers, sons of peasants, and sent them down the far side of the mountain to scrounge for tools, food, and clothing.

"Get back before nightfall," the major said. "Keep a lookout for the enemy."

Fred and the major ate an early lunch. They stood side by side in the clearing, sipping hot ersatz coffee made from acorns, swilling it in Italian Army mess tins while they chewed on hard chestnut bread and watched the men bring order to the camp. Steam from the coffee and their breath condensed in the freezing air. Tiny snowflakes fell on them, leaving a web of white covering heads and shoulders. Fred pulled his worn Seaforth Tam O' Shanter from his jacket pocket and put it on, over his right brow. The wind lifted the major's Alpini hat, and he tugged it down.

"Well, sir," Fred said. "How do you see things?"

"It's not good." He shrugged, a habitual gesture. "They'll fall apart if attacked. I worry if they'll ever become fighting men. I should've done more; I needed support; NCOs. No one here would accept the responsibility."

"They're not fit, and they don't like discipline," Fred said. "They're not ready to fight. I'll get them into shape, sir. You could order some of the veterans to assist me; promote them; establish a chain of command. What about Roncelli?"

"Not him. There's been rumours that he's robbed peasants. But I like the idea. We'll speak to the best of them when the foragers return," the major said. "Thank you, Sergeant Forte.

***

Fighting in Russia, the wounds suffered, the operations, had exhausted the major, sapping his will. After emergency treatment at a clearing station behind the front, he'd moved to a field hospital. The German surgeon operated on his hand, cutting away damaged flesh, reducing fingers to stumps, trying to save what he could. He removed the injured eye. The German was a decent officer caught up in a bad war.

"Your face will scar, but I'll do what I can," he said as he repaired shrapnel lacerations to the major's face. "I'll get to the wounds on your back as soon as I'm done with your hand and face."

Major Giuntoli, walking wounded, a weary traveller, depressed by his crippled right hand and ruined face, reduced to one eye, back and chest aching from healing shrapnel wounds, finally reached Udine, an Alpini base. There an Italian Army surgeon assessed the major's wounds.

"The German did a fine job on your face and hand, but it's a useless limb, I'll amputate. You need a prosthetic. Then convalesce here among your own."

Major Giuntoli's health and mood improved after leave in Pavia, his home town. The expectation that he'd return to the Alpini kept him cheerful, but when the doctor passed him fit only for light duties, depression enveloped him. The army sent him to Carrara to command a transit camp processing recruits for basic training.

"When Italy signed the armistice, we knew the Germans would occupy the country. I came up here with a handful of soldiers to organise resistance."

Fred felt sorry for Major Giuntoli. Wounds had knocked him up, depleted his will. The major had to know that the Germans fielded a hard-fighting army.

"You know who and what we're up against, sir?" Fred asked.

A bitter smile creased the major's face.

"I saw how they treated Russian prisoners. They shot partisans. Here, we face Smiling Albert and his legions."

"The field marshall," Fred said. "Kesselring the Capable." Albert Kesselring, commander of German forces in Italy, a formidable soldier.

"In Greece, after the armistice, the Germans got out of hand," the major said.

"I heard rumours. What happened?"

"They massacred most of the Italian garrison of Cephalonia, the Greek island," the major said. "An atrocity; murders. Tedeschi cazzo; Tedeschi bastardo."

The major pulled an off-white handkerchief from his side pocket and dabbed at his good eye, then he dabbed under the eyepatch. He looked toward the entrance to the camp. He blew his nose and tucked the handkerchief in his sleeve.

Fred shook his head. "Time to make them pay, sir."

* * *

The foragers returned late in the afternoon with tools and worn winter clothing.

"The peasants gave what they could," a former soldier said.

The haul of spades, picks, and a heavy hammer cheered Fred. He turned to the major. "Now we can get the camp into shape."

Fred and the major sat by a tiny fire burning dry timber inside the woodsman's hut. The faintest smoke escaped to the night sky through a hole in the roof. Sentries posted, and changeovers arranged, the men retired to their shelters to eat their meagre supper of stewed root vegetables and chestnut bread.

Fred spooned vegetable stew from his mess tin, and the major, a mess tin held in the pincers of his prosthetic, forked food with his left hand. They wiped up vegetable juices with chunks of chestnut bread.

The major pulled a small flask from a kitbag, held it in his left hand, and with the pincers unscrewed the top; he held it at eye level, filled it to the brim, and handed it to Fred.

"Grappa, for the cold."

"Thanks, sir." Sipping a couple of times, Fred knocked back the grappa. "By God, it's strong."

"That's the purpose," the major said. He poured himself a shot, gripped the metal top between the pincers, and downed it in one.

The major lit a candle, and the reeking smell of tallow pervaded the hut.

"Well, sir, you've taken the first steps and got organised," Fred said, "but you don't have fighters yet. So, what now?"

They discussed the band's affairs. Everyone had weapons and ammunition, but they needed heavier infantry weapons: light machine guns, rounds for the Brixia mortars.

The band had to learn hit-and-run tactics, for they had not arms, nor men yet hard enough to take on German soldiers on equal terms. The band might fare better against the Fascist militias and Black Brigades.

"Shoot and scoot, sir," Fred said. "Hit them hard from ambush, assassination; then scatter, split up to confuse them, and get away. But first the men need training."

"I agree," the major said.

"Sir, let's get them fit through digging defences, chopping and sawing wood. We can't have them shooting up here, for it'll attract the enemy. We can teach them arms drill, to handle their weapons."

"Yes," the major said.

They'd send out patrols of four or five men to gather intelligence about German and Italian Fascist units from trusted peasant families. Once the men's fitness improved, they'd deploy patrols further afield, defining an area of operations.

"I'll get them fit, sir," Fred said.

"We need to give them the courage to fight," the major said. "The men need to win the first fight."

"We can shoot at the Germans and the Fascists from a distance, but not too far away," Fred said. "It's easier to kill a man that way. The closer you get, the harder it is."

"Yes, I know," the major said.

"How are you managing, sir?"

The major wore a sidearm, an Italian Army-issue 1935 Beretta semi-automatic pistol—a sturdy, reliable weapon. But he'd be using it left-handed, awkward in a skirmish.

"I'm getting better with the left hand. I used to be a good shot with the Berretta."

The major stood and removed from a chest an object wrapped in light khaki canvas. He laid it on the floor between them and, holding the canvas under his boot, he unfolded the material with the pincers and his good hand.

"My weapons of choice," the major said. "I bought this old break-open shotgun from a peasant a few weeks ago. I cut the barrel and gave it a pistol grip. It's like the shotguns used in Sicily; the Lupara. Deadly up close. I'll sling it from my left shoulder."

The major held the shotgun between the pincers just behind the shortened barrel, and gripped the handle, fingered the trigger with his good left hand, and faced Fred.

Fred rose and pushed the shotgun barrel away.

"You want Dante and me to leave?" he laughed.

"No, no, I need both of you. Don't worry, it's not loaded. But that was careless of me." The major smiled. "I'm sorry."

The major pointed to another weapon in the canvas bag.

"That is a fine weapon," he said.

It was an immaculate Mauser C96 machine pistol.

"It's in beautiful condition," Fred said. "My platoon commander in North Africa called it the 'broom handle'.

"Yes, you can holster the gun in the stock," the major said. "I picked it up in Russia."

He lifted the weapon with the pincers, fitted the long stock, and raised it to his left shoulder, steadying the barrel on the pincers for good aim.

"I'll cope well enough when we attack the Germans and Fascist militia." The major pulled himself erect. "I am Alpini."

* * *

On patrol, Fred and the major led from the front. By the end of the year, regular patrolling, labouring in camp and daily weapons drill had made the flabby, would-be partisans fit men, but untested in a serious clash with German troops or the Fascist Black Brigades.

Patrols led by former soldiers and NCOs went out to gather intelligence and establish contact with supportive locals. They returned to dugouts, roofed with earth and stones, camouflaged with weighted branches, a camp perimeter defended by a machine gun, and a withdrawal route if a stronger enemy force attacked.

"We can't stay this way, sir. The men are too comfortable for guerrillas. They sleep on beds of soft grass; they're snug under blankets and leafy branches," Fred said after a morning inspection. "We need to reorganise."

"I know," the major said.

Fred and the major established common messing. Food was short. The peasants gave what they could, but also had to feed themselves, and nourishment was scarce in Italy at this point in the war.

Dante and Chiarina knew the mountains better than most of the partisans in the band, so they hunted, snaring mountain hares for rich, gamey stews. But there was a limit to how long game would last. The boy-girl duo turned to hunting birds with nets: thrush, starlings, blackbirds; snatching terrified creatures, all flapping wings and screeching. A quick pull and twist of thumb, fore and middle finger, breaking necks.

When the birds stopped singing, they turned to trapping hedgehogs and hunting badgers for the pot. They cooked game in tomatoes and perhaps pasta, given them by peasants, or roasted; just like chicken, an old woodsman said. They went after the wild boar that ranged in the woods in the high places. Dante, a marksman with a Carcano rifle fitted with a telescopic sight and silencer, dropped several of these dangerous animals with a shot to the head.

Then Dante and Chiarina loaded the donkey and brought the carcass back to the camp for butchering. A peasant might give the band a sheep once in a while, and they rustled the odd bovid when the larder was bare.

Dante loved being out on the mountain hunting with Chiarina. Desire for Chiarina tortured him; he had never known such torment, and wondered if she too suffered agonies. But to Dante, Chiarina was holy, and he'd sworn to protect her honour.

The food chain shrank and the hunting stopped. Feeding a band of fifty living in camp soon exhausted game and other wildlife.

The men, unused to living rough, grumbled about lack of food, and they became dirty, rejecting regular shaving and bathing and washing of clothes. A few days of this neglect of personal hygiene, and they stank. The major, Fred, Chiarina and Dante were the exceptions.

"If they don't keep clean, sir, they'll get lousy," Fred said. "At this rate, they'll have potatoes growing in their armpits."

"Yes, Fred," Major Giuntoli said. "Pride in appearance—that's what's needed."

"Leave it to me, sir. I'll fix them."

Fred had Dante and Chiarina go with him. A furious Fred lined up the men and paired them off.

"Take a look: Dante and Chiarina are clean and smart. I want you looking like that. Your mate will scrub your back. Now get it done."

The band had no uniforms, clad in an assortment of old Italian Army kit, some German Army items—especially boots—and civilian clothing, but within the hour, every man paraded shaved, clothing shabby but clean. Everyone wore a green scarf, folded thin and knotted at the throat neckerchief fashion; a conceit that said they were Fiamma Verde. They looked like soldiers.

* * *

The camp woke to a weak sun and winter sky. The fatigue party striking flints to make cooking fires of dry wood that did not smoke. The coughing and hawking as smokers emptied their lungs, then lit a hand-rolled cigarette. Men washing in cold water, shivering, splashing torso and armpits, maintaining healthy feet, and, on severe mornings, rubbing themselves with new snow. The muffled laughter as men wafted about the camp greeting friends, ready for the new day.

Not every morning, but when he and Chiarina were up and about, Dante brought his full mess tin of ersatz coffee to her dugout and shared the steaming liquid with her. He liked the intimacy, and the domesticity.

After meals, the men cleaned their mess kits. Fred conducted random inspections. A filthy mess kit meant extra fatigues. After some initial rumblings of protest, most of the men accepted the need for cleanliness.

Former Sergeant Paulo Roncelli, veteran of Abyssinia, Albania, and Greece, resented Fred's authority from the start. He smarted from the day Fred had thumped him. The job of assisting the major belonged to a real Italian, someone like himself enforcing discipline, not a former enemy, an interloper from Scotland. And he didn't care for Dante, resenting his closeness to Chiarina Inserti, a chit of a girl who should have attended to laundry, the kitchen, welfare, and yes, the comfort of the men.

After the midday meal, Chiarina cleaned her mess kit with hot water, scouring the insides with twigs and sandy soil. She'd rinse out sandy residue with cold water. Roncelli, feeling the grappa he'd been drinking, rose from his seat on a boulder and crossed the clearing. He scraped together the congealed remains of a thick vegetable soup laced with shreds of small birds' flesh and emptied the mess beside Chiarina, splashing her legs. He dropped the mess tin by her side.

"Clean it."

Chiarina caught the stink of his grappa-tainted breath. "Clean it yourself," she said, and threw the mess tin at Roncelli's retreating back, hitting him on the head and sending his bustina flying. She waited, hands on hips.

Roncelli cuffed her, and she staggered, struggling to keep her balance; she tripped and fell. He hauled her half up, breathing grappa fumes on her as she nursed her aching jaw.

"Clean it, I said; get on with it."

Dante, sitting outside the dugout he shared with Fred, had just finished pulling through and maintaining the Carcano rifle. Tougher now after months of patrolling, labouring and living in the field, Dante carried the Carcano at high port as he strode across the clearing.

"Roncelli!"

A swaggering turn and Roncelli faced Dante, who clipped him on the side of the head with the butt of the rifle, knocking him down. Roncelli, shaking his head, stunned, struggled to rise, reaching for his pistol. Dante chambered a round and aimed.

"Hands off the pistol or you're a dead man."

Roncelli raised one hand, nursing his swollen face with the other hand.

"Go near the girl again. I'll kill you."

Faraway, Dante heard the click of Major Giuntoli's prosthetic on the rifle, pushing the muzzle from Roncelli's chest.

"Disarm him and tie him up, he's drunk."

Dante went to a sobbing Chiarina, still nursing her bruised jaw. He held her for a minute until she stopped shivering, then walked her to her dugout next to the woodsman's hut where the major slept. He filled a mess tin with tepid coffee at the open kitchen, and brought it back to Chiarina.

"Drink this."

"Thank you." She reached for his hand and Dante sat down beside her.

"Don't worry, I'll not let anyone touch you."

Two days later Dante wondered why he'd not seen Roncelli.

"Where is he?" Dante said.

"History," Fred said. "You won't see him again. The bastard robbed peasants. They told Chiarina about his thieving and robbing when she was out. She told the major, and he asked her to keep it quiet. Roncelli committed the crimes. Unreliable; might have gone over to the Black Brigades."

"What happened?"

"He's gone for good," Fred said, "to his ancestors."

In a brief drumhead court martial, Fred and the major had beaten it out of Roncelli that he'd threatened peasants and robbed them. They took him to a quiet glade and, hands tied behind his back, forced Roncelli to his knees to administer summary justice. He had guts; looked Fred and the major in the eye, and spat at their feet.

"Do what you have to do."

"Give me your pistol, sir."

"No, sergeant; Roncelli's my responsibility."

Major Giuntoli unholstered the Beretta pistol with his steel prosthetic, and wrapped a handkerchief round the barrel to muffle the shot. He took the pistol in his left hand.

"May his soul and the souls of the faithful departed rest in peace," the major said.

He aimed at the back of Roncelli's head and squeezed the trigger. Roncelli toppled over.

Fred and the major bundled the corpse into a hollow deep inside a thicket, and covered the dead man with rocks and branches.

"He died better than he lived," the major said.

* * *

Major Giuntoli ordered the band dispersed. Fred completed the staff work: establishing two operational zones, forming two squads of twenty-five men, halved again, and again led by former NCOs of the Royalist Army. The major remained in charge of the band. Independent squads would operate inside an operational zone. Squads would live off the land, feed and clothe themselves, earning the trust and support of local peasants. Some operations would mean that squads combine in formations up to fifty men, depending on the job.

"I'd like command of a squad, sir," Fred said. "And to keep Dante with me."

"You stay here with me, Fred," the major said. "From time to time, we'll need to plan operations; you'll lead the headquarters squad. Chiarina is under my protection: she stays; Dante, too. The pair of them are as fit as fleas; I need runners to link the command."

"Thanks, sir," Fred said. "You'll have made Chiarina and Dante happy."

The men checked arms, and Fred organised re-distribution. Squads had Brixia mortars; squad leaders, Beretta submachine guns; the men, Carcano rifles. Dante and Chiarina, runners for the band, were each given a submachine gun and a Beretta pistol.

Before dispersal, the major decided to attack the enemy with the full strength of the band.

"I want ordinance and supplies," the major said. "Fred, organise a reconnaissance patrol and see if you can capture machine guns and identify a couple of potential targets."

"Yes, sir."

Fred took Dante and another two men to scout the enemy traffic on quiet roads in the vicinity of Pisa where the Germans worked, building a defensive line. Fred wanted to capture two MP 34s or MP 42s, German light machine guns with a high rate of fire, carried and operated by one man; they were often mounted on motorcycle sidecar patrols.

On a winding country road, traffic was quiet, but in the morning and again in late afternoon, a dispatch rider on motorbike with sidecar passed. The sidecar mounted a light machine gun. On this day the throaty exhaust of the motorcycle engine carried to the patrol hidden among trees, and they prepared to raise a thin, strong rope tied to a tree across the path of the bike.

The bike hit the rope, turned on its side, and careered onto the edge of the road. Fred and Dante emerged from hiding on one side of the road, and the two former Italian soldiers appeared from the opposite side. Dante stood guard, and Fred shot the two Germans in the heart with a silenced Beretta pistol. The ambush was over in minutes.

Dante, nervous at being close to mangled dead bodies, hung back and watched as the Italian soldiers took the machine gun off the side car. They stripped the dead Germans of weapons and useful clothing: boots, gloves, capes, and goggles. They took the field rations, hard crackers, preserved meat, dehydrated vegetables, ersatz coffee, and pea sausage.

"Might be horse meat in the ration packs," the machine gunner said. "Some people like horses, and would never eat them."

Fred shrugged.

"If I'm hungry enough, I'll eat horse."

Then they wrecked the motorbike.

"Dante, take the first spell carrying the MP 42 and the belts of ammunition," Fred said.

Dante wound the belts of ammunition round his torso, slung his Carcano rifle with the scope across his back, and hung the German weapon from his right shoulder.

"Heavy," he said.

"Weighs about 26 pounds," Fred said. "Carrying it'll get you fitter."

The partisans moved back into the hills, keeping behind the tree line, hidden from view. Fred set a hard pace to get them far from the ambush and well ahead of any pursuit. They marched all night, resting for a couple of hours, and continued at first light well into the next afternoon. Two thousand feet up at the edge of the trees, and fifteen miles from the ambush, the purr of a car reached them. Fred examined the country road through the San Giorgio 6 X 30 Italian Army binoculars.

Fred handed the binoculars to one of the former Italian soldiers.

"What do you make of it?"

"Lancia Aprilia Coloniale. Passenger car. Driver, armed guard, two officers; Fascist Militia. Don't see a light machine gun."

"Let it go," Fred said.

The soldier kept the binoculars trained on the winding road going back up the valley. They waited, the silence of the forest broken by birdsong and a soft breeze whispering through trees.

"Slow modified farm truck coming," he said. "A machine gun mounted behind the cabin roof."

Fred made up his mind. He knelt beside Dante, a hand on his shoulder.

Dante felt himself shaking, terrified that he'd lose control of himself.

"First time, son; take deep breaths, slow and calm," Fred said. "It's your job. I'm depending on you, the best shot in the squad.

Hide below the edge of the road. Use the rifle. Sight with the scope. Squeeze the trigger; don't rush; aim for the head. Kill the driver with the first shot. If it goes wrong we'll all die."

"I can do it, Fred," Dante said.

Fred jerked his head to the former soldier who'd spotted the truck.

"Site the machine gun in front of Dante; after he's killed the driver, then enfilading fire down the length of the truck. Get the men in the back and the tyres. Four of us attack when the truck stops. We'll surprise them; they won't be expecting it."

They deployed.

"Hold fire until I signal," Fred said. "Fire at twenty-five yards."

Dante lay prone, taking calming breaths, watching the black fez of the driver filling the scope as the truck approached. He shot the driver, revolted by the head erupting red like a ruptured pomegranate, blood and brains splashing the windscreen. The rapid *tac-tac-tac* of the MP 42 cut down the militiamen in the back and shot out the tyres, sending the vehicle sliding on its side for several yards before stopping. The injured guard struggled with the jammed door, until the machine gunner killed him.

"Strip them of useful kit," Fred ordered. "You too, Dante."

The partisans discarded the Fascist black fezzes, but removed tunics and warm comforters, belts, rifles, pistols, grenades, and ammunition. They took the rucksacks and filled them. Fred searched bodies for wallets and information; he kept any monies found.

Dante felt odd having just killed a man. He didn't mind the corpse of the militiaman he'd shot, but he couldn't bear to look at the shattered bloody face of the man he'd killed. Nor did he mind the rest of the dead, half-naked militiamen crumpled and twisted on the ground. Looting their clothing stripped them of manhood, made them detritus, their soiled underclothing clinging to pallid flesh. When Dante unlaced boots, hauling them off, he had to suppress the urge to boak at the smell of dirty feet. He unrolled foul-smelling socks from still-warm feet, and stuffed them into boots.

"Must wash the socks," Dante said. Then he croaked and retched through to a bout of the dry heaves.

"You'll get used to the dead and the smell. Here, wash out your mouth." Fred handed Dante a water bottle.

Dante gargled a couple of times, spitting out the foulness in his mouth. Then he swallowed a mouthful of water.

"Thanks, Fred. I think I'm okay."

Fred nodded.

"Map and compass, but no MP34 or 42; just the Breda."

The Breda 30, standard light machine gun of the Italian Army, had a slow but accurate rate of fire; the twenty-round capacity strip magazine often jammed. The weapon required constant maintenance of the cooling system. Used in the field, it needed a gunner and a loader.

The truck carried field rations for a company: a pack contained one tin each of ham and tuna, a packet of broth tablets, two packs of flatbread, and one pack of sweet biscuit.

"Ah, razione personale. I've eaten it overseas," the former soldier said. "It's poor feeding, but better than what we have. It'll keep the men going when we're out."

There was much to carry. Each man carried two weapons, and the rucksacks stuffed full weighed about fifty pounds. Without transport, the booty would slow them down and increase the risk of being overtaken by Fascist militia. The enemy would be looking for them.

* * *

An hour of forced marching—by now their shirts and underclothing were soaked and smelly, their hair damp under headgear, matted to the skull—exhausted the four partisans.

"Can't keep this pace up," Fred said. "Have to find a mule or a couple of donkeys." He looked at the map. "There should be a couple of hill farms up ahead."

Fred and the veteran Italian soldier went on ahead. Dante and the other soldier hid the loot and the packs in a thicket and stood guard in defensive positions.

Dante stood tense, mouth dry, belly shrunk to a tight knot, afraid that Fascist militia, maybe Black Brigade—or worse, the Germans—would find them.

"Be quick, Fred," he muttered, worried about shitting his pants.

After ten minutes, they came back with an old but sturdy mule, a big fellow. They'd offered payment for the animal and left the peasant with his two donkeys.

"Report us to the Fascists and we'll come back and kill you," the Italian soldier had said.

The old man had shaken his head.

"What do you know? I am no Fascist. Do not worry about me." He'd jerked his head toward the mule. "He is a good-natured mule. Use him for a day or two, then bring him back. I need him. I don't want any payment."

When Fred led the mule loaded with supplies into the camp, ragged cheering greeted them.

"We've not won the war, sir, but we did all right."

The major's good eye gleamed as the men unloaded the mule and emptied their rucksacks, laying down the captured ordinance.

"You've all done well. How are the men?"

"They fought well. Dante's a good shot. He has the makings of a sniper. I've got a couple of targets for you to review, sir."

* * *

The major sent out another squad of ten men led by a former sergeant of the Royalist Army, while Fred's squad raided and foraged. They travelled south into Tuscany in twos and threes, gathering at the rendezvous near Colonnta in the Apuan Alps. Four former soldiers garrotted the militia guarding the Viaduct of Vara, then set charges, blew up the line derailing the train, and shot up the soldiers on the train. The Fascists killed one man in return, and the squad withdrew into the hills, hiking in back to camp.

Fred's raiders had two easy skirmishes with unsuspecting enemies, and the ten-man squad had done well attacking the train. The fighting would get tougher; they'd suffered the first death in action. There would be more dead and wounded.

Fred trained the men hard, and soon had done all that he could. The results delighted the major: fit men, ragged still, but now looking and acting like soldiers. He prayed that combat would toughen the band, and not break its new spirit.

Fred gathered the men into an informal semicircle in the camp clearing. The major explained that he meant to attack the Germans.

"We'll fight as a brigade, fifty strong. We're tying down large numbers of enemy troops. If we were not in the field, the Allies coming up from the south would face thousands more German and Fascist troops.

The men applauded, and murmured approval went round the camp. Major Giuntoli was proud of his fighters. The men had come on since the winter of 1943 and the first cautious attacks on Germans and Italian Fascists. The men trained hard, learned to fight in the school of hard—sometimes fatal—knocks. Winning small skirmishes improved morale, as the band waged guerrilla war from the high mountains and forests.

* * *

The Kübelwagen led the convoy moving troops to the front using a minor road behind the main highway from Genoa to La

Spezia. A driver and officer in the front seats; in the back, two armed soldiers.

"Kill the driver; the car has to block the road," Fred said. "Then shoot the officer. I'll get the guards."

Dante got the driver in the scope and squeezed the trigger; the round entered the driver's head below the left ear and lodged above the right eye, blood and brains blotting the windscreen. The driver slumped across the wheel, and the Kübelwagen began a slow skid, overturning and blocking the road. The officer, a major, made it half out of the car, trying to draw his sidearm, but pausing, rubbing his left hand across his face to remove brains and blood. Dante had the man's head in the scope. The officer's peaked cap vanished when the bullet hit the side of his head, and he collapsed, torso on to the road, arms spread. The guards scrambled free, pointing their rifles, searching for targets. Fred killed them both with rounds to the chest.

Several yards to Fred and Dante's left, a Brixia mortar fired 45 mm rounds, hitting the rear truck of the convoy, wounding and killing several soldiers. The front of the convoy was stuck behind the wrecked Kübelwagen, and the rear truck was immobile. The Breda light machine gun fired: a *tac-tac-tac*king, traversing up and down the length of the convoy. Partisan grenades fell among the Germans, adding to their dead and wounded. The commanding officer had been killed, and the junior officers stunned by the ambush. But in less than a minute, the NCOs had infantry counterattacking. Men leapt from the trucks and advanced in open order on the mountainside. The machine guns gave covering fire to the advancing infantry, shooting ahead of the line.

They came on, tall men clad in winter kit: camouflaged smock and helmets, boots crunching and scraping stones, gripping the turf, advancing to the high ground.

"Jesus Christ, they're good," Fred said.

"Yes, they're good, the Germans," the major said. "I saw the Heer fight in Russia. You're ready, Fred?"

Major Guintoli meant to give the enemy a hard time; show them what a well-led band of Italian partisans could do.

"Give them a rough wooing, sir."

The major nodded, eyes flat, mouth pressed to a slit.

The half of the band that had sprung the ambush withdrew in a fighting retreat to prepared positions, through the trees and the rotting forest smells, back up the mountain, drawing in the enemy to where the other half of the band had dug in. Major Giuntoli meant to hurt the Germans and force them to retreat. Fred urged the men on, scrambling up the wooded slope to open ground. They'd killed and wounded some of the counterattacking infantry, but still they came on, and were not far behind. The partisans heard the Germans moving through pine trees.

Two wounded partisans kept up—just. One man, hit in the stomach and in agony, had fallen out, close to death. The Germans wouldn't treat him. They'd try to get information, then they'd kill him.

"Can't leave him for the enemy, sir," Fred said.

"I know," the major said.

"I'll do it, sir."

The major nodded.

A former NCO, a veteran of Italy's colonial war in Africa and the invasion of the Balkans, went with Fred.

"It's time," the NCO said.

The wounded man held on to a spreading puddle of thickening red daub clinging to his belly, seeping between his fingers.

"I'm going; do it now," he said. Fred shot him in the head with his Beretta.

The band had dug in on a line of forty yards in front where the pine trees grew, flanks anchored left and right on light machine guns. Foxholes manned by two men covered the open ground the Germans had to cross. Men armed with submachine guns covered the gaps between the foxholes.

"They won't be expecting us to resist on a defensive line," the major said. "They'll be thinking we'll run."

A file of infantry came out of the trees, machine gunners behind the leader. They were good infantry, each presenting a small target. A skirmishing line formed, men about five yards apart.

The band, dug in and hidden, opened fire when the enemy had advanced fifteen yards. Germans fell, dead and wounded. Machine guns returned fire. The reduced skirmishing line came on. The partisan machine guns laid down a suppressing fire. Chiarina, deep in the major's foxhole, fired her submachine gun. The major aimed and fired the Mauser from the shoulder. The German line staggered under the weight of the partisan fusillade and some retreated, taking their wounded with them. German dead littered the open ground.

Five of them, combat crazy or just brave, came on. They got to within ten feet of the major's foxhole.

Dante saw it.

"Oh, Jesus Christ, Chiarina's in there. Sweet Jesus, please, please, keep her safe."

The major—reckless, erect, exposed to firing; a true Alpini—the shotgun resting on the prosthetic, squeezed one trigger, then the other, and two young German soldiers fell, cut to pieces. The three surviving Germans ran for it, and made it back to their lines, out of the clearing.

The suppressing machine gun fire continued as the band withdrew. From the edge of the trees, Brixia mortars fired rounds into the German position, forcing them to take cover as the band's machine gunners retreated into the pine trees. Two partisans with axes, former Pioneers, toppled a couple of prepared trees, blocking the rough path.

A partisan loaded the mule the peasant had loaned them. He was a good-natured animal, so the major had kept him, and had sent the old man enough money to buy another mule or two donkeys. The mule stood, unfazed by the firing and the smoke, as they piled Brixia mortars, ammunition and rations onto the panniers bound to the animal's back. A gentle touch of the stick, and the mule surged up the mountain. He was a fine animal, and the partisans loved him.

Quiet fell, smoke drifted over the open ground, and the German infantry came on again. Several yards behind the toppled trees, a veteran Italian NCO and an assistant set the plunger and blew the dynamite buried in the heart of the open ground. More Germans died. One man fell into the crater left by the exploding mine.

Fred and the major encouraged the men to move out. In front of the column, an NCO set a hard pace as the band climbed through the fresh-smelling pine trees toward the snow and the high places. On the snow line, the men put on white camouflage garments made from rough sheets, and vanished up the mountain.

* * *

They recuperated in the smallholding of an old shepherd. The major had led them to a point on the map where he'd expected to find a shepherd's hut uninhabited in winter. Light from a paraffin lamp blinded Fred when he rushed the door, heat hitting him in the face. An elderly man looked up from a wooden table where he was sharpening a large-bladed knife. A wood stove glowed in the corner of the room, and two large dogs lay on the hearth. They growled and the man silenced them with a grunt and a wave of his hand.

"Do not worry, they are Bergamasco Shepherds—Doppio Pelo. They are good with the animals and they protect me. They like people. You are the partisans. Where is the Alpini major? I have heard of him."

"I'm Major Giuntoli. Why are you up here in January?"

"I follow nature."

When winter came, the shepherd moved his sheep and goats down the mountain to winter pastures. His daughter and son-in-law cared for the animals when he returned to the mountain. When spring came, the old man went down to the valley with his dogs and brought the sheep and goats back up the mountain.

"I have wine and grappa, and plenty of cheese from the milk of ewes. I make it myself. You must drink and take cheese. I have other food, but not much. My daughter is due to send supplies. My grandsons bring them."

"We have army rations," Fred said. "Wine, grappa and the cheese are welcome. Boiled water for coffee would be good."

"You fought today?' the old man said. "Faraway, I heard firing."

"Today, we won," the major said.

"That is good," the old man said. "But for every German you killed, they will take hostages from the people around here and kill them. It is the rastrellamenti. Rapresaglia? I heard that it is ten Italians for every dead soldier. Maybe they will kill me."

"We must fight them," the major said.

The old man shrugged.

"Yes, we must fight them."

* * *

Fred and Dante heard this exchange. Fred had been in the army since 1939 and took part in the fighting at Dunkirk, North Africa, and Sicily. For Fred, it was a practical issue. The way to put a stop to German and Fascist reprisals and attacks on civilians was to defeat them. To stop fighting would only prolong the war.

But Dante worried.

"Maybe the Germans and the Black Brigades will attack Garbugliago; take hostages; murder my grandfather and my grandmother; kill friends."

"That could happen. Let's pray that it doesn't," Fred said, ever a believer in the power of prayer. "You going down there won't stop them. We'll do more to protect them fighting with the band; keep the bastards busy."

They sat in the corner of the small barn. Fred poured two shots of the shepherd's grappa into small glasses. He handed one to Dante.

"Salute. Sip the grappa. You'll feel better, and warmer."

In the flickering candlelight, they spooned captured Italian Army field rations from their mess tins, wolfing down a thick potage flavoured with sorrel provided by the old man, into which they had stirred canned tuna and chopped ham, pushing meat and fish onto the flatbread. They saved a piece of flatbread to eat with the cheese, and they kept the biscotti for later to dip in hot black ersatz coffee that the old shepherd had promised.

"Not bad; Ah like the lemon taste of the sorrel," Dante said. "A change from the chestnut bread and the game Ah hunted with Chiarina."

Fred worried about Dante and Chiarina. They were so young, and he didn't want them captured, or worse, killed or wounded.

"Listen, son, don't get too attached to that girl, and don't let her get attached to you."

"That girl?" Dante stood. "You'll no' talk like that about Chiarina."

Fred had left it too late. Dante and Chiarina were already attached; a couple of innocent kids crazy about each other. The men liked it, and so did the major. And though he worried about them, Fred liked it. Dante and Chiarina's love flourishing on the run high on the mountain meant a blessing; it gave the men hope for an end to the war. The band believed good would come of it.

Fred poured two more shots of grappa. He walked a few steps and gave the bottle to one of the men, and came back to sit beside Dante.

"Here, sit down. Drink the grappa. Ah meant no offence, Dante. Chiarina is a fine girl. Ah don't want anything to happen to Chiarina or to you."

"Ah won't let anything happen to her."

The light of the door of the old man's hut lit Chiarina's pinched, white face; the day had been hard. The band had won, but the German soldiers had handled them roughly, killing two men, wounding one man whom Fred had to shoot, and wounding another two in the firefight on the open ground. The two Doppio Pelo, sensing a friend, nuzzled her legs, and she clapped their manes. Dante left the barn, the grappa burning a hot route into his gut, and went to Chiarina.

"Walk a little way with me." The dogs padded along and sat looking up at them when they stopped.

"I shot a man today. Perhaps I just wounded him," Chiarina said. "I feel I have sinned."

"He was German Army," Dante said. "They've massacred innocent people in reprisals."

"He was someone's son."

"He's the enemy that murdered your mum and dad, killed your brother; and they killed my father."

Silence struck them for a full minute. The dogs whimpered.

"Anything could happen to us," Dante said. "It's the war."

She stifled a sob. Her hand shook and he folded her hand in his hand.

"I'll never let anything happen to you, Chiarina. You know what you mean to me?"

Away from the door of the hut in the half-light, Dante saw the outline of her head and her beautiful hair, for she'd removed her bustina. He wanted to gaze into her dark eyes, to be certain. The dogs moved round them, rubbing against their legs.

"No; tell me what I mean to you," Chiarina said, regaining her composure.

Her voice was tender and he was sure that she cared for him as much as he cared for her. But for Dante it went beyond caring; he had to tell her.

"It's just that I love you."

He was glad it was out; the sweat ran down his back though it was cold up there in the high places.

Chiarina's hand tightened on his hand.

"Oh Dante, silly Dante, sweet and sentimental; my Dante. I know, I know. I love you so much." She kissed him for the first time.

Hand in hand they walked back to the old man's hut, the dogs capering round their legs.

The two wounded and some older, weary men slept in the hut. The handler had fed the mule and, content, the animal rested in a corner of the barn. Everyone else slept wrapped in a blanket in the small barn among the hay left from summer harvest. The shepherd gave Chiarina his bed, and she removed her moccasins and outer clothing. Fred posted sentries armed with light machine guns., and the partisans went into a quiet night—one of the few during the war.

Chapter Three

The major and Fred had chosen a flat surface on the top of the mountain for the band's camp. The campsite was protected by sharp rocks, and snow-covered low ridges to the front and sides. These natural contours would be difficult for attackers to cross.

Rocky surfaces on site prevented digging in. Facing southwest—the most likely approach of an enemy attacking force—a squad built a defensive wall of boulders. To the rear, the squad built a second defensive wall with a gap, easily closed. The gap led to an escape route down the mountain and into the trees, or on to higher ground to the north.

Fred walked to the edge of the camp. He raised binoculars, watching Dante silhouetted by the sun, running along the ridge half a mile out from the camp. Dante flew along the snowy ridge with a sure-footed, distance-eating stride, his arms pumping. The barrel of a machine pistol slung across his back edged above his left shoulder. The pistol holster on his right side swung up and down with the rhythm of his pace. Fred had been waiting for him. Dante had run fifty miles across the mountains, to and from the main band of the Fiamme Verde, carrying the major's written dispatch explaining the band's activities fighting the enemy, and bringing back information affecting the band.

Dante's familiar shape, face below a Tam O'Shanter, filled the lens. He stopped beside Fred, breathing easily.

"Ah like the bonnet."

"It's from one of the sergeants."

"You move fast. Up before dawn?"

"The sun lit the path. I ate bully beef.

Dante turned and pointed with his right hand.

"Five British. One officer—he's a captain—and four sergeants. One's got bagpipes."

"Jesus Christ," Fred said. "What do they want?"

"Join them on a raid. They're experienced sergeants. The captain's a snooty wee shite."

Fred gazed east at the smudges of men and animals moving along the snowy ridge. He turned the binoculars on them. Five British, and three mules with Italian handlers.

"They're bringing kit?"

"Bren Guns, a couple of mortars, explosives. Lee Enfields and Sten Guns. Bully beef, tinned potatoes, tea. Better than straight field rations. I came ahead to brief the major before they get here."

"No clothing?"

Dante shook his head. The friends moved back into the camp, walking over snow-dusted rocks to the major's bivvy. Dante described the British, and handed over the dispatch from the Commandant of the Fiamme Verde.

"The colonel said it's your decision, sir, whether to support the British on the raid."

* * *

The muffled clatter of hooves on snow-covered rocks woke the last of the sleeping partisans. The men gathered in groups, comrades watching the handlers unload weapons and food from the mules. Food! Men smiled and slapped friends on the shoulder. Major Giuntoli waited, Fred and Dante at his side. They wondered how the men would take to bully beef, tinned potatoes, and tea.

The four British NCOs wore khaki trousers, tucked into khaki canvas gaiters, and ammunition boots. The collar of sheepskin jackets jutted above belted white smocks. Each had a pistol holster attached at the waist. Khaki woollen mufflers wound round the neck, thick woollen gloves protected hands against the cold. The piper wore a Glengarry, the others woollen cap comforters.

"The Eyeties will unload the mules, sergeant," the British officer said.

A few minutes later, an ordered heap of ordinance and food lay on the snow-covered rocks. The captain, oblivious to his responsibilities of command, and with no thought for the welfare of the muleteers, waved his hand.

"Send them away, sergeant."

The sergeant looked around and caught Fred's eye. He shrugged. Fred grimaced. The handlers adjusted the panniers and harnesses of the animals.

"No," the major said, beckoning for a former sergeant, a middle-aged veteran of the wars in Africa and the Balkans. "Feed them before they leave. Grappa, coffee, and food. Fodder for the mules."

Major Giuntoli waited. The British captain approached.

"Hetherington, Grenadier Guards. You chaps are to assist on a raid under my command."

The major addressed Hetherington. Dante translated.

"I am Major Sandro Giuntoli, 3rd Alpini, Division Julia, 9th Alpini Regiment, L'Aquila Battalion of the Italian Royal Army, your superior officer."

The captain threw a shabby salute, and Dante didn't miss the flash of irritation in the quirk of the major's mouth.

"Attenzione, capitano! Saluto il vostro ufficiale superiore," the major commanded.

Dante caught Fred's eye. Fred shook his head. "A fuckin' tosser."

The British sergeants and the partisans shuffled feet, shrugged shoulders, exchanged awkward looks. A partisan spat.

The captain came to attention and saluted.

"Captain Ludovic Hetherington, Third Battalion, Grenadier Guards, attached to Special Operations."

Major Giuntoli returned the salute, the steel hook of his prosthetic touching the brim of his Alpini hat. He did not offer his prosthetic to Hetherington.

Hetherington's men had parachuted in, landing close to the main band of the Fiamme Verde to share intelligence, identify objectives, and attack the enemy.

"You appear to be well armed," Hetherington said, smoothing the sleeves of a brown leather, sheepskin-lined flying jacket. He arranged the hang of his khaki uniform trousers over the gaiters, brought his hands up, annoying the arrangement of a crimson silk paisley-patterned cravat glowing at his throat.

"We adapt and improvise," the major said. "We survive, and we fight."

Making do, and adjusting to circumstances—important behaviour for partisans. The major ordered Fred and the NCOs to organise parties to cross the enemy's lines and salvage discarded German, Italian, British, and American weapons, ammunition and kit. The provenance didn't matter, as long as the plundered ordinance and kit worked.

"You have a British sergeant here fighting with you," Hetherington said. "I don't know his name, but I want you to order him to join my force."

"Sergeant Alfredo Forte reports to me. But, if he agrees, you can speak to him."

Later, the major sent for Fred.

"Don't like the look of him, sir. He's like the officer who refused my request for compassionate leave. He's trouble."

"Talk to him, Fred. Find out what he's thinking."

* * *

The British set up quarters, bivvies for shelter, and storage of kit and weapons. Hetherington messed by himself, one of his NCOs bringing him rations. The four sergeants distributed food and rubbed along with the ex-regulars in the band. The piper made a point of having a word with Fred.

"Sergeant Major Jim McGregor, 1st Black Watch; transferred to the 6th Battalion when the 51st Division went back to Blighty. Got fed up and volunteered for this mob. What about you, son?"

"Sergeant Fred Forte, 10th Seaforths, Jim. You're a regular?"

"Right enough, son. Got eighteen years in. Ah got fed up hanging aboot doon south an' volunteered for Special Ops. The sergeants are volunteers, regular infantry, 2nd Battalion, Northumberland Fusiliers. Good lads."

Fred and Jim McGregor shook hands. He told Jim about his escape from the POW camp, the plan to reach Switzerland. The journey north.

"My family are from around here. The young fella is Dante Rinaldi, another Scots-Italian. He's ma pal, and a crack shot. His grandparents hid me. When he joined the band, Ah went with him."

"He's a good lad. Ah gave him the Tam O'Shanter. Ah tell ye, Fred, Ah didn't care for what happened to the Scots-Italians at the start of the war. Very bad. But Ah'm glad yer in the Seaforths."

Captain Hetherington had joined the squad at the last minute when the major commanding got laid up by malaria.

"A great fella, the major," Jim said. "Scots Guards. A bloody good infantryman. He should've been a regular. But Hetherington's a wee problem. He's a reckless, careless English fucker, an' he's no' a regular; he disnae like Italians, an' he's no' keen on the Jocks. Full of shite. Sup with a long spoon, son."

Fred walked across the position to where Hetherington had bivvied. He came to attention and saluted.

"Sergeant Alfredo Forte, 10th Seaforths, sir."

Hetherington rose and waved his right hand, a careless salute.

"You'll report to me from now on, sergeant. You'll be under my orders. You're back in the British Army."

"Begging your pardon, sir. Who gave you authority to move me?"

"God fucking damn you, Forte, for impertinence. I'm giving you the order. You'll obey me."

Like fuck, Fred thought. Aloud he said, "Ah never left the army, but Ah've permission to proceed to Switzerland, sir. Ah belong to the band until the war's over."

"You belong to the army. Do you want a court martial for insubordination and desertion? I'll put you in an army prison."

Fred stood easy, without Hetherington's permission, raging at this prick of an officer sitting on top of a mountain wilderness without one ounce of clout.

"You should talk to the major, sir."

Soon enough Dante, acting as translator, sat with the major and Hetherington near the major's bivvy. They warmed their hands over a feeble fire.

"Tell him he's not having Fred."

"I'll report you to the commanding officer of the Fiamme Verdi."

The major shrugged.

"I work with him, but he can do nothing. This is an independent band. We take orders from no one."

Hetherington's face flushed with anger, turning to the chalk white of cold rage.

"For this operation, you're to place yourself under my command, and I want Forte. He is a British soldier."

The major held up his prosthetic in reproof.

"He is my sergeant. Fred Forte should be an officer, outranking you. You look for my support, but you are insolent. Perhaps the band will work with you, but we will never take orders from you."

Dante read Hetherington's lips.

"He says we're fucking Eyeties."

The major rose and waved Fred over.

"You're staying. Tell the sentries to wait for my signal. Bring the British soldiers over, and the men not on duty."

Major Giuntoli addressed his men and the British NCOs. If Captain Hetherington agreed, the band would work with the British. If he did not agree, the captain would take his men back to the main force of Fiamme Verdi. The band would provide a guide.

He turned to Hetherington.

"You sent the animals away. I can't lend you mules. The ordinance and food will stay here. They'll be well used."

"He says his men will carry what they can," Dante said. "Men'll come back with mules for the rest."

In accented, halting English, the major said to Hetherington: "You go to hell, Captain."

The major beckoned to the sentries. They surrounded the British soldiers, rifles and machine pistols cocked.

"We're fucked, sir," the piper said to Hetherington. "If we're to get this job done, best to agree."

* * *

They sat on boulders in an open but sheltered spot where the rays of the winter sun fell. Hetherington brought the piper, Sergeant Major Jim McGregor, to the meeting. Major Giuntoli had Fred attend to translate and advise on tactics.

"Why come to me, Captain?" the major asked. "We're a small, independent band of irregulars."

"You have a reputation for military discipline and organization; you're dependable; and you've carried out successful attacks."

From the sour look on his face it clearly pained Hetherington to say anything good about Italians, especially partisans.

A thin smile creased Major Giuntoli's face, and he bowed.

"We've a stiffening of soldiers, and the young volunteers learn fast. I rely on Sergeant Forte, and I'm fortunate in having an oldtimer from the Arditi, an NCO. He fought on the Izonso in the Great War."

"He's a good man," Jim McGregor said. "We've had a natter. Ma half-arsed Italian and his broken English. He'd like to have been down south with the Co-Belligerent Army. Ah told him they'd done well at Monte Cassino. We got along fine."

Hetherington scowled at Jim McGregor. Fred and the major exchanged a look. Jim McGregor grinned.

"Thank you for that, sergeant-major," the major said.

In the north of Italy, the partisans operated in high mountains where few people lived—ideal terrain for guerrilla war, but the several bands lacked organization and unified command.

"The Allied Command wants to work with the partisans," Hetherington said. "To provide arms and equipment, and to coordinate attacks against the Germans. We'll fight alongside you."

"We'll not fight with the Communists,"

Before the 92nd Infantry Division launched an offensive, senior Allied officers wanted the help of local partisans to disrupt German operations on the network of roads connecting La Spezia-Parma, Spezia-Genoa, and Aulla-Reggio.

"Our job is to attack, kill officers, and damage the garrison at Borgetta," Hetherington said. "There'll be other attacks going in at the same time."

"I have a man who knows Borgetta," the major said.

Hetherington had aerial reconnaissance photographs with the Garrison HQ and buildings housing German troops pinpointed and marked. The Borgettian made sketch maps of the town and singled out targets where Germans had quartered.

"We'll create panic," the major said.

* * *

Ten men stayed guarding the camp, an NCO in charge. The former Arditi NCO commanded fourteen men and sealed off the road going south. The major and fourteen men secured the road entering the town from the north. Fred had nine men, including Dante, accompanying Hetherington's squad. When Hetherington's force entered the garrison headquarters, Fred's men would kill Germans escaping and prevent a rescue attempt by German soldiers.

The joint Partisan-British force descended Monte Groppo using shaded torches to light the path. The three squads were in position before dawn.

"Take care of ma pipes, son." McGregor laid the pipes beside Dante. "Ah'll get them when we're done."

Fred ordered three rounds fired from the two Brixia mortars, destroying the headquarters gate, killing two sentries, and demolishing the headquarters door. Fred with the Bren Gun and Dante firing the MP 42 poured suppressing fire into the guardhouse, killing the occupants. To the north and the south, they heard mortar explosions, rifle cracks, and machine gun fire, as the rest of the attack went in.

Hetherington led the squad into the German HQ. Lights came on, grenades bounced into rooms, killing soldiers and officers. Upstairs lights flickered. Pistols fired, the *brp-brp* of Sten guns.

A squad of German soldiers from a nearby billet charged towards the HQ and returned fire. Fred and Dante opened up with the Bren and the MP 42, downing six Germans.

Hetherington withdrew last, firing a Sten gun into the headquarters. The squad sprinted and weaved ahead of him across open ground for the cover of the position. Hetherington stopped and fired a final blast into the headquarters.

A shot of return fire hit Hetherington in the head, and he toppled.

The major and the Arditi NCO had shot up some trucks filled with troops attempting to relieve the headquarters.

Jim McGregor picked up his pipes.

"A'h'll play now," he said to Dante, "an' frighten the shite out the Jerries. They'll hide, thinkin' there's another attack going in."

He stood in shadow, piping. Partisans and British soldiers passed, lit by burning trucks and billets glowing red, withdrawing unopposed from Borgetta, to the wailing tune of *The Black Bear*.

The Britsh sergeants, led by Jim McGregor, prepared to rendezvous with a British submarine off a quiet stretch of the Ligurian coast. They left arms and supplies with the band.

"A great bunch of lads, sir," Jim said. He clasped Major Giuntoli's prosthetic. "Thanks for your support. We got the commanding officer and most of his staff."

Fred walked a short way with the British.

"Too bad about Hetherington," he said. "He wasn't shy."

Fred and Jim McGregor shook hands.

"Reckless, Fred. An idiot," Jim McGregor said. "He's well away. Save someone else the trouble. He'd have come after you one way or another. Ah got his dog tags. Ah'll see if we can get him a medal. Look after that young fella, Dante. He's got the makings of a soldier."

* * *

Dante emerged from his shelter and walked to Chiarina's low canvas bivvy. He shook her awake as the first rays of sun crept over the peaks from the east.

"Good morning, my love," he whispered.

Dante shaded a torch, smiling at Chiarina's tousled hair and sleepy eyes. Chiarina got up and pulled on her moccasins over her thick woolen socks, and wound the leather straps round her legs and tied them.

"You need army boots," Dante said.

Chiarina shook her head.

"I like my shepherd's moccasins," she said, pushing her hair under her cap. "And I like my bustina."

"So do I," Dante said as he pulled on his Tam O'Shanter.

"I like your new bonnet; just like Fred's."

Dante and Chiarina rubbed clean snow on their faces to wake up. He handed Chiarina biscuits from an Italian Army field ration pack, and a tin mug of English tea. They munched and swallowed, content for a minute or two.

"Coffee would be good," Chiarina said. "Even that ersatz dishwater. But this tea isn't bad."

They put on white camouflage outer garments.

Sunlight advanced through the position, revealing the humps of sleeping men. To the front and rear, sentries stretched, easing stiff joints, glad the night watch was over. Fred, up since before dawn, came over.

"All set for the patrol?"

He checked Dante's Lee Enfield and Chiarina's machine pistol. "Ammunition okay? Your pistols too?"

"Yes," Dante said.

Fred handed Chiarina a pair of looted 8 X 30 Italian Army binoculars.

"See what you can find out."

The major crossed the position. Sunlight flashed off the steel hook on his right arm. He worried about Chiarina and Dante, and he cared for them. He needed their speed and mountain craft for reconnaissance. But Major Giuntoli hated sending "his kids" out on patrol and into danger.

"We hurt the Germans the other day during the raid," the major said. "Tedesco and maybe Italians will be out looking for us. If you find anything, get back here right away. Be careful."

"Yes, sir," Dante said.

* * *

Dante and Chiarina kept to the snow fields on the descent where their white smocks and over-trousers helped them blend in, hidden from keen-eyed enemy patrols. Two hours out, they saw a press of white move out of the trees and assemble on flat ground.

"Down," Chiarina said.

They crouched, scooping soft snow, making a shallow foxhole.

"Look," Dante said. "You have keener eyes."

Chiarina placed the binoculars on the rim of the foxhole, and swept the mass of men below.

"Germans, and Italians, too. I can tell from their forage caps. There are mules way to the rear." Chiarina handed the binoculars to Dante, and he examined the enemy.

"You're right."

They watched the enemy formations form up by companies for the ascent of the mountain, the Germans taking the lead and setting a blistering pace.

"We have to hurry," Dante said. "If they catch up they'll shoot us."

Chiarina nervously licked her lips.

"You're okay?' Dante asked.

"Yes."

But Dante knew Chiarina wasn't okay. She was bloody frightened, and so was he.

"Come on. You set the pace," Dante said.

Chiarina led Dante into virgin snow where the white camouflaged outer garments kept them hidden from the enemy. She set a hard pace, but, with brief rest stops, a tempo they both could maintain for several hours.

Three hours later, Dante and Chiarina, exhausted by the punishing ascent, returned to the band, bringing word of the large enemy force ascending the mountain.

"They're coming after us," Chiarina said. "We were too far to tell what kind of troops, but we'd say mountain soldiers, battalion strength, say six hundred men. They have mules too."

"Yes," Dante said. "And we heard a plane flying over the mountain."

"He's here," Fred said. "A Storch."

The Storch, a German liaison plane, famous for its flying endurance, had spotted the band, gliding into elegant turns, swooping over the camp for an hour, above the effective range of small arms fire, reporting by radio numbers of men and dispositions to the ground force coming up the mountain.

"We can't stand and fight; they'll wipe us out," the major said. "Fred, organise a rear guard. Two squads of five to hold for twenty or thirty minutes, longer if they can. This is a strong position, and we occupy the higher ground. We'll split the band into smaller squads once we're away."

Two NCOs volunteered to lead the rear-guard squads, veterans from the old Royalist Army, with the band since the beginning. Partisans volunteered. Dante, the best shot in the band, also volunteered. The NCOs picked their men.

Fred assembled the volunteers for what might turn into a suicide mission. He had Brixia mortars, rifle grenades, two MP 42 machine guns, and Panzerfausts ready to distribute.

"You know what to do with these," Fred told the men.

The major ordered the band to prepare for withdrawal. A rush of activity ensued, men filling packs and cinching full rucksacks, relieved to be moving off the mountain.

Chiarina had her personal kit packed and machine pistol ready. She calmed the fretting mules excited by the flurry of movement in the camp. She whispered into their long pointed ears as she fitted a harness, then rewarded the creatures with a smidgeon of sugar filched from the rations. Men loaded panniers, filling them with ammunition packs, heavy weapons, and the band's meagre supply of food and medicine.

The column of men and mules completed assembly, ranks of sallow Italian faces turned pale. The men fidgeted with straps, re-slung rifles, kicked loose snow, ears straining for the major's order to move out. Brave men, dreading the German attack.

A frustrated partisan fired a few rounds from his Beretta submachine gun at the Storch. Fred pushed the muzzle to the ground.

"Too high. You're wasting ammunition. Save it for the fighting."

The major turned, training his binoculars on the col three thousand feet down the mountain. White winter outer clothing covered uniforms, but the field grey forage caps said mountain troops. He magnified the soldiers in the van, the men chosen to lead the attack, through the powerful glasses: edelweiss badges on the forage caps confirmed Dante and Chiarina's intelligence. German mountain troops, 5 Gebirgsjäger-Division. The German squads surged through the snow and poured over the col, ascending to the higher ground. He made a quick count: about 300 men.

"They're 5 Gebirgsjäger-Division. We attacked one of their battalions on the raid," the major said. "Battle-hardened from fighting in Crete, Russia, and I heard they fought on the Gustav line, near Cassino. The CO is the formidable Lieutenant General Max-Günther Schrank. We're up against it, Fred."

Major Giuntoli shifted the binoculars, magnified them and brought closer another formation of troops coming up right behind the Germans—about 250 soldiers of the Black Brigades, the Brigata Negra. He recognised them from the black forage caps. A few soldiers had left outer white tunics open at the neck, revealing the black turtle-necked pullovers typical of the Brigades. They followed the Gebirgsjäger formation over the col, making for the higher ground.

"Brigata Negra," the major said.

The Brigades gathered police, former soldiers and serving soldiers loyal to the Salo Republic that governed Northern Italy after the Italian government deposed Mussolini and signed the Armistice in 1943.

"Small for a brigade, sir," Fred said.

Brigata Negra came in all sizes, from weak battalions to strong companies. "That outfit is a hard company," the major said. "Ligurian. Tullio Bertoni from La Spezia, or the Generale Silvio Parodi from Genoa. Can't tell at this distance."

Knowing that he'd be fighting again in less than an hour rattled Fred. He'd felt panic and fear in North Africa and Sicily, and he'd managed to bottle it down. Maybe this time he'd crack and fall apart.

"We've got fifty minutes, maybe an hour, before they get here. We're in trouble, sir," Fred said. "We're outnumbered about ten to one."

Fred watched a couple of younger men vomiting, and two more pissing their pants.

"Major, some of the new men are in a bad way. We need to get them off this mountain."

"Soon, Fred, soon."

"Wish we'd rum; help get them get ready for what's coming. I've seen men drunk on rum fight. Why the hell do they keep on like this? They've been retreating and surrendering since we invaded. They can't last much longer."

The units hunting the band were tough soldiers, elites led by fanatical officers and NCOs.

"The war is what they have," the major said. "It's all they have. They'll fight on. Ahead of them is death or prison."

Fred borrowed the major's binoculars and focused on white-clad handlers and a cluster of animals, dark against the snow, bringing up the rear of the Black Brigade company. He studied this tight, mobile knot of men and five mules.

"They've got artillery, sir." Fred handed the binoculars to the major.

"A Cannon 65/17 model 13; lightweight and reliable. Five-man crew. Popular with the infantry. Ideal for the conditions up here. We're in point-blank range."

"Jesus Christ," Fred said. "That's a good gun. In Egypt I saw the damage they could do."

"Yes," the major said. "But now the gun crew is in extreme rifle range."

Black Brigade handlers trotted the animals to the rear. Smoke billowed from the gun barrel, whisked away in the breeze. A sharp report came after the smoke and the first round sailed overhead, exploding well to the rear of the band. A minute or two for adjustments, and another shell roared overhead and struck the rear of the position.

"That's good shooting," the major said.

Fred examined the Storch through the binoculars. He held on to the leather helmeted heads of the pilot and the observer.

"There's an observer in the Storch," Fred said. "Bastard'll radio map references to that lot down there. They'll plaster us with HE and shrapnel any moment."

"Got to do something about that damned plane," the major said. "Shoot him down now."

Then the whirr and buzz of the Storch reduced to a threatening, steady rumble, as the pilot throttled back the engine, slowing down, power gliding to below a thousand feet, loitering in a cloudless sky lit by a bright winter sun, turning in measured circles, a pterodactyl searching for prey.

"He's taking it easy, to let the observer adjust the fall of shells," Fred said.

Fred again trained the binoculars on the Storch, concentrating on its predatory circling.

"He passes above that rock spire about every minute or so. Lift and line up the MP 42s? Need to move fast, sir."

"Right, Fred."

The major worked out the angle of fire for the MP 42s, and ordered the guns elevated on two sturdy piles of stones hidden in the shadows at either end of the clearing. The gunners fed in ammunition belts. The second gunners were ready to guide the ammunition belt, and steady the legs of the MP 42. The main gunner trained the weapon.

The Storch continued flying the same threatening pattern.

"When Sergeant Forte signals, aim on a line above the spire, and fire," the major said. "Pour rounds into him."

The Storch came around again, heading for the spire.

"Fire!" Fred yelled, dropping his right hand. His harsh call bouncing through the position reduced the tension felt by the rear guard and the column awaiting the order to withdraw.

Two five-second bursts from one gun, and a hundred rounds shredded the plane's tail. The other weapon fired two bursts at the same time, and another hundred rounds wrecked the engine. The propeller swung and stopped. Flames from the engine smothered the cockpit, and the Storch fell in tight circles, striking the mountainside above the col, blotting virgin snow and rock with burning fuel and a ruptured air frame.

The partisans cheered. The gunners moved the MP 42s back to the line defending the position.

The major nodded to Fred. The Germans and Italians stumbled on the near side of the col, shocked by the loss of the Storch. Their cries of rage and frustration cheered the partisans and eased their fears.

"They won't stop for long," the major said.

"Even without the Storch, they'll find the range by the next couple of rounds," Fred said.

The major turned the binoculars toward a German officer stamping his foot and shaking his fist at the band. He sent for Dante.

"Can you shoot that clown jumping up and down? He's a good way off."

Dante cradled the Lee Enfield .303 rifle picked up from the debris of a skirmish between German and British forces. With Fred's help, he'd fitted a telescopic sight.

"Yes, sir. I can do that."

Dante got into position, legs spread for stability, head hidden by the rock wall, the muzzle of the rifle poking through a gap. He magnified the German's head and forage cap in the scope, judged the wind drift, and squeezed the trigger. The .303 round struck the German's face, killing him. As he fell, the men near him scattered for cover.

"Good shot, Dante," Fred said.

Dante had had a good eye for hunting game with the shotgun before he'd joined the partisans. Fred had tutored Dante on the harsher arts of the military rifle. First, the Italian Carcano, and lately, the superb British Lee Enfield. He gripped his pupil by the shoulder.

"You've done well, son, real well."

The mountain gun fired, and fired again. The gunners had the range, and the shells landed to the rear of the position. Chiarina, ducking low, threw herself flat on snow-covered rock, afraid of hissing shrapnel and rock splinters flying overhead. She rose, crouched, and rushed across the position towards Dante.

"Dante, I'm to go with the mules and the supplies." Her breath came in short blasts. She tried to smile and failed. "The mules like me. I'm good with them."

"I'm glad you're going down."

"Do you have to stay?"

"Yes, you know I must."

Through his clothing, Dante touched the medal hanging round his neck, given him by Old Mario, fingers searching for the features of Mithras, the God of Roman soldiers.

"I'll be alright. Oh Jesus, Chiarina, you be careful."

"Dante, Dante, I love you," Chiarina whispered. "Don't let anything happen to you."

The partisans standing nearby looked away.

Major Giuntoli glanced at the column and sensed the rising fear of his men. He gave the order to move out and directed the column. The animals and the handlers went first. The mules, hooves scraping on snow and rock, vanished over the far edge of the position. Chiarina turned and waved. Dante waved back, and she stepped over the edge and out of sight. The skliffing and crunching of nailed boots on rock as the men went over the edge rang in Dante's ears.

Dante touched his lips, wishing that he'd kissed Chiarina. He'd meant to tell her that he loved her, but the sorrow had overwhelmed them when they parted, and he'd forgotten.

"You alright, son?" Fred said.

Dante shrugged, swallowed his husky voice.

"Sure," he said. "I'm ready."

The major, weighted down by anxiety, rubbed his chin and shook his head. The rear guard would face a devil's symphony of fire and movement with scope for demonic improvised killing. He'd seen the hell coming to the rear guard when the Alpini fought beside the Germans in Russia. Major Giuntoli anticipated heavy casualties.

Fred's gut contracted and he mastered the impulse to shit. He wet his mouth with a sip from his water bottle. Fred dreaded the German assault of storming and movement; he'd been through the ordeal at Dunkirk, and often in North Africa and Sicily.

The major approached Fred.

"This'll be grim. When it's over, I pray we've men left to go on fighting."

"Do our job, sir."

They shook hands.

"We'll meet later," the major said.

Fred scurried to the rear edge of the position and gazed at the band's laden mules, guided by Chiarina, the handlers and an escort, picking their way down the rock-strewn reverse slope, heading for the tree line. The major turned and waved. Fred waved back.

The mountain gun fired again and a shell exploded against rocks, sending shrapnel and stony fragments singing through the position. Fred glanced at a dead partisan, a recent recruit, a straggler just out of his teens, his head shattered by daggers of flying granite. Fred's eye caught the freezing dry snow, stained from soaking up blood and brains. Who would tell his mother and father? Fred imagined the depths of their grief. He hawked, cleaning his throat, and spat out the filth.

"Fuck it; I'd better get on with it."

To save weight, the gun crew had not fitted the protective steel shield: they had no protection from rifle fire—a careless mistake by an Italian officer. Fred organised Dante and another two marksmen.

"Kill and wound as many as you can," Fred said. "I have to go and look after the rear of the column; push on stragglers. Get away as soon as you can."

Dante and the marksmen kept up a steady fusillade on the mountain gun, killing two gunners and wounding another, putting the weapon out of action for several crucial minutes. The mountain gun stopped firing as the Germans launched the advance along rough tracks. The Black Brigade followed close behind.

The Gebirgsjäger soldiers formed the assault, a section in loose formation, the light machine guns going with the infantry, firing as they moved. Squads followed, swarming up the high ground, men firing rifles and machine guns at will as they closed on six hundred yards.

The rear guard fired Brixia mortars as the assault approached four hundred yards. The Germans staggered, but reformed by the NCOs into single files, presenting the fewest targets. The NCOs, machine gunners by their side, led the assault on. The main body of Gebirgsjäger-Division and Black Brigade followed the assault troops. They moved and made expert use of ground cover, hiding in shallow contours, sheltering behind rocks, and, when the machine guns fired, suppressing rifle, machine gun and mortar fire from the partisans, they resumed their advance.

Files of Germans and Italian soldiers gathered for the final assault, jogging over open ground about two hundred yards downhill from the partisan line of defence. Two partisans fired looted Panzerfaust missiles into attacking infantry, killing and wounding several of the enemy.

Advancing Germans fell, but wounded and dead comrades did not dampen the bloodlust of the Gebirgsjäger. Doses of methamphetamine encouraged the recklessness of soldiers attacking the partisan defences. Part of the partisan rear guard pulled out, covered by the squad hiding in crevices and behind rocks.

They just made it as files of Gebirgsjäger-Division and Black Brigade swarmed onto the flat top of the mountain, formed a skirmishing line, and opened fire with rifles and machine pistols. The rear guard fired rifle grenades from looted German Mauser rifles. Then they fired two more Panzerfausts, leaving gaps in the enemy line, soon closed by the German NCOs.

Dante dropped over the rear edge of the position, the Lee Enfield at high port as he ducked and weaved left to right. The weight of the Panzerfaust strapped to his back slowed him down. He spared a glance at comrades running and shuttling left and right. He didn't see the NCO, probably dead now; the squad was down to four. A fleeing partisan dropped his rifle and threw out his arms as several shots riddled his back. He tumbled down the mountainside before striking a gathering of loose boulders. Now they were three.

Behind them, firing and explosions said that the last of the rear guard held on in the position, delaying the enemy. The firing stopped, and the three paused. Then they heard individual shots as the Gebirgsjägers or Black Brigades executed the last of the rear guard. The enemy would soon appear, cascading over the edge of the flat mountain top coming after them. There would be more skirmishing in a few minutes.

"Let's get into the trees," Dante said. "Set an ambush."

* * *

The two survivors of Dante's squad had sidearms and two Carcano rifles with grenade launchers. Dante had his Lee Enfield and the loaded Panzerfaust.

A rifle round bounced off the tube of the Panzerfaust and Dante went down, but hung onto the Lee Enfield, scrambled to his feet and sped to the refuge of the forest.

Dante fingered the Potato Masher grenade tucked in his belt. He worried about the damaged Panzerfaust misfiring. Surprised by his two surviving comrades looking to him, Dante suggested deploying on both sides of the rough track. Let the enemy squads pass; he'd fire the Panzerfaust; immediately, they'd fire grenades into their rear. Follow up with a couple rounds of rifle fire. Then it had to be every man for himself; head for one of the rendezvous points.

Gebirgsjäger-Division and Black Brigade squads entered the trees on a broad front, well spaced over five or six hundred yards, intending to sweep the forest and kill partisans. Dante listened for them coming. A mixed knot of Italians and Germans, weapons ready and confident of winning, strode down the rough track. Men broke off to search for partisans hiding in copses, in clusters of bushes, or behind rocks. Snow fell from the branches of conifers as they passed.

Dante, mouth dry, body pouring sweat in the freezing mountain air, terror loosening his bowels, thought he'd soil his worn, dirty underclothing. He concentrated on what he had to do and calmed down, watching the enemy soldiers flitting past. The Lee Enfield lay at his side. He sighted the Panzerfaust on the backs of the last enemy squad, squeezed the trigger, and immediately the rifle grenades fired. Dante dropped the Panzerfaust.

The volley of missiles fired in the confines of the forest killed five men. In the silence following the explosions, wounded men groaned. But the surviving Gebirgsjäger-Division and Black Brigadiers soon rallied. Dante's comrades fired rifles twice, but missed. Bursts of fire from submachine guns cut them to pieces as they ran through the trees. He drew the pin on the Potato Masher grenade and threw it. A couple of men fell in the explosion, cut down by fragments of metal, and Dante ran for his life.

He scampered away, afraid of death, blundering through trees, branches tearing at his clothing and scratching his face. But he did not abandon the Lee Enfield or the ammunition he carried. He'd packed no food or water, expecting to rejoin the band when the rear guard withdrew. His gut shrank to a walnut, hunger suppressed, but thirst nagging. The band's food and water, ordinance and meagre supplies and medicines had gone with Chiarina and the mules.

"Please, please, God, keep Chiarina safe," Dante whispered as he staggered on, already flagging. He had no idea how long he'd been running through the trees.

Darkness shrouded Dante, and he collapsed on his knees. He listened for the enemy and heard nothing. The Lee Enfield slung on his right shoulder slipped off. Dante rolled onto his side and fell a long way down into the depths of sleep.

Chapter Four

A canopy of conifers had sheltered the sleeping Dante, but now a morning wind moved the branches and a blanket of snow fell on him, and startled, he shot up. Birdsong; a tepid sun on his face. He rubbed his eyes. Tension seized him; flashes of yesterday's fighting and close combat terrified him, and the closeness of death haunted him for a few moments. Dante shivered, darting anxious glances, afraid that German soldiers or Brigata Negra would emerge from dense clumps of conifers and kill him. He took deep, steady breaths, just like Fred had taught him, and his racing pulse slackened; the jagged pains tearing into his stomach eased. Dante brushed the snow off his arms, legs and torso. A painful ache pulsated where the bullet had smashed the Panzerfaust into his back. The nagging, sawing pain in his arms and legs brought dizziness and nausea, and he pushed his hands deep into the snow until they found the earth and held him still.

The major and Fred had the maps, but Dante knew he'd have a good idea of his location once he had a look at the mountains and the position of the sun.

"Need to reconnoiter; fix my position," he muttered.

Coots chattered, and he reckoned he must be near water.

The coots ignored Dante as he slithered through wet snow to reach the shallow banks of a small mountain lake. He sucked in cold water, filling his stomach, then crawled back up the bank to the safety of the trees.

His greedy slurping of freezing lake water disgusted Dante, down on his hunkers, foul-smelling yellow gruel running out of him. Wet leaves would have to do for the business. Up on his feet, rifle slung on his right shoulder, ammunition pouches snug round his waist, an urgent boaking pulled his head down, and he puked up watery mucus and part-digested remnants of his last meal.

There followed two exhausting hours of steep ascent through the conifer forest, hampered by dense undergrowth and deep snow. Dante crawled out from the tree line near to the edge of the narrow ridge. The wind and weight of snow had formed a gleaming white cornice on the far edge. He kept back, worried that the cornice might collapse under him and cause an avalanche. South and west, the ridges descended. Dante had to fight the tug of home, the urge to go to Old Mario and Agate; hot food, a fire, a dry warm bed.

He looked northeast and recognised the mountain. On the far side, he'd find the cabin and the old shepherd with the friendly dogs; the place where he and Chiarina had affirmed their love.

* * *

Dante chambered a round into the Lee Enfield and, hidden by thick undergrowth, watched the hut for half an hour. No signs of the Gebirgsjäger-Division and Black Brigade. Knackered after spending a second night on the freezing mountain, Dante, haggard-faced and staggering from fatigue, came into the clearing in front of the shepherd's hut.

The shepherd dashed out the door, grabbed his arm and pulled him into the warmth of the hut.

"I've been watching you since you hid. You look terrible. You're lucky there are no Germans and Black Brigades about. What's your name, son?"

"I'm Dante Rinaldi."

"You were here with the major's partisans. I remember. Fred, your friend, the other Scots-Italian, came yesterday. I have news."

The surviving partisans, led by the major, had ascended to the highest level, marching a remote track to the main formation of Fiamme Verde, seeking recruits and treatment for the four walking wounded.

Dante had to know if Chiarina lived.

"Was there a girl with the band? She's called Chiarina."

"Yes, Fred left her with me," he said. "She'd have died on the mountain. I remember the two of you capering together, the last time you were here." He smiled. "My dogs were with you. They are good judges of character, and liked both of you."

"She's all right?"

"Chiarina isn't wounded, but she's not all right. She's ill. Pleurisy struck her down, and her nerves are bad. She's been through a lot these past few days. She's so young and she's a partisan."

"Where is she?" Dante asked.

"In there, sleeping." He jerked his thumb at his bedroom door. "I gave her a cup of strong poppy tea. Leave her for now; your girl must rest. No excitement."

A burden of darkness lifted from Dante.

"Thank Christ she's here."

"You must not take His name in vain, son," he said. "It is because of Him Chiarina lives."

Fred's four men had carried two young men on rough stretchers, wounded, and in a bad way. Fred had wanted to send them down the mountain to the village doctor, but they would not have survived.

"By the Blessing they were unconscious when Fred arrived. I laid them in the barn and an hour later they died. Fred stripped the dead of weapons and kit to carry away. I sat Chiarina by the wood stove and wrapped her in a blanket. Then I wrapped the bodies in old canvas and buried them deep in the forest; no one can find them."

"By yourself?" Dante asked.

"Yes, but I prayed for them; the De Profundis. 'Out of the Depths, I have cried to thee O Lord ….' "

"I remember it," Dante said. "It's the prayer for the dead. You might have been praying for me. I'm the last of the rear guard. Nine men killed. Two or three of them executed. I heard pistol shots."

The Gebirgsjäger-Division and Black Brigade had hurt the band: twelve dead and four walking wounded; down to thirty-odd fighters. But they had bruised the enemy.

"It's bad," Dante said.

"You'll all fight another day," the shepherd said.

Despite the heat radiating from the wood stove, Dante shivered. The shepherd handed him a glass of grappa.

"Drink it all, and strip off those wet clothes. Dry off."

Dante—wrapped in a thick, oiled wool pullover that smelled of sheep, and a pair of thick woolen trousers—toasted himself in front of the stove. He sipped from a second glass of grappa and relaxed.

"I'm Anselmo Rossi," the shepherd said. "Anselmo means 'the helmet', a protector. Rossi means red. I'm Anselmo the Red Protector." He laughed.

They shook hands.

"Good to meet you, Mr Rossi, and thank you."

"Aah, it is nothing, Dante. You must call me Anselmo."

Dante squirmed on the stool, his stomach swelling, and worried that he might puke again. He broke wind and his face turned crimson.

"Did you eat anything on the mountain?" Anselmo said.

"I drank from a small lake. I needed water. Afterwards I was sick and there was merde."

"Better you drink from running streams."

Dante mentioned the coots. Anselmo shook his head.

"You're in for some rough days. The lake is full of coot merde. Dante, you stink of sulphur and brimstone. The privy is outside."

Finished in the privy, Dante staggered to the stool.

"Cold out there."

"Hungry, Dante?" Anselmo asked.

"No."

"Drink this," Anselmo said, handing Dante a cup. "Sip it. It's tea I make from poppies and herbs. Good for your stomach. It'll make you feel good."

"I'll leave tomorrow and rejoin the band."

"You're going to be sick for a few days," Anselmo said. "Go out on the mountain and you'll die. Stay here. Get well."

Anselmo examined Dante's lacerated face.

"You have more cuts and bruises, I think. Let me look."

Dante sat on the stool in front of the wood stove, barechested, trouser legs rolled up. He glanced at his pallid flesh stuck on his bony frame, and shook his head. Partisan life meant a skinny body.

Anselmo cleaned up the scratches on Dante's face, then applied arnica to the bruises on his ribs. He laughed.

"Don't worry, when this is over, you'll fatten up. What happened to your back, son? Quite a bruise you have there."

"A bullet hit the Panzerfaust I had slung on my back. Knocked me over; I didn't feel anything. I got up and kept running. Then we fought."

"I'm going to bandage it," Anselmo said.

He folded cotton into a square, soaked it in arnica and bound it to Dante's back with bandages made from an old sheet.

Anselmo pressed a poultice of soap and sugar mixed in equal parts into an oblong of lint and bandaged it over a nasty, scabbed gash on Dante's right arm. He did the same to a bloody abrasion on Dante's lower left leg.

"The poultice'll draw out any pus and calm inflammation," Anselmo said. "In a couple of days, you'll be healing."

"Tell me what happened to Chiarina," Dante said.

"She worried that you might be dead. The girl will be glad to see you. The pain got bad when she coughed or took a deep breath; congested lungs too, and fever. Poor girl. When my wife had it, I used poultices to make her well. We had no doctor in those days, so I knew what to do."

"Tell me," Dante said.

Anselmo had ground flax seed with mortar and pestle, mixing charcoal powder with the flax meal. He added a cup of water and let it thicken, heating it, then leaving it to cool.

"I made two large pads from my wife's old underwear and spread the charcoal jelly on them," Anselmo said. "I made bandages from old sheets."

Anselmo had placed poultices on Chiarina's chest and back, and bandaged them. He changed the poultices every six hours. The treatment relieved Chiarina's pain, and she cooled down. Anselmo made her drink plenty of water.

"Congested lungs," Anselmo said. "I'm worried that the pleurisy might become pneumonia. That would be bad."

Anselmo looked into the bedroom. Chiarina smiled at him.

"You can go in, Dante," Anselmo said. "Chiarina is awake."

Wan and tired, dark shadows under her eyes, sweat shining on her face—Dante's beloved Chiarina looked terrible. Three days since they'd said farewell on the mountain. So much had happened.

Anselmo touched her hand.

"Chiarina... Chiarina, Dante is here."

Chiarina stirred, blinked, rubbed her eyes and smiled.

"Oh, Dante, Dante." Her hand went out to Dante and he grasped it.

Anselmo moved a hand-made wooden stool to the side of the bed. The dogs guarding Chiarina recognised Dante and came to him.

They held hands, both brimming with happiness, and wondered that they'd survived the fighting. Dante listened to Chiarina's rasping breath, the wheezing, congested lungs.

"I'm sick," Chiarina said. "Anselmo nursed me."

"I know," Dante said, cupping her hand in his hands. "I'm sick, too. I drank bad water. I'll be here for a few days. I'll help."

Chiarina's eyes fluttered, resisting sleep.

"I'm so tired. I worry the poultices won't work."

"They'll work. My grandmother uses them. Trust Anselmo; he's a good man."

Dante knew relief finding Chiarina alive, but his heart ached at finding her ill. Chiarina's heart soared when Dante came to her bedside, but pleurisy dragged her down to silence and exhaustion. The clasp of Dante's hands forced her eyes open. His eyes were full.

"You're crying," Chiarina said.

"No, no," Dante said. "Something in my eyes." He turned away, rubbing his eyes with his sleeve. He heard Chiarina sobbing. Dante turned, plucked the edge of the rough sheet and dabbed her eyes dry.

"We love each other," Chiarina said.

"Yes, always."

A tap on the door and Anselmo came into the room. The dogs brushed against his legs as he approached the bed.

Anselmo had Chiarina sit up.

"I'm going to try to drain some of the mucus from your lungs, then change the poultices."

"Will it hurt?"

"No, but you'll cough and spit for a while, and then you'll feel better as you get rid of the phlegm."

"Alright," Chiarina said.

"Help me, Dante. Prop her up on the pillows. You'd better stay. Learn how it's done."

"Okay," Dante said. "Where did you learn?

"In the army.

I still want the doctor to see you. I'll go down to the village at dawn, and bring him next morning. It's a good way down and there's snow."

"He'll come?" Dante said.

"Yes," Anselmo said. "Doctor Bartolemo Vico hates Fascists. He served with the Alpini on the Izonzo, where your father fought."

Anselmo formed a cup with the fingers and thumb of his right hand. He covered the congested area on Chiarina's chest with his cupped hand and placed his left hand on top of the right. As Chiarina took deep breaths, he vibrated his hands on the congested area, loosening and shifting mucus to the upper lungs where Chiarina could cough and spit out the filth.

Anselmo shifted Chiarina to a sitting position, leaning forward, and repeated the treatment to clear the upper back of the lungs. The coughing and hawking exhausted Chiarina, and Dante watching made her feel awkward. Anselmo dabbed her brow dry with a soft cloth.

"You'll feel better after that," he said.

Chiarina, re-poulticed and recovered from coughing and expectorating, slept. Anselmo and Dante sat by the stove. One of the dogs lay sprawled in the space between them. They'd finished supper: stale chestnut bread and hard cheese. They sipped from small glasses of grappa.

"You'll nurse Chiarina while I'm away?"

"Yes," Dante said. "You can trust me, Anselmo."

"Mind now, no capering, son."

"I'm too sick to caper and so is Chiarina. But, on my honour, no capering. I give my word."

"You'll need to help Chiarina use the chamber pot."

Anselmo told them to hide in the cellar if anyone came.

"Too much snow for the Brigata Negra," Anselmo said. "I doubt the Germans will show. They'll be sure to figure the band is elsewhere."

Dante's weapons, ammunition, and motley uniform were already hidden in an ancient cellar dug beneath the bedroom floor.

"The forest ranger comes by, but he's used to finding the place empty and the stove burning when I go out. If anyone comes, hide."

He showed them the trap door flush with the rough wooden floor, hidden by a shabby wool rug.

Anselmo gave Dante a worried glance. "Keep the pistol with you, Dante."

* * *

Anselmo left at sunup, taking Pietro, one of the dogs, with him. He slung a shotgun from his right shoulder.

"There's a pot of soup on the stove," he told Dante. "Soup I made with ham bones, dried white beans, pasta and sausage. Eat with chestnut bread, and get strong."

Pleurisy in Chiarina's case, and for Dante, fever and the runs, had ruined their appetites. He let her sleep most of the morning, looking in from time to time to see that she was comfortable. Late morning, she called for the chamber pot.

Dante moved the pot from beneath the bed, setting it well back.

"I have to get up," Chiarina said. "It's a crisis."

Dante rolled back the bedclothes and sat Chiarina up against the pillows.

"Hurry, please hurry."

Dante eased her to the side of the bed and swung her legs over the edge. Chiarina came upright, hands on the mattress, swaying. Dante steadied her, raised Chiarina to her feet.

"Can you walk?

"No."

Dante carried her—she'd been reduced to skin and bone by partisan life in the mountains. Although he liked her arms around his neck, her head on his shoulder, Dante felt sad that she'd starved. He lowered Chiarina onto the chamber pot.

"Call if you need me. I'll be by the door."

After ten minutes Chiarina called him.

"I'm ashamed," Chiarina said. "You seeing me like this."

Dante clasped Chiarina's hands and brought her to her feet.

"Don't worry, please don't worry."

She swayed, unsteady, but determined to walk.

"Give me your arm."

Dante held her arm, guiding Chiarina's cautious steps. He sat her on the edge of the bed and swung her legs up and under the covers. He tucked the quilt under her chin.

She gave him a weak smile.

"Thank you."

Dante took up the chamber pot.

"Don't look," Chiarina said.

He went outside, threw the contents down the privy and cleaned the chamber pot. Dante looked in the bedroom door, hoping that Chiarina would be strong enough to speak to him, but she'd fallen into deep slumber. When she wakened, Dante would renew the poultices.

* * *

"I have to do this," Dante said, as he helped Chiarina lift her night things and bare her torso.

"I understand."

A new mixture for the poultices, prepared by Dante, lay on a rough bedside table, along with fresh pads of flannel, cut from an old night dress that had belonged to Anselmo's wife. Dante spread the jellied mixture of charcoal and ground flax seed on the pads, unwound the bandages from Chiarina's back and chest, and re-rolled them. He wrung out a cloth in a basin of warm water and dabbed off the residue of the old poultice from Chiarina's back.

"You prefer to wash your chest yourself?"

"No, you do it. You're blushing, Dante."

"So I am. Can't help it."

"Look, Dante, I want you to look."

He gazed, but mastered the desire to caress Chiarina's small breasts. Precise dabbing with the warm damp cloth, and Dante removed the fragments of the old poultice.

"I'll make the bandages firm."

"All right."

Dante propped Chiarina up, but drew the covers up to her chin. He opened the bedroom door to let heat from the wood stove enter the bedroom.

"Don't go; stay a while. I'm lonely in here."

Heat wafted into the bedroom, and Dante and Chiarina relaxed.

"I like Anselmo's dogs," Dante said. "I'm glad he left Prince with us."

The dog, hearing its name, came to Dante, and he ruffled its thick coat. Prince laid his jaw on the edge of the bed, and Chiarina stroked his head.

"So do I," she said. "They're so friendly. They slept by the bed when I was quite ill."

"I'm glad he doesn't have cats," Dante said.

"You don't like cats?"

"Yes, I like cats, but I'm ashamed about what happened to my cat."

"Tell me."

"It happened last winter."

A German patrol had come to the house—ten men commanded by a sergeant—and demanded food.

The soldiers gave tinned sausage, cheese and hard biscuits from their ration packs to Agate. She made a stew thickened with crumbled hard bread and chestnut flour, covered in melted cheese. But the sergeant told Agate to bring more food. The soldiers ate into the Rinaldis' meagre store of ham, root vegetables, dried tomatoes, potatoes, and stale bread.

"And wine," Dante said. "They drank all the red wine apart from a demijohn Old Mario hid. They surprised us when they invited us to share the food."

The sergeant had a decent streak. He paid for the food and wine, gave Old Mario a cotton sock stuffed full of barley, and a bottle of schnapps.

"There's no point in giving money when there's no food to buy."

"What were the Germans like?" Chiarina said.

"Distant, correct," Dante said. "They didn't steal anything. They were army, not Waffen-SS. They put out sentries and slept in the barn. Next morning, they left early. But they just about exhausted our food store.

"The Germans who killed my parents and destroyed the farm were horrible, bad men."

After a couple of weeks of near starvation, the Rinaldis were desperate. Old Mario coaxed milk out of the family cow, squeezing the four teats, two by two, until a thick film of milk lay in the bottom of the milking pail. He wet a saucer white, offering it to the cat. She bowed her head, for she too ached from hunger, and before her tongue lapped up the milk, Mario delivered a fatal blow with a hammer. He skinned the family pet, threw the hide into the trees, and chopped up the carcass, braising the joints in a pot, thickening the juices with what little chestnut flour they'd left, making gravy. Agate mixed in barley to lend the mixture greater body, adding a trifle of chopped garlic for heightened taste, and old mashed polenta. Later, Agate made soup from the bones and shards of flesh of the cat, and thickened the soup with the last of the barley given them by the German sergeant.

"You ate the cat," Chiarina whispered. "And used her bones to make soup stock. Oh God."

"We had nothing," Dante said. "But we drank much of the last demijohn of my grandfather's red wine."

"I'm so sorry, Dante."

"Hunger," Dante said. "It makes you do the unthinkable."

Chiarina opened her arms and he bent over to her embrace.

"What happened to the band when I stayed with the rear guard?" Dante asked.

"Major Giuntoli and Fred—we'd never have got away from the Germans and the Fascists without them."

Major Giuntoli had chosen the escape routes wisely.

Chiarina whispered in the long, pointed ears of screeching mules. The terrified animals bucked, kicked back legs, protesting at crossing exposed routes along narrow ridges. The boom and crash of guns startled the mules. Chiarina guided the unruliest creature's hooves along the vertiginous edges. The rest of the mules followed.

"I felt sick, and the noise of the guns frightened me. The major walked to me through the gunfire. He grinned and pressed my shoulder. 'Chiarina, the animals need you. Comfort them. Only you can keep them moving. We'll get out of this fix.' But on one stretch of the ridge I thought we'd all die. I thought it couldn't get worse, but it did. I felt so ill, but I managed to keep going for my mules."

The ridge swept to the left, facing the ridge opposite, exposing the band to German Jäger troops leading the attack. The mountain fell away from the ridges on each side for one thousand feet. A duel of MP 42 machine guns and rifle fire echoed as the band traversed the ridge.

The oldest mule, the good-natured leader, Victor, caught a burst of machine gun fire, cutting up his rump and crippling his back legs. He fell and he cried, and he looked at Chiarina with sad eyes.

"I had to shoot him behind the ear with my machine pistol."

She burst into tears, and Dante held her close.

"It's all right, it's all right."

"I killed him, and he loved me and trusted me."

Chiarina and the handlers had no time to remove Victor's load, nor had they the means to carry the winter clothing, the medical supplies, and boots, always in short supply. The men helped Chiarina push Victor off the ridge, and the poor animal fell a thousand feet, tumbling over and over, hitting rocks all the way down.

Dante hugged Chiarina.

"After I killed Victor, I can't remember much. But Germans and Fascists hunted us along the narrow ways and high places. I couldn't look down for fear of falling. I was close to collapse."

While Anselmo had buried the two partisan dead, Fred had sat by the stove with Chiarina wrapped in a blanket.

"I asked Fred how we'd escaped, and he told me what happened."

* * *

Fred led the rear guard—the toughest fighters, hard men—holding back the Germans. Dogged running and fighting, lasting through late morning into the afternoon. Just before dusk, the major, alerted by gun fire at the rear of the column drawing closer, ordered an NCO to lead the van off the exposed ridge, and, once again risking death or wounds from German sharpshooters, strode toward Fred and the rear guard. On the way, he had a word with his men, encouraging a return of fire, standing erect as rounds flew past and ricocheted off rocks.

"Hot work, Fred?"

"Yes, sir; Oh Christ, they've fixed bayonets."

"So they have."

A spirited charge by Jäger troops came within twenty feet of the rear guard. The major rested the barrels of his shotgun on the shank of his steel hook, and blasted two Germans dead. He slung the shotgun and fired into the clutch of Jäger troops with his Mauser machine pistol. Fred led the rear guard in a counter-attack. They met the charging Germans head on, driving them back, killing with machine pistols, clubbing heads and bodies with rifle butts, denying the Germans the use of bayonets.

Fred and the rear guard held off the Germans until dusk came. In the lull following the mayhem, the major rejoined the head of the column moving off the ridge. Fred and the rear guard retreated. The Germans licked their wounds.

The partisans got away into the cover of darkness, by forced marching through the night into the high mountains.

"I tried to imagine what you went through fighting in the rear guard on the mountain," Chiarina said. "You and Fred are from Scotland, but your heart is Italian."

"The major and Fred, they're soldiers."

"You, too, are a soldier, Dante."

Chiarina dried her tears.

"It was awful. The dreadful cold. The noise. The machine guns and rifles, the fighting, the screaming, howling men. But we got away. Fred led the party carrying the two wounded men on rough stretchers. I'd collapsed. Fred nursed and half carried me along the way to Anselmo's."

Dante shook his head in wonder. He cupped Chiarina's hands in his.

"When he gave me the poppy tea this morning, Anselmo said everything would be good; Mr God, he said, smiled on the band and sent clouds covering the mountains. The Germans and the Fascists did not know the way. They could not follow, and their planes could not see."

"The cloudy weather is a miracle given by Him," Dante said.

* * *

Anselmo brought the doctor the next morning. They arrived before noon, following an early start and a brisk ascent of the mountain.

Doctor Bartolemo Vico bearded, hard-working country physician—a widower, much loved by his flock of rural patients—came into the room.

"You'll be Dante," he said as they shook hands. "I'm Bartolemo Vico. And you must be Chiarina."

Doctor Vico sat Chiarina up.

"I'll have to lift your night things, to sound your chest. Dante, Anselmo, you can leave now."

"I'd like Anselmo and Dante to stay, doctor," Chiarina said. "They've both poulticed and bandaged me."

"Ah, yes, of course. How silly of me."

The stethoscope moved over Chiarina's back and chest, locating the fluid in her lungs.

"Anselmo, your poulticing and cupping helped get rid of some fluid. I've pinpointed what's left in there. I'll drain your lungs, Chiarina."

Dante and Anselmo helped Chiarina rise from her bed and walked her to the living room. They sat her near the stove, which gave off a fine heat. Doctor Vico laid out his instruments on a small table scrubbed clean by Dante.

"It's just a small operation, called thoracentesis."

"Will it hurt?"

"Yes, when I put in the needle, and it'll hurt a little when I extract the needle. I'm sorry, but I have no local anesthetic."

Doctor Vico had Chiarina sit upright, hands resting on her thighs, her night things raised and resting on her shoulders, revealing her naked back. He cleaned the area around the insertion point for her left lung with a swab soaked in iodine. Dante and Anselmo held her hands.

Chiarina gasped as the needle entered between her ribs. Doctor Vico connected a tube to a bottle to carry off excess fluid from Chiarina's lung.

"Sit, child. Let your body work. It won't be too long."

Silence; and Dante and Anselmo squeezed Chiarina's hands.

"Hold tight, boys," Doctor Vico said. He extracted the needle and covered the puncture with a cotton dressing, fastening it with sticking plaster.

"Now for the right lung," he said, and he repeated the procedure.

"Dante, throw the fluid down the privy."

Doctor Vico bandaged cotton swabs soaked in iodine around Chiarina's torso.

"Rest a while, Chiarina. You're in good hands. After tomorrow, get up for a few hours, but no work for a week."

Doctor Bartolemo Vico washed his hands, ate stale chestnut bread and cheese, and drank a glass of Anselmo's grappa. He had a look at Dante's cuts and abrasions.

"Clean. Anselmo does a great poultice. He'll re-bandage. Dante, you have the hot breath of hell. There's sulphurous fumes in your system. Anselmo told me you drank water from the coot lake. Take these." He gave Dante two pills. "You'll be squatting on the privy for most of the day. Tomorrow, you'll be fine."

But he had more to say to the young people.

"Chiarina, you're a shepherd girl?"

"Yes. I've cared for sheep and goats, and I understand mules."

"I'm your doctor now, and I'm advising you not to go back to the partisans. Anselmo told me all about you, and about Dante, on the way here. You have seen too much. What are you, sixteen or seventeen? You have done enough, more than most. Stay with Anselmo; heal. Help him with his animals when they come up in the spring."

The doctor told Dante to rest until he felt well enough to travel.

"But why go back? Stay here, and when it's safe, go to your grandparents."

Dante wanted to stay, to be near Chiarina, but he knew that he belonged to the partisans until they defeated the enemy.

"I have to go back. You know that."

The doctor shook his head sadly. "Yes, I know; all you young men trying to get yourselves killed. You're seventeen. You've done enough. Live for your family. This war has taken your father and your brother-in-law. Stay alive for your mother and your sister; return to Scotland."

"I'm going back to the Fiamme Verde."

Doctor Vico shrugged.

"I know. I'll pray for you. I'm leaving. I'll go down the mountain and get to the village before dusk; I'll sleep in my own bed."

* * *

After three days, Chiarina got up for a few more hours and insisted on preparing their simple meals. But Anselmo refused to let her rise early to prepare their meagre breakfast. He did that, and Dante brought a scrap of chestnut bread and ersatz coffee to her bedside. Then he sat with her.

By the end of the week, Dante felt well enough to leave and make the long trek across the mountains to the main band of Fiamme Verde.

After breakfast, he brought up his motley uniform, the Lee Enfield, and ammunition pouches from the basement.

"Keep the oiled wool jersey and thick trousers," Anselmo said. "You'll need them up there."

Chiarina had washed and combed out her thick hair. It hung below her shoulders, framing her face when she came into the living area.

Dante liked this new feminine Chiarina, dressed in blouse and skirt, with a shawl around her shoulders and slippers on her small feet—clothing that had belonged to Anselmo's daughter.

"You're lovely," Dante said.

"I'll take the dogs for a walk," Anselmo said. "Let them attend to their duty."

An awkward silence descended as Dante pulled on his outer garments and buckled the ammunition pouches round his waist. He slung his small kitbag containing food, water, a set of clean underclothing and socks given him by Anselmo, and adjusted the straps.

"You're going back to the band," Chiarina said. "Why didn't you tell me?"

"You think I want to go? I want to stay with you and Anselmo until this war is over."

Chiarina came close, and adjusted Dante's Tam O'Shanter to the proper angle.

"There, that's better."

Dante brought a note from his pocket.

"This is my mum's address. Maybe she's bombed out by the Germans. And this is where you can reach my sister, Graziella, but maybe she's bombed out too. I just don't know. You know where to find my grandparents."

Chiarina slipped the note into the pocket of her skirt.

"I'll try to get back here to see you. I want you to come to Scotland. But it's the war, the bloody war. Please stay here and keep safe."

"I'll wait. I'll stay here with Anselmo. Send for me; I'll come."

"I'll always love you."

"And I'll always love you."

A kiss—a chaste, loving kiss—and they clung to each other, afraid to part.

"If I can't come for you, if you don't hear from me, come to Scotland. I'll be waiting."

The lock thudded home, fastening the door, and Chiarina felt shut off, anxious they might never meet again.

Dante swallowed the lump in his throat, hunching his shoulders against the cold wind. He tugged on the sling of the Lee Enfield, bringing the rifle close to his shoulder, and attempted an even pace.

Chiarina gazed after Dante as he walked to the tree line, glad that his faltering steps soon found the marching rhythm. She still had the binoculars, and magnified Dante, bringing him close enough that she felt she could touch him. Chiarina watched her beloved from the window until he cleared the tree line, and, making rapid progress towards the ridges, he vanished from her view.

Chapter Five

June 1945: almost a month since Germany and the Salo Republic surrendered to the Allies. The police station at Pontremoli, a quiet town, held Brigata Negra officers and local Fascists, some in custody for several weeks before the collapse of German and Salo forces. Major Giuntoli refused to wait for politicians preaching reconciliation in post-war Italy. After trial, sentencing, and time in prison, Fascists released slipped back to ordinary life.

"We're going to do something about these bastards. They killed Italians and committed atrocities," the major said to Fred.

Fred led an armed party to old battlefields littered with the detritus of war. A partisan, a good mechanic, got a couple of abandoned British Army trucks working, salvaging parts from wrecked vehicles and touching up the paintwork. They mounted MP 42 machine guns in the turrets above the driver's cabin.

"A better weapon than the Bren Gun," Fred said to Dante.

Faces charcoal-blackened, the major led twenty partisan veterans whose families had suffered at the hands of Fascists, armed with rifles and Sten guns. Fred led the guard; Dante volunteered for Chiarina's sake.

The partisans entered the station two hours before dawn, overpowered the passive duty officers who, having no wish to die shielding Fascists, handed over keys to the cells. Major Giuntoli watched his men unlocking cells, then bundling Salo soldiers and Fascists into the corridor. They locked the police in the cells.

Some of the Fascists and Salo soldiers, depressed by jail time, broke down and wept, guessing the partisans meant to kill them. The tears did not register with Major Giuntoli.

"Get them on to the trucks," he said to Fred.

Three officers of the Salo forces and a ranking Fascist official remained defiant and resisted. One big man head-butted a partisan. Fred broke his jaw with a blow from his Lee Enfield rifle butt.

"Communist scum," the Fascist said through blood and broken teeth.

His two companions lay on the floor, nursing bruised kidneys.

Fred pointed to his green scarf.

"Fiamme Verde. Catholic, and Conservative, but I salute the Communists for killing Mussolini. Get on the truck, or you'll die here."

Partisans leveled Lee Enfields and Sten guns at the Fascists, while Fred, Dante, and a couple of other men bound their wrists behind their backs, pushed them into the rear of a truck, and made them lie on the floor.

"Guard them well. Any trouble, kill them," the major said to Fred.

The lead truck carried the prisoners and their partisan guards; the second truck with the remaining partisans followed. They took ten men and a woman to a quiet place in the hills and parked the trucks. A partisan who knew the area led the way. They ascended through the forest to the mountain. In a hidden glade near the edge of the tree line, where the runoff from melting snow softened the earth, they stopped and untied the prisoners' hands. Spades handed out, the prisoners dug their own graves in random positions deep in the clearing. Fred and Dante covered them with Sten guns.

"Kneel," the major ordered the prisoners, but they would not.

"This is murder," an officer of the Brigata Negra said. "You'll suffer for this."

"No one out there cares about you now," the major said. "This is justice for your crimes."

Partisans forced the prisoners to their knees at the edges of their graves.

"Blindfold them," Major Giuntoli said.

But they didn't want blindfolding.

"Hard-cases," Fred said to Dante.

The major shrugged.

"Blindfold them, anyway."

Dante thought about the murder of Chiarina's mother when German and Salo soldiers shot her to pieces in front of her husband, and then clubbed him to death with rifle butts. Chiarina had seen their murder just before she ran for the refuge of the band. He remembered lost comrades and volunteered to take part in the executions. Fred volunteered, too, but the major shook his head.

"It's Italian business," he said, looking at Fred and Dante. "You are Scots-Italians. Soon you will go home; forget about this execution."

The major withdrew a Beretta from its holster and fitted a silencer. He killed the woman with a bullet in the back of the head. She tumbled face down into her grave. He passed the pistol to an NCO. He shot the senior Salo Officer and passed the pistol to another partisan, who shot a Fascist and passed on the pistol, until all the Fascists and Salo soldiers had keeled over and lay in their graves.

"Leave them face down," the major said. "Let them stare at hell for eternity."

Deep in the hills on a dirt road, the partisans left the trucks. Men showered petrol about the vehicles. The sun edged above the horizon. The men pushed the trucks to the rim of the precipice and set fire to them. The flames caught, and they heaved and pushed the trucks over. The blazing vehicles tumbled and crashed a good way down until boulders held them, and they blew up when the fuel tanks ignited.

The men shouldered arms, and formed a loose double rank. The major glanced at his men.

"All right, Fred, let's head for the camp."

Fred formed the men in single file and they marched into the hills.

* * *

The time had come to disband and hide most of the weapons and ammunition against the possibility of a Communist insurrection and civil war. Major Giuntoli had Fred assemble the men. He walked to the front of the band and spoke from the heart.

"We will not go to the British or the Americans and disarm. We disband here on the ground we defended and won. And we hide our weapons against an uncertain future.

"You have fought a long, hard war for Italy with courage against terrible enemies. We have shared dreadful moments in battle. Many of our comrades have died.

"We survivors are bound by circumstances of battle. You men of the Fiamme Verde are a special company, like soldiers of Rome. I am proud to have served with every one of you. You have done enough. You deserve peace and a long and happy life. It is time to go home."

He moved through the ranks and shook hands, embracing and naming each one of his men in a personal farewell, wishing them good luck.

The men took their time packing and hiding weapons. Release from the band after two years and more of fighting came as a shock. In the bleak days on the run, amid combat, and seeing comrades killed and wounded, they'd dreamt of an end to this life. Now that the moment had come, some of them did not know what to do.

"I'll hang on tonight, and maybe for a day or two," a veteran sergeant of the Royalist Army said.

A handful of the experienced partisans murmured approval and laid down haversacks and kit.

The major brought them to attention.

"You're all going home. The longer you hang about here, the harder it will be to leave."

"You're right, sir," the sergeant said.

The command drifted away and went down from the mountain in twos and threes, on their way home.

"What about you, Dante, and you, Fred?" Major Giuntoli asked.

"I'll walk to Florence," Dante said. "I hear there's a centre there for displaced British subjects and refugees."

"I'll walk with Dante to Florence and report to the British Army," Fred said. "I hope they'll send me home. I think I'm ready for demob."

"And what about you, sir?" Dante said.

"Report to my battalion for medical checks and discharge. Then I'll go home."

The major gave them letters in Italian detailing their loyal and distinguished service.

"These documents might be useful. My battalion and home addresses are there if any official wants to contact me."

An awkward, embarrassed silence followed, and feelings overcame British reticence.

"Fuck it, sir, but you're the best officer I ever served with," Fred said. He came to attention, and gave a last immaculate salute to his commanding officer.

"Same goes for me, sir," Dante said, coming to attention and saluting the major.

The major came to attention.

"Thank you, Fred, and you, Dante. You made me stronger." He raised the steel hook to the brim of his Alpini hat.

* * *

When the Band dispersed, Major Giuntoli divided food, clothing and tools among the men to take home. A couple of young farmers asked for the mules. The major and the partisan accompanying him packed what they could carry.

Fred and Dante filled their kitbags with British Army field rations packed on top of personal kit.

"Across the mountains, Fred, to Anselmo's place. Chiarina will still be there. Then Garbugliago to see my grandparents."

"We've Modestino, the mascot," Fred said. "She'll carry stuff."

"Why's she called Modestino?" Dante said.

"Back in school I read a book about a donkey called Modestino."

"Never heard of it. But you went to the high school. Ah got stuck in St Mary's; Ah finished with school here when Ah was thirteen. The war."

Modestino was patient, feminine, a sweet-natured, dignified creature, liking company. The animal did not complain when they loaded the panniers with field rations and army clothing. They turned northeast, heading for Anselmo's small holding. They planned to thank the shepherd, but what Dante wanted was to see Chiarina, and to hold her.

They meant to walk two or three days across the mountain to Anselmo and Chiarina, and turn south through the forest to Garbugliago to say farewell to Dante's grandparents, Mario and Agate Rinaldi.

Fred and Dante, warriors of the forest and high places, carrying arms, coming back to the world. Both men wore the Tam

O'Shanter, British Army battle dress, gaiters and ammunition boots. Around their necks they wore the green scarf of the Fiamme Verde. And they kept their arms, for the authorities had not cleared the countryside of armed bands of Allied and German deserters no better than brigands. If they had to fight, Fred reckoned it would be up close, so they each carried Beretta automatic pistols and German MP 40 submachine guns, a superior weapon to its Allied equivalents.

October brings to Liguria bright mornings, sunny cheering days to enjoy the changing colours of the forest, and evenings mild enough for sleeping out. Fred and Dante prayed for clement weather.

They arrived at Anselmo's farm late afternoon of the first day and the weather held. No smoking chimney welcomed Fred and Dante. The dogs did not race out the door of the house to caper and frolic. They tried the door to the house; locked against marauding deserters from the several armies. Fastened bolts suggested a lengthy absence. The barn door opened on an empty stall, straw stacked against the walls, enough to make a mattress.

"They're not here," Dante said. "Where the hell are they? Christ, Ah hope nuthin's happened to them."

Dante brought Modestino into the barn and began unloading her. Fred closed the barn door, then turned and loosened the small package of sacking nailed to the back of the door.

"You open it, Dante."

The sacking contained a note for Dante from Chiarina. Anselmo could not see through blurred vision. She had first gone down the mountain with the animals and passed them to Anselmo's daughter. Then she ascended the mountain and brought Anselmo down to the care of Doctor Bartolemo Vico. The doctor had an old car and would take Anselmo and Chiarina to a hospital in Bologna where he knew an eye surgeon who'd remove Anselmo's cataracts; a tricky operation. Chiarina would look after Anselmo until he could see, and bring him home again.

Dante left a note wrapped in the sacking telling Chiarina to go to his grandparents if she needed help.

* * *

November is the rainy month, but that year the skies opened early. Dante and Fred made a sad descent through a curtain of precipitation, water trickling down the neck of their capes, wetting battle dress, dampening shirt and underwear. But their misery paled beside a sad Modestino weighed down by the load, stepping, faltering among rocks, her mane saturated, dripping, and chill reaching into her bones.

By dusk the wind got up and they found damp shelter under a rocky overhang. They unloaded Modestino and moved her load under the projecting rock. They hobbled her front legs and kept her in the limited shelter of the overhang edge. Fred foraged for twigs and dead wood to light a fire. He found a cache of dryish wood in the back of the overhang, left there by earlier visitors. Cold food and hot tea for supper; and they banked the fire to warm up and dry out.

Dante took the driest side of their capes and dried off Modestino, leaving her damp. She warmed her rump near the fire. Dante draped the capes over the load to dry. Then he fed and watered the animal.

Snug, lying on a groundsheet inside an army sleeping bag and covered with capes, Fred and Dante slept. In the small hours, with the fire reduced to dull red embers, Dante felt a pawing at his legs and then a wet nose on his face. He woke to find Modestino staring and shivering. She sneezed and coughed.

"Good Christ! The poor thing is sick."

He woke Fred.

"Got to get Modestino warm, or she'll collapse."

Fred piled wood on the fire, and Modestino looked ill in the yellow light of the flames. Dante dried her off again, but still Modestino shivered. He brought her right inside the overhang.

"Ah'm not sleeping with a donkey," Fred said.

"Too right you are, Fred. Ah'm not letting her die. Ma grandfather is good with animals. Got to get Modestino to Garbugliago."

They fastened the ground sheets and opened out the sleeping bags. Dante unhobbled Modestino and she came right under the overhang.

"Come on, girl," Dante said, and coaxed Modestino onto her side, lying on the groundsheets. He covered her with the sleeping bags and the joined capes. The fire gave off a good heat. Fred piled on the last of the wood.

"Come on, Fred. Get under the covers and cuddle up. Keep Modestino warm."

Fred wrinkled his nose and slipped in next to the animal and pressed against her. Dante made sure the donkey was comfortable, and then he, too, slipped in beside her, pressing against a happy Modestino. The donkey smell did not offend, for she was a clean animal, and soon they all slept, the silence broken by the gentle fluttering of Modestino's puckering lips as she exhaled.

Modestino was spry, but not recovered, when she got up. Dante fed and watered her. He knew that the poor creature could not carry her full load of the day before.

Fred and Dante squatted beside a small fire and sipped tea and munched hard tack. Glad they were that the rain had passed over.

"Fred, we need to help her," Dante said.

"Ah can see that."

With the axe, Dante and Fred cut wood from a dead tree and stacked it in the back of the shelter for the next weary travelers.

They broke down the load and filled slack spaces in their packs. Fred, adept at packing and arranging kitbags, fashioned two rough packs from the capes held with rope and lashed onto the kitbags. They reloaded the panniers, and Modestino neighed and capered with her lighter load. Fred and Dante each now carried an eighty-pound load.

They passed over open ground coming near to Garbugliago, Dante in front, Fred leading a subdued, ailing Modestino behind. As they passed through the main street, doors slammed, and women afraid of strangers peered from behind curtains.

They stopped in the small vegetable garden where Old Mario worked at the compost heap. Agate was inside the farm house.

The old man came forward and embraced them.

"We've been expecting you for the last couple of months. Agate, come! They are here."

Agate embraced and kissed her grandson, then held him at arm's length.

"You've grown. I hope you've been behaving yourself."

Fred grinned, and Dante blushed.

He gestured to the donkey.

"She's sick; a bad cough, and she stumbles. Can you have a look at her? Her name's Modestino."

"Ah, my grandson is still a sentimentalist."

"She's our mascot. If you can't be kind to her, we'll not leave her here."

Old Mario held up a placatory hand.

"Unpack her. I'll make up some feed."

He wiped a large bottle of iodine free of dust.

"I'll put a dose in the feed for a few days, and the cough will go away. Let me look at her hooves."

He examined Modestino's hooves and withdrew a clasp knife from his jacket pocket.

"Hold her steady, Dante. Be nice to her. She doesn't know me, but she likes you."

With the point of the knife, he picked out fungus, casting it aside, then added a dash of bleach to warm water, and washed the hooves.

"I'll do this twice a day for a few days, and pack her hooves with clean rags soaked in iodine. She needs a paring."

Old Mario spent several minutes paring and smoothing the frog of the animal's hooves, getting rid of damaged and infected tissue.

"Don't worry, we'll look after her; and thank you for bringing Modestino."

They gave most of the food and some of the clothing to Old Mario and Agate, along with the axe and spade. Fred reached deep into a bag on the panniers lying at the door of the house. He withdrew a clay jar of army rum. Old Mario's eyes lit up.

"Let us drink to your safe arrival."

They went inside, and Agate brought out four small glasses.

"Pour, Mario," Fred said.

"Aaah," Mario said, filling each glass to the brim with dark rum.

"We thank Him and Our Blessed Lady for your deliverance."

Mario raised his glass, and they all touched glasses for good luck. Mario downed the rum in one. Agate sipped; Fred downed his in two; and Dante, following his grandfather, swallowed his in one. He coughed.

"More than a hundred proof," Fred said. "Good stuff." Fred refilled all the glasses but Agate's, who said she'd prepare the meal. Mario got up.

"Your crusade is done. Let us go to the church and offer thanks to the crusading knight, Nicolo the Lombard."

Mario, Dante, and Fred walked in the twilight to the church. Going in, they dipped their fingers in the stoup and blessed themselves. They laid right hands on the pommel of the sword held by the knight on the bas relief of the sarcophagus.

"Nicolo the Lombard, we offer thanks for your blessing that kept my grandson and Fred safe on their crusade against evil."

At the door, again they dipped their fingers in the stoup and made the sign of the cross. Fred and Dante put on Tam

O'Shanters, and moved by the dignity of it all, turned as one man, came to attention, boots crashing on the flagstones, and saluted the long-dead knight.

"I am proud of you, Dante and Fred," Old Mario said.

Outside, Mario put his arms round their shoulders.

"There is another we must thank: Mithras, god of the Roman soldiers."

Mario wished he knew the rituals of the Roman legionnaires.

"Let each of us thank Mithras."

They stood in silence. Mario had his head bowed, hands clasped before him. Dante and Fred touched the medals of the god underneath their shirts, given them by Mario when they set out to join the partisans; and they offered grateful thanks.

* * *

Agate had the meal ready when they returned to the house—hard chestnut bread, a hot dish of pork spam thickened with oatmeal, broth and crumbled hard tack.

"Like All In," Fred said, thinking of an army stew served in the Seaforths. "It's good."

Later they had tea and sweet biscuits. Mario put the clay jar on the table. Agate brought four glasses. They drank rum until mellow.

"What about that lovely girl you brought here, Dante?" Agate said.

Dante told them what had happened.

"If she comes here, you'll help her? I left her a note saying you would help."

"Yes," Mario said.

"I want her to come to Scotland, and we'll get married."

"Married!" Agate said. "But you've not turned eighteen."

"You weren't much older when you got married and came to Scotland," Dante said.

Agate looked down at her slippers.

They drank more rum. Dante felt the spirit kick in and slowed down.

"We heard about the raid on Borgetta and the running battle you had with the German mountain troops and the Brigata Negra," Mario said. "You did well. What happened after you escaped?"

They described the retreat, and Fred taking Chiarina and the wounded to Anselmo.

"I got sick and separated from the band. Anselmo looked after me for about a week," Dante said. "That was the last time I saw Chiarina. Then I walked across the mountains to rejoin the band."

Dante told them that after refitting with British arms and kit at the main camp of the Fiamme Verde, the band worked with British SOE operatives and Italian SAS attached to the British.

"Did you fight at the liberation of La Spezia and Genoa?" Mario said.

"We kept back from that, and fought our old enemy, the 5 Gebirgsjäger-Division as they retreated north," Fred said.

"We're good at ambushing, and attacked them all the way to the outskirts of Turin, where they surrendered to the Americans last May. Hard fighting, and we paid them back. Then we pulled back to hold the ground we had won."

They said nothing about the raid on Pontremoli gaol.

Dante and Fred slept in Dante's old bed. They rose early and breakfasted on oatmeal, hard tack, and tea.

They thanked Agate and Mario for their hospitality, and got ready for the march on Florence some way to the south.

"Thank you, Dante and Fred, for the food and all. Don't worry, I'll take care of Modestino."

Dante went to the barn where Modestino stood. She came to Dante at once, nickering, nuzzling Dante's face. Dante hoped Mario would keep his promise. He patted Modestino's forehead.

"Goodbye, old girl," he said, turning away and swallowing the lump in his throat.

Mario embraced Fred and Dante. Agate shook hands with Fred and kissed her grandson on the cheek. Dante and Fred moved off.

"You'll help Chiarina if she comes here?" Dante called back.

Mario smiled, waved and nodded his head. A stony-faced Agate lifted her hand in farewell.

* * *

On the march to Florence, Dante and Fred passed through countryside and towns ravaged by fighting. Everywhere, the scars of war disfigured the land. Outside Florence, they dumped their German machine pistols, but they both hid a Berreta M1935 pistol in their clothing.

Dante and Fred said farewell. Fred got ready to report to the army.

"See you in Westburn, Dante. You'll be home before me. Tell my mum and dad I'm okay."

"I'll do that, Fred. Look after yourself."

Dante went to the British Consul, who sent him to a military camp full of friendly Polish soldiers.

"No idea how long you'll be there. Wait for transport. You could always walk to Naples."

Dante shook his head. He'd had enough of walking through war-ravaged Italy.

After a week, he got a lift from Polish soldiers going down to Naples in a truck.

The Sicilian bandit, Salvatore Gulianom, and his band operated in the south.

A grinning Polish Sergeant patted his Sten gun.

"We see him, he's a dead man."

In Naples, Dante reported to a hostel for displaced persons as directed by the British Consul in Florence. He slept in a dormitory and was fed once a day. After two weeks, he joined a ship sailing for the UK.

* * *

His last day aboard ship: Shaved and bathed, Dante, clad in fresh underwear and socks, laid out one of the two British Army battle dress issued to the Fiamme Verde in the closing months of the war. The well-worn kit was marred by ingrained food and dirt stains, patched tears on the seat, and holes at knees and elbows from living and fighting over rough country. He kept the good battle dress pressed and folded in his kitbag.

Dante was proud of his uniforms and took good care of them. To keep calm, he sponged blouse and trousers of his fighting battle dress free of dust, and made a futile attack with wet cloths on stains, borrowed an iron and ironing board, and pressed the garments with regulation razor-sharp creases. A sailor lent him polish to shine his well-used black ammunition boots. His Tam O'Shanter and pressed green scarf lay on the counterpane of his bunk. A kitbag contained his best battle dress, spare ammunition boots, a few belongings and the mountain garb given him by Anselmo. Everything was packed and ready to leave the ship.

Sailing from Naples to Southampton, Dante enjoyed what for him amounted to luxury: the quiet ship, the six-berth cabin, and he the sole occupant; the steward who appeared each morning to make up the bunk and tidy the cabin; the clean showers and heads a few steps along the alleyway where he washed and stood under the tingling arrows of endless hot water. And the food. Porridge, eggs and bacon, toast, margarine, and jam for breakfast. Prodigious meals at noon and early evening; solid British Merchant Navy grub: thick soups, stews, roasts, potatoes and vegetables, plates piled with fresh white bread; duff and custard. Dante couldn't get enough to eat. Soon his clothing hung almost fitting him, rather than draped like a shroud on his bony frame.

The other passengers, lost souls like himself returning to God knows what, bid Dante a quiet good morning or good evening.

He shared a table with a Coptic woman and her daughter, a bubbly girl of eight.

"I'm Kristina Taylor, and this is my daughter, Hannah. My own name is Aziz. I am a Copt, from Egypt."

She'd married a British man, a canal pilot working for the Suez Canal Company. She worried about leaving Egypt and making the family home in England. They exchanged polite conversation. Dante told her about his time on the farm in Italy.

"But you wear a uniform," Kristina said. "You're a Scots-Italian, in the British Army?"

"No. I belonged to the Fiamme Verde; Catholic Partisans. I got the uniform from the British Army when we helped them fight the Germans and Fascists. The refugee administration in Naples gave me civilian clothes, but I threw them over the side."

"My husband has taken a job as a Mersey pilot. The pay is good. He's in Britain now finding us a house. I worry. Some British don't like Egyptians. I'm not a Wog. I'm a Christian, a Copt."

Hannah, a sweet, pretty child, started to cry.

"I miss my daddy. I wish we'd stayed in Port Said. It's our home. My gran and grandpa and my cousins are there."

Dante took Hannah's hand.

"I hear Liverpool is a great city. You'll like it." He smiled. "We're the same colour. No one ever called me a Wog. You'll be all right, and you'll meet your British gran and grandpa, and your new cousins."

He didn't tell Kristina and Hannah about the harsh treatment of Italians, damned as Eyeties and Tally bastards at the start of the war, their businesses wrecked and looted, internment, and deaths. Dante worried for this little girl and her mother.

Hannah smiled through her tears.

"You're so kind," Kristina said.

A young Scots Fourth Engineer took Dante round the engine room and stoke hold. On deck, he spoke to sailors. Homesick soldiers on the way home for demob chatted to him on deck.

"Is that you, Dante?" a Scots voice called.

A tall, familiar figure grabbed his right hand and shook it.

"Sergeant Major Jim McGregor, 1st Black Watch. You remember me, lad?"

"Ah do, but Ah never expected to see you again."

"You're wearing the bonnet I gave you. Good."

Jim McGregor took Dante to the mess. He ordered two beers.

"Ah'm goin' back to the battalion. There's a bunch of lads goin' home for demob. Ah'm lookin' after them."

Jim McGregor had served with Special Operations Executive behind the lines until the enemy surrender.

"What about you, Dante?"

"Ah stayed with the band until Major Giuntoli decided to disband, but we didn't go to the Americans or the British to surrender weapons and supplies. The major wasn't having it. We ended it on the ground we'd won and held."

"Ah like that. A fine soldier, Major Giuntoli. What about that bonny girl, Chiarina?"

"I left Chiarina with Anselmo, the shepherd. She was sick and had enough. She needed to get well and rest. Ah got sick, too, and Anselmo looked after us. Then I walked the mountains to rejoin the band."

They'd finished the beers, and Jim McGregor ordered two more.

"Ah'm not sure how, but one day soon, Ah'm going to bring Chiarina to Scotland."

"You do that, son. She's a fine girl."

Dante spent time with Jim McGregor and his men. They were all Jocks, and he found it comforting, being more or less among his own people. Some of them had not been home in five years, having soldiered in North Africa, then moving to the Italian Campaign. A couple of men in their early twenties meant to stay on in the army.

"Ah like the army. Goin' for a Regular. Back to the east end of Glasgow, to Bridgeton? No thanks," one said.

The single men seemed to be most at ease with going home for demob. Some men talked of migrating to Canada, Australia, or New Zealand. One hardy young man mentioned the Southern African Colonies.

Going home unsettled the married men. One man got drunk often. An anonymous "friend" had written to tell him that his wife went out with the Yanks; and he'd find a year-old surprise waiting for him.

A married soldier in his mid-twenties said he'd no idea what to expect.

"Ah've no' seen her in four years. We write letters, but will she still be the same lassie Ah married? Christ! Ah'm no' sure Ah'm the same fella *she* married."

And Dante slept often, tempted by neat clean sheets and warm blankets tucked round his bunk. It came to him that he didn't have to sleep clothed and shod as he did in the band.

But the greater part of the time at sea, Dante kept to himself. He had much to think about, but was consoled that others too had troubles. Even so, he worried about how he'd seem to his mum and Graziella. Would they like him? Would *he* like *them*?

Would he find in Westburn the friendship and camaraderie so freely given in the band? He couldn't be sure.

He missed Chiarina, and it hurt to think about her. He just had to see her again, and for keeps.

In the band, be could always turn to Fred and the major for advice and counsel. In Westburn he'd have to stand alone, and support his mum and his sister. He prayed that he'd be ready.

On the twelfth day, the Admiralty rerouted the ship to Westburn when a report said mines in the English Channel threatened the vessel. The ship turned southwest into the Chops of the Channel, rounded The Lizard, and steamed north into the Irish Sea; two days sailing to the Clyde Estuary. Dante didn't mind the extra time at sea—an interlude to ready himself for the shock of home.

The last day, as the ship entered the Clyde Estuary, Jim McGregor spoke to Dante.

"You get Chiarina over here to Blighty and get back to yer family. Tell Fred Ah'm askin' for him."

They shook hands.

"Thanks, Jim."

Dante went on deck, shunning the port side, the views of the north shore of the Clyde, the the Argyll Hills and the mountains to the northwest. He ignored the freighters and the men-of-war anchored at the Tail of The Bank.

The seventh year of exile, and the longing for his family and Westburn smothered the simmering pool of anxieties about coming home. The Clyde river steamers berthed at Kempock Pier, the mottled grey and red stone facade of the torpedo factory, and the Esplanade lined with fine Victorian villas did not register with Dante. But yearning for home did not shift memories of the band and Chiarina.

Dante stared at Princes Pier and rail terminus where his father had begun the journey ending in his drowning when the U-47 torpedoed the Arandora Star. Rage contracted his stomach. He cleared his throat and spat the filth into the river. Calmer now, he turned his back, and went below as the tugs coaxed the vessel along like meddlesome border collies.

* * *

A knock, and the cabin door opened. Sergeant Lachlan Ponsonby, Westburn Police, filled the doorway, arms folded, displaying three white chevrons. He stepped into the cabin, right hand out.

"There ye are, son. Welcome home, Dante."

Dante remembered Sergeant Ponsonby from days capering in Holmscroft Street, before his grandfather took him to Italy. He grasped the offered hand and nodded.

"Hello, sergeant."

"You've been away a while."

"This is the seventh year."

The sergeant had an order to bring Dante home.

"Does ma family expect me?"

"They know you're on your way. I telephoned. The station got word yesterday."

Dante fastened the battle dress blouse and cinched the waistband. He looked at his polished ammunition boots, making sure his pants hung over the khaki gaiters. The green scarf of the Fiamme Verde he placed under the collar of the blouse, a triangle decorating his back. Over his breast, he tied a sailor's knot. Last, he put on the Tam O'Shanter, and tugged it over the right brow.

Sergeant Ponsonby recognised the combat wear on Dante's uniform.

"Ah didn't know you'd joined the army, son."

"Partisans; Green Flames, the Catholic Fiamme Verde."

"Would ye no' be better in a civilian suit, Dante?"

"The refugee people in Naples issued a suit. Shabby rubbish. Ah chucked it over the side."

Rage consumed Dante, having to walk the ground where his father set out on the path to his death. He wanted anyone who looked to know where he came from, and pointed to the miniature Italian flags stitched to his blouse sleeves.

"Ah'm no' some repatriated internee fae the Isle of Man or Canada. Ah fought for Italy; aye, and Scotland as well. Ah'm no walkin' home slinkin' along Holmscroft Street, a bloody refugee; a fuckin' tramp."

"Ye'll not be talkin' tae yer mother that way?"

Dante turned away, swallowing hard at the mention of his mum. He tried to picture her, not as she had been when he'd left, but as she might look now, and couldn't. He'd been away too long.

"Ah won't."

Sergeant Ponsonby brought transport to take Dante home in style.

"Ah wangled a car. Get ye home quick."

"Ah don't want a lift. Ah'll walk home."

"Yer no' twenty-one, son, so Ah've tae hand ye over tae yer mum."

"Then walk wi' me."

"Ah'll do that, Dante. But first Ah need to take the car back to the station. Then we'll walk."

Dante slung his kitbag, and stepped up the companionways leading to the main deck to disembark.

"No pistols or the makings of a Sten gun in there, Dante?" Sergeant Ponsonby laughed.

"Not a thing. Ah left it all behind in Italy. Ah'm glad to be home."

"Ah know fine well how ye feel, son. Bad things happened here when Italy declared war."

"A sergeant in the Seaforths, Fred Forte from Kempock, told me about it. We joined the Fiamme Verde."

"Ah know the family. Ah put some people in jail for thieving and rioting. But it's over. Ah'm glad tae see ye back, son."

* * *

Sergeant Ponsonby drove the vehicle to the police station. A bus or two passed, and there were few cars on the road. Dante said little after seeing the bombed-out West End Baths. A slow transit along Brougham Street took them past an undamaged St. Mary's Church. A brief look at his primary school, St. Mary's, as the car passed Patrick Street to join Grey Place, and Rinaldi's Cafe established by Old Mario. The car passed the King's Theatre, showing "In Which We Serve".

"Good picture, son."

"Never heard of it."

"You'll catch up."

They navigated a quiet Dalrymple Street, passing the fire station. Sergeant Ponsonby pulled into the police car park and handed in the keys. He jerked his head at a red-brick building.

"The Sailor's Rest, built in 1944. Look Dante, what is it ye want to see? Is it the Blitz? Let me tell ye about it, and it's no' pleasant."

Fifty German bombers came over on the night of 6 and 7 May 1941.

"The bastards dropped bombs everywhere. Incendiaries, parachute land mines, and high explosives. In the East End, people hid in the railway tunnels. The distillery went up, and the fire drew in the bombers."

When the all-clear sounded, huge fires lit the town. The docks were damaged and the ships anchored in the river attacked. Sugar refineries, the yards and foundries were all hit hard. The outer walls of houses and churches tottered above rubble, reduced to burnt-out shells.

"Grant Street in the East End, Waverley Street and Thom Street, up by the dam got hit, and South Street in the West End. It was a grim night. When the Germans finished, two hundred and eighty people were dead and one thousand two hundred injured. Ah'm tellin' ye, Dante, a thousand houses destroyed and more than half the housing stock damaged. Mothers and children evacuated."

He led Dante up William Street to Cathcart Street. To the east lay a wasteland of rubble and half-buried masonry.

A loud report and Dante leapt, a gazelle in flight, landing on his side behind rubble, head well down, taking cover from incoming fire. Sergeant Ponsonby extended a hand.

"Come on, son, get up. A bus backfired. You're in Westburn."

"Instinct; couldn't help it."

He brushed loose dirt and gravel from his battle dress uniform.

"Was ye in the army?"

"Flanders, 1918; HLI. Ah got out at the end of 1919 and joined the police. Ah was too old in '39."

They gazed at the empty quadrant next to the east gable of the municipal buildings where Cowan's Corner had once stood. Sergeant Ponsonby knew how Dante felt, his senses fine-tuned to the threats of death. It had taken him a few months getting used to being home from Flanders.

"Take it easy for a while, son. Everything'll be fine. You've seen enough of the Blitz?"

"Ah think so."

They tramped up steep Provident Street, past Gault Place, and turned right on Roxburgh Street, passing the red sandstone of Westburn Cooperative Society's head office. Dante gazed at the sloping street running downhill to the West Station.

The first sight of his hometown in almost seven years, leaving a child and returning an eighteen-year-old veteran of the Italian Resistance, a proud fighter in the Fiamme Verde, but the lingering scars of the Blitz and wartime austerity, and it seemed to him the war had exhausted Westburn. He'd seen worse destruction and ruin in Italy where armies clashed. He'd longed for the certainties of home before the war. The new optimism and confidence, Westburn shaking free of the Depression, the people cheerful, better dressed, enjoying decent food; but the war had drawn Westburn into a time of rationing, and made the people glum and shabby.

The walls blocking tenement entrances surprised Dante.

"The brick walls in front of the closes," Dante said. "What're they for?"

"Baffle walls, son," Sergeant Ponsonby said. "If a bomb hit the street, the blast would go right up the close and wreck the building."

"Ah see."

Westburn's young men were at work, or away serving in the forces, leaving only old men on the streets, women and young mothers pushing prams.

"The women," Sergeant Ponsonby said, "they're out for the messages."

"The messages," Dante said. He laughed, hiding the lump in his throat. He liked the familiar words that made him feel more at home, remembering when his mum sent him with Graziella to buy food.

The war had hurt Westburn. Rationing kept people scruffy and down-at-heel. Small boys and girls hurried to school wearing oversized hand-me-downs from big brothers and sisters. Meagre displays of fruit and vegetables in grocers' windows: an onion or two, fragments of turnip, potatoes, perhaps an apple. Wriggles of linked sausage, a dab or two of sliced sausage, and dollops of mince adorned the display slabs in butchers' windows.

They passed Morretti's Café at the corner of Roxburgh Street and Trafalgar Street. The Morrettis were friends of his parents. Dante wondered how they'd survived the war. The café was shut in the early morning, fading marks of damage on the shop front patched after the anti-Italian riots in 1940.

"It's shortages and rationing, Dante," Sergeant Ponsonby said. "It'll take time, but we'll get on our feet again. Ye'll see."

At the corner of Duncan Street, a knot of three threadbare corner boys and a conscript soldier on leave loitered by the wall of the old St. Patrick's Church.

"Good morning, boys," Sergeant Ponsonby said.

Muffled laughter as they passed and the rasp of a throat cleared; the splat of phlegm hitting the pavement.

"He's a fuckin' Eyetie; a wee Mussolini," the soldier said.

Dante turned, ready for battle, slipping the kitbag off his shoulders. Sergeant Ponsonby's hand restrained him.

"Now boys, away home. Ah don't like bad language, but if Ah hear another word, Ah'll lift the fuckin' lot of you."

Truncheon in hand, he closed up, and caught sour breath tainted with cheap wine. The neck of a bottle jutted from the jacket pocket of a corner boy. Sergeant Ponsonby hit the bottle with his truncheon, filling the boy's pocket with broken glass. Sweet, sticky red wine stained his clothing and dripped on the ground. Sergeant Ponsonby turned to the soldier.

"That young fella has seen more fighting than you've had hot dinners. Ah'll let him knock the shite out of you."

Dante, nursing a balled right fist inside his left palm, waited.

"'S'at a fact," the soldier said.

One of his companions tugged his sleeve. "It's the fuckin' sergeant, Big Lachie Ponsonby; an' the Eyetie's ready tae gie ye a fuckin' doin'. Come on."

"Now for the last time, boys, clear off."

They turned.

"Sorry," one said, and they sped toward the Avenues.

"Damned hooligans; pay no attention to them, son."

Dante slung his kitbag, and he and Sergeant Ponsonby turned left into Bruce Street. Dante stopped.

"Ah'm no' ready for this. No' after near seven years away. Can ye no' put me up somewhere like the Sailor's Rest for a couple of days?"

"Well, Dante, yer mum's ready,

They turned right on the corner of Holmscroft Street, and passed Mount Pleasant Street, stopping to admire the vivid red brick grandeur of the new St. Patrick's parish church, completed in 1935.

"Ah'm no' Catholic, myself," Sergeant Ponsonby said, "but Ah do like the new St. Pat's. It's a fine-built church."

Dante quickened his pace, and the crash of his ammunition boots shattered the morning quiet.

"Get this over with," he whispered.

"Shhh," Sergeant Ponsonby whispered through the finger on his lips.

Two hundred yards more, and the journey from the Apennines ended. Though glad to see that the tenement containing the family apartment remained undamaged by the war, the baffle wall protecting the entrance vexed Dante.

He worried; would his mother and sister understand what it had been like in the partisans? Would they grasp a fragment of what he had been through fighting in the Apennines? And what could they know? They were strangers to each other. He'd left home a child of twelve and returned a tough guerrilla fighter, older than his years.

A cluster of women and a few older men burst from the close. Dante recognised his mum and Graziella leading the rush.

"Here's Dante, Mrs Rinaldi, Graziella. He's a fine young man."

"Thank you, thank you, Sergeant Ponsonby." Mrs Rinaldi wrung his hand. And then she had her son in her arms, hugging and kissing him. Then she held Dante at arm's length.

"Oh Dante, Dante, ll mio bambino, mio figlio. Let me look at you. Why, you're a man now."

Graziella took her young brother in her arms.

"Dante, mio fratello. I'm so glad, so glad you're home at last. We missed you."

"Welcome home, son," an elderly neighbour said, "an' yer a soldier. Well done, lad." He reached over and shook Dante's hand.

They passed through the welcoming women of the close, the good neighbours clapping Dante on the back. Dante relished the familiar smells of home. His mother and Graziella held onto his arms as they climbed the stairs and the landings scrubbed clean. But the drabness of the walls, unpainted since before the war, made him sad. Surging emotion, happy childhood memories of his dad, his mum, and Graziella gave way to sadness at all the innocent days lost during his years of exile. The war had stolen Dante's childhood. His eyes filled when he saw the brass name plate, and the letters of the family name faded by his mother's habitual polishing. His mum and Graziella stopped outside the main door of the family apartment. Dante managed to speak.

"Often, when Ah was in the mountains, Ah wondered if Ah'd ever get home again."

"If only Luigi was here to see you, Dante, his son," his mother said.

Graziella sobbed, and they cried, and Dante hugged his mother and sister.

"Mia mamma; mia sorella."

And they hung onto each other a while. Graziella dried her eyes, put the key in the lock, opened the door and they were home.

* * *

Porridge, fried duck eggs, a couple of rashers of Ayrshire, toasted slices of buttered plain loaf, taking most of the butter ration for the week. Dante was replete, sipping strong, sweet, milky tea.

"Hen's eggs are not to be had," Graziella said. "I got the duck eggs from the farm in McGeachie's Glen, not far from the allotments."

His mum and Graziella wanted Dante dressed in civilian clothes. And Dante didn't mind, realising that his time in partisan uniform had ended. Suits, shirts, underclothing, and shoes belonging to Dante's father remained, but the clothing required alterations. Dante had still to fill out. Despite gorging himself on the voyage home, he'd stayed skinny after near-starvation in the partisans.

The chain and medal he wore round his neck were visible at his open, collarless army shirt. Graziella fingered them.

"What is it?"

"A holy medal, for protection."

"Let me see," his mother said. Her eyes widened when she got a good look. "It is not holy, it's pagan!"

Dante explained that the day he and Fred Forte left Old Mario and Agate for the Fiamme Verde, his grandfather had taken them to the village church, seeking blessings at the tomb of the crusading knight, Nicolo the Lombard.

"Old Mario's a good Catholic, but he called on the ancient gods for Fred and me." Dante pushed the medal out further. His mum and Graziella came closer. "It's Mithras, god of Roman soldiers. Nicolo the Lombard and Mithras, they brought me home. I'll never take it off."

Dante pulled on the thick wool pullover given him by Anselmo over the battle dress blouse.

"It smells of sheep," his mother said.

Dante shrugged and had a good look at his mother. He remembered a pretty, young, vivacious Mum. The death of his father and the war had worn her down. She looked underfed, and her skirt, blouse and cardigan—neat, but worn—hung on her.

"It's a warm jumper. A good man, a shepherd, gave it to me."

He removed the khaki gaiters, but for the moment had to wear the khaki trousers and ammunition boots.

Dante went out with Graziella late morning. He carried a parcel containing two of his father's suits. They walked to the corner of Holmscroft Street and Mount Pleasant Street, making their way through the West Station roundabout, to Newton Street, to Eddie Nicol, Tailor. He measured Dante and said he'd have the suits ready by the weekend.

"Mum's going to see about getting you a ration book," Graziella said. "No ration book means no food, no clothing; nothing."

"I ate your rations at breakfast?"

"Duck eggs aren't rationed. Most people won't eat them. And the butcher did Mum a small favour with the bacon. I pleaded with the grocer for a little butter."

McCulloch's clock chimed noon. They looked along Nelson Street, neat tenements on the right. On the left, Greenock Academy, the school for Westburn's posh families; beyond it, Ardgowan Primary School, and visible, too, the red glazed brick of the Eye Infirmary.

The sun shone and the air was crisp.

"Let's walk," Graziella said.

It was a typical November day—the razor-edged winter light, the peaks and ridges of the Argyll Hills and the Arrochar Alps etched into the horizon by His hand. The blue winter sea stretching from Kempock Point to the Tail o' the Bank, cargo ships, a cluster of men-of-war at anchor. The azure waters of the Clyde spreading northwest to the deep rias of the Holy Loch and Loch Long, a legacy of the Ice Age.

"Ah missed this," Dante said.

"It is beautiful," Graziella said.

"How are things with you, Graziella?"

"Oh, all right. The government didn't conscript me to work in the shipyards. I'd have hated that. They listened for once when I said I had to help Mum run the family business. I keep busy with Mum in the shop, and I worry about when I'll be able to open the café in Kempock."

Graziella was in her mid-twenties, a widow, hiding her good looks behind an impassive face, a black beret covering her hair. He wanted to see her smile again, wanted her to shed the drab grey winter coat covering her good legs, and kick off the clumpy shoes. Graziella needed to look young again.

"Oh, our house in Kempock; I have three Polish paratroopers billeted there," Graziella said. "Nice young men, and the rent money comes in handy."

The Polish sergeants kept the house tidy. Graziella cooked for them on weekends when they brought rations and insisted she use any leftovers with her mother. They planned to remain in Scotland when discharged from the army.

"I met some Poles in Italy. Good soldiers."

He stared at his sister.

"Please, please don't look at me like that. I'm alone, Dante. These Polish boys, they're just lodging in the house. I'm just not interested in meeting someone else. Please don't ask. I hate talking about it. I can't get over Tony's death."

Graziella wept. Dante dried her eyes and hugged his beloved big sister.

"Ah'm sorry. Ah'm home; Ah'll get to work in the chipper, starting tomorrow, and I'll help you get the café open again."

"Oh, I knew you would. I'm all right now. Come on, I want to show you something. It's a bit of a walk."

They moved away from the viewpoint on Lyle Hill and walked down the slope of Newton Street, heading east to Fox Street, ascending its last steep part and entering Westburn Cemetery by one of the back gates.

"The Cemetery, Grazi," Dante said. "Where are you taking me?"

"A shortcut to a good place. You'll see."

A sombre refuge, quiet on a weekday. Stark trees bereft of leaves, rustling survivors nestling against gravestones, floating, falling, swirling in the sharp breeze. Brother and sister averted their eyes from lairs. Graziella led Dante through a labyrinth of narrow paths, thick overgrown bushes and trees touching them as they passed neglected sanctuaries of long-dead Westburnians.

"Green Lady's Swamp," Graziella said.

A sorry-looking dried-out pond lay before them, an irregular gossamer of water shining in the middle, grass and weeds clinging to the sides.

"You brought me here just after my fifth birthday," Dante said. "Scared me half to death, telling me the Green Lady would take me away." He grinned.

"I remember. Was I a bad girl?"

"No, not ever."

They exited the cemetery through the Bow Road Gate, turned left, a short walk to cross Inverkip Road. A turn through a shabby Lady Alice swing park, up the steps to the Second Dam, pausing at the culvert linking it to Murdieston Dam—a popular place for model yacht enthusiasts.

"The wee boats are all right in the summer, but I like to come in the winter when it's quiet and the water's still," Graziella said.

They turned onto Cornhaddock Street from Murdieston Street, then right on Lemon Street.

"We're going to the allotments?" Dante said.

"Yes," Graziella said. "Our patch is just over the railway footbridge."

Graziella had taken an allotment in 1941. Dig For Victory, the government had said. She had dug for her mum and for Tony's family, producing vegetables and sometimes surplus crops exchanged for a pat of butter, a rasher or two of bacon or meat, and the occasional luxury of hens' eggs. And flowers; she could not resist planting out the seasonal flowers, filling the apartment with fragrant blooms, to her mother's delight.

After word of Tony's death, her husbandry had faltered and then renewed with greater vigour. Joining the rhythms of the seasons—planting, growing, harvesting—had strengthened Graziella's faith in this world.

But now she worried about Dante who, she guessed, had seen and done things outside the cycle of normal life, and though he declined to talk about it, she worried he carried burdens from the war.

Graziella had heard stories about demobbed soldiers, sailors, airmen, older than Dante, coming home unsettled, some of them violent, taking to drink. One young man was so restless he rejoined the infantry, upsetting his mother. She worried about Dante, and meant to look after him and keep him from breaking their mum's heart.

Graziella opened the garden shed. Dante weighed the spades, the forks, the rake, and the hoe, one by one in his right hand. A couple of old chairs, a work bench, a tool rack with hammers and screwdrivers, forks, hand trowels, and a potting scoop. Sister and brother sat on the bench outside and against the wall of the shed. Feeble heat from the November sun came through their clothing.

"There's a paraffin stove, a kettle and a couple of pots. Old plates, cups, a few pieces of cutlery. In the summer, I make picnics with Mum; Sundays, after Mass. She likes that.

Lately, I've not been able to do as much," Graziella said. "The place is untidy."

He gazed at the weedy vegetable patches and the empty flower bed, and the remnants of the compost heap.

* * *

"What was it like," Graziella asked cautiously, "in the partisans?"

Dante couldn't speak; not at once. What could he tell his adored big sister? Would Graziella understand? She'd suffered in the war, and wasn't over it: Tony, her husband, had been killed in Sicily fighting with the Seaforths.

When could he tell Graziella about Chiarina? It was bliss, being with her at sunrise, clasping her hand, standing on the rim of the stronghold and gazing on an inversion, a tapestry of unbroken clouds beneath. As far as the eye could see, islets of snowy peaks, breaking through the counterpane of mottled white.

"All right," Dante said. "Terrible food; Ah often went hungry."

"That can't be all. There has to be more."

Dante glossed over the real life of the band, but told Graziella about meeting Fred and joining the Fiamme Verde. Major Giuntoli and Fred training the men, teaching them to fight. The days when the band attacked the enemy and won, the men grim but cheerful, sitting by weak fires on icy mountains, singing partisan songs. The belief, held in common, that what they did might bring good.

"Fred told me about Tony."

Graziella stifled a sob.

"I see.

Were you afraid?"

"Sure. Look, Grazi, Ah belonged to the Catholic Fiamme Verde, a guerrilla band. From the mountains, we fought Germans and Fascists. Ah was the best shot. When the major wanted a sniper, he picked me."

Graziella hugged her brother.

"But, Dante, Dante, you're just a boy. Why did you go?"

Dante shrugged.

"I heard about Italian boys who joined the partisans. Right thing to do. You don't tell Mum. Ah'll tell her I worked in the camp. That Ah was too young to fight. Ah'm glad I'm done with it."

"You know the government'll call you up up for the army when you're eighteen," Graziella said.

"I heard about that on the ship."

"Maybe you won't have to go."

Dante shrugged.

"There's one other thing. I met a girl, Chiarina Inserti. She came to the band after the Germans and Fascists killed her mother and father. Burned the farm; destroyed the flock. That was before I joined with Fred. The major picked Chiarina and me to be the band's hunters for game, and we were the band's runners and scouts."

Dante pulled out his looted, battered Italian Army wallet, and handed a small black and white picture to Graziella. It showed a group of twenty, taken after a raid. Sombre faces; Dante and Chiarina in the front row; Dante holding a Lee Enfield; Chiarina cradling a Schmieser Machine Pistol.

"Her legs are bound with leather thongs. What is it she's wearing on her feet? And the sheepskin jacket." Graziella looked closer, at Chiarina's abundant hair. "I think I'll like her. She's so young and pretty."

"Moccasins. She's a shepherdess, a mountaineer."

He handed Graziella another picture, a head and shoulders snap of Chiarina and himself. They stood shoulder to shoulder, hair blown awry by the wind; he was gazing down at her, and she looking up at him. Two kids in love in a bad place.

"You do love her," Graziella said.

Mid-afternoon, and Dante and Graziella walked home from the allotments and reached the junction of Mount Pleasant and Holmscroft streets.

"Show me the shop," Dante said.

They walked east toward the Avenues. The Rinaldis' fish-and-chip shop was located to the east at the far end of Holmscroft Street. The outside was unpainted since before the war.

"No paint," Graziella said. "Shortages." She knocked the main door, and one of the Moretti daughters, sixteen, opened the door. She'd been getting the shop ready for opening time at five o'clock.

"Sylvanna, this is my brother, Dante. He came home from Italy this morning."

"Welcome home, Dante," Sylvanna said and took his hand.

The inside of the shop was spruce and clean, the walls covered in a pale distemper, but like the outside it wanted fresh painting.

The serving counter had been scrubbed clean, and the fryers were heating and gleaming, reflecting the light.

"Chris is peeling and chipping potatoes in the back shop," Sylvanna said. "He knocked on the door and asked if he could help."

Chris McCoull, a boy from Holmscroft Street. A neglected adolescent. His father married again after his wife, Chris's mother, died. The new wife, an Irish widow, brought two of her own to the union, a boy and a girl, older than Chris and favoured by their mother. She'd drawn Chris's father to the pleasures and the rot of red biddy, a cheap, potent Empire wine. She neglected Chris, fed him scraps, thrashing him when his father was at work, a punishment redoubled when the father came home and beat his son for insolence.

"Who's Chris?" Dante said.

"A local boy," Graziella said. "He's a nice lad, lives near the shop. His stepmother thumps him, and leaves him hungry. He calls her the Good Mother. He has a wry sense of humour."

Graziella called Chris. A head appeared at the door of the back shop.

"Hello, Mrs Rebecchi."

"Come down, Chris, and meet my brother, Dante. He's come home from Italy."

They shook hands.

"Hello, mister," Chris said.

"Ah'm eighteen, Chris. No' much older than you, so call me Dante."

The boy blushed.

"Ah'm thirteen, but Ah'll soon be fourteen, and then Ah can leave school."

Graziella had the night off, and Arturo Moretti, Sylvanna's older brother, said he'd come in to fry the fish and chips. Sylvanna would serve the counter, and Chris would cover the back shop until after eight o'clock.

"Chris would stay until the shop closes, if I let him, but he has to go home to bed," Graziella said. "There's school in the morning. It's a poor house he goes back to. We feed him, and it's warm in the shop."

Sister and brother got ready to go home and walk west on Holmscroft Street, just a few hundred yards distant, but with tiled closes, bathrooms and WCs inside the apartments, it was a world away from the east end of the street.

"What about your tea?" Graziella asked.

"I'd love fish and chips, and snacks too," Dante said, picturing golden battered haddock, pale tender chips, and snacks: sliced potatoes dipped in flour batter and cooked in the fryer.

"Me too."

Graziella arranged with Sylvanna to double-wrap the food and have Chris bring it to the apartment at seven o'clock.

"Give him this," Graziella said, handing Sylvanna a florin. "Tell him it's for himself, and not drinking money for the Good Mother."

"You pay Chris?" Dante said.

"I slip him a few shillings now and then. If he'd regular pay, his parents would have it off him for drink. We feed him, which is more than they do. I gave him a warm overcoat, one of Tony's, and they pawned it for drink money."

Later that evening, Dante, replete—sweet, milky tea washing down snacks, fish and chips, bread and margarine—backed away from the table and stretched.

"You're tired, son?"

"Ah am. Ah'm turning in."

Dante kissed his mother and Graziella goodnight.

He undressed, kicking off a pair of his father's slippers, folded the battle dress pants, collarless shirt and undergarments, and wriggled his toes in the unheated bedroom he'd shared with Graziella when they were young.

He looked at the set of folded pajamas and robe lying on the pillow. They'd belonged to his father. He smiled and put them on.

A knock came at the bedroom door.

"Come in, Mum. Is something wrong?"

"No, no, I just wanted to see that you're comfortable."

Dante smiled, and gestured to his bed.

"It's been a long time since Ah slept in a bed. Ah mean, this is luxury, better than a ship's bunk or a partisan bivvy."

"I worried so much all the years you were in Italy. I'm happy to see you safe and home again." She kissed Dante on the cheek and held him in her arms.

"Ah'll turn in, Mum." But he saw that she meant to see him into bed. He removed the robe.

Dante slid under the sheets, and his Mum tucked him in and laid her hand on his cheek.

"Good night, my son."

Lying on his back, hands behind his head, Dante grinned in the darkness.

I'm still her wee boy.

* * *

Friday afternoon. Brother and sister walked back from Eddie Nicol's tailor's shop. Dante carried the altered suits. They turned into Holmscroft Street from Mount Pleasant Street.

"Hello, Mrs Rebecchi," a boy's voice piped up. "Ah like yer jumper, mister."

"Ah, Chris, it's you," Graziella said.

"Behaving yerself, Chris?" Dante said.

"Aye, mister."

Chris had a few schoolbooks tied with coarse string slung over his shoulder. He'd deposit them in the flat, hoping that his

Good Mother would be out, or more likely, sleeping off an afternoon session with the red biddy, getting ready for an evening on the batter.

"Ye need help with the spuds the night, Mrs Rebecchi?"

"Come to the shop for an hour or two at six."

Dante liked the boy's polite, open way. He could use young company and the friendship of someone who might, from time to time, take him back to the years before the war, to memories of his own boyhood. He hoped Chris would help him in the allotment.

"Are you up early on a Sunday, Chris?"

"Aye, mister."

"Right, then. After eight o'clock Mass, help me in the allotment?"

"Aye, mister."

"Chris, Ah'm too young to be a mister. Ma name is Dante; okay?"

"Right, mister. Sorry, Ah mean, Dante."

* * *

Dante's mum gave him a pat of lard, a rasher or two of streaky bacon, wrapped in grease-proof paper, and four slices of plain loaf wrapped in clean newspaper. She also gave him a thermos flask of tea. Dante packed the food in his haversack.

"You can fry the bacon on the stove, and the bread too," his Mum said.

A quiet, early morning Mass followed. Dante and Chris were half asleep as the Irish priest droned through his sermon. Neither went to Communion. Dante was not ready to confess, had no idea what he might confess—a necessary step before taking the Blessed Sacrament. Chris avoided confession and Communion, and attended Mass when the spirit moved him. Teachers kept him in the faith, forcing him to attend confession and Communion once a year, about Easter, the least for a Catholic to stay in the Faith.

The pair of them left St. Patrick's Church, walking to the allotment, clouds of steaming breath wreathing their heads as they hiked up steep Mount Pleasant Street. Dante opened the shed.

"You had breakfast, Chris?"

"The Good Mother gave me a half slice of bread and margarine. This mornin' she sprinkled sugar on the margarine. Gi'e the boak. Ah hate it. She has a cup of stewed tea and a couple of Woodbine. Smokin' herself to death, she is."

"We'll have a bacon sandwich later on, a doubler."

The new friends sat on the bench outside the hut, surveying the allotment, enjoying the faint heat of winter sun.

"What happened to your mum, Chris?"

"After the Blitz, she went to Clyde Square to look at the damage. At the foot of Provident Street, a wall collapsed and crushed her to death."

"Ah'm sorry, Chris."

Chris wrung his hands.

"Ah'm ready," Chris said. "Ah like being up here wi' you, outside an' away from the stink of stale Woodbine smoke and wine breath. She set the bed on fire one night. Ah threw water on her and put it out, but she cuffed me for soakin' her. Ma father, he's a disaster as well; hardly ever sober. He's an idiot wi' fires. Near the end of the war he lost the place.

January 1945. Blackout enforced. Chris's old man, mad from guzzling red biddy, took an armful of newspapers and cardboard into Holmscroft Street and made a fire—a brief, intense blaze. Old Man McCoull railed at the darkness.

"Come on, Mr Hitler, drop yer fuckin' bombs here!"

"If your mum and Mrs Rebecchi had no' been passing from the shop and got him home, Big Lachie Ponsonby would've taken him to the cells."

"Why did he do it?"

Chris shook his head.

"He's an Irish mental case. Get ye a bad name. He's no laughin' matter. Always ravin' on about The Troubles. That night when he shot out the door, he wis yellin', 'The Blue Noses hate us! Ah'm fae Ulster, the black north, where they cut the heid aff the drake 'cause it wis green! Ah'm a fuckin' Fenian!'"

They forked over half the allotment; back-breaking work. Then a start to hand-weeding perennial and annual weeds, work that thwarted Graziella.

By noon, Dante stopped and dried his brow with the sleeve of his thick pullover given him by Anselmo.

"Let's see if we can burn some weeds," Dante said.

They sorted the weeds into dry and wet heaps.

"Let the wet weeds dry. We'll burn them next week," Dante said.

"There's two rabbits," Chris said, pointing to the west edge of the allotment where the doe hopped here and there round her young buck, nibbling at leaves.

Dante picked up two good-sized, smooth stones, weighing them in his hand. He gauged the distance, aimed, and trusting his arm, threw the first stone. As it flew, he threw again. The first missile hit the doe on the head, killing it, followed by the second missile killing the buck. Chris dashed over and picked up the rabbits by the hind legs.

"Where did ye learn to do that?" Chris said, amazed. He laid the rabbits on the bench.

"In Italy. In the mountains, Ah hunted with ma girlfriend when we were in the partisans. We belonged to the Catholic Fiamme Verde, the Green Flames."

"A partisan; is that like a soldier?"

"Something like a soldier. Do ye want to be a soldier?"

"Ah'm no sure. Never thought about it. It's hard enough gettin' through the week here."

"Take up soldiering only if you have to."

"Yer girlfriend; what's she like?"

Dante handed Chris the small snap of Chiarina and himself, the one with her beautiful hair framing her face.

"Her name is Chiarina."

Chris's breath whistled through pursed lips.

"She's a cracker; Ah mean she's nice-lookin'."

"She is that; and she's a fighter."

He showed Chris the other photograph.

"That's me with the rifle and Chiarina with the machine pistol."

"Jesus," Chris said.

And Dante believed he could trust Chris, close enough to him in age, streetwise but innocent, and with little chance of escape from a hard and wasted life.

"You wait till you see her. She's lovely. You'll like Chiarina. Ah was crazy about her the first time Ah met her up in the mountains."

Chris shuffled his feet, embarrassed at Dante's talk of love.

"You've a girlfriend, Chris? Maybe a lassie ye like?"

Chris shrugged and looked down at his shabby and none too clean clothes.

"There's nae chance o' that."

Dante removed a knife from the haversack, pulled it from the sheath, and fingered the edge of the blade. He held it out to Chris, who had a good look. Chris touched the diamond-shaped, white enameled badge set in the middle of the hilt, embossed with a black swastika.

"Don't touch the knife; it's sharp. Ah found it, near a wrecked German truck."

Dante didn't tell Chris he'd looted the knife from the body of a dead German soldier, a boy on the verge of manhood, killed in an ambush on a lonely Apennine road.

"Pick a good bunch of dry weeds, Chris." He handed him a box of matches. "Light a fire. We'll have heat."

While Chris kindled the fire, Dante skinned the rabbits, bled them, and washed them under the cold tap. He got rid of the inedible parts. Dante wrapped the carcass of the doe, its liver, and kidneys in grease-proof paper. His mother and Graziella would pot roast it and have rabbit for the evening meal instead of Woolton Pie.

Woolton Pie, dreamt up by the Ministry of Food: a swill of potatoes, parsnips, cauliflower, swede, carrots, turnips, oats, spring onions, and cheese, lurking in tepid water below a potato crust.

Chris and Dante would eat the buck. The fire caught, and hard weeds blazed finely.

Dante placed lard in the pan over the lit stove, and fried the streaky bacon and the bread. He liked the snapping and cracking of hard weeds burning in the heart of the fire. He handed Chris a double bacon sandwich. They washed the food down with tea from the flask.

"You always go to St. Pat's?" Dante asked.

"Aye. When Ah have to. Ah've always lived in Holmscroft Street. Never been farther than Kempock. Someday, mebbe Ah'll see Glasgow."

"We'll do something about that, Chris. What about First Communion and Confirmation?"

"In St. Pat's."

"Me too."

"You'd have been dressed up. The Good Mother sent me tae the church like this. Ah had a white sash over a dirty old jersey."

The boys of Chris's class had dressed in their Sunday best, had had proud mothers with them, the fathers at wartime work or away at the war. After Mass, a breakfast in the church hall, women of the parish had served porridge, rolls on margarine and tea. A boy had insulted Chris.

"Yer nuthin' but a dirty clat," he said.

Outside the hall, Chris thumped him, bleeding his nose. Next day the class teacher thrashed Chris with her Loch Gelly tawse, leaving him with raw hands and blood blisters on his wrists.

"Ye must have deserved it," the Good Mother said when he got home, slapping him round the head.

"Confirmation, that was better. The old man came and the Good Mother sent me shabby, but clean. Ah picked St. Peter for ma Confirmation name. He was Jesus's pal, an' boss of the Apostles."

Dante laughed.

"That's who Ah picked, and for the same reasons as you." He stuck out his hand. "Here, we'll shake on that."

Dante re-lit the stove, melting the lard and bacon fat congealed in the pan, adding a small lump of lard. He butchered the buck with the German dagger, dropped liver and kidneys into the sizzling fat, forking them cooked onto the plates. Chris gulped down his share.

"Hand me the plates, Chris." He placed a half of rabbit on each plate and they ate with their hands. Silence, as they devoured legs and haunches and the flanks, then sucked marrow from bones.

"Tasty?"

"It is. Never had rabbit. Best grub ever."

Dante poured the last of the hot tea over the greasy plates. Chris rinsed them at the coldwater tap. When the fire had died out, Dante threw cups of water on the smoking embers.

Chris shivered under an old jacket way too big for him. He wore canvas summer sand shoes beneath long short pants held up by thick string. Much as he treasured the pullover given him by Anselmo, Dante figured Chris needed it more than he did. The pullover, though whole, gave off the pungent odour of sheep. Chris's boozy father and stepmother wouldn't take it to the pawn, nor would they want to wear it.

"You'd like the pullover?"

"That'd be great."

"No long pants?"

The boy shrugged. "The Good Mother sold ma ration book on the black market for drinkin' money. A' ye get in there's scraps tae eat an' the rags fae the backs o' the Good Sister an' Brother."

"Ah'll give you a warm pair of long pants that go with the pullover when we get back to Holmscroft Street. An Italian shepherd gave them to me. No boots, Chris?"

Chris pulled a face.

Dante removed his ammunition boots.

"Try them on."

Chris kicked off the sand shoes. His dirty socks had holes and his big toes stuck out. He blushed.

"Ah had socks like that in the partisans," Dante said.

"The boots are a wee bit big for me," he said. "But Ah can put in paper."

Dante, in stockinged feet, went into the shed, rummaged around, and found cardboard from an old box. He laid it on the ground beside the boy.

"Stand on that. Keep your feet apart, and keep still."

Dante removed the German knife from the haversack, pulled it from the sheath, and fingered the razor-sharp blade.

Dante outlined the shape of Chris' feet with the point of the knife.

"Okay, you can sit down."

With deft cuts on the cardboard along the outline of the boy's feet, Dante fashioned a pair of insoles. He placed them inside the boots.

"Try the boots now."

Chris stamped his feet, walked up and down the path, skipped, and ran a few yards.

A wide grin split his young face. "Jesus, the boots are great."

"Good. You can have them when we get down the road. Ah've another pair. Tell yer old man and the Good Mother if they take the boots to the pawn, there's no more tick at the chipper."

Chris laughed.

"Thanks, Dante."

Dante liked Chris; it pleased him to give the boy clothing and boots to keep him warm. He'd dig into his kit, and see if he could find him a belt to hold up the pants and a pair or two of whole clean socks.

Chapter Six

Springtime 1946, and the family chipper in Holmscroft Street was running well. Dante started work on Graziella's café in Kempock, passed his driving test, and bought an old van, a Ford Y, for thirty-five pounds.

Chris lent eager hands in the chipper. Over the Christmas and New Year school holiday, he added swift chipping of potatoes to his skill as adept spud peeler, and Dante hired one of the Moretti girls full time. Dante's mother came in several times before the shop opened at five o' clock, but withdrew again, happy to let Dante run the business.

"Here's a few bob, Chris."

Chris counted the five shillings.

"Ah'd like tae save a bit. Ah'll take a couple of bob. Keep the rest for me?"

"Sure."

Dante put the money in the small safe in the back shop.

After a few weeks, Chris had saved a pound.

Dante studied racing form and made careful bets on horses; calculating odds, challenging the mind, winning a few pounds on nags with an outside chance. He picked a good horse running at five-to-one and bet Chris's pound, and a couple of his own. If the horse lost, Dante would replace the pound. The horse won by a head.

Dante heard Chris come into the shop after school.

"I'm in the back shop, Chris."

"Something wrong, Dante?"

Dante handed Chris a large, white, Bank of England five-pound note.

"This is for you, and here's the pound you saved."

"Jesus, a fiver, *and* ma pound; six quid. A fortune."

Dante told Chris about the bet.

"A wee flutter on the gee gees. Our horse won."

"Ah'm glad it didnae lose."

"Don't you worry, Chris. I'd have made it up had it lost."

Dante returned Chris's money to the safe.

"Saturday morning we'll go the Post Office and open savings accounts. Ah won a few quid as well."

Chris, now fourteen, would leave school in June, launching him into the world of work. Dante worried about the boy, counting on Chris working in the shop.

"What about getting a job when you leave school?"

"The old man's talkin' about havin' a word wi' the Council foreman to start me as a boy labourer alongside him. Later, Ah'd get a navvy's job."

"How much pay?"

"A pound odds a week to start."

Digging roads and holes in the ground, labouring on building sites, clearing bomb sites. Heavy, physical work in all kinds of weather among the hard drinking navvys. A two-year break in the army when he turned eighteen. Navvying and soldiering; a short road to nowhere. Chris deserved better. The old man and the Good Mother would take most of Chris's wage off him, funding their boozing on the red biddy. Chris needed to find a better job and a place to live.

"How about workin' for me?"

"Ah'd like working with ye; are ye no' kiddin' me?"

"Ah don't kid ma best friend, Chris. Ah've got plans, and there's a place for you."

Dante decided to buy and fetch his own fish from the market. He could save money. Fish delivered nightly to Glasgow fish market from Aberdeen docks. He'd use the Ford Y van to pick up and bring the fish to Westburn.

* * *

Dante and Chris had worked on Graziella's café.

"You like the shop?"

Graziella looked around the café that she and Tony had established soon after they married in 1937, but that had been wrecked by the war.

"It's wonderful, Dante," she said. "It's great to have it opened again."

Sunday evening, brother and sister sat at a table drinking Camp Coffee.

"This is like the ersatz coffee we drank in the partisans."

Dante examined the Camp Coffee bottle. He read from the label.

"It's a right concoction, this: water, sugar, coffee essence and chicory essence. All shook up."

"Let me see it. One of these days we'll get real coffee again."

He handed the bottle to Graziella. She studied the drawing of a seated Gordon Highlander and a Sikh soldier outside a tent. The Sikh held a tray of coffee. A scene from British India, the Jewel in the Crown. Now being given up. Graziella read from the label.

" 'Ready Aye Ready. Always ready.' The country is exhausted, worn out. I hope Britain will be strong again and ready for anything. I wonder if I'll ever be."

She stared past her brother, remembering the happy time before 1939 when she and Dante were children; Graziella, the big sister looking after Dante, her wee brother. Luigi, her kind and loving father. Celestina, her sweet, gentle, affectionate mother. Falling in love and marrying Tony Rebecchi.

But the war destroyed everything. Sure, it had to be fought and won, but Sweet Jesus, at a heavy price: Dante stranded in Italy and joining the partisans; her father interned by the British; jailed by the country he loved, then drowned at sea. Her mother heartbroken. The wreckage and death of the Blitz. Tony killed in Sicily. Graziella wept.

Dante got up and went to her side of the table, put his arm round her and hugged her.

"What's wrong?"

But he knew what was wrong; the damned war.

"Don't cry, don't cry. Ye'll have me bawling in a minute."

"It's so hard to forget the war. I'll never forget the telegram telling me Tony had been killed. I had to get tablets from the doctor. One day I'd like to go to Sicily and see his grave."

Mass burials often preceded interment in a proper grave for men killed in action.

"Leave it for a year or two."

"Right now, I couldn't face it. At times, I'd have given anything just to get away. But you had to carry on. It's been over for a while, and I can't forget what happened to us."

"Time; we have to give it time. Let's get Mum happy and the family business going again, and your café opened."

* * *

Dante and Chris worked magic, using the old Ford Y to bring scarce new timber, stain and varnish for the interior, booths, chairs and tables. Light grey paint would do for the shop front. God knows where Dante got the materials—on the black market? Graziella didn't ask.

Dante discussed his plans to buy fish for the family chipper. He needed money, but wouldn't go to the bank. He felt he was too young to qualify for a loan. The bank might lend it to his mum, making her liable, and he wasn't having it. He meant to make a success of things with Chris and the Moretti girls helping in the shop.

"Ah need the van to bring the fish from Glasgow. Ah got it for thirty-five quid. The savings are down to fifty quid. It's not enough to set up the deliveries of fish from Aberdeen."

"How much do you need?"

"All together, a couple of hundred. It's a fair amount of cash. Ah'd start payin' back right away."

"Ask Mum?"

Dante shook his head.

"Ah want to do this under ma own steam."

Graziella admired her brother's single-mindedness and his independent spirit.

"I'll let you have two hundred. Don't even think about saying no."

"How did you manage to save that amount of money?"

"I lived with Mum for most of the war. Soldiers were billeted in the house Tony and I bought when we got married. It's the rent money."

"Are you sure?"

"You're my wee brother; of course, I'm sure. You don't need to pay me back until your business is on its feet."

"Ah'm doin' it for the family."

Graziella smiled, reached across the table and kissed Dante on the cheek.

"I'm going to stock the shop, get the ice cream machine going again. I'll open next Saturday. And now that the Poles have gone, I'll move back to my own house. Do you think Chris would help me, after school? You can spare him?"

"Sure, he'll jump at it. He likes us."

"Dante, we're his family."

Sister and brother left the café at Cardwell Bay and, as the sun set, started the walk home to Holmscroft Street. They strode east on Eldon Street, passing the Battery Park shrouded yet in its wartime livery of Nissen huts and sea plane berths.

"I hope the town gets the park back to normal," Graziella said. "I like walking by the shore."

Dante jerked his head in the direction of the open-air swimming pool, the infamous Battery Baths, silhouetted on the shore line. A spring board, the diving dale, the cement pool. Swimming with the fishes in unfiltered sea water, clean enough to start with, but cold. The water always warmed up as the days passed, fouled by plunging, dirty bodies.

"Ah hated going there. Murky, freezing water."

Dante remembered the Hen Hut, where, on busy summer days, boys had to change. The rare heatwaves brought out the farting unwashed, the reeking bodies, and stinking feet.

"The stench in the Hen Hut; make you sick. Once Ah boaked before Ah got ma trunks on. Ah never went back."

"Oh, Dante. Stop it."

Graziella smothered a grin.

They passed the torpedo factory, a series of grey and red sandstone buildings with a sawtooth-patterned roof. It stood close to the shore, built on the riverside before the Great War, relocated from Woolwich Arsenal to Westburn, and still going strong for the Royal Navy. Dante gazed past the main gate.

"Are there any Woolwichers working now?"

"There might be a few left."

The neat, semi-detached villas built in the mid-thirties, opposite the factory, caught Graziella's eye.

"I always liked these houses. Dad wanted to buy one just before you went to Italy, but Mum was nervous about the expense, so we stayed put."

"She likes Holmscroft Street, and the folk who come to the shop. And the memories of days before the bloody war with Dad alive. Ah doubt she'll ever move."

In the faint glow of street lights, they turned left from Eldon Street onto The Esplanade. Shadowy edges of grand Victorian villas visible. On the river, the lights of anchored merchant ships and men-of-war glistering on the water.

Dante stopped.

"Okay. Thirty-five to forty minutes, and we'll be home."

He led Graziella across the street, and stopped at the low wall of the villa bordering the pavement.

"Jaggy," Dante said, running his hands over ugly iron stumps on the coping stone. "You could hurt yourself. What happened to the railings?"

"Gone; every metal garden fence and ornamental iron railing, taken for the war effort. At the Battle of Britain, people gave their pots and pans. The government said they needed the aluminium to make Spitfires and metal to make guns. I doubt they'll ever replace the fences and railings. It looks terrible. Everywhere scarred. At least there's no bomb sites out west."

* * *

Dante exited Saint Patrick's Church by the back door onto Holmscroft Street after eight o'clock Mass and Communion. The entrance to the Rinaldi apartment lay opposite on the south side of the street. Dante was hungry. He thought about breakfast. He'd fasted the previous evening until receiving the Blessed Sacrament at Sunday Mass. A quick breakfast, meet Chris in an hour and the pair of them would go to work on the allotment until well into the afternoon. He let himself into the apartment, changed into his clean work clothing, his old British Army Battle Dress, went to the bathroom and washed his hands. Celestina stood rigid at the gas cooker frying a couple of duck eggs, fatty bacon rashers, slices of plain loaf. He came behind his mum and bent to kiss her cheek, but she turned away.

"No nonsense you."

"What's wrong?"

"Nothing wrong."

She banged the plate down and poured tea, rattling the cup and saucer.

"Here is breakfast."

Dante's appetite vanished. Silence broken only by the click of knife and fork on the plate, he forced himself to eat all the food. What had upset his mother? He didn't wait long to find out. Dishes and cutlery rattled as she placed them in the sink, then slammed the door as she left the room. A few minutes later the kitchen door burst open and his mother sallied in.

Celestina's worry for her son had vanished when Dante came home from the war. His safe return made up a sliver for the loss of Luigi, and the woe of Graziella when Tony died fighting in Sicily. But the discovery that Dante had been a fighting partisan, and had a *girlfriend*, made her angry and jealous.

"What you do to me?"

She waved the photographs of Dante and Chiarina kept hidden in a drawer under his shirts. Celestina had been prowling in his personal property.

"You shouldn't spy on me or poke into ma things."

"This my house. I do what I want. You tell me no fight, and you carry guns."

She pointed at a picture.

"Ah!"

Dante, always quick-tempered, snapped. Rage filled him, and he spat out the unvarnished truth.

"Ah was nobody's skivvy cookin' and washin' dishes. Ah was the best shot. When they needed a sniper, the Alpini major called for me. Ah killed Germans and Italian Fascists. Ah made ma duty."

His mother cried and sobbed herself to the edge of hysteria.

"You tell me lies!"

"Ah tried to protect you."

Celestina had wound herself tighter than a set booby trap. She held a photograph in each hand, waving her arms.

"This girl; trovatella; she is gypsy, zingara, no?"

She pointed to the picture of Dante and Chiarina together, her hair framing her face. He looking down at her, and she gazing up at him. Two young people in love in a wild place.

"And you, moon-eyed. Stones you have for brains."

Dante snatched the photograph from his mother. But her diatribe wasn't over. She held the remaining photograph between thumb and forefinger, and waved it in Dante's face.

"And this; men with guns. Bad men: Ladri e brigante. You with silly hat and holding rifle. And girl with machine gun, dressed like soldier."

Dante plucked the picture from his mother's hand.

"They are brave men, not brigante. Good Italians. The girl is Chiarina Inserti. The Germans and Fascists murdered her mum and dad, destroyed their farm. Major Sandro Giuntoli, of the Alpini, our commanding officer, protected her." Dante thumped the work top surounding the sink. "Lei è un' amazzone; un leopardo."

"Ah, listen to him, Chiarina this, Chiarina that. She is alley cat. You want girl? I find good Italian girl, here in Scotland; good wife for you."

"Be quiet."

"You no tell me be quiet. This one, she go with soldier. You put whore, puttana, la prostituta before your mother."

"Gesu Cristo; sta zitta; shut up, and listen to me. Chiarina is brave and pure. Ah'm no' some wean you can push around. She'll come here or Ah'll go to Italy and we'll get married."

"You stay. No go Italy. Before twenty-one need to be okay from me for passport."

"Ah've ma old passport."

"Pah; baby passport. No good."

The last of Dante's self-control collapsed.

"You've said enough; too bloody much. Ah'm movin' out. Graziella'll put me up. And if she won't, Ah'll get a bed in the model."

The Bogle Model Lodging House for indigent men, where the jakies and ne'er-do-wells of Westburn lived when they reached bottom. The Hotel de Bogel.

"Go with vagabondi and ubriachi."

"Ah'll tell you this: Ah'll soon be eighteen and Ah'll be called up. The army'll grab me with ma experience. Ah'm goin' to Maryhill Barracks to volunteer; sign on for three years, a regular, a professional soldier. Ah'll run yer damned chipper until I go into the army, but Ah'm no' stayin' here."

In less than ten minutes, Dante had filled the kitbag and an old case with his belongings. Wailing and sobbing came from the kitchen as Dante pulled the door shut.

Celestina's love for her son had overflowed. She'd handed Dante freedom to restore the family business, and recapture the respect won by his father. But her outburst had wounded Dante. She had expected Dante to submit to her will, but her love, curdled by jealousy, had driven him away.

* * *

He'd quickly calmed down; joining the army for three years would put Chiarina further away.

Dante, mature beyond his years, but love-struck for Chiarina, had struck back and shattered his mother. Shame enveloped him for what he'd said. Perhaps he should have told her about the girl, but whenever Celestina found out she'd have fomented a bloody row. He'd not live with his mother and her resentment of someone he cared for, a girl she'd never met.

Dante didn't mean to come between his mother and Graziella. He'd stay with his sister, and run the chipper until joining the army.

Chris waited for Dante at the corner of Holmscroft Street and Mount Pleasant Street, eager to work with Dante in the allotment.

"Somethin' wrong, Dante?"

"No. Ah'm goin' to ma sister's for a few days. Help me wi'this?

"Okay."

With petrol scarce, the friends went to the West Station and Dante bought a day return ticket for Chris and himself to Fort Matilda Station. From the station, it was a short walk to Graziella's café, and her nearby house. Dante said nothing during the short train journey. The silence unsettled Chris. Something had upset Dante, but he didn't dare ask. Halfway to the café, they rested against the boundary wall of Battery Park.

"Ah'll still be workin' in the chipper, until Ah join up, but Ah need you to help Graziella the odd time. Will ye do that, Chris?"

"Ah'll help Mrs Rebbechi anytime. What's wrong, Dante? Yer no' gonny join the army?"

"The army it is. Ma mother lost the place and we had a blazin' row about the partisans, and ma girlfriend, Chiarina."

"Ah'm very sorry, Dante. Can ye no' make it up?"

"No Chris, Ah can't. She said terrible things about Chiarina; Ah'm ragin' at her."

Chris left the moment they reached the café. He did not want to witness an embarrassing encounter between Dante and Graziella, for he liked and respected both of them.

* * *

"Yes, please," Graziella said, turning her back on the gantry and its meagre display. The near empty shelves were laid here and there with jars of boiled sweets, chocolate delights, assorted cigarettes and pipe tobacco. She laughed.

"Oh, it's you, Dante; out for a walk, and dropped in to visit?"

"No' exactly."

Dante eased the kitbag straps on his shoulders, and he moved the old suitcase against the shop counter.

"My God! What's happened? Tell me you've not left home."

"Mum lost the place at breakfast. She went berserk, and we fell out."

The solitary customer finished his sweet, milky coffee and left the café. Dante told Graziella what happened. They went to the back shop.

"Oh God, she didn't say that, did she?"

"She did. Ah'll still run the chipper and the fish delivery. Can you put me up for a while? Ah can't go back."

The Polish paratroopers had left, so Dante had a room.

"Take the bedroom facing the bay."

"Ah'll run the chipper an' use the van for the fish run; but Ah'm no' stayin' wi' Mum."

Late afternoon, brother and sister ate fish teas, bread and margarine in silence. Dante drained his tea cup.

"More tea?"

"No, thanks. Ah'm fine."

Silence overwhelmed them.

"Wednesday, the half day, Ah'm goin' up to the city. Maryhill Barracks. Ah'm due soon for call-up. Might as well go in now; a regular soldier. Get it over with."

"Dante, for heaven's sake, grow up. You're needed here. That means three years at least. You'll kill Mum."

"Well tae hell wi' you an' all. Don't you dare tell me to grow up. Ah'm goin' to the Hotel de Bogel."

Graziella pushed her chair back from the table, the legs scraping the linoleum. She shoved her brother back into his chair.

"Don't be daft. You're staying here."

* * *

Wednesday morning, Dante left Kempock for Glasgow, determined to go through with his threat to join the army as a regular soldier. Dante was far from sure that an army career, even a short enlistment of three years, was what he wanted.

The devil on his shoulder urged him on. *Good, do it. Get away from your mother and your sister. Let them worry about the chipper and café.*

What the hell are you trying to prove? Be man enough to make it up with your mum. Tell her you're sorry you lost the rag.

Dante listened to the devil and tried to dismiss the angel. But the good angel refused to be silenced, reminding him of Fred and the major, who'd urge him to grow up, act like a partisan. Stop acting the daft boy. And Chris, who looked up to him, might say he was plain stupid.

Graziella didn't open the café, but caught a bus to the centre of Westburn and walked to the family home in Holmscroft Street. Her mother, in thrall to the vapours, depressed, given in to Black Dog—eyes rheumy, angry red nose—sat at the kitchen table with Mrs Moretti.

"Celestina, you've made yourself ill," Mrs Moretti said. "Dante's a good boy. Think what he's done for your business and for Graziella's café. A good Catholic, too. I see him at Mass and Communion He's young, but he's a man. He'll come home soon. You'll see. Here, have a nice cup of tea."

Mrs Moretti turned when Graziella came into the kitchen. Frustrated by Celestina's melancholy, she grimaced. Graziella walked Mrs Moretti to the door.

"Thanks for coming."

"Celestina's got herself worked up. She's in a bad way."

"Yes; I'll have to do something about it."

Graziella made a fresh pot of tea. Dante had lost the place, but her mother had fomented the row. What if her brother came home having signed on for three years, or longer? The thought made Graziella afraid for her mother. After the anxious war years, Dante enlisting in the army and being sent to some hostile empire outpost might be the end of her.

"Where is Dante?"

"Dante's away to Glasgow to join the army. You're up to High Doh, and so am I. Stop it, Mum or we'll both have a heart attack."

The events of the last couple of days had exhausted Celestina. Resigned to losing her son again, she shook her head.

"For God's sake, Mum, why did you say those things to him? He's very upset."

Graziella reminded her mother of everything they knew about Dante's time with Old Mario and Agate: joining the Fiamme Verde with Fred Forte from Kempock, and blessed by Old Mario.

"Old Devil, that Mario; and Agate, suoceraccia; a fiend. No' nice to your father." And quite bereft of irony, Celestina said, "Bad to me; call me trovatella."

"But Mum, you were thirteen, a foundling, when you came to Scotland. You were alone when you met Dad. You called Chiarina trovatella, and worse."

"She take Dante away."

"Well, he's away now to the last place he should be going, the bloody army. Someday he'll find Chiarina."

"Graziella, please, no swear. When he leave?"

"A few weeks. You have to make it right. You might never see him again."

Tears ran down Celestina's cheeks; she buried her face in a handkerchief, and harsh sobbing shattered the quiet of the kitchen. Graziella reminded her of Luigi's service, an Alpini on the Izonzo: the fighting and slaughter, wounds suffered. The lethargy when he came home, the legacy of wounds, and ugly memories of the White War.

"The partisans fought a different war. The Fiamme Verde was a small band, but the fighting was awful. Dante and Chiarina went through hell, just like Dad. Your son wanted to spare you. He's a brave young man, and he kept Chiarina's honour. You should be proud of him."

"I'm so sorry."

"So is Dante, but you'll have to tell him yourself."

* * *

Dante got off the train at the West Station at 8:30 a.m. He hoped to spot Chris heading for St. Mary's School. Dante wanted company for what he was about to do. At eight forty-five, Chris sprinted round the corner of Holmscroft Street onto Mount Pleasant Street. Dante waved as Chris passed the Glengoyne Bar and crossed Roxburgh Street.

"Ah'm goin' to Glasgow. You've never been in the city. Come with me; skidge the school?"

"Okay; fed up wi' school anyway. I'll say the Good Mother kept me off. Mebbe you'd write a note?"

"No bother."

They were in Glasgow Central Station by ten past ten, and they had breakfast at Sloan's Restaurant on Union Street.

"Are you really goin' to join the army?" Chris asked as they waited for a tram.

"Ah might sign on as a regular."

Chris didn't want his good friend to do anything rash.

"What about yer mum, an' the shop an' Graziella's café?"

"You help them, Chris."

They boarded a tram for the barracks. Neither said much as the vehicle lurched and rattled its way over the rails and crossings to the north of the city and the HQ of Glasgow's Own, the HLI—Highland Light Infantry. Dante gave Chris a few bob and left him in a café near the barracks on Maryhill Road.

"Ah'll be as quick as Ah can. Have a walk about. Ah'll come to the café when Ah'm done, so keep checking."

Dante met indifference at reception. A sergeant in kilt and battle dress blouse passed him to a corporal, dressed the same, who had him fill out forms. He cast a bored eye over the paperwork.

"Rinaldi, eh? So yer an Eyetie; jist back fae the Isle o' Man, or Canada? Ye'll be goin' to the Pioneer Corps."

Dante caught his eye and stared. The corporal stood up.

"Who the fuck are ye lookin' at?"

Dante recognised the green, white and red medal ribbon of the Italian Star, and the pale buff, red stripe and the narrow stripes of dark and light blue of the Africa Star on the left breast of this wee Glasgow hard ticket. A regular. He was about twenty-three.

"Ah'm no' long back from Italy an' the war. Ah see ye were in Africa and Italy. A friend of mine has the same medals, Sergeant Major Jim McGregor 1st Battalion, Black Watch."

"How the fuck did ye meet him?"

"SOE; parachuted into the Ligurian Mountains. Fought alongside the partisans."

"Fuckin' Eyeties, nuthin but Teagues. Yez can fight fuck all."

"Ah belonged to the Catholic Green Flames. That's Fiamme Verde, in Italian. Did ye no' hear the Italians were the last to surrender at El Alamein, when the Germans packed it in? An' the partisans chucked the Germans out of La Spezia and Genoa, before the Yanks got there."

"Fuckin' bullshit."

"So me an' Jim McGregor, Sergeant Fred Forte, a Scots-Italian Seaforth, a couple of Northumbrian Fusiliers, an' a bunch a pukka Italians, kicked the shite out of the 5th German Mountain Division. They're real soldiers."

The corporal tapped Dante's forms into a perfect rectangle on the desk.

"Here; get yer arse into the doctor. Ah'll tell ye somethin', sunshine. Ye'll dae yer basic training here. Ye might run intae me again; cunt."

* * *

Dante liked the appearance of the civilian doctor, a man in his late fifties: tall and lean; a weather-beaten tanned complexion, in vivid contrast to his white coat. He came from behind his desk. Razor-sharp creases on his dark grey trousers, white shirt and RAMC tie, polished black brogues reflecting the office lights.

"Good morning, Mr Rinaldi. I'm Doctor Thompson."

They shook hands.

"You've met Corporal Smith, I see."

Dante liked Thompson's polite Kelvinside accent.

"Tell me about yourself."

Dante, having got as far as the medical with his decision to enlist as a regular soldier, struggled whether to go on, or get up and leave; no legal rules bound him. As the traveller falling into conversation with a stranger unburdens himself, Dante told Dr Thomson his personal, intimate life story up to when he came home and settled in. He surprised the doctor, telling him of his love for Chiarina, and, having lost touch, that he had to find her.

"And you want to be a regular soldier. Why?"

"Ah'm due for call-up, an' decided to join early. Get away from home for a while."

"But you're just back from the war in Italy. Haven't you done enough? Why not wait until you're called up? And what about your girlfriend, Chiarina? Have you considered the army can send you anywhere in the world? You might never find the girl. And after three years in the ranks, if you find her, she'll be married, having given up on you?"

Confused and angry, a callow, impetuous Dante had rushed to the barracks to enlist. Now it sank in; a few months from now, he could be sent to Germany, to fight in Palestine, sweating his life away in West Africa, British Honduras, Aden, Malaya.

"No. Ah've not thought about it."

"Well, Mr Rinaldi, it is time you gave it some thought. Look, go home, wait until you're called up. I hear National Service is to be cut from two years to eighteen months. That would give you more time with your family,

The doctor reached across the desk.

"Give me your hands."

He held on to them.

"Let me tell you something else that might cause you to wait. Several Scots-Italians called up were sent to the Pioneer Corps. They're an honorable corps, but you'd be labouring, working in a military store, operating a crane.

"Hmm; now look straight ahead."

"Hmm."

Dante stood and removed his shirt and undershirt. Thompson placed a stethoscope on several points on Dante's chest and back, listening. The stethoscope warmed up as it travelled over Dante's torso. Thompson listened longest to Dante's heart. He removed the stethoscope and laid it on the desk.

"Drop your breeks. And the underpants. Cough. Hmm."

Thompson made notes in Dante's file.

"You can get dressed."

While Dante dressed and adjusted his clothing, knotting his tie, Thompson washed his hands, sat at his desk and finished making notes in Dante's file.

"I served in Italy in 1917. Captain, a surgeon in a casualty clearing station near the Izonzo. Dreadful slaughter. All those dead and wounded young men, British, Italians, Germans, and Austro-Hungarians."

"Ah saw men in the Fiamme Verde killed and wounded."

Doctor Thompson had visited Italy several times after the war.

"I stopped after Mussolini invaded Abyssinia. I'd like to go back."

Dante wondered what the doctor might be thinking, giving him a leisurely medical.

Doctor Thompson waxed about the injustice and indignities heaped on the Italians by the British authorities when Italy declared war, the rioting and looting by hooligans, the sinking of the Arandora Star.

"Ever suffer rheumatic fever? In the mountains, you'd often be living in cold and damp."

"Don't think so."

Doctor Thompson pored over his notes.

"There's a wee murmur at your heart, Mr Rinaldi. I don't like it."

"Can you no' give me an X-ray; to be sure?"

"Would I tell you how to make a fish supper? The stethoscope tells me all I need to know."

He stared hard at Dante, then smiled. Dr Thompson grinned again, and gave Dante the broadest wink.

"I'm marking you unfit for service. But you'll be all right, son. You understand?"

"Ah understand."

Dr Thomson met many young men, and he'd grasped early in this interview that Dante wanted to enlist for the wrong reason. Rinaldi had seen more fighting and horror than some of the regulars in the barracks and more combat than most of the National Service men would ever see during two years of service; and he'd only turned eighteen. Dr Thomson got up from behind his desk and escorted Dante to the door of his office. He laid a hand on Dante's shoulder.

"It's a pleasure meeting a fighting partisan. You've done enough. The war has hurt your family. Away home, and whatever is wrong there, you put it right. You're the man of the house now. Be good to your mum and your sister."

Dante turned and faced the doctor. They shook hands.

"Thank you, Doctor."

"Don't come back here, son. Away down the road to Westburn, and good luck to you."

Dante's mood fluctuated between disappointment and relief: the let-down by his rejection for army service, then euphoria that there would be no basic training, no orders from thugs like Corporal Smith. But what to do about his mum?

Dante reached the end of the corridor linking Dr Thomson's office to the vestibule and the main door. Corporal Smith came marching through the swing doors, Tam O'Shanter tilted over his right brow, kilt swinging, white gaiters flashing, heavy regimental brogues crashing on the tiles. He stopped, barring Dante's way.

"Ah, the fuckin' Eyetie. Are they sendin' ye tae the Fish Supper Rifles, or the Ice Cream Fusiliers?"

Dante had had enough of this malign, poisoned dwarf. He closed up to the corporal.

"You, ya wee cunt; get the fuck out o' ma way."

Corporal Smith's eyes bulged and his lips compressed to a reptilian slit. Dante got his weight behind a blow, his right fist accelerated from his waist and sped to the point of Corporal Smith's jaw. Just the way Fred had taught him to punch. The corporal's eyes rolled, his knees buckled, and he fell, the kilt awry as he hit the floor, Tam O'Shanter lying beside his head.

Dante pushed up the hem of the kilt with the toe of his boot.

"Christ, it's true; nae drawers."

He laughed at Corporal Smith's pale, uncircumcised, wilted tadge.

"Good for you, lad. That wee shite has been askin' for it for years."

Dante turned to face the sergeant he met earlier, grinning from the hatch to the main office.

Chris, fed up sitting in the café drinking tea, wandered around Maryhill, finishing up at the barracks gate, waiting for Dante. Dante's buoyant stride raised his spirits.

"Dante, yer laughin'. What happened?"

"Ah'll tell ye on the tram, Chris. It's okay. Everything's all right."

The friends reached Westburn by three o'clock.

"Let's take the van," Dante said.

They alighted from the train at the West Station, went to the van parked in Holmscroft Street near the chipper, and drove to Graziella's café at Cardwell Bay.

Graziella frowned when they entered the café.

"Mum's in a terrible state. Mrs Moretti came to see her, and there's no one to help in the chipper tonight. We won't open."

"Leave it to me, Graziella," Dante said. "Ah said I'd do it."

"Leave it to you? That's rich."

"Mrs Rebecchi, Dante. Ah'll see yez later," Chris said, embarrassed.

Dante, his hands on Graziella's shoulders, turned.

"Wait, Chris. Help me in the chipper the night?"

"Sure."

Dante gave Chris a sixpenny ice cream wafer, and his bus fare back to Westburn.

"Here's the keys. Open the shop. Ah'll come as soon as Ah can. We'll start servin' a bit late."

Dante walked Graziella into the back shop and closed the door.

"Mum's up to High Doh with your carry on, Dante."

"Ah failed the medical. Between you and me, Dr Thompson let me off."

"Right, m'lad. We're going to see Mum; pack your things. We'll sort out this mess. She's anxious to see you."

* * *

Graziella used her key and went first through the front door of the Rinaldi apartment followed by a sheepish Dante, kitbag slung on his shoulder, right hand clutching the old case. He dreaded meeting his mum.

Dante followed his sister into the kitchen. His mum looked a wreck sitting at the edge of an easy chair, face pinched, eyes red from crying, hands folded in her lap. Their row had diminished her.

Graziella went to the kitchen tap and filled a kettle. She put the kettle on the gas and prepared tea and biscuits.

"Ah'll put ma things in ma room, Mum."

Celestina kept her eyes on the fire.

"That's fine," she whispered.

Dante put off returning to the kitchen, unpacking at tortoise speed. He created more delay visiting the bathroom, flushing the cistern a couple of times, kneading soap and water into his hands, holding them under tepid water for a minute. A careful drying of hands.

Celestina stood, her back to the glowing coals, hands by her sides, when Dante returned to the kitchen.

"Mum, Ah'm…"

His mum turned the palm of her right hand towards Dante, as though in reproof, not letting him speak. Dante turned to Graziella, but her eyes were on the tray as she laid out the afternoon tea.

Jesus Christ, Dante thought. *If she starts up again, Ah'm out of here; an' for good this time. Ah'll try the navy or the bloody Marines.*

"So, so sorry, my son. You forgive me?"

Tears ran down her face. She opened her arms and embraced Dante, and he hugged his mum.

"No leave, Dante, no leave."

And Dante stayed.

* * *

One morning at the fish market, Dante felt a hand on his shoulder. He turned, and a man grabbed his hand and shook it.

"You must be Luigi's boy, Dante. Yer a dead ringer for yer father. Ah'm Jimmy Adams, yer dad's partner before the war."

Jimmy Adams and Luigi Rinaldi had distributed fish, refining and shipping beef dripping imported from Argentina to chippers throughout the west coast. Their business collapsed when war broke out.

"Bad what happened to yer dad and the Scots-Italians—internment, the riots, and the Arandora Star getting sunk."

A Glasgow Italian who delivered fish to the west coast wanted to retire, and Jimmy Adams needed a new partner. He'd been watching Dante and Chris buying fish and loading the van.

"Ah know you buy yer own fish and work with that young fella; he's a great worker."

"He's a right beast."

"Ah need a man to come in to the business on the west coast; you interested, son?"

"Definitely."

Dante expected he'd need capital and his mind worked on raising it; and he'd need a bigger van. Jimmy Adams had another important question.

"You're about eighteen. What about National Service?"

"Grade four. Failed the medical. Don't worry, Ah fought for near two years in the partisans in Italy. Ah belonged to the Fiamme Verde. The Green Flames. Ah'm strong. Ah'll bring the letter the commanding officer wrote when we disbanded. Major Sandro Giuntoli, Alpini Regiment."

"Ah'm impressed. There's no need, son. Can you raise five or six hundred quid, Dante? Ah'll lend ye money, as well. Pay me back, interest-free from the profits. Ye should be clear in a year. It's a good deal, son."

Dante stayed quiet, reckoning he must be paid on delivery of fish. No exceptions.

"Ah reckon yer thinking what Ah'm thinking, Dante. Cash on delivery. Good. There's one eejit in Westburn, Ricardo. A tight-arsed Italian. He never wants to pay on time. It's easier drawing blood from a stone. Yer dad could handle him."

"Ah can get the money, Mr Adams. And Ah'll deal with Ricardo. No pay, no fish."

"Great. Look, son, call me Jimmy. Everybody calls me Jimmy."

A straightforward method. The fish arrived by road in the small hours from Aberdeen. Dante phoned with his order, and Jimmy Adams bought. Haddock, the preferred fish, followed by whiting. Jimmy Adams got the pick of the delivery: he paid cash on the spot.

"It's the way, son. Ah'll let everyone know you're taking over. Make sure the Westburn Italians pay on delivery."

"Do Ah sign a contract?"

"A handshake? Good enough for yer dad and me. Shake on it?"

They shook hands.

* * *

At home, there was ground to make up. Dante loved his mum, and she loved him, but his outburst following the emotional goading and provocation had wounded her.

When Graziella told Celestina about Dante's need of a loan to buy a bigger van—he'd settled on a pre-war Bedford—and fund the new business with Jimmy Adams, she saw a way to thaw chill lingering between them, and gave him five hundred pounds.

"Jimmy Adams; nice man, good man. I meet with your father before war. Bring here later."

She handed Dante an envelope stuffed with one hundred white fivers.

"No loan, Dante; no pay back. Money for family business."

"Oh, Mum, thank you, thank you."

"No say nothing, my son. You do good for family."

She hugged her son and kissed him on the cheek; and he, less tense, kissed her, too.

Celestina and Dante did more than go through the motions of a loving mother and son; hugs and kisses, a deeper warmth. But an underlying chill remained. That his sweet-natured mum had acted out of character caused Dante's deepest wounds. Celestina, after talking to Graziella, thought bringing Dante round meant she must recognise Chiarina.

Dante worked hard. He gave Chris a job on leaving school, working in the back shop, preparing potatoes and fish for frying, cleaning the fryers, keeping the shop tidy, filling shelves; and he paid him a good deal more than a boy labourer's wages. Chris never stopped, and learned quickly. If the shop was quiet, he looked for work.

Dante and Chris enjoyed the rhythm of the working days. The early morning drive to the fish market, loading the van, delivering fish to the Westburn chippers; getting to the shop by eleven o' clock to prepare for the evening's business; the storage and preparation of the best potato for chips, Maris Piper, delivered daily by a local merchant. Chris operated the hand-cranked potato peeler, joining Dante when finished, to hand-cut chips, storing them in water-filled, stainless steel tubs, bought long before the war.

Dante preferred haddock, a delicate fish requiring careful preparation and cooking. Whiting followed haddock, when haddock was not to be had. Less flavourful, but still good eating. Lawson's of Dyce supplied boxes of solid fat, which Dante heated to liquid in the fryer.

Assisted by Chris, Dante mastered the running of the chipper. They operated the three-pan, gas-fired fryer, and, as rationing eased, sold cigarettes, lemonade, deep-fried Scotch mince pies and black puddings, with chips.

From the start, Dante and Chris loved the thrill of early evening: the first batches of fish and chips going into the fryer, the hiss of the bubbling fat swallowing the fish and chips, the unvarying sizzle of the cooking fish and chips.

Some months later, responding to customers' requests, Dante made snacks, an old favourite in the district: sliced potato discs dipped in a flour-and-water batter, cooked in the fryer until transformed into golden, crispy roundels, tender on the inside, considered a delicacy by the people of the Avenues, Holmscroft Street and the immediate neighbourhood.

One of the Moretti girls had worked in the shop for two years. Dante asked her advice on cooking the perfect fish and chips.

"Serve them right out of the fryer," she said. "You have to turn over cooked fish and chips every fifteen minutes, and put on a new batch. Otherwise it's not fresh. Doing it this way limits queuing. Customers don't like waiting too long. And keep the fat clean."

Freshness came from pacing, frying batches of twenty to twenty-five fish, and sufficient chips.

Cooking chips in the fish pan cleansed the fat. Throughout the evening, Chris or Dante, using a long-handled fine mesh sieve, removed burnt fragments of batter, fish, and potatoes.

Staff held a serving to the customer: glistening chips cooked in hot fat, crispy pale on the outside, white, tender, melting, tasty on the inside, laid on a square of white paper. A haddock fillet fried to perfection lay on top. Salt and vinegar to taste. The food was wrapped first in white paper, and double-wrapped in newspaper to keep it warm and fresh.

They wasted nothing. Dante sold used fat and potato peelings to pig farmers for brock, and when he'd taken a delivery of unfilleted fish from the market, added fish heads and guts to the pig feed.

"Don't you worry, Dante," one farmer said. "The pigs'll eat anything."

Flour for batter came in white linen bags. With clothing rationing in force, Dante and Chris washed the empty bags, fashioning serviceable aprons to wear behind the serving counter. The experienced girls who served wore their own floral-patterned peenies, and, with personal hair arrangements and discreet makeup, brought a welcome elegance to the shop.

Together, they brought the Rinaldi chipper back to pre-war levels of popularity. New customers came from outside the neighbourhood. Often, on mid-week evenings, the shop fried twelve to fourteen stone of fish, and the chips to go with them. On a good week, the shop sold seventy-five stone of fish. Dante counted it out: sixty fish suppers came from a stone of fish; one thousand and fifty pounds of fish. In the till, it meant cash for selling four thousand five hundred fish suppers.

On Sunday mornings after Mass, before they worked on the allotment, Dante drove Chris in the van to Graziella's at Cardwell Bay. They helped to fill shelves. Dante even learned to make ice cream.

The profits increased from the chipper and the fish delivery. Now eighteen, Dante had earned the respect of Westburn's Scots-Italians, and the people of the neighbourhood. One elderly lady, a customer since his dad opened the shop, voiced her approval.

"It's good to see ye here, son. Yer so like yer dad. An' the fish an' chips are just as good."

Dante felt a surge of pleasure.

"We try. Thank you. Ah appreciate you telling me."

One Sunday morning, with Chris busy washing the floor of the front shop, Graziella pleaded with her brother in the back shop.

"Mum wants it to be like before. She's trying very hard. Have you any idea how much she worried all the years you were stuck in Italy? No word. Dad dead, and Tony killed. She said the rosary every day, praying to the Virgin to protect you. On your birthday, she had the priest offer prayers for your safe return. God, at times it all got too much for her, and she'd break down, convinced you were dead."

"Ah'm tryin' as well. But she said bad things about Chiarina. Do ye think she meant it?"

"Of course not. She was upset. Mum's been through a lot with this bloody war."

"Christ, Ah wish Ah'd been man enough to hold ma tongue."

"Then tell her. Dante, for God's sake, give Mum a chance. When you're done at the allotment, she has a present for you. I helped her choose. She's getting a surprise Sunday dinner ready; the rabbit, the one you snared and brought home a couple of days ago. Invite Chris to have his dinner. Let him go home and change." Graziella smiled. "He's put up with your moods, too."

* * *

Working for Dante for several months, Chris had made good money and saved about a pound a week. Every Saturday morning Chris and Dante went to the post office bank and made a deposit. He traded rabbit for clothing coupons and bought a suit, a couple of shirts, tie, underwear, and his first pair of adult leather shoes.

Chris looked smart as he walked to Dante's place; he liked the click of his steel-tipped heels on the pavements.

Dante answered the door and took Chris to the good room, to where they were banished until dinner was ready.

"Yer lookin' good, Chris. Eddie Nichols did a good job with the suit."

Chris had brought two boxes of chocolates, one for Celestina, the other for Graziella, purchased in Marletti's Cafe at the West Station.

"He refused at first; Ah'd nae ration coupons. But he trapped when Ah reminded him about the rabbit and fish we gave him."

The friends sat on the settee looking onto the red Lancashire brick of St. Patrick's Church's soaring back gable.

"Ah like St. Pat's, Chris. It's well-built. What happened to yer face?"

Chris fingered a pale blue swelling bruise on his right cheek.

"Barney wi' the old man."

"Tell me."

The father threatened to pawn Chris's suit and shoes on the Monday. He'd needed a bob or two to tide him over. Then he bummed money for a drinking session in the Gunners Mess on South Street.

Chris knew that once his kit entered the pawn he'd have to redeem it. He told his father he'd get nothing.

"Ah'll stiffen ye if ye touch ma things."

The old man's punch caught Chris on the face as he turned to avoid the blow. He punched his father on the stomach, sending him reeling and falling over a chair onto the floor. He puked up the red biddy from the late Sunday morning drinking session over the linoleum.

The Good Mother, shrieking like a banshee, flew out of her chair, claws searching for Chris's face. The Woodbine cigarette between her lips glowed bright, then dull red, as she breathed. Ash fell on her soiled cardigan.

"Yer a wee fuckin' bastard, McCoull."

Chris shoved her back in her chair and told her to go to hell.

"It's wild. They're never off the drink. Her two have scarpered. The Good Brother's joined the army, and the Sister is livin' with her boyfriend's married sister. Ah've got to get away from them."

"That's bad, Chris. We'll talk later."

Graziella brought the boys in from the good room. An awkward Chris turned over the small brown paper parcels in his hands. He wasn't used to being an honoured guest. When the

Good Mother fed him, he ate from a plate or paper wrapper on his knee.

"Ah brought you these, Mrs Rinaldi, and you as well, Mrs Rebecchi."

He handed the chocolates to Celestina and Graziella. They unwrapped them, and both embarrassed Chris by kissing him on the cheek.

"Grazie, Chris; thank you. You are good boy," Celestina said.

"Yes, so you are, Chris," Graziella said.

Graziella brought a silver tray with four small glasses of red wine.

"I know you're not eighteen, Chris, but never mind."

Celestina raised her glass.

"Chris, Dante. Salute. Mille Grazie. The family comes good again."

She embraced her son and kissed him on both cheeks, and for the second time that evening she made Chris blush when she kissed him on the cheek. Celestina nodded to Graziella, who went to the sideboard and brought out a slim package.

She smiled.

"Go on, Chris, open it. You're a part of this. It's something for you."

A wrist watch: a sturdy, used Newmark. Chris put it on his left wrist.

"Mrs Rebecchi, Mrs Rinaldi, Ah don't know whit tae say. You're right good tae me. Jesus, Ah never had a watch in ma life, and never thought to."

He turned away, overcome. Dante laid a firm, reassuring hand on his friend's shoulder. Graziella wanted to embrace this good, shy boy, but she knew he'd have cried.

* * *

Graziella and Celestina had spent the afternoon preparing the feast. The family dined several times on rabbit hunted by Dante.

Quick cooking, a pot roast with gravy, potatoes and vegetables from the allotment. As Dante and Chris had hunted beyond the allotment, moving to the hills above the town and foraging in the acres of wilderness below the Lyle Hill, the take had increased.

Dante drew on a skill from his partisan days, laying snares at the centre of the rabbit beat, the loop set at seven inches high. When the rabbit ran along the beat, its head went into the loop and tightened on the neck, dispatching it. The snares seldom failed trapping an animal.

With the increased harvest of game, Dante traded rabbit for fruit and hens' eggs, and ration coupons. He established a climate of sharing, giving rabbit to neighbours, and Scots-Italian friends.

But this rabbit, a fine plump doe in her prime, he'd skinned with the razor-sharp German dagger, removed the guts and cleaned the carcass. The hide he'd buried, and the guts discarded, carrion left out for crow and hawk to eat.

Celestina butchered the rabbit, reducing it to serving pieces. She laid the liver and kidneys to one side for chopping.

Graziella peeled potatoes for boiling and mashing, chopped onion, a couple of garlic cloves, and celery brought from the allotment, then prepared bay leaf, rosemary, and thyme, taken from the family herb garden established by the wash house out back by the drying green.

A trickle of goods came again from Italy, and she'd managed to buy a small container of olive oil, a jar of black olives. Wine, too, but no pinoli nuts.

Graziella set the table for four, laying out the best china dishes, fine silver cutlery and wine glasses. She placed a packed vase of small perfumed yellow roses, brought by Dante, at the centre of the table.

Celestina made a soffritto of onion and garlic sautéed in the olive oil. She added the rabbit pieces, letting them brown lightly, absorbing the aromatics of onion and garlic, before seasoning the pot with salt and pepper. A splash of red wine. The rabbit braised for forty-five minutes, turned occasionally to keep the meat moist. Half way, Celestina added kidneys, liver and olives.

Dinner began with a salad of lettuce and turnip leaves from the allotment, and tangy, unripe tomatoes from the greenhouse Dante and Chris had built with salvaged timber and glass. Olive oil, salt and pepper. Good crusty bread Celestina had made. Water to drink. Rabbit and mashed potatoes. And they drank the red Ligurian wine. Custard and stewed apples for dessert; all the provender their ration coupons could obtain. Last, cups of Camp Coffee.

"Best grub ever, Mrs Rinaldi, Mrs Rebecchi," Chris said. "Ah'm full."

* * *

Graziella poured the last of the Ligurian red wine into four small glasses and handed them round. Content after the dinner, they sat round the fire side sipping the red nectar. Graziella rose, went to the sideboard and removed a square brown paper parcel bound with white string. She handed the parcel to her mother. Celestina rose from her chair.

"Dante; a present. Graziella helped me decide."

He opened the parcel, laid the contents on his chair, rolled the string, folding the brown paper, placing them on the mantelpiece. The matching glistering silver frames caught his eye, and he ran his fingers over the entwined silver rope adorning the edges.

"Look inside the frames," Graziella said.

The fine enlargements pleased him, especially the picture of Chiarina and himself. The one with her hair framing her face, she gazing at him, their eyes locked. The picture of the band, he and Chiarina armed, took him back to the hard days, the fighting; and he remembered comrades lost.

"You like them, Chris?"

"Ye both look great."

Dante's throat swelled; he turned away mumbling, "Thanks, Mum, Graziella; Christ, Ah don't know what to say."

"Dante, can we put pictures on mantelpiece?" Celestina said.

"We'd like everyone to see them," Graziella said.

"Here, Mum, you put them up," Dante said.

And they knew the family would be all right.

Chapter Seven

Dante worried about his friend's future. Chris would happily spend years working with the Rinaldi family, and did not look ahead. The café and chipper business in Scotland belonged to the Scots-Italians, and Chris wasn't an Italian. He could do well outside the the family business.

"Next year or two, Chris, what would you like to be doing?" Dante asked one day.

Chris looked up, grinned and stopped cranking the potato-peeling machine. "Workin' 'wi' you and Mrs Rebecchi. There's the army when Ah'm eighteen. Ah'd change digs; find a new place to live."

"Ah'll see what's doin', Chris."

Vasco Parasella, a naturalised Italian from La Spezia, head waiter at the The Old Hotel, came to the chipper to test Dante's interest in supplying a variety fish. Dante and Vasco agreed a price, and payment on delivery.

"Call me the night before with your order," Dante said. "Ah'll make you first delivery the next morning."

They shook hands.

"How are things at the hotel?" Dante asked.

"Trouble, today," Paracella said.

Whole fish too came from Aberdeen. The second chef prepared the fish. He fell ill with flu and took to his bed for two weeks.

"We're busy, and no one can fillet fish like the second chef. I can fillet, but I'm dead slow."

"Chris's a dab hand. He'll fillet your fish."

Dante left Chris at The Old Hotel and came back for him when he'd completed deliveries.

Vasco Paracella levelled a keen eye on Chris working with the knife, making an angled cut under the fins on either side behind the head, severing it, and removing the guts. A surgical incision beneath dorsal fin, running the blade from top to tail along the bones. Feed the blade midway through to the underside, moving it along the fillet for trimming, and extracting the pin bones.

Vasco liked Chris's neat and tidy work and asked Dante for his services whenever whole fish came.

"Sure. Ah can spare him for an hour or two. How about you pay him, say a pound a time for work done?"

After several visits, Vasco Paracella handed Chris a fiver.

"Take it. I asked Dante. It's okay. He said to pay you. Good job, Chris. Thank you."

* * *

An unexpected phone call in November gave Dante the chance to steer Chris to a brighter future. He didn't want to offend his best friend, and he'd be happy to have him working in the shop for as long as wanted. But it was not the best option.

Sunday afternoon after four o' clock. Dante and Chris had finished working in the allotment, and Chris went back to the apartment. There'd be relief from the misery; his old man and the Good Mother were out on the batter from noon, guzzling the red biddy at the Gunners, and later to a squalid tenement flat with boozy cronies for more potent cheap wine and drunken maudlin talk.

Chris had attached a lock and bolt on his bedroom door to keep the old man and the Good Mother out. There might be no peace later in the evening when they returned, but he'd secured his privacy.

Dante answered the phone. "All right, Ah'll come to the hotel at half past seven."

"Who phone?"

"Vasco Paracella, Mum. He wants to discuss a job for Chris."

"Chris is nice boy. Good friend to you. Take care, my son. No hurt Chris."

* * *

A slow Friday evening. They sold the last fish supper at half past ten. Dante and Chris helped the girls on the counter clean up and sent them home by quarter to eleven. He and Chris finished tidying and closed the shop at eleven o' clock. They went to the back shop. Dante took a slim, long-necked bottle of grappa from the cupboard.

"Homemade. Joe Barilli brought it back." Dante set two small-stemmed glasses on the table. "These belonged to ma dad." He filled the glasses. "Sit down, Chris."

Chris sat, looking slightly apprehensive.

"Salute," Dante said and took a sip. The grappa burned his tongue. "Strong stuff."

Chris wrinkled his nose. "No' half. No' sure if Ah like it. Something wrong, Dante? You and me havin' a drink this late on a Friday night."

Dante shook his head and sipped liquor. Silence.

"Come on Dante, what is it? Tell me."

"Vasco Paracella called me. There's a job for you at The Old Hotel. The chef likes the way you fillet fish. But first, John Turner, the manager, wants to see you. He's heard about you from Vasco."

Chris, face working, swallowed grappa. Dante wanted to avoid awkwardness, but he'd not handled it well. He'd upset Chris.

"Have Ah screwed up; you want rid of me?"

"Chris, we're good friends. Yer ma right arm. No, you haven't screwed up; an' no, Ah don't want rid of you."

"Are you showin' me the door?"

"Before you jump to any conclusions, listen, and Ah'll tell you about the job."

The Old Hotel needed a porter-cum-kitchen assistant. Portering meant cleaning public spaces and lavatories, moving furniture, carrying luggage and, if asked, cleaning and polishing guests' shoes. These jobs came in the morning. In the kitchen, he'd learn from the chef to prepare and cook food, and he'd be paid overtime in the dining room, at weddings, dances, and other busy periods. Vasco Paracella would teach him to wait tables. After a year, they'd move Chris to the kitchen full-time.

Chris's face brightened, but his eyes remained guarded.

"Did you line this up?"

"No, Vasco approached me."

Dante tried to guess at Chris's thinking. Their friendship, the Sundays at Mass, working on the allotment, and the chipper business. He knew Chris loved being there and on the early morning runs to the fish market.

"You'd have time off, two half-days, and we'd meet. And Ah told Vasco about our goin' to Mass and workin' on the allotment."

Chris nodded but kept his eyes on the floor. Dante said Chris had to think ahead. In the hotel he'd have a career. What Chris had learned in the chipper was the first step into the hotel and restaurant business.

"You'd stay in staff quarters; three square meals day. No charge. Vasco said you'd get a rise."

A grin lit Chris's face. "Jesus, a move away from home, and more money."

"Correct. Chris, we're best mates. Ah'd never give you a bum steer. It's a good offer. Go see John Turner. If you don't fancy it, stay here and keep workin' with me."

* * *

Chris slumbered light and got up early on Saturday morning. The old man and the Good Mother slept off last night's red biddy while he made tea and spread margarine on a slice of toasted outsider.

At eight o'clock as he made his way west on Holmscroft Street, Chris wondered at the differences a few hundred yards made to people's lives. He came from the poor end of the street. Cramped apartments with set-in beds and outside jakes. Cross Mount Pleasant Street, and people lived in tenements with tiled closes, and apartments with bathrooms and inside jakes.

Chris was afraid of losing the warm affection he'd found with the Rinaldis.

He thought about walking further west through the streets with the affluent, detached houses on Inverkip Road, but instead crossed the street and entered St. Patrick's by the side door.

A deep-seated superstition drove him to the church, hope from childhood lingering into adulthood, optimism that had survived the ministry of the cursed Irish priests. Dipping fingers of his right hand in the stoup by the door, Chris made the sign of the cross, then worked his way to the end of a pew in the middle of the church. He genuflected to the altar and knelt, hands joined.

Chris murmured an Our Father, several Hail Marys and a Glory Be To The Father. His knees hurt and he raised himself onto the seat.

The church was empty save for a couple of old biddies kneeling in the front pews, rosary beads folded over hands, fingers counting Hail Marys, whispering prayers to Our Lady.

The light flooding through the dormer windows brightened the altar. The stillness, the waxy smell of burning candles, murmuring aged voices, made Chris drowsy. He drifted off, and his desire for guidance waned.

The faint chimes of McCulloch's Clock striking the hour penetrated the church walls, startling Chris. He shrugged, optimism and hopes dashed. No guidance or revelation had come. He checked his Newmark watch. Nine o'clock. Chris had spent close to an hour in St. Patrick's.

Chris genuflected to the altar and left the by the side door. He turned toward the Orangefield Café for a cup of coffee, then headed home, dressed for work, and went to get the chipper ready for Saturday night opening.

"Good morning, Chris."

"Oh, good morning, Mrs Rinaldi."

"Wait for me. I go to butcher for rations."

Celestina returned in a few minutes from the butcher shop, with her small parcels of mince, slice and link sausage in her message bag.

"Not much for Sunday." She smiled. "You and Dante bring home rabbit tomorrow."

"We'll try."

Celestina gazed at Chris and he grew uncomfortable under her eye.

"Dante speak, Chris?"

"He did."

"You worry. Come with me."

They walked past Balfour House down the brae to the roundabout and north along Nelson Street. Celestina stopped outside Rossi's Café.

"Joe, the son, is home from Navy. Nice man; makes good coffee."

They sat in a booth, and Joe came.

"Hello, Mrs Rinaldi, and you must be Chris. I've heard about you. All good." Joe grinned.

He brought the coffee, and they sat sipping the steaming liquid. Celestina nibbled a chocolate biscuit. Chris took out his handkerchief and wiped the crumbs from his chin.

"Chris, we never do a bad thing to you. You are family to us."

"You've all been good to me. But Dante surprised me. Ah'd never thought about leavin' the chipper. Ah like workin' there wi' Dante and goin' to Mrs Rebecchi's café."

"You trust Dante?"

"Ah'd trust him wi' anything."

"You go to see John Turner."

* * *

Chris got the job as porter-cum-kitchen assistant, and moved to staff quarters. He shared accommodation with a waiter, the barman, and another kitchen assistant. He had a clean bed and decent food, and advancement several rungs up the social ladder away from the squalor of home. Staff quarters, a paradise far from the old man, the Good Mother, and their careless ways.

Chris realised that Dante had rescued him from a grim life navvying for the council, or labouring in the shipyards, an interlude in the army, a life of boozing, low pay and hard labour in atrocious conditions. He was grateful that Dante had saved him from an early grave.

But trouble came early. Joe Marshall—a big, aggressive man—took a job at The Old Hotel for the summer season. An experienced waiter, a veteran steward, who'd spent his early years deep sea in the Merchant Navy, and later, on the river steamers, and Glasgow hotels. A middle-aged drifter of no fixed address, moving between work in the city and life afloat on the Clyde.

Marshall drank like a fish, a trait shared with many veterans of the sea, catering, and hotel life: he was a plonker, a piss artist, smashed when off duty, and often half shot on the job.

Joe Marshall stayed in the staff accommodation. On principle he disliked Chris, a Catholic, and worse, he considered the younger talented and energetic man a threat. Marshall gave Chris a hard time, running him ragged, assuming superiority, chivvying him into extra work clearing up around the kitchen, mocking Chris's lowly duties: portering, cleaning guests' shoes, scrubbing out the lavatories, vacuuming, dusting, and sprucing up public rooms.

He'd hiss in Chris's ear, "Yer a wee skivvy, McCoull; a fuckin' Teague. Ye'll amount to fuck-all."

Marshall made Chris's life miserable. Chris told himself that he wasn't afraid of the big man, and resolved to endure. Marshall would leave in September and Chris wanted no trouble.

John Turner, manager—a solid Ulster-Scot—liked Chris's hard work. He'd brought Chris on, arranging overtime in the dining room, Sunday lunches, weddings, dances. Vasco Paracella trained Chris, and John Turner asked Chris to help the second chef prepare Sunday breakfasts.

Chris discovered a flair for working tables; he studied the head waiter's mastery of French service, and off duty, practiced the movements of fork and spoon from the serving dish to the diners' plates. Chris took pride in his appearance. He felt good in the brilliant white jacket, the dark trousers pressed with sharp creases front and back, his black shoes polished until they shone like glass. He became a discreet, popular waiter at table, garnishing roasts and fish with potatoes and vegetables, lifting rolls with fork and spoon from the bread barge.

Chris didn't mind portering. Furniture in public rooms gleamed from his dusting and polishing. His careful vacuuming brought carpet pile to a rich fullness, and the lavatories he scoured spotless and left smelling of fresh disinfectant.

Part of Chris's wages and all tips went into his post office savings account. One Thursday afternoon late, his father and the Good Mother came to the back door of the hotel looking for a share of his new prosperity.

"How're gettin' on, Chris? Ye never come by an' see us," the father said.

The Good Mother exposed stained false teeth in an ingratiating smile. Chris stepped back from the stink on her breath of last night's El D, a cheap potent wine. He felt sorry for his old man, ruining his life, wasting himself on the jake. Chris held the Good Mother in contempt; a swine of a woman he wished had never left Ireland. She'd brought on his father's ruin, and Monday to Friday had thrown Chris out on the street to attend school, or pass the time at weekends, clad in rags, half starved; a stepmother who'd nagged his father until he'd beat Chris several times a week for giving her lip.

"Go on, clear off," Chris said.

The Good Mother hawked and spat a gob of phlegm at Chris's feet. "Yer nuthin' but a wee shite, McCoull; a right bastard."

Marshall passed, going off duty. "Trash; Westburn, Fenian scum,'" he said to Chris. His old man and the Good Mother had no shame, begging Chris for drinking money. Chris mopped up the Good Mother's muck, and drew the mop head down the front of her dress. He handed his father a ten-shilling note.

"Take her away, and get out of ma sight."

That night Marshall came in drunk and emptied his bladder over a sleeping Chris. The hot, stinking flood woke Chris, soaking his bed. Marshall pinned him to the bed with his foot and shook the last drops of piss over Chris and put his dick away.

"Stay out of the fuckin' dining room," he said, and drove a heavy kitchen knife into the headboard above Chris's head. Marshall staggered back, gagging, honk bubbling on his lips. He swallowed his own puke.

Chris went to the bathroom and was sick. He got rid of the knife.

Piss on people; a standby for West Coast toughs. When Chris was twelve, a pupil in St. Mary's, a lout of fourteen had sprayed jets of piss on him. Chris had thrown one punch, and come away wet and stinking, nursing a bloody mouth.

A waiter helped Chris clean up and fetched fresh bedding.

"Complain about that bastard. See Mr Turner and get the fucker sacked."

It was a matter of honour for Chris to deal with Marshall himself. Bringing his troubles to John Turner would show weakness, a want of manhood. Chris shook his head.

"Ah solve ma own problems."

Sunday afternoon, Dante and Chris finished working on the allotment. They sat on the bench outside the hut sharing cheese-and-tomato sandwiches, drinking tea.

"The young fella from Garbugliago," Dante said. "He's settling in fine in the shop. He's a quick learner, a hard worker."

"That's good."

Chris told Dante about Marshall.

"Can't have that. Sort him out, Chris."

"This week, on Thursday, his day off. Ah'll get him. Ah'm no' scared of him, but he's a big bastard."

"You want me to come?"

"Thanks, but no. Ah'll deal wi' Marshall."

"Wait a minute." Dante got up and went inside.

From inside the hut, Chris heard the rasping of a saw cutting wood. Dante returned and sat down beside Chris and sandpapered the rough edges off twenty inches of pick shaft. He wound brown garden twine round the bottom of the shaft, making a tight, six-inch grip. He held it up for inspection and fingered the square head.

"Here, this'll even the odds. Let him know you're there, then say nothing. Hit him. Don't mark his face or his head. Give him it on the ribs and shoulders, the arms. Hurt him so he won't throw punches or grab you. Get him down, rap him on the shins. Warn him off when you're done."

"Where'd you learn this?"

"In the Fiamme Verde. With a rifle. Ah'll show you how before Thursday."

Chris poured tea from the flask. They had another sandwich.

"Chris, any trouble at The Old Hotel, if you get the bag, come back to work in the chipper. Drive the van and deliver the fish. Help Graziella."

"Thanks, Dante."

* * *

Thursday, Joe Marshall's day off. By late evening he'd be out of his skull, drunk and belligerent. He staggered into the staff quarters, looking right and left.

"Where's that wee bastard McCoull?"

"Right here, ya fucker."

A sword-thrust to the belly with the sawn-off pick shaft as Marshall turned, his hands grabbing his gut; hammer blows to Marshall's upper arms. He let go of his torso, and Chris laid a volley of blows on both sides of the ribcage, driving him to his knees, then whacked him on the shoulders. Marshall fell back, spread-eagled on the floor. Chris rapped him hard twice on both shins.

"Enough, enough!" Marshall pleaded.

But rage consumed Chris, now twice pissed on in his life, and Marshall's appeal only goaded him to greater fury. A blow to Marshall's head left a swelling, bloody welt.

Chris pinned him to the floor, the end of the pick shaft digging into Marshall's breast bone. "Stay away from me or Ah'll finish ye," he growled.

Marshall passed out. With the help of the barman, Chris lifted Marshall and threw him onto his bed.

The following Sunday afternoon, Dante and Chris were weeding the vegetable patch side by side. Chris took a slug from a bottle of water, wiped the top and passed it to Dante. He put the neck to his lips and swallowed, banishing his thirst.

"No marks on yer face, Chris. Any bruising?"

"Clean as a whistle. Marshall never got near me."

"The job okay?"

"John Turner sent for me and told me to behave myself. No more fighting. But Ah told him Marshall fell when he was drunk. The waiter and the barman were there, and they supported me. Ah thanked John Turner. He understood: Ah'm still there."

The manager knew that he'd been right to employ Chris, but hiring Marshall had been a mistake.

"John Turner's a decent man," Chris said.

* * *

A year on, and true to their word, John Turner, Vasco Paracella and the head chef, Dick Devlin, eager to have him on board, transferred Chris full-time to the kitchen. But for the first month, Chris spent time with the new porter, making suggestions about the job and answering his questions.

During that first year, Chris had read Escoffier and understood making sauces, soups and garnishes, as well as perfected his skills with kitchen knives. Chris took on fish filleting from the start, preparing salmon, sole, haddock, flounder, and herring, along with intense practice of basic kitchen skills. Preparing vegetables, enjoying the texture of potatoes, carrots, turnip, leeks in his hands, trimming and cutting to suit various dishes.

He bought a quality Sheffield blade, a steel sharpener, honing stone and small bottle of light mineral oil. Sunday morning was honing time, music to his ears the rasp, the slip and slide of Sheffield steel on oiled stone. The edge was sharper than a highland broadsword. The second chef taught Chris how to use the steel sharpener. First thing in the morning Chris rang blade on steel, a few minutes' continuous ringing, banishing the dull edge from yesterday's cutting.

Chris controlled the knife, left hand holding lamb leg, cutting away fat; boning gigot of lamb; cutting chops; the brief rasp of butcher's saw on bone; sirloins, removing the filet, cutting down the back bone, trimming sinews and cutting away ribs. From beef trimmings and chicken offal and carcasses he made stock for soup. His first success was soups. Thick barley broth, lentil chicken barley broth, chicken with rice.

"You're better at it than me," the second chef said.

And so, Chris mastered the four corners of the kitchen: vegetables, soups, fish, roasts. In the larder he assisted with the preparation and cooking and baking of bread, pastry, desserts, cakes.

He never refused work, seeing requests for help—even when footsore and tired—as a chance to learn, adding to his repertoire of culinary skills and knowledge.

Breakfast was a plated service, and Chris worked with the second chef frying a stock of bacon, and sausage, tomatoes, potato scones, kept moist and hot to go with eggs. The eggs were cooked to order: poached, boiled, fried scrambled, and omelettes. Breakfast was a busy time, never a break to sit at table, so Chris made do with two buttered morning rolls filled with bacon and egg, washed down with cups of tea.

Every morning early, Chris relished the feel of fresh-smelling laundered kit: the chef's hat, white jacket, neckerchief and crisp, gingham pants. If the kitchen turned quiet, Chris mucked in with the women keeping the kitchen clean and tidy. His efforts pleased Dick Devlin, a fanatic for an immaculate kitchen. The smells of frying eggs, bacon and sausage vanished, and the freshness of the pots and pans, the cleaned air, signalled the end of breakfast.

Chris knew the value of organisation. He'd learned that working with Dante. So he adapted to the daily rhythms of the kitchen. The head chef established the menu, working a day ahead. Square away the kitchen after breakfast, and lunch got underway: vegetables prepared and cooked. The second chef prepared meat stews, and steak or chicken pies for cooking on the next day.

Dinner preparation started at lunchtime, the menu built around a roast and dishes cooked to order: steaks, chops, fish.

On Friday, the pace quickened. Bookings came and the chef attended to planning and ordering. The rest of the week was quieter, but on Sunday, more diners came for lunch, and the kitchen had all staff on duty. By Sunday dinner, the dining room quieted. From time to time the chef left after Sunday lunch, leaving the kitchen in the capable hands of the second chef and Chris, who looked forward to the day when he'd be ready to run the kitchen.

In the winter months, and over Christmas and New Year, local companies organised dinner dances, and throughout the year, but often in the summer months, weddings. That meant paid overtime, and Chris saved the money. Preparing and cooking for fixed menus was straightforward, striking a balance of sixty percent meat, thirty percent chicken, and ten percent salad.

The chef sourced food from local suppliers. The butcher kept beef on the hoof on hill pastures above the town. Dante supplied fish. Fruit, vegetables and flowers came from Westburn family businesses. Local supply guaranteed fresh produce.

For Chris the passage from working in the chipper to hotel porter, kitchen assistant and promotion to second chef was a matter of getting on with the job. But his mentors, and Dante too, saw the young Chris becoming a man.

* * *

Dante had written to Chiarina but his letters had come back and he gave up writing. He'd written to Old Mario and Agate, but they said they had no news of Chiarina.

* * *

Chiarina and Anselmo had stayed in Bologna while Anselmo was in and out of hospital, having the cataracts in both eyes removed. Then they'd come back to the village for Anselmo to convalesce. The operation was a success, but he had to wear glasses, which he did not like. He settled for a stainless steel frame with rimless lens that gave him a severe look, masking his warm disposition.

In their movements, Chiarina had lost Dante's address. All she remembered was that her beloved lived in Westburn and the family owned a chipper.

By May, Anselmo had recovered from the cataract operations. He loved remote places. He and Chiarina, took the sheep, the goats, his animals and the dogs back to the mountain.

A deep and lasting affection bound Anselmo and Chiarina. To Anselmo, Chiarina was another daughter, younger than his natural daughter. And for Chiarina, he became the father that she'd lost. Chiarina seemed content but kept hidden her longing for Dante. Anselmo, a wise old owl, understood how she felt.

Anselmo's son-in-law came up from the village to look after the animals. Anselmo and Chiarina crossed the mountains to Garbugliago to find Dante's grandparents, and found no help there. Agate said she had no knowledge of Dante's address.

Anselmo, furious at Old Mario and Agate's hostility, declined their offer of food, but for Chiarina's sake he asked whether they might sleep in the barn.

Later, Mario with greater heart than Agate, brought bread, cheese, coffee and wine to the barn.

"My wife's heart is stone. I remember you, Chiarina, from the war. I saw then you cared for each other. Here is Dante's address."

Mario slipped Chiarina a folded note.

"When you find Dante, tell him I tried to save the donkey, Modestino. Tell him she is not here. Agate nagged me. I slaughtered Modestino and we ate her. We were very hungry."

Try as he might, Anselmo could not convince Chiarina that Dante waited for her in Scotland. Chiarina was afraid about meeting Dante again. She had heard nothing from him. Chiarina had convinced herself that Dante had forgotten her.

"Why doesn't he come for me?"

"Britain has been at war, too. I suggest Dante is looking after his family. You remember, his father drowned and his sister is a widow, her husband killed in Sicily."

Anselmo and Chiarina left Garbugliago at dawn, breakfasting on the hoof as they walked, chewing on saved stale bread and cheese.

Anselmo patted the money belt under his shirt.

"We shall go to Pavia and find Major Giuntoli. He will help us."

From Garbugliago they walked down the mountain to La Spezia and from there travelled by bus to Pavia.

They soon found Major Giuntoli, now set up as a wine merchant. He'd married the widow of a fellow Alpini officer killed in Russia. She had two children, and was now pregnant with Major Giuntoli's child.

He delighted at finding again his old comrades, inviting them to stay while passports were obtained.

* * *

Saturday night, well past eleven after the shop closed. Dante sat in the kitchen drinking coffee with his mum. The phone rang and Celestina answered it.

"For you, Dante. Sergeant Ponsonby."

"Hello, Dante. Ah had a call from the Dover police. There's a lassie there just off the boat from Calais, Chiarina Inserti. A man's with her, says he's her guardian, Anselmo Rosso. Do you know them? She's claiming she's your fiancée."

"Ah certainly know them. Chiarina was in the partisans."

Dante, filled with excitement, felt his love for Chiarina grow stronger, knowing that she'd landed at Dover, just hours away by train.

"Yes, she's ma fiancée. Anselmo looked after Chiarina when she was sick. That's the last time I saw her."

"When was that?"

"January 1945, at Anselmo's cabin up in the mountains, the Apennines."

"Right Dante. Hold on, I'm going to the other line."

Celestina came into the hall.

"Something wrong, Dante?"

He put his finger to his lips as Sergeant Ponsonby came back on the line.

"Right, right. They're all right. We'll be at the West Station tomorrow night. About seven o 'clock."

He went back to the kitchen with a happy grin on his face. He plucked Celestina from her chair and hugged her, then spun her round.

"Chiarina and Anselmo are in Dover just off the Calais ferry. The police are looking after them tonight. Tomorrow they'll be on the train. Big Lachie's going to meet them in Glasgow Central off the London train and bring them to Westburn. They'll be here about seven o'clock."

"Get things ready; tell Graziella."

"First thing in the morning, Mum."

Chiarina and Anselmo, having staved off hunger with a Dover Police breakfast and survived the postwar joys of railway fare, needed wholesome food.

Next morning Dante called Chris at The Old Hotel.

"Chiarina and Anselmo are in Dover. They're arriving the night. Can you help? We need a meat sauce."

"Ah'll make it myself. It'll be perfect; don't worry. And Ah'll make an apple tart, a big one. In the afternoon, Ah'll send the porter over with the food."

"Thanks, Chris. Come and eat with us; try to make it for eight o' clock."

"Count on it. Ah'll be there."

In the afternoon, Celestina and Graziella made pasta, with Chris's meat sauce, and herbs from the herb garden. They had bread and wine.

* * *

Chiarina and Anselmo left Dover at first light for London. They'd spent the night in the cells; not prisoners, but guests of His Majesty. As Sergeant Lachlan Ponsonby promised, the Dover police fed and watered the travellers, gave them each a bed in the cells, and access to the ablutions in the morning to prepare for the journey north to Scotland; and a breakfast: porridge, toast and margarine and mugs of sweet, milky tea.

Sunday, Chiarina and Anselmo found themselves in a quiet corridor train north from London; they had a compartment to themselves. The travellers changed trains at Crewe Junction. A hurried snack of strong, sugared, milky tea and toasted dried egg sandwich spread with margarine killed appetites. Making their way to the platform for the Glasgow train, they sensed the furtive looks of shabby locals.

Anselmo, a countryman to his fingertips, strode along the platform, the metal heel tips of his sturdy boots echoing of the hard surface. He remained indifferent to the prolonged stares of locals fascinated by his foreignness: the well-worn brown corduroy suit, the brown worsted flat cap. A stogie clenched between his teeth, he exhaled a thin stream of acrid smoke. The rucksack on his back and the case he carried did not slow his pace.

When they had had enough of looking at Anselmo, they shifted their gazes to Chiarina, hurrying beside him burdened by two suitcases containing her few belongings.

She had brought a wedding dress and veil that had belonged to Anselmo's married daughter. The garment had been altered in Pavia by Major Giuntoli's wife to fit Chiarina's youthful figure.

They boarded the Glasgow train. It was a sunless English day, and a journey across a bleak, shabby land recovering from the long years of war. The curtain of rain drenching the countryside and towns depressed them. The rubble-strewn bomb sites disfigured streets near railway stations. Anselmo, a stoic, shrugged at the stains of war. Doubt assailed Chiarina. She felt she was tempting fate bringing the wedding dress and she'd be punished for her presumption.

Chiarina's fidgeting and wrinkled forehead worried Anselmo. He reached across for her hand to reassure her and banish her concern.

"Dante is an honourable young man, he meant what he said about marrying. Trust Dante; and trust in Him."

It had been close to two years since Chiarina had seen Dante, but she cheered herself up with the thought of seeing him that evening.

* * *

Three anxious Scots-Italians waited on the platform of the West Station, a curtain of drizzle dimming the light. Dante looked around at the bunches of weeds and moss sprouting from the pointing of the retaining wall, the puddles on the platforms, the vending machines attached to the platform walls. Fry's chocolate bars stood next to anonymous brands of cigarettes, the brand name worn off the display plate. The machines hadn't worked since 1939. He turned to Graziella.

"Ah hope Chiarina and Anselmo are no' put off by this."

"It'll be all right," Graziella said.

Celestina patted Dante's arm.

Two years since they'd been together. How would Chiarina look? How would he look to her? Maybe it wouldn't work. Perhaps their love for each other had been the consequence of a wartime romance where emotions were heightened by the dangers of partisan life. Could their love flourish in the real world of shabby, austere Westburn still licking its wounds from six years of war?

Dante, quite forgetting his duty to family, thought he could survive Italy if Chiarina grew unsettled in Westburn. He dismissed the thought. Surely Chiarina could adapt to working in the chipper, or the best option, work in Graziella's café.

He walked a few steps along the platform, muttering, "It must be alright. Ah can only imagine the trouble Chiarina and Anselmo have gone through to get here."

He walked back to where his mum and Graziella waited.

The train screeched to a halt, clouds of white steam shooting from the engine's cylinders, floating up, vanishing into the driech and the damp retaining walls of the railway cutting.

A handful of travellers got off the train and vanished.

"Jesus Christ, where are they?" Dante said. "The bloody train'll be heading for Fort Matilda in a minute."

"Calm down, my son," Celestina said.

Big Lachie came out of the gloom carrying two cases, drizzle shining on his waterproof cape. In vain, Dante looked for Chiarina wearing an Italian Army bustina, a sheepskin jacket and moccasins, with soiled yellow leather bindings wound round thick woollen mountaineer's socks covering her lower legs. And Chiarina, eyes searching for Dante clad in worn khaki British Army Battle Dress, a Tam O'Shanter tilted over his right brow, didn't spot Dante either. They looked past each other.

Then a girl stood in front of him. She spoke Italian.

"Dante. It's me, Chiarina."

He looked down, for her head came to his shoulder. Dressed in a prewar grey wool coat, belted at the waist, given her by the major's wife, with woollen stockings and shoes suitable for a long journey. He cupped her face in tender hands, and she smiled.

"I looked for a partisan."

"And I too; the police sergeant brought me right to you. He is a good man."

An embrace, a chaste kiss in front of family and guardian. Dante brought Chiarina to where Celestina and Graziella waited.

"Mum, Graziella. My girlfriend— my fiancée, Chiarina Inserti."

There was no frostiness with Celestina; she embraced Chiarina and kissed her on both cheeks.

"Welcome, Chiarina, daughter."

And Graziella embraced Chiarina, and kissed her on both cheeks.

"I'm so glad to meet you, Chiarina. I've heard so much about you from Dante. Soon we'll be sisters."

Now Dante had time to see Anselmo. He was, as expected, a tidy countryman in a brown three-piece corduroy suit, a matching worsted cloth cap, and sturdy countryman's boots. The stogie clenched between his teeth set a filigree of acrid smoke to wreathing his head. Dante wondered what the well-used but whole Italian Army rucksack contained.

Dante took a couple of steps, and put his arm round Anselmo's shoulder.

"And this is my friend, and Chiarina's guardian, Anselmo Rossi."

More handshakes. Anselmo put his hands on Chiarina's and Dante's shoulders.

"I'm glad that you have found each other again."

Sergeant Ponsonby, carrying Chiarina's two suitcases, came as far as the entrance to the tenement.

"Come in, Sergeant," Graziella said. "Have supper with us."

"Thanks, Graziella, but I have to go back to the station. Finish the shift."

He turned to Dante, and Celestina.

"You'll come to the station tomorrow? Bring Mr Rossi and Miss Inserti with you. There's a few forms to fill out. It'll no' take long."

Dante shook Sergeant Ponsonby's hand.

"Thanks for all your trouble; for everything."

"No trouble, Dante. Glad to help."

Dante walked him to the door.

"She's a fine girl. Take good care of her, son."

Dante smiled.

"I've dreamt of this day since I got home. I'll look after Chiarina. I'll make her happy."

* * *

They entered the living room-cum-kitchen. Anselmo opened the rucksack and removed a round cheese wrapped in muslin, two bottles of grappa, and two thick sausages covered by a protective net that just fit in the rucksack. He laid them on the kitchen table.

"Salsiccia Ligure, Bruzzu cheese from the sheep, and the finest grappa. From Major Giuntoli."

"Thank you, Anselmo," Celestina said. "But it is so much you bring."

Anselmo raised his hands. "It is a small thing from the old country."

Celestina liked the look of Anselmo, his quiet dignity and good manners. She felt that they could become friends.

Chiarina and Anselmo stayed in the apartment in Holmscroft Street. Anselmo shared Dante's room and Chiarina had the set-in bed in the good room. But after registering Chiarina and Anselmo with the police, Dante planned to drive them to Graziella's house in Kempock. Celestina had suggested it and Anselmo approved. Two young people so much in love, and apart so long, must be kept from temptation.

The next morning after breakfast, Dante and Chiarina sat in the good room while Celestina and Anselmo, new friends, tidied away the breakfast debris and washed the dishes.

Dante and Chiarina sat awkward in their nearness to each other.

"Sleep well?"

"Si, Dante; you?"

"Me too, but for a while Anselmo snored like a bull."

"Sometimes up in the cabin the noise came through the walls right into my bedroom."

Dante reached behind the cushion and withdrew a neat bundle of envelopes bound by an elastic band. Dante had kept them, a talisman strengthening his confidence that one day he'd see Chiarina again.

"Here, the letters belong to you. I worried myself sick every time one came back. I kept them hoping one day we'd meet again."

Chiarina took the bundle of letters.

"We went to see your grandparents and asked for your address, but Agate refused to help. Anselmo declined the food she offered, and we slept in the barn. Later, your grandfather brought food to us and gave me your address. That's when Anselmo said we were coming to Scotland to find you."

"She can be hard-faced."

"Your grandfather said to tell you that he tried to save the little donkey, Modestino."

Dante explained that Fred and he had given Modestino to Mario and Agate.

"A sweet little thing. Affectionate and hard-working. We brought her from the Fiamme Verde, carrying some of our kit. Modestino liked me."

Dante told Chiarina how he and Fred had looked after Modestino on the mountains on the way to Garbugliago.

"She was shivering and coughing. We banked up the fire, dried her off and Modestino lay beside us covered with our sleeping bags and waterproofs. She shared our bed."

Dante grinned at the memory.

"I hope Mario and Agate are looking after Modestino. Mario could make her well. She was a grand wee thing. You didn't see her?"

"No, she was not at the farm."

"Maybe they sold her?"

"No, Dante. I'm so sorry to tell you, but your grandparents slaughtered and ate Modestino. Your grandfather said they were very hungry."

Dante's stomach shrank, and his eyes stung.

"Christ Almighty; they killed Modestino and ate her! I'll bet they had her all to themselves. Agate'd be behind it; bloody old vixen. I don't care how hungry they were. It's unforgivable."

"Oh, Dante. I know how you feel. I felt awful that day on the mountain when we fought the Germans and they wounded Victor, the mule who loved me. I had to shoot him.

"I'll read the letters."

* * *

Dante came back to the room, and he and Chiarina were alone together again for the second time since she'd arrived from Italy. On the surface, they were shy. She looked prim, sitting in the chair, hands in her lap, legs pressed together, wearing sensible shoes and woollen stockings.

Dante found Chiarina's primness irresistible, and hot blood extinguished guilt and fear of mortal sin laid on him by demented Irish priests. He longed to be hidden with Chiarina in a warm partisan shelter, on a remote Ligurian mountain where he could make love to her.

Chiarina felt awkward. Desire blotted out her Catholic virtue. The words of wild village girls rang out in her head. *Sto morendo esso.* "I'm dying for it." She moved in the chair and shifted her legs further to the side. Her knuckles turned white. She remembered shocking words from the village. *Oh Dante, mi gobba.* "Oh Dante, hump me." If Dante touched her, or kissed her, she'd give in.

"I've read your letters. I wish I'd got them when they were posted."

"Me, too."

"Your letters must have missed us at the farm and Bologna when Anselmo was in hospital."

The Italian post office, struggling in a war-torn land, had forwarded the letters to the Bologna address, but by the time the letters arrived, Anselmo and Chiarina had gone back to the mountain cabin. Failing twice to deliver the letters, the post office had sent the letters back to Dante.

Dante, struggling with overwhelming temptation, got up from the chair.

"I'll come back later."

"No, Dante. Sit down. Stay with me."

Chiarina had read the letters in the order written. She handed Dante a letter from the end of the bundle.

"Read that one. The last part."

Dante's eyes raced across his own handwriting, and he felt the blush rising from his shirt collar. He took a deep breath to cool down. He'd meant it when he wrote the letter to Chiarina, plunged into loneliness and longing, half mad, praying that his words might bring Chiarina to him. But he cringed at having to read it now.

"I loved you from the first day I met you. But since we've been apart I have loved you more. Life without you is a prison on the cold side of the mountains. You are the reason why I live. I have loved only you without question. We will find each other and be together always."

Chiarina got up and sat on the arm of Dante's chair.

"And now that I've come?"

"The same; but more. You?"

"Dante, love of my life. My only one. But we have to wait."

"Yes, my love. We have to wait."

* * *

"I want to work. Do you think I can find a job?"

Dante explained that she and Anselmo would be living with Graziella.

"More room. It's a nice house right by the water at Cardwell Bay. You could help her in the café, and it's near where she lives."

And so Chiarina went to work, struggling with the language, but learning quickly. Anselmo, steady as Gibraltar, kept to his native Italian. Being handy, he worked behind the scenes, doing odd jobs, and trying his hand at sea fishing from the naval jetty using a hand line.

A gregarious man, Anselmo was befriended by a couple of local sea anglers who had a small boat and took him out into the river, to deep water where the cod, plaice and herring were healthier and the water cleaner. Though new to sea fishing, Anselmo caught on, becoming proficient at gathering bait: mussels from rocks on the beach, and hairy worms from the sand at low tide.

But Dante, not one for hanging about, prepared for the wedding. He and Chiarina wasted no time visiting Mr Monty Solomon's pawn shop and purchased a Victorian engagement ring: two small diamonds on a twist setting. Mr Monty had his assistant, Ma Forrest, clean and polish the ring until the gold burnished to a new lustre and the facets of the small diamonds reflected brilliant points of light. Anselmo had given them his wife's wedding ring, a fine band of rose gold, and Mr Monty resized the ring to fit Chiarina's slim finger.

Wedding arrangements were made and within a fortnight of Chiarina and Anselmo's arrival, the couple were married in St. Patrick's Church. Fortune smiled on the happy couple. The parish priest, Father Toner, had gone back to Ireland on holiday, and they were married on a Saturday morning by one of the young curates. Anselmo gave Chiarina away, with Graziella standing as matron of honour, and Chris as best man.

There was a wedding lunch for twenty guests at The Old Hotel. Chris made the arrangements and much of the preparation on the eve of the wedding. Dante and Chiarina caught a late afternoon train for Edinburgh where they spent a week on honeymoon.

On their return from Edinburgh, they stayed with Celestina for a month until their flat, rented at 4 Watt Street, was ready to occupy. And Chiarina continued working with Graziella.

* * *

Fred Forte had been abroad with the army for almost six years, apart from embarkation leave in 1942, when the battalion deployed for North Africa. When he and Dante separated in Florence, Dante heading for home, Fred had thought about getting out of the army. But he knew he wasn't ready. Fred looked forward to being a sergeant again in the British Army, after the harsh wildness and uncertainties of life in the Fiamme Verde.

The thought of becoming a civilian, taking up his old job working in the family café, made him uneasy. Fred was afraid of ennui. Sure, life had been hard and dangerous in the partisans, but it had never been dull. He valued the powerful sense of competence that came with his belonging to the Band, being Major Giuntoli's right hand, and second-in-command. Soldiering remained in his blood. He'd been away too long.

Fred considered volunteering for the Far East, but the Japs had surrendered. He'd heard talk of trouble in Malaya. The Chinese Communist guerrillas, who'd fought the Japanese, were about to turn on the British. Fred volunteered for Palestine. Keeping the Jews and the Arabs apart might be interesting. A captain interviewed him.

"Why don't you go home?"

"Not ready, sir."

The captain had interviewed several soldiers who didn't want to go home. He wasn't ready himself. But this sergeant had seen enough fighting for a while; he didn't need to put himself in harm's way again.

"You look a bit tired and worn out for the infantry. Fighting in North Africa and Sicily. The time with the Fiamme Verde."

"I'm an infantry sergeant, sir."

"Exactly, and you speak fluent Italian.

There's thousands of POWs coming home and refugees, too, plus slave labour coming back from Germany. You're staying here. You'll report to me. The army needs interpreters."

Fred realised he'd been fortunate. Still, after a year of interpreting, he was not yet ready to go home.

After service in the Seaforths and the Fiamme Verde, the thought of working in the family business nagged at Fred. He dreaded tedium; did not want it. He reported to another C.O., a hard-nosed captain, and within a month he found himself in Palestine with the training cadre, Third Infantry Division HQ, as the British Mandate ended. But after a year in Palestine, having witnessing Arabs and Jews fighting and killing in a bitter guerrilla war, Fred wanted to go home.

* * *

The Westburn Scots-Italians arranged a ball in the town hall. It was the first time they'd gathered since 1939 to celebrate who they were: Italians and Scots, glad to belong to Britain, and proud to be Italian. They had moved on from the horrors of 1940 when Italy declared war on Britain. The Scots-Italians didn't forget the wrongs done to them, but they declined to look back and bear grudges; they forgave those who'd attacked them.

The Westburn Italian families found pride again, picking themselves up and getting on with the business of serving their Scots neighbours, as before the war. Their sense of worth and self-respect soared.

Fred, demobbed and released from the army three days before, slept late, rose, and looked to his toilet. He walked the streets of Kempock, wanting to get in touch with his home town. Late forenoon he caught a bus to Westburn for a decent haircut at Roy's, the old-time barber at the West Station, and, as an indulgence, the barber shaved him.

Late afternoon he got ready for the ball. His mother had pestered him until he said he'd go.

Glad that some of his pre-war civilian clothing still fit, Fred got rid of the ugly suit and the rest of the demob rig. He'd brought home a couple of jackets and pants made in Haifa by a Jewish tailor.

Deciding to attend the dance in uniform, Fred brushed and hung the tailored battle dress blouse and shirt made for him by the Haifa tailor. He unfolded the khaki wool tie, and hung it over the battle dress, touching the miniature Italian tricolour he'd stitched to the upper right sleeve. Not pukka, but to hell with it. He gazed at his medal ribbons: the Africa Star, Italy Star, Palestine Medal, and Distinguished Conduct Medal awarded for an action in Tunisia. Hadn't he fought for Britain and Italy? The regimental MacKenzie tartan trews pressed to razor-sharp creases had worn well, and he hung them with the battle dress. Ingrained army habits still on him, Fred spent half an hour shining his regimental brogues until they reflected the light in his bedroom.

His father would drive their old Ford, taking them to the dance, and would have nothing to drink.

Fred had gone with women in Italy and the Middle East, but had never felt affection for any of them. He wondered what the Westburn Scots-Italian talent would be like. He wasn't expecting much in the way of beauty. He hoped Dante would be there.

* * *

Graziella, just twenty-six, had cast herself the budding matriarch locked in widowhood for four years, marooned in grief and loss for her beloved Tony. And though lifted out of this slough of despond when Dante came home safe from the war in Italy, she fell again to sorrow, hiding her looks in dark, drab clothing and heavy shoes. In the street, she enveloped her figure in a long, shapeless coat, hiding her fine hair under a floppy black beret.

With the war behind her, Graziella grew cheerful and slipped away from grief and worry. For the dance she dug out one of her best dresses and fine shoes from 1939. She was a quiet, demure presence sitting with Celestina, Dante and Chiarina. Anselmo had extended his stay, and agreed to come to the dance. He stuck with the corduroy suit, but Graziella had persuaded him to let her sponge and press the garments.

Any man with half an eye could see Graziella looked striking. Her dark hair was arranged in a classic, straight up-do, curls on top and a soft waved fringe. The elegant blue dress with white polka dots showing her good figure and shapely legs. A complementing navy leather belt at the waist and elegant navy court shoes completed the outfit, of superior quality to anything on sale in austere, post-war Britain.

A soldier's step rang on the wooden dance floor as Fred followed his mother and father into the hall. Dante shot out of his chair, taking rapid steps across the space separating them.

Handshakes, back slapping, and scrutinising glances followed, as Fred and Dante looked to establish if the other had changed much since their days with the Fiamme Verde on the Ligurian mountains.

"When did you get home?"

"Three days ago. I didn't call. I knew I'd find you here."

Much catching up when Fred saw Chiarina, and noted the wedding band on her finger. He was delighted seeing Anselmo, beside Chiarina, in his countryman's brown corduroy suit.

Dante introduced Fred. He left Graziella to last.

"Fred, my sister Graziella Rebecchi. Graziella, my friend, Fred Forte. We served together in the partisans. Fred and Tony served in the Seaforths."

"Hello, Fred. I recognised you from pictures Tony sent."

Fred also recognised Graziella from pictures Tony had shown him. He thought her fetching; more beautiful in the flesh.

Graziella was taken with Fred's smart turnout, and his Colour Sergeant's stripes—a handsome Scots-Italian soldier.

A fleeting moment, and she wondered if Tony might have reached the rank of Sergeant had he survived the war. Strange that she hadn't known Fred before the war, from the small Scots-Italian community of Westburn and Kempock.

In the lull between numbers, the town hall was quiet, apart from the faint buzz of conversation. The band, Charlie Hardy and The Kit Kat Orchestra, vocal refrains by June Connor, sorted through sheet music as Charlie hurried the musicians with impatient waves of his baton, trumpet tucked under his left arm.

The band struck up with a quickstep, "In The Mood," made popular by the Glenn Miller Orchestra. Fred thought he might be pushing it asking Graziella to dance, but he went ahead.

They cruised the edge of the dancers.

"Were you with Tony when he was killed?"

"Yes."

"You'll tell me what happened?"

"Yes, but not here."

Tony had been killed by a burst of machine gun fire—a quick but bloody end. He'd spare Graziella the gruesome details.

Dante brought drinks from the bar. Fred talked to Anselmo. He caught Graziella's eye, and she held his look for a moment, and then looked away. She felt warm and proud that Fred, a handsome man in uniform, found her attractive. The band played a slow number. Fred glanced again at Graziella. Their eyes locked, and Fred raising his eyebrows, nodded to the dance floor. Graziella smiled and stood, and Fred went to her and led her onto the floor.

They kept to the floor, waltzing, then another quickstep. They held on for the slow number, "Isn't It Romantic." June Connor sang.

'Isn't it romantic
Music in the night
A dream that can be heard...'

"That girl has a sweet voice," Fred said. "Nice name too, June Connor."

"Yes, she has. That's her band name. Her real name is Philomena O'Donnell. She comes to the café some Sundays with her boyfriend."

Fred held Graziella and she came close to him.

Across the room, Celestina tugged on Dante's arm.

"That Graziella, already she dance four times with him."

Dante smiled.

"Wednesday afternoon, I close the café for the half day," Graziella said. "Meet me there at two o'clock."

"I'll be there."

* * *

Fred waited outside Graziella's café, lounging against closed doors. He'd been particular about his grooming, dressed in tailored clothes made for him in Haifa, and for protection against the winter cold, a fitted double-breasted overcoat purchased before the war. He saw Graziella walking on the shore side of the short promenade of Cove Road.

"Hello, Fred. You're looking well. Being out of uniform suits you."

Fred's eyes lingered on Graziella's face, framed by a small navy beret set at a jaunty angle, her knee-length, navy wool coat showing off her good legs.

"You're looking pretty good yourself."

They decided to walk west to Ashton and the Cloch Hotel, and there have afternoon tea in the secluded lounge with superb views of the river and the mountains from the expansive bay windows.

Fred poured tea.

"Well, Fred, you said you'd tell me. How did Tony die? I want the truth."

"Sicily; a place called Francofonte. Defended by Fallschirmjäger. That's paratroops. Tough soldiers."

A German platoon held the crossroads at the entrance to the town. The major commanding the company ordered Fred's platoon to open the road. In the opening attack, a sniper killed the lieutenant commanding the platoon.

"I was platoon sergeant, and took over. Tony had just made corporal. I ordered him to lead his squad to attack the left flank of the the German position. A burst of machine gun fire cut him down."

"You ordered him to attack?"

"Yes. It was my responsibility to lead the platoon."

"Did he suffer much?"

Fred shook his head.

"He died as he fell. If it's any consolation, we cleared out the Germans."

A vision flickered in Fred's subconscious, of the sandbagged German position strewn with bodies—fair-haired warriors shot to bits.

"I hated the war. I lost my father and my husband. I worried myself sick about Dante stuck in Italy. I'm glad now I didn't know he was a partisan. God help the mothers, the wives and the lovers of those dead Germans."

"Later, the Germans captured me."

They left the hotel and walked in silence to Graziella's house. Fred harboured guilt about Tony's death, and knowing he'd been carrying out his responsibilities as an NCO did not ease the weight of the burden, the feeling that he'd sent his friend to his death.

"I feel responsible for what happened. I'm sorry."

Graziella tugged Fred's arm and they stopped at the bottom of the elevated foot bridge crossing the Kempock-Glasgow railway.

"You mustn't feel that way. It's the war; just the bloody war."

Glad to be forgiven by Graziella, a feeling of relief surged through Fred.

They crossed the railway and walked the short promenade, stopping at the gate of Graziella's house. Knowing how Tony had died lifted a shadow from Graziella, and she wanted time alone to think about Tony. He would always be part of her, but she realised now that her years of grief and mourning were ending, and her life would move on.

"I'd like to ask you in, but I need time alone, to think about everything."

"That's all right. I understand. I'll say goodbye, Graziella."

Fred shook her hand. Graziella looked up and smiled.

"Thank you for telling me what happened. We can meet again if you like."

Fred grinned.

"I'd like that."

"Call me."

"I'll do that."

A brief, intense romance ensued, and the long shadow of the war gradually lifted from Graziella and Fred. They went to the cinema, the old standby for courting couples, and they went dancing, making the malicious gossips simmer.

Their romance pleased Dante, who delighted in Graziella's new blooming; and he was glad that she was with Fred, his friend and brother-in-arms.

Celestina expressed a cautious optimism about Graziella and Fred. She felt her daughter had spent enough years in mourning. Graziella was just twenty-six, too young for widow's weeds. But she prayed that Graziella would not become Fred's mistress, to be discarded after a shabby hole-in-the-corner affair, leaving her daughter damaged beyond recovery.

"I'm happy for her, Dante; but I worry. This Fred, he is soldier for too long."

"Mum, Fred Forte is a brave and decent man. You'll see."

Mother and brother didn't have long to wait. A few months into the romance, on a Sunday evening, Fred was invited for the evening meal with the family.

Graziella broke the post-meal silence tentatively. "Mum, Dante, we have something to tell you."

She turned to Fred.

"Mrs Rinaldi, Dante, I've asked Graziella to marry. She said yes, and we ask for your blessing."

It was the news that Celestina, Dante and Chiarina had wanted to hear.

Graziella, long resident in Kempock, and Fred, a native of the burgh, had avoided Toner, the parish priest at St. Patrick's, and his peat-bog Catholicism. Arrangements were made with the kindly parish priest at St. Ninian's for a Nuptial Mass. Dante and Chiarina, the witnesses, Celestina and Fred's parents, and a handful of close friends made up the the wedding party. Chris, busy at The Old Hotel, prepared the wedding reception.

Later, the happy couple borrowed Fred's dad's old Ford, and drove to a quiet hotel beyond Inveraray for a few days' honeymoon.

* * *

Two years passed. The second chef at The Old Hotel left for a head chef's job in Glasgow. Chris, still in his teens, had matured and become a valued member of staff, and an asset in the kitchen of The Old Hotel. John Turner appointed Chris second chef. To keep his grasping Good Mother and his poor, ruined father from coming to the hotel and begging, Chris gave them two pounds from time to time. He knew they'd get paralytic on the red biddy. They'd never stop guzzling. But he warned them that if they came near the hotel he'd send for the police and never give them another brass farthing.

With Chiarina come to Scotland and married to him, Dante became the happy and settled family man. Chiarina expected their first child, a second grandchild for Celestina and a cousin for Francesco, Graziella and Fred's first child.

Dante did everything for his family, his beloved Chiarina and his mum, and kept a hand ready for Graziella and Fred. And, being an aunt and uncle chuffed Chiarina and Dante.

The family's businesses prospered. Graziella and Fred had added to the pre-war popularity of their café in Kempock at Cardwell Bay. Dante continued to buy fish at the Glasgow market and distribute it to Westburn and its environs. Recently he'd opened a new chipper on Newton Street, next to the West Station and the La Scala cinema, the popular local bug hut. But he'd not given up the original fish restaurant in Holmscroft Street. An Italian from Martinello, a village behind La Spezia, had taken a lease that provided good steady income for the family, and the new man employed the staff.

Chiarina and Dante lived in a rented apartment at 4 Watt Street, a comfortable two-room and kitchen. One tenant had bought his apartment, and Dante meant to be the second.

Chris, established in The Old Hotel, settled for the rosy future ahead.

Dick Devlin, the head chef, suffered a heart attack, and had a long convalescence of many months in front of him. With the man now pushing into his mid-sixties, keen though he was to get back to work, John Turner knew it was odds on that Dick the chef might never be fit again for work. He sent for Chris.

"How do you feel about taking over as head chef? It's permanent, but if Dick comes back and fit, I'm obliged to give him back his job. I'll promote from the kitchen staff to second chef."

"Promote the sous chef, Mr Turner. He's a good man. Thank you, I'll take the job."

Chris reckoned if Dick came back, he'd be in a strong position to find a job elsewhere as head chef.

* * *

Another year passed. The guests from afar and the middle classes of Westburn coming to The Old Hotel knew what they liked: plain food, cooked well. Chris had the kitchen fine-tuned. The staff could do their jobs standing on their heads. He tried new dishes, but not far from the mainstream taste of the clients. Minced collops, a traditional Scottish dish—ground beef mixed with minced onion and oats, seasoned, with a dash of Worcester sauce, and a poached egg on top of the collops and served with mashed potatoes. And Cullen skink—a thick, creamy, Scottish soup made of smoked haddock, potatoes and onions.

Chris found an outlet for his creative urges on Sunday visits to Dante's and Chiarina's apartment. Usually Celestina came, and often Graziella and Fred, too. With guidance from Celestina and Chiarina, he soon mastered Italian dishes—as much as rationing allowed—using vegetables from the allotment: pasta with meat and tomato sauce, various rabbit dishes, grilled, braised, pot-roasted. They always had wine. The Rinaldis treated Chris as family.

* * *

On Monday morning in early May, John Turner sent for Chris, letting him know that important guests, Mr and Mrs Stavros Michas, would be staying at the hotel for a week.

Stavros Michas owned Michas Lines, a well-run company with ships sailing under the Panamanian flag, but maintained and insured by Lloyds. The fleet was manned by British officers, Indian crew and Goanese catering staff.

The Michas fleet comprised eight cargo ships engaged in worldwide tramping. He had four American-built Liberty ships, three Victory ships, all reliable and cheap to run. Mr Michas had bought his first vessel from her British owners, Clan Line. The ship had been built by the Westburn Dockyard Company, the engines installed by Reid's Foundry. He'd renamed her the Peliopadus and made her his flagship.

One of his ships, the SS Agamemnon, would dry dock at the Garvel Graving Dock for work on the hull and an engine overhaul, the tail shaft coming out and a new screw fitted. Mr Michas liked to keep an eye on the work.

Mr Michas always reserved a suite, and breakfasted in the dining room. He spent much of the day aboard the ship dry docked for repairs. His wife liked to visit Glasgow, or explore the West End of Westburn. In the evenings, the couple liked private dining in the dining room after it closed and other guests had left. On one or two evenings of his stay, he might invite guests for dinner.

"He enjoys British food," John Turner said. "He's fond of fish, but this time he's asked for some Greek food."

"Ah'll see what ah can do," Chris replied.

"I'd like you to take charge; see to the cooking and presentation of the food. Vasco will take care of the wine and serving. Mr Michas likes ceremony at table, a celebration, but there's nothing pretentious about him. He came up the hard way; a self-made man."

Chris had mastered the essentials of Escoffier, but this Greek shipowner's taste was new ground. He visited the Mitchell Library, and made notes about Greek food. He visited the grocer shops of Greek Cypriots and arranged for the delivery of what he needed.

The day Mr Michas arrived, for dinner Chris made rabbit stifado, a classic Greek stew in rich sauce with oven-roasted potatoes. He laid it on a serving tray, covered it, and had one of the kitchen assistants carry it into the dining room. With a flourish, Chris presented the dish.

Vasco served the food.

"Delicious rabbit, Mr McCoull," Stavros Michas said. "Farmed?"

"Wild rabbit. Fresh, snared by my friend yesterday. A special order. I prepared it for cooking personally."

The next morning, Chris came out of the kitchen and offered Mr Michas and his wife each a pair of kippers for breakfast. That went down well. After breakfast, Chris suggested a variety of Greek dishes for dinner.

One day Mr Michas came back to the hotel for lunch. Chris suggested Cullen skink he had ready, and as it was a cold day, steak pie with boiled potatoes and root vegetables.

"My goodness, Mr McCoull, you look after me," Michas said afterward as he dabbed at the corner of his mouth with a serviette. "That was a delightful lunch."

Near the end of Michas's stay, with hen's eggs being scarce, Chris bought a duck and a dozen duck eggs from the farm in McGeachie's Glen. The strong flavours of the duck eggs pleased Mr Michas; he liked the bold taste. And that evening for dinner,

Greek duck—breast marinated in apple cider, seasoned with cinnamon, ginger and coriander, served with apples—delighted Mr Michas and his wife.

Chris strayed from the highlights and served established Greek dishes: crusty white bread; whitebait, fried in onions and served with slices of lemon with Cretan salad. A slice of dried bread, softened and topped with chopped tomatoes and crumbled feta. He pulled in tomatoes and herbs from the allotment, and made egg and lemon soup mixed with white beans, cooked with onions in a fresh tomato sauce. Lemon garlic chicken followed, and with potatoes, lamb with yogurt, and oven potatoes. For dessert, halva: semolina pudding sweetened with syrup, studded with nuts and raisins; baklava; and a spoon of sweet oranges.

"You run the kitchen? It's your responsibility?"

"Yes."

"And your age?"

"Ah'm twenty-one."

Stavros Michas had a proposition for Chris: come and work for Michas Lines. Carry out an audit on catering on the flagship of the fleet, SS Peliopadus.

"I want to know if the crew is being well fed, and the books balanced by an honest butler. There could be more ships to audit, leading to an appointment as chief steward. What do you think, Mr McCoull?"

Stavros Michas stroked his chin and smiled.

"What about the army; are the military likely to grab you?"

"They knocked me back. Ah had rheumatic fever when Ah was a kid. But Ah'll pass any medical. Anyway, Mr Michas, Ah've heard if you're at sea, you're exempt from the army."

"Well, what do you say?"

"Ah hardly know what to say." Chris smiled. "Goin' to sea; it never crossed ma mind. Ah'll say yes, and thank you."

"You'll get a raise." He mentioned a figure. "My ships are registered in Panama, and you'd be out of the country long enough to avoid income tax."

"That's good money."

Mr Michas anticipated Chris's concern about leaving The Old Hotel and explained that while John Turner would be sorry to see him leave, he would be happy about his success.

Chris prepared for his new life: passing the medical, reading the manuals given him and preparing for the train journey to London and boat train to Antwerp. He loved being chef at The Old Hotel, but Mr Michas had offered him a better job. Chris worried about coping as auditor and perhaps chief steward. He didn't want to disappoint Mr Michas, and he could not fail and let down the Rinaldis, his true family, who had done so much to make his life worth living. But seafaring would take him away from his drunken, sponging father and the Good Mother. Life aboard ship meant visiting new lands and presented levels of responsibility he'd considered out of reach. Chris made up his mind to follow the sea.

A day before Chris left Westburn to join the ship, he went to Dante's house in Watt Street to say farewell.

"Take care of yerself, son," Dante said.

They shook hands. Chiarina rose from her chair, took Chris by the shoulders, and kissed him on both cheeks.

"We'll miss you. Write; let us know how you're getting on."

Chris, embarrassed, felt the tugs of affection and friendship, and his eyes smarted. He gave an awkward shrug.

"Ah'll miss you too. Ah'll be away for a year or two."

Chapter Eight

With the roughness of Westburn behind him, Chris came aboard the Peliopadus feeling good, experiencing a scintilla of self-importance after traveling first-class rail to Antwerp, where the ship was discharging a cargo of cotton. He'd stopped in London to attend an intense first aid top-up course, adding to skills learned as first aid man in The Old Hotel. Stavros Michas had asked Chris to deal with first aid on the ship.

Chris anticipated camaraderie afloat, but the British officers gave him a curt handshake, and a brusque, "How do ye do?" It dawned on him that the officers wanted to see what he could do before offering friendship.

He had no idea what to expect when he signed on the Peliopadus as supernumerary. The ship bunkered in Antwerp and the pungent stench of heavy fuel oil and the lighter diesel oil fumes filled the vessel, doing for his sense of smell what winter smog did for eyes and lungs.

The constant movement of a ship at sea tired his legs, with the muscles twitching and straining for balance. On the third day out, a long swell sucking and sighing at the hull, the Peliopadus heaved and twisted, sending Chris flying into the bulkhead in the working alleyway, bruising his shoulder.

"A hand for yourself for safety, and a hand for the ship," the Second Mate said.

A few days at sea, and the officers, getting used to Chris on board, became friendly.

One day after lunch, a day of the Peliopadus surging through a troubled sea, Harry Blenkinsop, Third Mate, a Geordie from Newcastle who'd passed First Mate's ticket, took Chris round the vessel. He handed Chris a waterproof jacket.

"Put that on. Don't want you getting damp. Let's start aft."

Chris and Harry walked aft to the poop. They stared at her wake straight and true as a bowline, stretching back for a mile.

"She's getting on a bit now; built in Westburn in 1936," Harry said. "But she's a cracker. I love sailing on her. If she bumps the quay when coming alongside, the mate sends me to check if she's damaged the quay. She's built like two brick shithouses."

The Peliopadus, a foot short of five hundred feet in length with a beam of sixty-six feet and a draught of thirty feet, weighed ten thousand four hundred and ninety-six tons. The crew's quarters lay down aft.

"I like sailing with Indians. They're a mix of Hindus and Muslims; and the Goanese, Catholics of course. Never any trouble. But keep your distance. Get too friendly and some of them'd take advantage. The bogeyman is the butler. He's bad at his job. The food is terrible."

"Right; Ah'll be havin' a look at that."

"Let's go down. I inspect the deck's quarters twice a week. The Fourth Engineer checks the engine room crew. The Serangs keep everything hunky-dory."

They descended the companionway and walked port and starboard sides past open doors of cabins. Thick heavy air hit them, laden with aromas of spices and curry. Harry laughed.

"Strong, eh?"

Men off duty looked out at them from inside cabins. Dark faces smiled, and teeth gleamed. Men saluted, and said "Roz bākhair, Sahib," as they passed in the alleyway, dressed in vests and lungis, sandalled feet pattering on the maroon, bitumen-covered steel deck as they made for the heads.

"Roz bākhair means good afternoon. If you're down here and you see a couple of them shagging, turn a Nelson's eye."

Strong earthy odours wafted from the heads. Harry jerked his head towards the smell.

"Roses it's not. They don't use paper. They wipe their arses with the left hand, then wash it. If some bandit offers his left hand, don't touch it. He's insulting you. Get the Serang to tear a strip off him and kick his arse."

"Ah'll remember that."

They walked forward on the port side on teak decks holystoned white, past hatches four and five to the accommodation where the engineers had cabins.

"Tropical hardwood," Harry said. "Soles of your shoes don't wear out."

The sound of hammers on wood broke into the sounds of the ship and the sea.

"That'll be the chippys, the carpenters. We can chat to them later."

The Peliopadus carried two British carpenters, rated officers, to look after the wooden decks and the wooden sheathing of the hatches.

"It's a full-time job."

Harry held up his hand and they stopped by the number three hatch.

"I've seen a few punch-ups here. Some officers settle a difference of opinion on number three. Fisticuffs; Marquess of Queensberry rules. Drink taken. Avoid it; strictly for idiots."

A tall man in his mid-forties came from up for'ard, dressed in a white polo-necked sweater beneath a well-worn double-breasted uniform jacket fastened by four gold buttons, uniform trousers tucked into oiled leather sea boots. His face was masked by a trimmed beard the same sandy colour as his mane of thinning hair.

"That's the Chief Engineer, Ken Barnes, from Liverpool, a Scouser. Knows everything about steam engines and turbines, and he's got a diesel endorsement. Fluent in Urdu. The crew love him. Been with Michas Lines since the beginning. Remember to call him Chief."

The chief stopped by Chris and Harry to light his pipe, a large jaw-warming Meerschaum with a yellow mouthpiece. The wind blew away clouds of aromatic tobacco smoke. He nodded to Harry.

"Hello young man. You'll be Mr McCoull? I missed you when you came on board. I'm Ken Barnes, Chief Engineer."

They shook hands.

"Chris McCoull, Chief."

"Going round the ship? I'll have a word with the Fourth to take you round the engine room."

'Thanks, Chief.'

"When you're finished, lads, come by my day room and we'll have a peg."

Chris and Harry moved for'ard, passing the slim black funnel with a broad red stripe, an approximation of Clan Line colours. A sliver of smoke broke from the top, whisked away by the wind. They stood by the number two hatch with the heavy-lifting derrick in front of the bridge and accommodation for deck officers.

"What's a peg?"

"Any drink, but for the chief, Plymouth Gin and bitters; pink gin. Popular in the RN," Harry said. "The chief pours a mean one. Intoxicating electric soup."

Chris knew of it from the bar of The Old Hotel; Angostura bitters, a concentrated bitters, made of water, 44.7% alcohol, herbs and spices, but good for an upset stomach.

Harry pointed to the heavy-lifting derrick.

"We've loaded steam and diesel locomotives with the derrick. Carried topside."

Standing far for'ard next to the anchor winches, the bow rising and falling eight feet and more, a salty spray showered Chris and Harry Blenkinsop. Chris turned pale, his grey complexion matching the overcast sky, and a cold greasy sweat smeared his face. He puked once, twice, over the side and soon gave a final dry heave, careful the wind didn't blow the mess back in his face.

"You're green about the gills, Chris," Harry said. "You'll be all right after getting the bile up. That onion soup we had, pure rubbish."

Chris wiped his mouth. "Ah'll be checkin' on that and a few other things in Catering."

"The pink gins will help; but take it easy; small sips. Make it last."

A few minutes later they sat warm and snug in the Chief Engineer's day room.

"No gin for you. Bitters and tonic water, son," the chief said. "Help you get over the *mal de mer*."

The chief and Harry took swallows from their gin and bitters.

Chris noticed the three gold rings, the last gold stripe with a left closed loop and a gold E in the centre.

"You don't have four stripes, Chief?" Chris said.

"Of course I do, lad; on my Merchant Navy uniform. This is my Royal Navy Reserve uniform. Commander E, RNR. Served on corvettes and frigates during the war; North Atlantic mostly. Senior Engineering Officer in a frigate squadron." He laughed and glanced towards the bridge. "Captain Robert James, Old Jangler Jim up there, he hates it; I outrank him. He never got past lieutenant in the RNR."

Ken Barnes relit his pipe. He stuck out his left foot. "These boots I got from a German officer when he surrendered his submarine. His spare pair. First class. I traded pipe tobacco for them."

The chief had docked in Westburn on the SS Hercules to discharge a cargo of raw sugar for Westburn refineries.

"I dined in The Old Hotel several times. Great food. Funny, I never saw you, son."

"I'd have been in the kitchen."

"Of course. But it's good for the ship you're on board. Four months of this caper the old man and the butler are working is enough. I mentioned the food to Stavros Michas the last time he visited the ship. Athena must have whispered in his ear."

"Athena?" Chris asked.

"The Greek goddess of wisdom," the chief laughed. "Perhaps she brought you to the Peliopadus. But watch for the butler, Chris. He's an arse bandit; a mean bastard."

Chris reckoned he had at least two supporters for his work: the Third Mate and the Chief Engineer. He hoped to find more allies.

The conversation shifted. The chief reminisced about the years spent out east. He rose from his easy chair and pulled a thin volume from a book shelf above the desk.

"An Urdu primer, Chris. Learn the important words and phrases. I've marked them. The crew will respect you for it. If you get stuck, knock on my door."

The next day the young Scots Fourth Engineer, Willie Baxter, from Clydebank, on the four-to-eight watch, gave Chris a tour of the engine room.

Willie, wearing a white boiler suit, a hand-towel-made-muffler at his neck, and a sweat rag hanging from the hip pocket, spread his arms and jerked his head left and right at the main engines. He wiped his brow with the sweat rag.

"She's a beauty. Twin triple expansion engines," he shouted. "Connected to two Bauer-Wach exhaust turbines powered by exhaust steam from the main engines. Twin screws; she can do seventeen knots. Come on."

He pointed to three steam generators. "Power; electricity for the galley, and the ship. One genny running, another on standby, and one on maintenance. Ah take care of the electrics."

Chris, glad to move away from the throb of the generator hammering his ears, followed the Fourth on to the engine plates between the main engines and stopped at the controls. He steadied himself against a metal table fastened to the bulkhead with an electric kettle, cups, sugar, tea and coffee on a shallow lipped tray. The thump and whoosh of the engines pierced his skull.

"Noisy."

"You get used to it."

A Junior Engineer moved away and the agwallah on watch vanished.

"Where are they off to?"

"The Junior Engineer is checking round the job and the agwallah's away to pump bilges."

Chris watched the connecting rods driving the crank shaft round, the rotating heavy steel crank webs filling the engine pans. He glanced at the control panel. The gauge showed one hundred RPM.

"Follow me, Chris. Ah'm goin' to feel round."

Willie Baxter hung on with his left hand to the port engine frame below the high-pressure cylinder. As the crank web reached its apex he moved his right hand in and out matching the speed of the engine, touching the space between the edge of the bottom end and the main bearing. He wiped his fingers on the sweat rag, checked the medium and low pressure cylinders. Then he examined the starboard engines. Chris stood well back. Baxter showed Chris his fingertips, covered in thick lube oil.

"They're fine. But Ah'll add a wee jag of lube oil."

The Fourth went round both engines again, lube oil can with the long spout in right hand. He hung from the engine frame by his left hand, right hand sketching an elegant arc, moving up and down, matching the stroke of the connecting rods, squirting oil on the down stroke into the reservoir attached to the cross head, lubricating it and the bottom end.

"Dangerous," Chris said. "You'll die if your hand slips and you fall."

"Aye, right enough. Ah make sure Ah don't fall in."

Chris's eye followed Willie's pointing finger to a piston connected to the port engine, plunging up and down in a forty-gallon drum.

"The washing machine; clever, that is."

The engine room Serang directed two agwallahs, day workers, to sweep up round the controls.

"Good afternoon, Sahib," he said to the Fourth.

"Hello, Serang. Chris, meet the Serang. He's the man to ask for a curry from the crew's galley. Good curries; better than the shite the butler serves up. The Serang's in charge of the engine room crew. Serang, this is Chris McCoull, a new man in Catering."

"So pleased to meet you, McCoull Sahib." The Serang smiled and rocked his head from side to side.

They shook hands.

The Serang, dignified and middle-aged, wore a white collarless cotton shirt and pants hanging above his ankles. On his feet he wore heavy leather sandals, called chapples.

"Tonight, I bring you curry; lamb or chicken, boiled rice and chapattis?"

"Lamb. Thank you, Serang. Ah'd like that."

The Serang and the two day-workers moved to another part of the engine room.

"Give him a few bob," the Fourth said. "The Serang knows his stuff. A good man. Right, to the stoke hold; meet the boilermaker."

In the stoke hold, the roar of the burners from eight Scotch boilers deafened Chris. The Indian Donkey-Man smiled at Chris, wagging his head from side to side. Chris smiled and nodded to him.

"For two packets of cigarettes he'll give you a good haircut in your cabin," Willie said.

Dick Ostler, ex-Royal Navy, a Mush from Southampton, shook hands with Chris. He shouted in his ear.

"Good kit, the Scotch boilers. Working at 220 PSI. Get the ship to 17 knots."

"That's what the Fourth said."

Dick Ostler indulged in a lengthy, technical description—well beyond Chris's understanding—of how boilers worked and linked to the main engines. Dick Ostler loved his work.

"What do you think of the grub, Chris?"

"So far not a lot."

"Glad to hear that. Helluva noisy in here. Come round to my cabin after dinner and we'll have a couple of beers. Some of the boys'll be there."

"Thanks, Dick. Ah look forward to that."

Two more officers on his side, and Chris felt better. After a few beers with several officers in Dick's cabin, he had several more allies.

Chris adjusted to life afloat, but the first few nights the creak of timber, the screeching of rubbing metal edges and surfaces, the loose objects rolling about inside the bunk casing drove Chris mad and kept him awake. He found it hard to get used to drawers shooting out and slamming home in time with the surging, disturbed seas, and a bucking, heaving, twisting ship.

But days passed, the din faded, and he grew used to the subdued background cacophony, finding in it a discordant lullaby, a prelude to deep sleep. Chris heard the song of the Peliopadus, his ear tuned to changes of key when the ship altered course or the engineers on watch changed over pumps or generators.

Chris had prepared for difficulties with the butler, but hadn't expected naked hatred. Bonifacio d'Souza lorded it over the

Goanese crew. He detested and feared Chris, a usurper threatening his job, his power, and income from the racket he had with the captain, skimming off the top from the crew's ration allowance and pocketing the cash.

That first week at sea, day by day the butler's confidence grew and he sniggered when Chris passed in the working alleyway or on deck, whispering to the Goanese. He delayed handing over the books, so Chris went to the office, opened the desk and removed them.

"My office, you leave now. You are boy on ship. You know nothing," the butler said in his sing-song voice, waggling his head from side to side. Ten o' clock in the morning and Chris had to back away from the stink of rum on the butler's breath.

"The food on this ship is shit, you understand? Fuckin' shit. You buy rubbish at half price, and put the full price through the books."

Chris grabbed the butter dish he'd brought from the saloon, and stuck it under the butler's nose.

"Smell it; it's rancid."

The butler turned his head away.

"You're pocketing half the daily food allowance for the crew."

The butler faced Chris and leered, exposing mottled red teeth and gums stained from chewing betel nut. "Prove it, Scottish man."

Chris had had no notion of racial pecking order before joining the Peliopadus; he treated the Indian and Goanese crew with respect. But a few days after signing on as supernumerary, he'd gained a grip of the social order aboard the ship. The crew—Hindu, Moslem, and Goanese Catholics—addressed the British officers as Sahib, white man, prefaced by their rank. So the First Mate was "Chief Officer Sahib." A steward told him when officers' wives visited the Peliopadus in home trade waters, the crew addressed the wives as "Memsahib."

"It's Sahib, you black bastard," Chris told the butler now. They stood, Chris facing the butler in the small catering department office. "Stay out of the office." Chris took the butler's keys. "Knock before you come in."

The butler stuck his face into Chris's. "I come when I want. My office; you, fucking bastard." D'Souza's left hand went to his hip, and with a mincing sway of his arse, right hand squeezing his dick, he shoved his pelvis at Chris. But it was no seductive gesture; it was an aggressive move by a seasoned hard case. Chris recoiled, startled and disgusted by the knowledge that the butler was an arse bandit, likely engaged in the corruption of one of the boy seamen who'd helped Chris with his luggage when he came on board.

But Chris was no snow cake. He grabbed the butler by the shirt front and drove his right knee into the butler's balls. "Don't fuck with me, you black turd, or Ah'll break you."

The butler dropped his bloodshot eyes and drew back. Chris held him erect, shoved him to the door—hooked open for cooling draughts—and shot him into the alleyway. The butler, gasping, bent, hands cupped on his scrotum nursing his aching knackers, collided with the Second Steward who'd waited in the alleyway, drawn by the raised voices, and obviously delighted at the butler's loss of face.

Chris went to Captain Robert James, old Jangler Jim, a man reaching the end of his career; he loved the weight of cash in his pocket.

"I've checked the books. The butler's thieving. He's stealing the food from the officers' mouths. And I wonder what he's doing to the crew's allowance. The quality of food served on board doesn't square with the expense."

"The books balance, McCoull; all receipted and in order. I signed them off."

The captain filled a pipe, fingers working the tobacco flakes into the bowl. He lighted the pipe, sucking and blowing till the tobacco glowed a dull red and a cloud of smoke wreathed his head. He exhaled smoke in Chris's direction. Chris waved it away. He got the message: the captain and the butler operated a neat racket, sharing the cash, say a third to the butler and two-thirds to the captain.

"My last trip to Gabon. I never want to see Port Gentile again. I retire when we discharge in Rotterdam; six more days. The Peliopadus is a happy ship. I don't know why Mr Stavros Michas signed you on as supernumerary. Why did he?"

Chris reckoned he could stand his ground. He was Michas's man, and he'd bide his time. "Ask him."

The captain relit his pipe. "We understand each other, Mc-Coull?"

"We do."

* * *

The Peliopadus left Rotterdam with a mixed cargo for Bombay. Two months before, Chris, then head chef in The Old Hotel, had never dreamt of leaving Westburn. Now he looked forward to his second voyage. Places remembered from school geography lessons: the English Channel, Ushant, the Bay of Biscay, Straits of Gibraltar; and new regions, eastwards down the Mediterranean past Malta to Port Said, Suez, and down the Red Sea, the lights of Aden on the port side, out of the Red Sea through the Bab el Mandep, across the Arabian Sea to Bombay.

On clearing Rotterdam for the channel, the new captain sent for Chris.

"Rodney Graham." He gave Chris a dry, firm handshake.

"Chris McCoull, Captain. Pleased to meet you."

Chris liked the look of Rodney Graham, a sliver over six feet. Beneath his receding hairline, he had well-spaced almond eyes, a sallow complexion and a warm smile that revealed even white teeth; a handsome man.

Rodney Graham's relieving Jangler Jim had brought a mixed response from the officers. The majority were neutral. Two old India hands were hostile.

"Rangoon Rodney; a fucking Chi-Chi," the Third Engineer said.

"Aye, a half-chat, a bad mix of wog and white man," the Second Mate added.

The Third Engineer, Arthur Wiggins, fourteen years at sea, was a practical engineer without qualifications and no chance of promotion. He was tall, heavy-built, mid-thirties, violent when roused; wanted to be home with his wife and sons, but couldn't afford it. Ashore he'd be a low-paid fitter in a Hartlepools shipyard or engine foundry.

Chris had Wiggins taped for a big awkward bastard, and avoided him.

"What's a Chi-Chi? Is it the same as a half-chat?" Chris asked the radio operator, Beastie Willie, an Aberdonian, a pleasant gentle soak who loved a dram, his nerves wrecked after twice spending days in a lifeboat when a U-Boat torpedoed his ship in the North Atlantic in 1941 and 1942.

"Someone of mixed blood. Captain Graham's mother's Burmese; he showed me a photograph. His mum's tiny; a good-looking woman. The captain was born in Rangoon; father's a Scot from Glasgow. He's a first-class seaman. I sailed with him three years ago on the Peliopadus. He knows the ship.

"Wiggins is a clown; he's from the Hartlepools, a monkey hanger, a bag of wind and piss. But don't call him monkey hanger, unless you're wanting trouble."

"A monkey hanger?"

"A Hartlepudlian with a head full of bricks."

The Anglo-French Wars; a French ship wrecked off the coast of Hartlepool. The ship's mascot, a monkey, survived, captured wearing French uniform. Hartlepudlians held an impromptu trial on the beach. But the poor dumb animal couldn't answer questions, and the local half-wits believed that the primate had spied for the French, and they promptly hung the creature from the mast of a fishing boat.

"Christ, I met thick folk in Westburn, but Hartlepudlians take the biscuit," Chris laughed.

"Fucking idiots!" Beastie Willie said. "Maybe they hung a ship's powder boy, and the story got mixed up with the pathetic wee monkey spy. Don't let Wiggins hear you laughing; he'll take you on."

"Mr Michas told me you know your stuff, Mr McCoull," Captain Graham said. "Can you get the galley into shape; sort out Catering?"

"It's a solid crew in Catering, and the Second Steward is a good man. But they need encouragement."

"And you can provide it?"

"Yes, sir. It'll take a week or two."

Rodney Graham poured two stiff gin and tonics. "Let's drink to that." They sipped the cool tonic and refreshing sting of Gordon's Export Gin.

"How did you and Mr Michas meet?"

"You know Westburn, Captain?"

"Yes, I attended the Watt School. I joined Clan Line as an apprentice from Westburn, and I've docked several times; repairs and discharging sugar."

"Ah worked at The Old Hotel. Head chef when Mr Michas stayed about a week. He kept an eye on his ship, the Agamemnon, in the dry dock. He liked the food and the way Ah ran the kitchen. Ah looked after him and Mrs Michas, Voula, a polite woman."

"Tell me about it."

Chris explained how he'd delighted Stavros Michas and his wife.

"Can you get the galley and the saloon to that standard?" the captain asked.

"Definitely; first the butler needs sorting out."

"I'll leave it to you, Chris; you can count on my support."

Two days at sea, and bad weather since Rotterdam. The Third Mate told Chris the ship would soon be out of the Biscay and into better weather. He was right; windy, sunny days came, and the Peliopadus's skittish behaviour, pitching and rolling in the following sea, exhilarated Chris. Two days they spent sailing down the Portuguese coast; ahead lay the Straits of Gibraltar, and passage into the Mediterranean.

First of April found them a day's easy sailing from Gibraltar. A regular workday with watch keepers and day workers turned to. Chris went to the galley before sunrise to assess preparations for breakfast. He expected the butler to attend; Chris had told him to be there.

The butler had not lit the oil-fired stove. Chris lighted the torch—a metal rod, three feet long, with a wad of cotton waste soaked in paraffin attached. He inserted the torch through the observation port and opened the fuel valve. A blast of yellow flame shot out the port. Chris turned away at the moment the flames seared his right hand, and scorched the right side of his face and head. He staggered back and collapsed on the deck.

The reek of singed hair poisoned his sinuses, tears filling his eyes. He sneezed, once, twice, and winced—afraid of a disfigured face. The pain came, drawing his streaming eyes to his burned right hand. How the hell would he manage with his right hand damaged and useless for several days?

The capable Second Steward, Fernandez Xavier, stared at Chris, eyes rolling. "Sahib, Sahib, butler hurt you. He is bad man; break my nose; hit cook when drunk. Make jiggy jig boy sailor. Maybe butler try to kill you."

Chris hated the butler for attacking him. His antipathy increased, knowing the man was a drunken pederast shagging a boy seaman, a doe-eyed Muslim from the Indian Punjab, corrupting him with money.

Chris nodded through the pain of his aching right hand and the worry about his blistering, swelling face. Maybe the butler had tried to kill him.

"Fernandez, can you clean out the stove and organize breakfast?"

"Yes, I do that, McCoull Sahib."

"When you have a minute, come to my cabin. I'll need help dressing my hand."

"Yes, Sahib."

Cracking open the inlet valve to the stove burner and depositing fuel on the base of the stove—a cunning, dirty trick of d' Souza's to catch Chris in the blowback.

In his office, Chris glanced at the calendar pinned to the bulkhead above the desk. April First—All Fools Day. Fury and rage consumed him as he got out the first aid kit. In the minute it took to reach his cabin, cold hatred and a resolve to get rid of the butler replaced anger. If Chris failed, the butler would have him ashore—dead or alive.

Grunting through pain, Chris applied dressings and bandages to his head and face, and fretted about permanent scarring. His right hand hurt worse than a rotten tooth loose in its socket, but he could move his fingers. He'd suffered no damage to tendons or ligaments. The blisters on the back of his fingers and the swollen fluid tennis ball on the back of his hand would drain. Chris could see; his eyes were okay.

The Second Steward knocked, came into the cabin, and gasped in horror at the burnt and bandaged man sitting at the desk. "I bring tea, McCoull Sahib. You feel better."

"Help bandage my hand," Chris said to Fernandez when he returned with the mug of tea. They applied a dressing to the injured hand and bandaged it, but not too tight. Fernandez made a sling from an old tablecloth and set Chris's arm up on his chest. His arm needed to be high to get the blisters draining. Chris held the mug in his left hand and swallowed scalding tea. Fenandez was right; he felt better.

Chris, still in pain and shock, sent word to the captain by the Second Steward that he'd had an accident and had returned to work in the office, writing with his left hand.

The captain came at once. "It could've been much worse, Chris," he said after he'd inspected the wounds. "Maybe I should put you ashore in Gib. What happened?"

Chris being discharged and put ashore would leave the job unfinished, and the butler triumphant. He wasn't having it.

"Somebody leaked diesel into the stove. It's your decision, sir. Ah'd rather stay aboard. Ah know first aid, and Ah've dressed the burns. Give it three or four days and Ah'll be on the mend."

"Good; I'd be sorry to lose you," Captain Graham said. "Take the rest of the day off. I'll call on you later."

A knock at the open office door; d'Souza hovered there. "Come in," Chris said.

"McCoull Sahib hurt. You no understand galley stove. Must be careful." The butler came closer and stared at Chris's face. Chris caught a whiff of stale rum. "Captain put you ashore, McCoull Sahib. Good hospital in Gibraltar. Then you go home."

The butler's eyes glinted, and a smile tugged at his lips. "April first, bad day for you. Leave galley, I fix everything. I go now."

"You're pushing your luck, d'Souza. Ah'll be at work tomorrow," Chris said to the retreating butler. He resolved again to deal with this villan.

The Peliopadus passed through the Straits of Gibraltar into the Mediterranean. Beastie Willie said the ship would head straight for Port Said and the Suez Canal, a five-day sail.

The officers commiserated with Chris about the "accident," certain the butler had made a deliberate attack to injure or kill Chris. But no officer voiced that opinion. They offered passive support. Chris concluded that he'd best deal with the butler on his own terms.

The chief waited three days before coming to Chris's cabin.

"I waited till all those platitudinous buggers had finished. What did the captain say? I didn't ask him."

"He told me to stay well and look after myself. I think he's on my side."

"Hmm. You've done well to get this far."

The Chief Engineer reflected on his family's struggles to find and support him in an apprenticeship at Cammel Laird on the Birkenhead side of the Mersey, and the years of study driven by a determination not to disappoint them.

He reckoned Chris had survived without help from his family, a graduate of the School of Hard Knocks. The chief liked Chris and wanted him to succeed. He paused; filled and lit his pipe. Several strong puffs set the tobacco going well. The chief inhaled a lungful of the aromatic smoke, and blew it out contentedly.

"Pardon my French, Chris, but that fucking butler is having you on. He's taking the piss out of you. Don't let all the hard work and your good name end here, aboard the Peliopadus."

Chris nodded. "Ah'll be seein' to the butler, right soon."

"You know what to do. Good lad."

The chief's words put iron in Chris's resolve.

Sunday fifth of April, a quiet day at sea; watch-keepers and Catering on duty; deck and engine day-workers stood down; the butler buggering the boy seaman.

For the last few days, Chris had enjoyed the sun and warm Mediterranean air on his face and arms, felt his wounds healing.

Chris felt the weight of what he had to do. He alone must defeat the butler or suffer the contempt of the officers and the crew.

He thought about Dante, Graziella and Celestina, their kindness, putting him on the right path, making his life good. He couldn't live with the guilt of failing and letting them down.

If Chris lost, his sea career was over.

That morning he removed the dressings from his face and head. The blisters on his fingers and the back of his hand had drained. With Xavier's help, Chris bandaged on a light dressing for his raw right hand. Morning and evening he puffed penicillin powder on the new tegument on his face, head, and hand; and Chris wished for the return of his straight fair hair and freckles.

On a vivid blue sea dabbed with white surging breakers, a rolling swell hissing and sucking at her hull, the Peliopadus steamed at a steady twelve knots, the breeze singing through the rigging, along with the creak of metal and wood as she moved with the sea. Shipboard Sabbath routine calmed Chris.

Four days had passed since the burning. The Peliopadus was well down the Mediterranean. Chris watched the butler grow lax, his guard down, unconcerned by the stewards' soiled white jackets and napkins, the indifferent food, the crumbs and stains on tablecloths.

The butler surrendered to drink, boozing away the day, and by night met his catamite. Chris knew that danger increased the closer the Peliopadus ran to a port. A half-cut or sober butler could attack, and Chris would finish up ashore in hospital.

One night in the small hours, the watch-keepers of the twelve-to-four on duty. The butler, dallying in late evening with his ganymede, went aft, thinking about God knows what, loins warm from screwing arse, slugging rum; he stood staring at the wake of the ship.

Chris now slept with the cabin door locked. Were it open, the butler could've entered his cabin and finished him.

Chris had planned his moves to deal with the butler, to finish him in one shot. At one thirty Chris rose, dressed in dark blue pajamas, slipped his feet into rubber sandals and pulled on rubber kitchen gloves. The sawn-off pick shaft brought from home he secured behind the waistband of his dark blue pajamas, with a rag tucked down the front. He masked his face below the eyes with a blue neckerchief. The right hand hurt as he pulled himself, feet first, out of the cabin porthole and dropped to the teak deck. The watch on the bridge was looking for'ard, no activity on deck, and the engine room watch were busy below. No one coming on duty until the watch changed at four in the morning.

The moon waned in a cloudy sky, and the stars gave no light to the ship, dark save for her running lights. The Peliopadus, maintaining a steady twelve knots, cut through a short, heavy swell.

Moving astern, crouching, keeping to the shadows, past hatches four and five, and right aft to the stern of the vessel, Chris looked up to the poop lighted by the aft running light, and spotted the butler's left hand resting on the hand rail.

"If I don't get this bastard first, he'll get me," Chris thought, scaring up courage for the violence he meant to wreak. "Anyway, Ah'll fix him and we're close enough to Malta to put him in a hospital ashore."

Chris's right hand ached from his tight grip on the sawn-off pick shaft. He ascended the internal companionway, gripping the hand rail with his uninjured left hand, passed the seldom-used sick berth, and crept to the poop door, hooked open in the mild weather. Chris faltered; his courage left him for a second or two.

"Ah can do it; it's him or me," he thought. "Ah'm no fuckin' cream puff. Ah'll finish this fucker off."

The butler stood by the flag staff, slugging from a bottle of rum. He rested the bottle on the flag locker, a steadying hand keeping it from falling on the deck. Chris gripped the sawn-off pick shaft, relishing the increased pain of a tighter grip with his injured hand.

He swung down and the pick shaft smashed into the left side of the butler's head, opening a wound that would need stitches.

He caught the butler by his arms as he slumped, out cold, laying him on the deck, head near a mooring bollard. With the rag, Chris smeared blood and hair on the bollard and dragged the butler until his head lay by the bollard. He threw the rag over the side. Then he stretched the butler's right hand across the narrow space and placed it on the jamb of the door. He unhooked the door and let the swell swing it shut, crushing the butler's fingers, then gave it a hard push on the return swing, smashing the fingers beyond remedy. A soft moan escaped the butler, but he did not come round.

Chris had finished d'Souza's sea career. "Rot in Goa, cunt, for all Ah care; an' keep a civil tongue in yer breeks." He threw the kitchen gloves and the pick shaft over the side.

At three forty-five a quartermaster, about to go on watch at four, stepped aft for a breath of cool air and a bidi, the leaf-wrapped dry tobacco cigarettes favoured by the crew. He found the butler.

A sweating Chris lay awake, worried that the captain or the First Mate had discovered his assault. He waited for a knock on his cabin door. "Sahib, Sahib," the Second Steward called. "Come, butler hurt."

Rodney Graham and the First Mate stared at the inert butler, who lay in a different position than when Chris had left him. Dried blood and cold vomit stained the deck; a smell of rum and sour puke. The mate shined a torch on the butler. "Jesus Christ," he said. "His right hand is a mess."

"The butler doesn't need first aid, Mr McCoull," the captain said. "He's dead, and dead drunk: left the door to the poop open, collapsed, cracked his head on the bollard, hand caught in the door. The gash on his head? He got up, puked, and collapsed again, striking his head; that's what killed him." He turned to the mate. "What do you think?"

"It looks like it," the mate said.

The butler had attacked Chris, who had meant to injure the butler, not kill him. The butler had brought death on himself, yet Chris feared an accusation of murder. "Ah agree," he said, relieved not to be answering questions, and feeling a growing confidence that the captain was on his side.

"Draw up a report for my signature," the captain said to the mate. "Get the body into the fridge. We'll get rid of it in the afternoon."

Rodney Graham came to Chris's cabin soon after.

"I'll conduct the service. We're the only British Catholics on board. The Goanese want you to recite the Lord's Prayer. They respect you for the work you've done on the Peliopadus."

The captain looked at Chris, the hint of a knowing grin tugging the edges of his lips.

Work; what work? Chris frowned. "Okay, Captain."

The Goanese had washed the body and dressed the butler in his best whites, wrapped him in a canvas coffin made by the deck Serang, and weighed the corpse with scrap metal placed at the feet. They laid d'Souza on a plank resting on trestles by the number four hatch, and covered the coffin with the Portuguese flag. At two in the afternoon, the deck Serang raised the church pennant.

The British officers, Goanese and Indian crew, excepting the watch-keepers, gathered on the starboard side, facing North Africa over the horizon. The officers stood apart from the Indian crew, and the Goanese stood on either side of the trestles where the canvas coffin lay by the port side. The chief caught Chris's eye, grinned and gave a satisfied nod.

"We are gathered to bury our shipmate," Captain Graham intoned. Officers and crew, bareheaded now, bowed their heads. "We therefore commit the earthly remains of Bonifacio d'Souza to the deep." Rodney Graham nodded to Chris, who stepped forward; had the captain winked?

"Our Father who art in Heaven, hallowed be Thy name." Chris heard the murmurs of the officers and the Goanese, their voices hurrying to the last words, "...as we forgive those who trespass against us, and lead us not into temptation, but deliver us from evil. Amen."

The butler had made it personal. Chris could not leave Bonifacio d'Souza free to attack him, but he'd meant to send the butler to a Maltese or Egyptian hospital; not kill him.

"Second Steward!" Captain Graham commanded. Fernandez walked to the head of the coffin. Four Goanese moved, two to a side. They grasped the plank. "Atencao," the Second Steward said. They lifted the plank and slid the remains of Bonifacio d'Souza from under the Portuguese flag and over the side.

Chris heard the splash of the corpse hitting the sea. His shoulders levelled, torso and arms slackened, and the sweating stopped; he felt clean with his enemy gone to the deep. Chris imagined sharks gathering to desecrate the butler's remains, a close circle, following the sinking canvas coffin down through chilly currents; a rush of dark, living torpedoes, sharp teeth cutting and tearing through canvas sailcloth, biting into d'Souza's corpse, crazed by his blood, shredding the cadaver. A tattered sailcloth coffin all that remains, empty bar a few bones and shards of flesh, sinking into deep waters. Chris stood until the deck Serang lowered the church pennant.

The butler need not have died. Chris had injured his right hand, but drunkenness had killed Bonafacio d'Souza.

"It was him or me," Chris thought again.

The assembly broke up, and officers and men returned to duty. The chief crossed the deck and stood beside Chris. He laid a hand on his shoulder.

"It's finished, lad; you're no weakling, no shrinking violet. Not by a long shot."

A strong sense of relief coursed through Chris as his guilty conscience waned. He gave thanks that his ordeal was over.

The chief walked Chris to the side of the ship where, a few minutes before, the butler's corpse had slid into the sea.

"There's no substitute for victory. You'll get Catering lad; make it your own."

Half an hour later, Captain Graham sent for Chris. "Sit down, Mr McCoull. Too bad about the butler. Anything more you should tell me?"

"A thieving drunk, sir. He ruined Catering."

"Yes; I've sent a report by radio to Stavros Michas. Accidental death caused by his drunkenness. Mr Michas will deal with the Panamanian authorities."

Chris nodded.

"I also sent him your report. Sending the butler over the side saved the company firing him and sending him back to Goa."

The captain held a copy of a radio message appointing Chris Chief Steward. "You accept?"

"Yes, and thank you, sir."

Chris felt the captain's eyes on him, an approving look. "You saw him off, didn't you?"

"He did that himself, Captain."

"Yes. Anyway, you're looking good, Chris; burns healing; smart new khakis. Except for myself and the chief, you're the only man aboard the Peliopadus who looks like an officer."

Captain Graham handed Chris a pair of epaulettes: four gold stripes, each one separated by the white stripe of Catering. "They're a spare pair of mine. I had my steward stitch in the white stripes. You're now the Chief Steward. Wear them, Chris; you've earned the right."

Chapter Nine

A few days later at sea, Captain Graham sent for Chris to put the finishing touches to managing the welfare of the officers and crew.

"There's not much in the way of a slop chest aboard, Chris," the captain said. "How'd you like to manage it for me?"

"Sure thing, sir. I can do that."

Chris had noted the paucity of the Peliopadus's slop chest. Some toiletries, and little else. The ship was bound for Rotterdam—a good port in which to replenish the chest.

"I'll get the agent to run you up to Botlek. You can negotiate a good price. You decide. I'll come with you, if you like."

"Thanks, sir, but no need. Ah can handle it."

Chris asked about supplies for the crew.

"They can buy from the slop chest," the captain said. "But they prefer to bargain with local merchants. There might be the odd request for a toothbrush or toothpaste. Ask the Serangs what the crew might need."

The crew relished market time: Half a day off in port to visit local markets and haggle. The First Mate and the Second Engineer arranged market time for half the deck and engine room crew to leave the ship for a half day. The other half went next day. At any time, enough hands remained on board to work the ship.

"No alcohol for the crew, ever," the captain said. "Company orders. The Indian government don't want their citizens fond of drink."

"What about a markup, sir?"

"Five percent, and we'll put profit into the ship's welfare fund. Holiday treats and the like.

Oh, last thing, Chris. Would you handle the ship's films and library exchanges? Look after the bond—spirits, beer and tobacco."

"Certainly, sir."

* * *

Sundays, the captain invited his officers for drinks and light food before lunch. Goanese snacks, chamuças, samosas, and pakora were popular.

Captain Graham, the chief and Chris, dressed smartly in crisp khakis, black footwear, shoulder boards and black tie in line with company regulations for officers. That Sunday the officers' uniforms just passed muster.

Under Jangler Jim's misrule, standards had slipped—the unkempt dining saloon of grubby linen and bad food; several officers taking to wearing pullovers over uniform shirts, and slippers instead of proper footwear; one or two abandoning the uniform for white, polo-necked naval sweaters and several colours of corduroy pants.

Just before moving to the saloon, the captain reminded the officers of their duty and that in Rotterdam the slop chest would be restocked with everything needed: work wear, toiletries, toothbrushes, shoe laces, polish and KDs to order.

"Personal orders, let the Chief Steward know."

* * *

With Rodney Graham in command, the weeks passed. Officers turned to on watch, looking smart. Sartorial improvement carried over into off-duty time, insofar as an officer at sea is ever off duty.

In parallel, the quality and quantity of food was transformed from rubbish to a general consensus that, fitting for the flagship, the Peliopadus had to be the best-fed ship in the fleet.

The service in the saloon would not have shamed a good hotel. Crisp, white linen tablecloths and napkins changed daily, napkins tucked in a silver ring with the rank of its owner typed on the outer face.

Saloon stewards served tables in brilliant white jackets changed daily, and the galley—from the cook down—put on clean kit each morning.

Breakfast became a choice of cereals, bacon, sausage, fried tomatoes, toast and morning rolls, eggs to order. Silver pots of tea and coffee stood on the table. Fresh bread and rolls daily.

Chris's shipmates knew what they liked at lunch and dinner: British Merchant Navy favourites—nourishing soups and salads; roasts of lamb, mutton, pork or beef; thick stews and braised dishes of liver and kidneys with potatoes and two vegetables. And from time to time, the cook made Goanese fish curries, and individual dishes came from the crew's galley.

The Moslem crew ate Halal food. Chris bought the provisions, and the engine room Serang approved the Halal meat and chicken. Chris and the Serang went to the meat store in Hamburg.

"This good, McCoull Sahib," the Serang said, touching a carcass of mutton. "Butler say is best."

"Did he?"

Chris and the Serang moved among the hung, frozen sheep carcasses and shelves of chicken stamped MK—Mohammedan Killed—In blue. Chris stopped where the smaller lamb carcasses hung.

"How about this, Serang?"

The Serang's eyebrows shot up. "Oh, very good, McCoull Sahib. Lamb number one. Make crew very happy."

"It's going well, Chris," the captain said later that day. "Best food I've had in all my years at sea. The boys are putting on weight."

Chris stayed in shape. He had a chinning bar installed in the laundry, and carried out sets of bodyweight exercises several times a week.

"I'm buying with care; spending a little less than the full daily allowance, Captain. Put the surplus in the welfare fund?"

"I checked the books. Good job, Chris. Yes, in the welfare fund. Was there something else?"

"Well, sir, the Topaz washes work clothes in the engine room washing machine. The officers give him a carton of cigarettes a month. Buy a washing machine for the laundry room. Do better than washing kit in tubs. Charge a modest fee to pay the Goanese for washing and ironing. The machine will pay for itself."

"Excellent, Chris. I like that. We'll dock in Antwerp in three days. Buy a good one. Get the agent to help. I'll speak to the chief and have an engineer install it."

Several of Chris's catering crew were adept tailors. He turned from the door of the captain's day room.

"Yes, Chris; what is it?"

Chris fingered his uniform shirt. "Tailoring, sir. There's some good tailors in Catering. If you like, Ah'll organize it; part of the laundry service."

"Great idea, Chris. You can start with me. I'll have my steward pass on some kit."

"Right, sir."

* * *

One spear in Chris's side remained: Wiggins, Third Engineer, a monkey hanger from the Hartelepools. No one on board faulted his technical abilities. He knew his stuff. But he had no qualifications, had not studied for his Second Engineer's ticket. Without it he was stuck at his rank.

Wiggins was an awkward big bastard, threatening in his cups. Few of the officers regarded him as a shipmate. The engine room crew feared him.

Chris found an upset new Junior Engineer, who'd recently joined the Peliopadus, standing aft at the end of the twelve-to-four watch. Wiggins, irritable beyond reason, had cuffed him.

Chris took the young man to the office and sent for coffee. He had a look at the boy's swollen cheek. He was more humiliated than hurt. Chris poured a tot of whisky.

"Drink up. You'll feel better."

"Called me a useless Scotch cunt."

"Go to the chief and report him."

"Not going to complain. I have to work it out."

Wiggins moaned about the food and the service in the saloon. He worked at being scruffy, and did not care for observing company regulations to dress in starched KDs with badges of rank displayed.

The Chief Engineer, Wally Barnes, fed up with Wiggins whingeing, sent for him and told him off. The story spread throughout the ship.

"Get out of the ship if you don't like it. I'll take your resignation right now. You've never been better off or looked after in your life. There's something about you monkey hangers. You're all bloody thick."

"I'm the best Third in the company; I should get a rise in pay."

"Get your Second's ticket. You might get promotion. Several young Seconds have Chief's tickets. You're struggling, Wiggins. Smarten up. Now get out."

Wiggins was due leave in a couple of months. The ship's company hoped the next Third would be an improvement.

* * *

Unloading in Le Havre, Chris went down below to speak to the Serang about crew's rations.

"What the fuck are you doing, McCoull?" Wiggins barked. "Stewards have no business in the engine room. Ask permission."

"See the chief if you have a beef, big man."

Wiggins moved a step closer to Chris.

"Get out of the engine room, you fucking glorified waiter."

"Go and hang a monkey, Wiggins. You're a bag of wind and piss."

"You're fucking pushing it, McCoull."

Chris closed the gap between them, invading Wiggins's personal space.

"Anytime you feel like pushing it, let me know. Right now, if you like. Put your money where your mouth is; number three hatch, when you're ready."

They stared one another out. The Indian firemen on duty, hating rows and fights, vanished into dark places. The main engines were silent but for the gentle hiss of warming through steam, the fluttering of auxiliary machinery in the background. The Junior Engineer working with Wiggins approached.

"Third, about the genny…" he said.

Wiggins shot Chris a threatening look and turned away. Chris didn't move for several seconds. He wanted to avoid trouble, but he'd not walk away from Wiggins.

"Come, McCoull Sahib," the Serang said. "I take you topside."

The Serang accompanied Chris to the engine room door. His face had turned pale and he glanced down at Wiggins standing by the controls.

"You all right, Serang?" Chris said.

The Serang compressed his lips and nodded.

"Thank you, McCoull Sahib."

* * *

The Peliopadus would sail on the high tide at midnight. Chris had a look in the saloon as his stewards served dinner. Wiggins came in and Chris thought he looked half-cut. Appearance-wise he barely passed muster. Chris went to the galley to speak to the cook about the next day's lunch and dinner menus, leaving the saloon in Fernandez's capable hands.

Chris had a cup of coffee in the galley. Beastie Willie stuck his head round the galley door.

"You'd best come now, Chris."

Fernandez sat at table, his white jacket covered in drying soup; diced vegetables stuck to his face; a welt was growing on his forehead. He dried his eyes with a napkin. The officers stood around the table, embarrassed.

Chris laid a hand on a humiliated Fernandez's shoulder.

"Who did this?"

"Ah, McCoull Sahib, terrible, terrible." His shoulders shook.

A truculent Wiggins had chucked the soup over Fernandez when he'd asked him to move his arm from the place setting. Then Wiggins had struck Fernandez on the forehead with the edge of the soup plate.

"Where is the bastard?" Chris said.

"Take it easy, Chris," Willie said. 'The chief's dragged Wiggins to see the captain. He's gone too far this time. I hope he gets sacked."

Murmurs of approval from the officers.

"Come on, Fernandez," Chris said, taking him to the office.

Chris wet a hand towel and Fernandez cleaned up.

"Your forehead's okay; a bruise. I'll put arnica on it. How are you feeling?"

"I am shamed, McCoull Sahib. Third treat me like animal."

Tears spilled down Fernandez's cheeks. Chris handed him a handkerchief. He got out the office bottle and poured two shots of whisky.

"Drink this, Fernandez. Ah'll see Wiggins. He's not getting away with this."

They drank off the Scotch.

A knock at the office door and Captain Graham and Chief Engineer Wally Barnes came in.

"How is Fernandez, Chris?"

"Humiliated, sir. No serious injuries."

"Fernandez," Captain Graham said. "I am sorry that one of my officers did this. I apologise on behalf of the ship's officers."

"I am sorry an engineering officer struck you, Fernandez," the chief added. "It won't happen again. I sacked Wiggins. The captain has double DR'd him and told him to be off the ship within the hour."

"I'll take the Second Steward to his cabin," Chris said.

"Double DR; decline report on conduct and ability," Chris said to the chief a few minutes later. "Well, he asked for it. I'm glad to see the back of him."

"Wiggins is finished in the Merchant Navy," the chief said. "He's gone to the Rex Hotel. The agent will arrange travel to the UK tomorrow."

But it is an ill wind that does not bring some good. The Fourth Engineer made up Third, the senior Fifth Engineer promoted Fourth.

"There'll be no day worker until we come back to Europe," the chief said. "A new Junior Engineer will join. But there's a Junior on each watch."

Chris finished his beer.

"Ah'm goin' to pay Wiggins a visit, Chief."

"What was that, Chris? Never heard you. Remember, she sails at midnight."

Justice had been served by the captain and the Chief Engineer sacking Wiggins, but not honour. Chris could not let the incident pass; Wiggins had vanished into the Peliopadus's history, reduced to a line or two in the ship's log. Thumping Fernandez, just another Wog, meant nothing to him. Wiggins the hard case engineer remained unsullied.

Letting Wiggins go sullied Catering. But above all, it left Fernandez, a gentle soul, unable to fight back, humiliated and unavenged. Chris prepared for the ancient ritual of combat.

He looked at the club he'd had made and put it back in the drawer, hidden beneath uniform shirts. Chris believed in an eye for an eye. He selected a pair of tight-fitting, silk-lined black leather gloves with a stud fastening at the wrist. The leather and lining were thick enough to protect his knuckles, but not blunt the force of his fists. There was no other way to deal with the affront to Fernandez and Catering. It had to be the old way.

Chris dressed in dark clothing and peacoat, gloves tucked in a side pocket, head covered with a seaman's navy wool cap comforter. The Hotel Rex was a twenty-minute walk from the dock. At ten thirty Chris left the Peliopadus. He counted on Wiggins being in his room.

At the hotel, he asked for Wiggins's room number, explaining that he brought monies due to the engineer going home.

"He's expecting me. You don't have to call him."

Chris paused outside Wiggins's room and fitted on the gloves. He'd kick the door in if Wiggins had it on the safety chain.

"Who's that?" Wiggins called through the room door.

"Room service; management's compliments," Chris said in what he hoped sounded French.

A drunk Wiggins opened the door.

Chris kicked the door open, and in thirty seconds it was over.

He left the hotel by an emergency door, arriving back on board twenty-five minutes before midnight. He went to Fernandez's cabin.

"How are you feeling?"

"Better, McCoull Sahib."

"Don't speak of this. I went ashore and saw to Wiggins. No one hits one of my men."

Fernandez smiled. "Thank you, McCoull Sahib. I sleep now. Work tomorrow."

Chris stayed on deck, calming down, breathing lungfuls of cool night air. The Peliopadus rocked as the Seine met the open sea. Soon she'd be steaming down the Channel. The ship slowed and the cutter came alongside to take off the pilot; faint bells from the bridge and engine room; standby finished. The throb of the engines increased; the Peliopadus gathered speed, a silhouette manouevering into the Channel.

A hand on his shoulder. The chief had come from the engine room.

"You're okay, lad?"

"Half a minute, Chief; Ah took care of Wiggins. Ah put the head on him. He never laid a hand on me."

Chris examined his gloves in the glow of the Peliopadus's running lights. A smear of sticky drying blood stained his fingers.

"Good job, Chris. That's the last bad egg away. Get rid of the gloves, they're ruined. I'll give you a new pair."

Chris tossed the gloves over the side, and they vanished before hitting the sea.

"Come on round for a peg before turning in."

* * *

Chris loved the Peliopadus, built in Westburn back in 1936. Her creature comforts were spartan, but she had class—an understated, quiet beauty, like his idea of the perfect girl that he'd yet to meet. When called on for stern duty, the ship became a saltwater princess, steaming at sixteen or seventeen knots, rainbows in the spray coming over her bows. He relished the comparative luxury of the communal officers' heads and showers, kept spotless by the Topaz's frequent cleaning.

On fine evenings close to the Line, Chris stood midships and rubbed his hand on the hardwood top of the ship's rails. The Peliopadus's pulse and movement, a twist, a heave in the swell, and her power surged along his arm, into his body.

Stavros Michas found charters for his ships. Vessels were never idle or laid up in Piraeus waiting for trade to pick up.

The variety of charters pleased the crew, like carrying whisky to America and Canada.

A brilliant June morning. Chris and the Chief Engineer stood well for'ard for a complete view.

"I never tire of this," the chief said.

He swept his arm across New York's majesty. Southport, the Brooklyn Navy Yard. The Statue of Liberty and Ellis Island. Ahead, the Manhattan skyline, familiar from countless old films.

They'd watched "A Tree Grows in Brooklyn" the previous evening, an unexpected preparation for the city.

Chris felt like he knew the city. Lloyd Nolan as the cop, marrying a widow, saving the family; and James Gleeson, the tavern owner supporting their two children, giving them jobs after school.

"Reliable, decent people. Just like my friend Dante. The pictures I grew up with: the Bowery Boys, Dead End Kids. Can't wait to get ashore."

"You'll never see anything like it. Look at it, Chris."

Chris absorbed the marine panorama. The cargo and passenger ships manoeuvering through glistening, sun-dappled blue waters. A white Coast Guard cutter making for a berth. A Fletcher Class fleet destroyer, a busy crew moving about her deck, slipping out from the Hudson River on her way to the Atlantic.

"It's terrific."

The chief went below for standby.

Chris looked again at the city. He came to love New York, his expectations enhancing that first run ashore. Buying personal kit: shirts, boots, KDs, and formal clothes.

* * *

Chris enjoyed the runs from Europe to the Cape, cruising off the west coast of Africa, the ship laden with general cargo, the deck behind the heavy-lifting derrick packed with big tractors for discharging at Walvis Bay. The days unloading in Cape Town, Port Elizabeth, Durban. Then sailing north to Mozambique, calling at Beira and Laurenco Marques.

Leaving Mozambique, they sailed south for Cape Town to load fruit for Europe or the UK. Feverish preparations at sea as the Mates drove the crew cleaning the holds to receive fruit, the Fridge Engineer getting ready to cool the holds, to freeze the cargo.

The excitement of heading east: exiting the Suez Canal and the Gulf of Suez, into the Red Sea, out through the Bab el Mandep—The Gates of Hell—past Aden, heading for Bombay or Calcutta, carrying machine tools. Chris gazing into the heat haze, taken by the rhythms of white horses blown by the wind, racing across an azure Arabian Sea. The return voyage to the Continent, the holds packed with copra, tea and coffee.

Cargoes of raw sugar from the West Indies, a brief unloading in UK ports. Chris felt homesick, but resisted the temptation to phone Dante or make a quick trip back to Westburn. He dealt with his longing for the Rinaldis and Westburn by sending postcards.

The Peliopadus arriving in home waters, the seas between the Elbe and the Brest, the English Channel a day ahead. Some officers aboard for six months or more, succumbed to melancholy.

Chris, seated in Beastie Willie's cabin for a peg, asked about the Second Mate.

"His face is tripping him," Chris said.

"He's got the Channels," Willie said. "He's wanting his own fireside. I've seen shipmates so fed up they quit the ship, gave up the sea."

Chris grinned.

"Not me. Ah like the old girl too much. Peliopadus is home."

"Right enough," Willie said. "She is a grand old girl; and you're a rover, Chris."

Chris went on deck. He looked the part of ship's officer in his tailored khakis, epaulettes with four gold stripes, and dress Wellingtons. Willie had touched on something deep inside him; he loved roving, the unsurpassed variety of life at sea on a Michas ship. The cool climates of Northern Europe, the warm Mediterranean, the fierce heat of the tropics. A week of sweet passage; then days of turbulence, the Peliopadus battered by wicked heavy seas.

It would have taken the rack to have Chris admit it, but he liked the power and influence that went with being Chief Steward. As chef at The Old Hotel, he'd had it, but at sea he had more. Weeks from port, the ship's company depended on Chris and Catering to keep body and soul one.

The prospect of distant ports and discovering new things excited Chris. Several days docked in Piraeus, and a couple of runs ashore with the chief to visit the Parthenon and the Plaka, left Chris in a bouyant mood, a condition strengthened by the passage through the Sea of Marmaris and the Bosphorus, to gaze on Istanbul and Uskudar on the shores of Asia Minor before entering the Black Sea.

The Peliopadus, loaded with grain, lay outside Constanza, the port shielded by a minefield, waiting for a minesweeper to take her in. It was a long week discharging cargo and loading textiles for Italy and hides for Germany.

Constanza disappointed Chris. The impoverished dockers offered to buy clothing off a man's back and shoes off his feet. But none of the crew wanted the worthless lei.

Chris held off judgement, keen to see behind the shabby docks, and sold a few packets of Pall Mall to dockers. Going ashore he had his first brush with Communist State Security. A sentry on the brow armed with an assault rifle checked his passport, seaman's book and shoregoing pass.

His spirits rose as he walked into the port. He had a good look at an ancient Romanian Navy corvette in dry dock, then watched the cargo ships with counter sterns and Woodbine funnels that had seen better days, schooners and caiques, discharging and loading. It felt Levantine; the Near East. He wished he had his camera with him. But the Mate had warned him taking pictures would invite charges of spying.

The mood darkened with his second brush with Red security; a policeman at the dock gate hauled him into a shack of an office. This officious corrupt thug, armed with a huge pistol, scrutinised his passport and seaman's book. With an ostentatious flourish, he stamped the shore pass, then threatened to frisk Chris "for contraband." Chris palmed him a couple of packets of Pall Mall and passed.

Dirt roads, worn buildings. The streets filled with Russian soldiers in heavy jack boots and shabby uniforms. An army of occupation?

Excellent Turkish coffee. The friendly café owner took Chris for a German. He'd served in the Romanian Army on the Russian front, fighting alongside the German Army. He didn't like Russians.

A tavern meal: hard bread, tomato and green salad, a meagre dressing of oil and vinegar, sour pungent cheese, thin local beer. An accordion playing a mournful tune. A fat Russian officer tried flirting with him, and bummed a few Pall Mall.

Chris felt depressed by this bleak and shabby town. He'd thought Westburn impoverished, but it was a treasure house compared to Constanza. He'd had enough of the place; it browned him off. The gloom lifted when the Peliopadus cast off, sailing for Italy and Germany.

He dreamt of Japan, drawn by the stories of Japanese women told him by old sea dogs on board who had cruised the home islands.

Chartered for a run to the Far East: Singapore, Indonesia, Hong Kong, and North Australia. Chris hoped for a new cargo in Darwin for Japan, but not yet. The Peliopadus loaded beef and butter for Europe.

* * *

The first couple of years at sea passed, and Chris had settled to life afloat. He declined leave at the end of the first year, deciding to remain aboard the Peliopadus for another year. Throughout the year, officers went home on leave and replacements joined the ship.

The Indian crew too changed after a year. Chris suggested to Captain Graham that it would be useful to have a pool of Goanese Second Stewards, giving stability, adding a permanent cadre of men familiar with Michas Lines' methods. Stavros Michas liked the idea and adopted it. Catering came into line with the deck and engine room and their pool of established Serangs.

Michas Lines, a small company operating a handful of ships, meant old shipmates often served again on the same vessel.

That second year, Chris was sorry to see Captain Graham, the Chief Engineer Wally Barnes, and radio operator Beastie Willie leave the ship. Chris waited by the brow as they departed. Three sailors carried their baggage to the quay and the waiting taxis to Antwerp station.

Captain Graham shook his hand.

"Look after yourself, Chris. Maybe we'll sail together in a year or two."

Beastie Willie mounted the brow, turned and waved. "Ah'll be seeing you. Go on leave, Chris. You can stay too long on board."

Wally Barnes, the Chief Engineer, grabbed Chris's hand.

"I'd sail with you anytime, Chris. The word is out in the company. You've made the Peliopadus the best-fed ship in the fleet."

And later, it was with sadness he said farewell to Fernandez, his valued Second Steward, leaving the ship in Aden where the Peliopadus changed the Indian crew.

"I say goodbye, McCoull Sahib. With the Blessing I sail with you again."

"You're working for Michas Lines now, Fernandez. We'll be shipmates again."

They shook hands.

Chris got on well with the several replacements who came aboard. But he enjoyed solitude, kept his distance, and concentrated on running Catering.

* * *

Chris's third year aboard the Peliopadus, and still he declined leave. Before joining the ship, he'd not known such contentment. He liked the taste of success, the good salary, and the hard work.

And life got better. The captain, Chief Engineer and the radio operator went on leave, and old shipmates rejoined Peliopadus. Captain Graham, Beastie Willie, and Wally Barnes came back. A few months earlier, Fernandez had come on board in Cochin.

The Peliopadus, outward bound from Montreal where she'd discharged general cargo, was now a day out of the Gulf of St Lawrence, in ballast, bound for Halifax Dockyard for refit. Under grey skies, she buried her bow in a troubled pewter sea, plunging deeper into troughs between mourning white waves. Translucent curtains of spray flew aft, dampening Chris. He stood on the upper deck midships, deep in the song of the wind in the rigging. From deep in the hull came the creak of timber and screeching metal. The Peliopadus, at twelve knots, bucked and twisted through a disturbed North Atlantic. A bolt of pain hit a left upper molar, drawing his tongue to the tooth second from the back. His forefinger probed the gum above the tooth and explored the mushy, painful surface; an abscess. He'd suffered one as a child, and his mother had taken him to a dental butcher who'd numbed it with novocaine and pulled it, a first tooth. Chris winced at the memory of pus taste, tears, howls and blood.

He left the deck, went below, got a bottle of oil of cloves from the medical cabinet, soaked a wad of cotton wool, and jammed it on the aching tooth, tight between gum and cheek. He looked at the elevator and extracting forceps. Oil of cloves would do until the Peliopadus docked at Halifax in two days.

The tugs coaxed the Peliopadus into dry dock. The Mate trimmed and stabilised her for resting on the blocks, and supervised the hoisting and placement of timber support props along the hull.

Chris watched as the crew and the shore gang brought the gangway on board. He would begin the restocking of the Peliopadus with supplies for the period in port, and lay out a schedule of requirements for the long voyage through the Panama Canal across the Pacific to the Antipodes. Then he'd ask the agent to arrange a dental appointment.

* * *

The agent arranged an appointment with Dr Solene Aimie for two o' clock in the afternoon. The surgery was a twenty-minute walk from the dock. A French name in Halifax, Nova Scotia, the heart of Scots Canada, surprised Chris. He wore fresh khakis, epaulettes and well-polished Naval Wellingtons; a futile attempt at lifting his spirits. The thought of having a tooth extracted depressed him. The warm sun did nothing to cheer him up.

The receptionist, a dour, heavy-set Scots-Canadian matron, showed him to the fresh, impersonal waiting room. The floor was covered in a beige carpet, a table displaying several neat rows of current newspapers and magazines. Chris sat in a comfortable easy chair.

"Dr Aimie will see you shortly," the receptionist said.

He gazed at pictures of Canadian ships from the war hanging on the facing wall, then rose from the chair to study the view of the naval dockyard, the men-of-war and merchantmen alongside. The Peliopadus rested in dry dock, a pale feather of smoke coming from her stack.

"Good afternoon. You'll be Mr McCoull?"

Chris turned. "Good afternoon. Yes, I'm Chris McCoull from the Peliopadus."

She held out her hand. "I'm Dr Solene Aimie."

"Pleased to meet you, Doctor Aimie."

He told her how he'd treated the tooth with oil of cloves. Chris heard his own voice rather far away. This petite girl in a fitted white coat was so pretty. More than pretty; an understated beauty. Her slender legs, fine features, aquiline tilted nose, stylish black hair, smooth black complexion, the sweetest red lips; Dr Solene Aimie had bowled him over.

"Are you all right, Mr McCoull? You seem distant."

"No, no, Ah'm fine, Doctor."

She looked in his mouth, working with a probe. Chris dared a look into her huge dark eyes with the long eyelashes.

"Yes, an abscess. Has it hurt much?"

"Now and again. Are you going to extract?"

Dr Aimie meant to treat the tooth: remove the infection with a root canal and cap with a gold crown. Clean and polish, and put gold inlays in three teeth. She named a price.

"It's a lot. Can't you just pull it?"

"No, not when I can save it. But I'll send you to a butcher if that's what you want. It's up to you. You have nice strong teeth. Take care of them."

Chris felt at a disadvantage, lying in the chair, suffering under her cool eye. Her frank gaze appraised his expensive boots and tailored khakis, the epaulettes showing his rank. He knew that she knew he could afford the treatment.

"Well, Mr McCoull?"

"Ah'm in your in hands."

"You're unusual. British and Russian patients often have mouths full of steel. You don't. I'll have the treatment finished by the end of the week."

"I'm glad of that. I'm dead scared of dentists. I hate needles."

Solene Aimie suppressed laughter.

Chris's breath hissed as the needle went in and out, and in and out again on the other side of the abscess. They waited while the novocaine kicked in. The left side of his face grew numb.

"Well done, Mr McCoull. I know that hurt."

"Are you from France?"

"Martinique. I'm a French citizen, but I've never been to France."

"You have a nice accent; attractive."

She looked at him, and smiled. "Thank you. I like your Scots accent, Mr McCoull. Dignified."

Chris blushed.

"Ready?"

A nurse came in to assist.

On the Friday afternoon came the fitting of the gold crown and the cleaning and polishing, Chris's mouth felt clean; his smile dazzled. Solene Aimie told him about brushing and flossing to maintain his dental health. After he'd paid the receptionist, Solene—for he thought of her as Solene—came to reception to say farewell.

"You're a good patient, Mr McCoull. Goodbye."

"Ah'll say cheerio, and thanks, Doctor, thanks for everything."

* * *

Sunday, late morning, the officers finished with breakfast. The captain was ashore for a round of golf with the agent. Ship's officers went ashore, leaving the deck and engine room watch on board and the Indian and Goanese crewmen at leisure. The Second Steward had left a cold buffet for the watch-keepers in their messes. The galley crew shut down for the day. No officer wanted dinner; Chris meant to stay ashore for a while.

He left the Peliopadus to explore Halifax. He breakfasted early on porridge and toast, leaving room for a Canadian lunch. The dockyard foreman recommended an old-fashioned family diner.

He'd suggested taking a taxi or a bus, but the sun shone, the air was warm and mellow, and so Chris decided to walk. He shifted out of his day khakis, looked at the soft, well-washed blue Oxford Hathaway shirt with the button-down collar, brown Bedford cords he'd had made in Hong Kong, and the tan boots and belt made in Bilbao. They'd cost him a packet. He gave the boots a careful polish, bringing them to a glossy finish.

Chris found the Nova Scotian restaurant, crowded for Sunday lunch with Catholics and Scotch Presbyterians let out of church, but the lady on reception found him a small table for two.

"We can always find a place for a Scots sailor."

Chris studied the menu, undecided, wanting food different from the staples of the Peliopadus.

"Excuse me, sir."

The lady from reception smiled.

"The restaurant is full, but for this table. Would you mind sharing with one of our regulars?"

"No, not at all."

Chris rose as Solene Aimie appeared, waving to the table by the receptionist. She was so lovely in her beige summer dress with the full skirt and three-quarter sleeves. He caught the click of her heels as she approached the table.

Solene had her hair pulled back in a chignon; it suited her pert nose and high cheekbones. He looked at her, a long glance. She was exquisite.

"Ah, Mr McCoull. So nice to see you again," Solene Aimie said. She extended her gloved hand. Chris pressed her hand, firmer than he'd meant to, and she gave him a quizzical look.

"Hello again, Dr Aimie. Very happy to share the table with you."

An awkward silence descended on their unexpected meeting. They studied the menu. Solene ordered eggs Benedict. Chris asked for scrambled eggs with smoked salmon.

"Eggs and lox. A patient likes it served with bagels," Solene said, breaking the silence.

They made small talk throughout the meal. Chris finished his food, and Solene set down her knife and fork a moment later. They lingered a moment or two over the last of the coffee.

When her cup rang on the saucer, he found he didn't want her to leave. Chris felt if she left he'd never see her again. He caught the waitress's eye and nodded for the bill.

"I can't let you pay."

Solene smiled. "Thank you."

They stopped outside the entrance. Solene pulled on her gloves.

"Can I walk with you, Miss Aimie? I mean, if you don't have somewhere to go. Would that be all right?"

She laughed. "Oh, Mr McCoull. You're my patient."

"I'm Chris, the patient who likes you."

She smiled. "I'm Solene. Come, I'll show you Halifax."

* * *

Halifax was a navy town through and through. Home to the Atlantic Fleet of the Royal Canadian Navy; blue jackets in the streets. They looked down on the naval base from Citadel Hill. Solene pointed to Dalhousie University.

"I studied there; dentistry, and French. Hard work. I like the town. Cold winters, but the port is ice-free."

"There's my school."

Chris pointed to the docks where the Peliopadus dry-docked.

"How long have you been at sea?"

"More than three years; all service on the Peliopadus. I've not been home. I take a day or two off if she's in port for a while.

"Don't you miss home?"

"No. My mother died in the war. A wall fell on her after the Blitz. My father married again, and my stepmother is a vixen. We never got on. I'll go back one day. See the Rinaldis."

Chris told Solene about the Rinaldis and how Dante, Celestina and Graziella had made his life good.

"I'm family to the Rinaldis. They kept me right. Dante's wife is called Chiarina. A lovely girl. They fought together in the Italian partisans during the war."

They walked from Citadel Hill to the town, where they lingered a while in Pleasant Park. Solene told Chris about her family. Fabien, her father, a lawyer, the patriarch. Her mother, Morgane.

"I have two brothers and three sisters. I'm the eldest daughter. My father is very strict. He wanted me to study in France. There was an awful row about my coming here. My mother saved the day."

There was a chill in the evening air. Solene looked tired. Chris didn't want to overstay.

"Should you be going home?

"Yes. Walk me to my car?"

"Glad to."

"I'll run you back to the ship."

"That's kind of you, but I think I'll walk. I don't get the chance at sea."

Chris would've been proud to be seen anywhere with Solene, but didn't want nosey officers or crew seeing him coming out of a car driven by a beautiful woman, then put up with the questions and the wisecracks.

They stopped at her car, not far from the restaurant where they'd dined earlier.

Solene held out her hand "Thank you, Chris. It's been a lovely day. I'll say goodnight."

He held onto her gloved hand. *Sweet Jesus,* Chris thought, *but she is wonderful.*

"Can I see you again? I'd like to."

"All right."

"Tomorrow? I could leave the ship early."

"I'd love to," Solene said, "but I'm sorry, I can't. Tomorrow I'm flying to Montreal to attend a dental conference at McGill University; and on Wednesday to Quebec to a conference on French language. Thursday I'll have lots to catch up on at my practice."

She could see the disappointment on Chris's face, and it vexed her. She liked him.

Solene mentioned a quiet place, Lindy's. By day a deli-cum-café. On Friday night, jazz musicians gathered there to play and sit in.

"There's a small dance floor. The owner clears away tables."

"I'll meet you there. Outside, say eight o'clock on Friday evening?"

"I'll look forward to it."

* * *

Somehow Chris got through the week until Friday. The days dragged, but burying himself in work helped the time pass.

It was a fine June evening, and with dinner over, the galley shut down, and Fernandez supervising the tidying of the saloon, Chris prepared to step out.

"Looking smart, McCoull Sahib. Good night."

Chris grinned. " 'Night, Fernandez."

He arrived at Lindy's fifteen minutes early, anxious that he might miss Solene, and burying a deeper anxiety that she wouldn't come. Five minutes later Solene appeared by his side.

"Hello, Chris. I came early. I didn't want to be late."

"Me too."

Solene, even more lovely than he remembered, wore a lilac fitted summer dress, navy leather gloves matching her T-strap shoes. He felt flattered that she was so well turned out. Discreet makeup; her eyes sparkling, so beautiful, her hair framing her face.

"Can I have my hand back?"

"Oh, sorry."

Chris flushed, anxious that he'd gotten off to a bad start.

"You're looking smart, Chris."

Solene admired the grey wool jacket, dark slacks, shiny dress Wellingtons, blue Hathaway Oxford shirt all of it topped off by a maroon Rooster wool tie.

"Thanks, I bought the kit in New York."

"You look American. I like it."

Solene knew all the band members. One Canadian black man, the owner of Lindy's, and two from the U.S., dockyard workers, one a store man, the other a labourer in the engine shop. They preferred life in Canada. And, to Chris's surprise, there were also two Scots emigrants from Glasgow: a drummer and a tenor player. Both worked in the dockyard, one a shipwright and the other a ship's draughtsman. The Scots were gregarious, but the black Americans, though polite, were distant.

"The Yanks; not friendly."

"They tend to be cool until they get to know you. They were like that when I came at first."

Chris wondered if the coolness had to do with his being with Solene.

Between numbers they chatted about Solene's visits to Montreal and Quebec, her life in Halifax, and Chris and Michas Line. They sipped a Newfoundland rum, Screech, mellowed with ice, Coke, and lemon.

"How long will you be in Halifax?"

"A month. Probably five weeks with the sea trial after the refit."

They danced a couple of times.

"You like the music, Chris?"

For Chris, music was incidental to his life. He'd never had money to buy records. His father had bought a radio, but one Monday, crippled by a hangover, he'd pawned it to raise cash for a curer.

"Yes, the slow numbers. The fast ones, well, they're hard to understand."

The quintet played Stardust, the last number. A measured warm tenor led, stretching the romance of the tune to the discreet swinging accompaniment from piano, bass and drums.

His hand moved across the table and touched her hand. Solene looked up and smiled. Her fingers laced with Chris's fingers.

"Ask me to dance."

"Alright; dance with me?"

He held her at half-arm's length. A mellow trumpet took the lead, coaxing more romance from the song. Solene moved closer.

"You dance well, Chris; but you haven't done this before?"

"No. First time I've felt like this."

"You're fond of me?"

"Right from the start. You knew, didn't you?"

Solene tightened her hold on Chris's hands. He felt her sweet breath on his cheek, and closed the hair's breadth gap between them as they moved across the small dance floor.

"Am I doing it wrong?"

"Perfect. You're doing fine."

"But you knew?"

"I knew."

A swish of the brushes, the last chorus of Stardust. They stopped on the dance floor.

"Jesus, Solene," Chris whispered.

Solene kissed him—a swift, tender brushing of lips.

"It's all right, Chris."

The owner of Lindy's called a cab. They waited outside, relishing the cool air. When the Peliopadus had dry-docked, Chris had felt that more than a month in port was forever. Not now. He'd found love and respect for this beautiful girl.

"I'll drop you; then he can run me to the ship."

And Solene sensed Chris's mood.

"We have a bit more than a month, Chris. It's not long enough. Tonight, stay with me a while."

They heard the crunch of the cab's tyres coming near.

"It's okay if I stay? I mean, you're sure?"

"I'm sure, Chris. Stay with me."

* * *

Chris asked Captain Graham for leave; four days. Fernandez would look after Catering. Michas Lines owed him months of leave.

"Glad you're taking leave, Chris. A break with your girl?"

"You know about the girl, sir?"

"The Peliopadus is a small world, Chris. Everyone wants to meet her."

"Her name is Solene."

Solene had arranged for the rental of a cabin by a lake out in the woods of Nova Scotia two hours from Halifax. She picked him up at noon on the Thursday.

Several of the crew and the Goanese not on duty gathered on the port side of the ship, waiting for Chris going ashore. Officers off duty watched from the boat deck.

Chris emerged from the accommodation, weekend luggage in hand, dressed in soft, washed out jeans, blue Hathaway shirt and dress Wellingtons. When he got to the head of the brow on the ship's deck, Solene, watching for him, got out of the car and waved. Even at the distance of a hundred yards she looked gorgeous in a trim blue dress, the skirt and high-heeled sandals flattering her legs.

When he reached her, Solene kissed Chris; then he packed his kit in the car.

"Nice car."

"It's a surprise, an MGA; a present to myself."

The Goanese stewards applauded and cheered while the off-duty sailors and firemen gathered on the deck. She frowned, and turned to look at the ship.

"It's all right, Solene. They mean well. The man with the moustache, that's Fernandez, my Second Steward. First-class bloke."

Chris pointed to the grinning and waving engine room Serang.

"He's a friend of mine. We work together buying halal food for the crew; a good man. Let's give them a wave."

Solene changed her sandals for flat driving shoes, then pulled on driving gloves.

"I love driving the MGA. It's a great British sports car."

Solene drove to the outskirts of Halifax.

"We're a mixed bag on the Peliopadus: Goanese Catholics, Hindus, Muslims, and British officers. We rub along; I like that."

Solene glanced at Chris and smiled. "So do I."

"Captain Graham sets the right tone. He's half Burmese—mother's from Burma, father's Scottish. A great skipper; an exceptional seaman."

Clear of Halifax, Solene's face became a map of concentration, and the sky-blue MGA glided through tight corners, tyres gripping the road. The wind whipped their hair, and growls and roars from the engine triggered Chris's excitement as Solene accelerated into the open road. She had expert control of the vehicle, like an F-86 Sabre on a strafing run. Chris, whose driving had never risen above the level of Dante's fish delivery van, glued himself to the passenger seat. He gave up looking at the passing scenery, admiring Solene's skill at the wheel. The car stopped at a road junction, Solene looking right, left and right, checking traffic.

"Terrific driving. I've seen nothing like it. You're wonderful."

She glanced at Chris, grinning. "I'm crazy with my MGA, but I'm careful when you're by my side."

Solene put the car in gear and made a sharp left turn on the road. Chris caught a glimpse of her left leg as she worked the clutch, right hand gripping the gear stick, guiding it through second and third gear, into fourth gear. The MGA shot along the open road, a flash of blue and chrome.

The MGA cruised at a steady sixty. Chris felt safe with Solene; she was taking care of him. He stole glances, admiring her looks, the high cheekbones, the pert tilted nose, her hair swept back in a chignon, her lips that he'd kissed.

"Solene, Solene, I'm crazy about you," Chris said, his whisper hidden in the purr of the engine.

The cabin had one bedroom, a kitchen and a bathroom with a shower. Water was heated in the tank behind the open fireplace meant for burning logs. It was summer in the Nova Scotian woods, with cool evenings, and they welcomed the time to light the log fire and heat the water. There was a gas fridge and a gas three-burner stove, gas bottles outside the cabin wall, with an oven and grill. But the cabin's appointments were not what Chris had come to admire.

* * *

She lay in his arms. The morning sun shone on her smooth black skin.

"I wondered about falling in love; I wanted it to happen. Then I met you, and I knew you loved me. Oh bébé, to love and be loved."

Chris held Solene, she who'd come from heaven; caressed her; kissed her; touched her. Dug into himself to find the words for her.

"Solene, my heart. I love you."

"We can feel this way forever."

"Yes, forever."

Solene stiffened.

"What's wrong; have I done something?"

"Oh no, Chris; not you. It's my father and what he might do. He's a difficult man. If he found out about us, he'd be in Halifax like a shot, dragging me home."

"Do you think he'll find out?"

"No, but it would be awful if he did."

They slept again after making love.

Hours later, Chris stirred.

"Can I make breakfast?"

Solene held him. "Not yet."

After breakfast of eggs, bacon, toast and coffee, they sat outside on a wooden bench by the cabin door.

"A walk, Chris?"

"Good."

They followed a footpath through the woods, skirting the edge of the lake. Pine trees, conifers, maple; trees still green; pungent resin from the conifers made for an exhilarating walk. He told Solene of days hunting rabbits with Dante on the moors above Westburn and in the Lyle Hill wild acres beneath the cliffs.

"Tell me, what does Solene mean?"

"My name means *with solemnity*."

"Dignified and beautiful, but never solemn."

Solene, her stern father's favourite, had always felt his affection and love, but had also suffered punishment for minor transgressions. She'd learned to walk the boundaries of her father's will.

When Solene made her First Communion, her father had rebuked her for looking up and smiling as she approached the altar to receive the Host.

"I was seven, demure and holy in my pretty white dress. He said I was undignified and scolded me. I'd fasted before Communion. When we got home I got nothing to eat, and he sent me to my room. I cried myself to sleep."

For a few minutes, fear haunted Solene's face, the confident, competent young woman now a faun, afraid of pursuing darkness as memories of a childhood horror returned.

Chris put his arm around her, and she turned into him. They held each other for a moment.

"That's awful. My First Communion my stepmother sent me to church in shabby clothes. A boy said I was dirty, and I punched him. Next day the class teacher knocked hell out of me."

He told Solene how the Good Mother had egged his father on to beat his only son.

"When I turned fifteen I fought back and left the house for staff quarters in The Old Hotel."

"I was glad to get away from my father when I came to Canada."

They held each other a moment longer.

"Your father won't like me?"

"No; it's just that you're white."

They walked on for a couple of minutes.

Chris stopped, tilted Solene's chin, and looked into her eyes.

"The Rinaldis, they're my family; guaranteed, they'll love you."

She kissed him.

* * *

"Can you fish, Chris?"

"Never tried. I'm a dab hand at preparing and cooking fish."

Back at the cabin, Solene removed a rod and a box of tied flies from the storeroom.

"There's speckled trout in the lake. I'll catch our dinner."

"I'll dig up worms for bait."

Solene laughed. "That's cheating." She selected a tied fly from the box, holding it for Chris's inspection. "Fishermen like a sporting challenge."

Solene stood at the end of a small jetty thirty yards from the cabin door. Chris admired her skill at casting and spinning the line. A flick of the rod sent the line out to rest on the water. She manipulated the rod and line, the fly seeming like a moving, living insect. On the fifth cast a trout rose and took the bait. The line tightened, and the rod bent to an elegant arc as the fish went deep, fighting the hook.

Solene fought back and, careful not to offer hard resistance and break the line, brought the fish toward the jetty.

"Help me land him."

Chris held the net as Solene brought the handsome trout from the water. He got him into the net, laying him on the jetty. Solene removed the hook but turned away as Chris wielded the gaff and despatched the trout. He weighed a good two and a half pounds.

Back in the cabin kitchen, it was Solene's turn to admire skill as Chris gutted and filleted the trout, reducing the fish to two generous filets.

"Where did you learn to do that?"

"I picked it up working for Dante, and in The Old Hotel. I keep my hand in aboard the ship. When the flying fish land on deck, the sailors gather them for a fry-up; I help the galley fillet the fish."

Chris seasoned the trout with salt and pepper, and melted butter in the frying pan. He coated the filets in bread crumbs, then laid the fish flesh-side in the pan. Five minutes a side and it was cooked to perfection. Solene handed Chris a lemon.

"I was sure I'd catch something, so I brought this."

"What else can you catch?"

Solene laughed. "A Scotsman." She kissed Chris.

They sat by the log fire, sipping rum and Coke made from Cuban Bacardi Reserve rum that Chris had bought from the ship's bond.

Each evening Chris cooked the meats and vegetables Solene brought for dinner.

The days passed in walks through the woods and round the lake. On another day they spent an hour fishing but caught no trout.

Each evening after dinner they spent time in each other's arms.

On the penultimate evening, Solene opened up about her family. Her father, Fabien, from a humble family of shopkeepers, had become a successful lawyer. He'd married Morgane, from a family of farmers and fishermen, a teacher of children.

"My father did well. The family's comfortable. But he's so damned strict."

The eldest brother, Matthieu, a lawyer, worked with the father.

"The younger brother, Yann, my father sent to France to study law. It's not what he wanted, but he seemed to go along with my father's wishes."

"What happened?"

"When he arrived in France, he joined the navy. My father raged against him. But my mother accused him of driving Yann away. That cooled my father down, and it made it easier for me to study in Canada."

"What about your sisters?"

"Still in school. I worry about them."

* * *

They arrived back at the ship after six. The evening meal was over for the officers and crew. Chris meant to stow his weekend luggage and dine out somewhere with Solene. He'd not reckoned with his friends aboard the Peliopadus. The quartermaster on the gangway, dressed in fitted navy jersey, navy bell bottoms, a white titfer and black hat band, with *Michas Lines* in gold letters, waited for their return.

They got out of the sky-blue MGA and Chris removed his weekend bag. They turned to the ship and the quartermaster cried, "McCoull Sahib is back!" The cry rang along the dock, echoed by a throaty chorus.

"McCoull Sahib is back; McCoull Sahib is back!"

Fernandez and the engine room Serang led the deck and engine room crew surging down the brow.

"Come, Miss," Fernandez said to Solene, and he escorted her aboard the Peliopadus.

The Serang organised the sailors and fireman who raised Chris shoulder high and carried him up the brow to the deck of the Peliopadus. They stood him beside Solene. Chris introduced her to Captain Graham and the chief, Wally Barnes.

"Welcome aboard, Miss Aimie," they said, and shook hands with her.

"Why, you're so popular, Chris," Solene said.

Chris shrugged, flushed with embarrassment.

"The Serang asked me could they welcome McCoull Sahib and his Good Missus," Wally Barnes said.

"Fernandez came to see me," Captain Graham said, "and here we are."

Chris and Wally Barnes walked together, following Captain Graham and Solene. They climbed the stairs to the upper deck and the captain's day room.

"What's a Good Missus?" Solene said to Captain Graham.

"They're being polite. A Good Missus, well, she's a man's wife."

"Oh!"

"She's a fine young woman," Wally Barnes said. "You're a lucky man, Chris."

The Captain's Steward served gin and tonics, Chris's favourite. Captain Graham discussed Solene's dental practice, and Wally Barnes mentioned his one visit to Martinique.

A knock came at the door.

"Come in," Captain Graham said.

A smiling Fernandez entered the room.

"Serving dinner, McCoull Sahib."

* * *

A beaming Fernandez showed them into the office, now an intimate dining room—the desk removed, a table set for two. A vase of mixed crocus filled the room with sweet fragrance. Silver service, crisp, brilliant white linen and the Peliopadus's prized crystal jug filled with salted lime juice.

"Oh Chris, this is lovely."

Another perfect G and T.

Fernandez and another steward brought Goanese delicacies to begin: chamuças, samosas, and pakora.

"Delicious, Chris; such variety."

"We must eat everything. Fernandez and the Serang have gone to a lot of trouble. There's more to come from the crew's galley."

The table was cleared and tidied by Fernandez, and the cutlery straightened.

"Serang and Bhandari bring next dish after few minutes. You and Good Missus rest."

"I hope you're not mad when they call you Good Missus," Chris told Solene when Fernandez had left again. "They're showing respect."

"I'm not mad; are you?"

"Oh no, not at all."

He caressed her hand. She raised it to her cheek.

"Isn't it wonderful that we met?"

"Jesus, Solene. Every day I give thanks for it."

"Why did you join the Merchant Navy?"

"A Greek ship owner—that's Mr Michas—stayed in The Old Hotel. I was the chef. He liked the way I ran things and asked me to audit catering on the Peliopadus. Then he appointed me Chief Steward."

"What did you have to do?"

Chris explained the lax state of affairs aboard: the abominable food, the dishonest captain, Jangler Jim, and the crooked butler, taking money from the crew's ration allowance.

"The first few months were hard, but I sorted out Catering; I made things right. Captain Graham came aboard and supported me."

"That's a lot of responsibility, and you so young. You've done well; and you like your job, its power and influence?"

"Yes; I've stayed on board; four years without home leave. I wanted it that way."

Minutes later, knuckles rapped the door.

"Come in."

A grinning Serang, perfect teeth shining in his brown face, led the Bhandhari carrying a tray into the room.

"Salam, McCoull Sahib."

"Salam, Serang, Salam Bhandhari."

Both men were dressed in their best: blue chequered cotton lungis, solid leather chapples, and white collarless cotton shirts with three-quarters sleeves.

They'd borrowed from the ship silver serving dishes, and they gleamed in the light. The Serang placed them on the table, and the Bhandari set the tray to one side. With a flourish, he lifted the lid on lamb marinated in a spinach sauce. The

Serang removed the lids on two smaller dishes to show four chapatis—unleavened bread—and a heap of steaming saffron rice.

"Number one lamb, McCoull Sahib. Bhandhari make special for you and Good Missus."

Chris looked at Solene and she acknowledged.

"Thank you so much, Serang and Bhandari. I'm touched."

"It's wonderful," Chris said.

The Serang smiled and bowed from the shoulders. The Bhandari, grinning, waggled his head from side to side.

"Oh Miss," the Serang said, "McCoull Sahib, is Number One damn fine fellow."

Chris showed Solene how to scoop up the food with a wedge of the unleavened bread.

"That's how the crew do it."

With dinner finished, they stood on the boat deck drinking coffee, watching the lights of Halifax.

"How long, Chris?"

"With the sea trials, about two weeks. We'll dock each evening."

"It's not enough time."

"I'll come back."

"I want that. But what then?"

Solene and Chris had rushed their love. They had no time for genteel courting. Soon to be separated by oceans, they faced the spectre of loneliness.

The Peliopadus was chartered for a long voyage, bound for Montevideo to discharge Canadian whiskey, then to load frozen beef. From there they were to sail north for the Panama Canal and Vancouver, discharge the frozen beef, and load general cargo for Australia.

Chris expected the Peliopadus to be in home waters after a year.

"I can't leave the ship early; I'd let down Mr Michas and my shipmates. I'll pay off and come straight to Halifax."

Chris didn't want to push events more than he had. But he'd shown that he was serious, and worried that he might scare Solene off.

"I'm not coming to Halifax for fun. I'm a good chef. I'll find work. I've saved, and I'll get a restaurant of my own."

Solene smiled and grasped Chris's hands.

"I'll wait."

"You want to be with me?"

"Above all things."

Chris took a deep breath.

"Marry me?"

"Yes."

* * *

The Peliopadus was sailing on the morning tide and scheduled to cast off at 6:00 a.m. Solene came to say farewell, and Chris descended the gangway to her.

The screw turned, creating a thickening dirty foam. Bridge, deck and engine room watch-keepers were on standby.

The First Mate hailed and waved to Chris from the wing of the bridge.

"Chris, ten minutes, and we cast off."

"Open it."

She gazed at a carved gold Victorian Scottish Celtic Cross inlaid with agate of deep autumnal colours.

"I got it in town, at a little antique shop."

"It's beautiful. Put it on."

Chris fastened the gold chain round her neck and turned her around. He held the cross between the thumb and forefinger of his right hand.

"I swear on this cross, I'll come back."

Solene placed the fingers of her right hand over Chris's fingers.

"I swear too; I'll wait for you. You know I will. I love you."

They hung on to each other, sharing a last lingering kiss.

The gangway lowered to the dockside and, mooring ropes cast off, the Peliopadus moved away from the dock. Tugs took charge and manouvered her for the open sea.

Chris watched Solene in the early morning light. The sun was rising, but even the promise of summer failed to lift Chris's gloom at leaving Solene. The tugs cast off. Chris and Solene waved until the ship had moved far from the dockside. The Peliopadus picked up speed, heading south.

Chris turned away. Deep sadness shrouded him as he lost sight of Solene. Worry about the year ahead vexed him. He felt sure of Solene, confident she'd wait for him. Satisfied, too, that he'd convinced her of his honourable intentions.

Sometime Solene's family might learn of Chris, perhaps from a "friend." The thought of her father meddling in their lives made his heart race; but right now he could do nothing.

Chris entered the galley and buried himself in the morning schedule. Afterwards he weighed up the arrangements in place at the several ports for replenishing ship's stores.

Chapter Ten

Weeks at sea and far from Solene, driven mad by the lonely deep ocean, Chris depended on the company of his shipmates for his sanity. In port he looked forward to Solene's letters, a welcome relief.

The days passed, and the ship settled into her sailing routine—watches changing every four hours; day workers on deck and down below, five and half days in the week; visits to shipmates' cabins for a peg. Most days Chris met Beastie Willie, and Wally Barnes. On Sundays he attended Captain Graham's day room with his brother officers for drinks before lunch.

Days of sailing until the ship was south of New York; deck officers kept an eye on the radar for icebergs drifting south, while sailors on watch scanned the horizon. The captain placed lookouts on the bridge.

"Can't be too careful," he said to Chris one morning spent reviewing the ship's books. "Bergs come down from Greenland."

Next morning, Chris was on deck at dawn for the sunrise. Captain Graham hailed from the bridge and waved for him to come up.

"Bring your camera."

A mile to starboard a white massif with blue tints—a frozen cathedral—soared out of the sea. The sheer majesty of the berg took Chris's mind off Solene for a while. A groaning, creaking, mountainous berg; the stench of rotting cucumbers reached the Peliopadus.

"The berg's ill and in pain," Chris said.

Ocean currents carried the opaque mass south. An avalanche of ice fractured, and slabs tumbled; shimmering fragments flew, glistening in the sun's rays. Waves, white horses, disturbed the ocean surface, rushing towards the ship. Captain Graham ordered the quartermaster to steer to port.

"No point in getting too close."

Each week Chris kept an eye on the galley and the saloon, planning menus with the chef and Fernandez. The department ran well. The chef had the galley running in harmony, and under Fernandez's guidance, dining surpassed many a passenger vessel.

For interested officers, the engine room Serang arranged for tangy lamb, or creamy, subtle chicken curries, and a plate of chapatis, made by the Bhandari. Chris loved the food of the Indian subcontinent.

Life afloat made a few shipmates soft. Chris avoided flab, exercising daily on the poop, and performing a brutal round of pullups with leg raises on the chinning bar in the laundry room.

From Halifax to the Carolinas, the Peliopadus sailed through calm azure seas under deep blue skies. But one early morning on the twelve-to-four watch, the klaxon blared and had the crew leaping from bunks. Chris and Wally Barnes met in the alleyway.

"Fire down below. The Second's on top of it."

Chris roused Fernandez and alerted Catering. The Mate had the deck crew ready for an emergency.

Fuel leaking from a burner had carbonised. This tarry mass caught fire, and roaring whooshing yellow flames shot twenty feet up the boiler casing—a frightening eruption for the crew, with the Peliopadus's holds packed with seventy proof Canadian whiskey.

Wally Barnes had fire hoses run out and extinguishers to hand. The Second and the Serang braved the flames and the scorching heat, hands protected by asbestos gloves, probing and fencing with steel pokers, stabbing a burning mass of solid crude oil through the observation port until it fell to the bottom of the boiler and burned off. They replaced the burner.

The emergency was over in forty minutes.

Chris organised tea, coffee and sandwiches for the engine room watch, and sat with Wally Barnes and the Second in the Engineers' Mess.

"Good job it didn't spread," the Second said. "The old girl on fire, bow to stern. Christ, drifting in a lifeboat, freezing water and bergs around. No one screwed up. Burner's working fine one minute and knackered the next. The Serang's a bloody good man."

* * *

Each day love for Solene made Chris's heart soar. He was sure of her love. They'd keep promises made.

The father threatened their happiness, though. A meddlesome severe patriarch, he might intrude on their love and wreck it. At sea, Chris was powerless to help his beloved. He prayed for Solene's father to stay away from her.

The ship skirted the Caribbean and encountered shoals of flying fish. Chris gazed at these glistening torpedoes from the bow, often a foot long, beating tails on the sea, green to blue dorsal fins extended, flying at fifteen miles an hour, gliding forty feet at a time, skimming the waves.

The Peliopadus steamed along at fifteen knots, low freeboard, cutting through a fair swell and steady breeze, flying fish landing on the main deck.

The deck Serang set sailors gathering fish for the crew. He gave Chris a bucket of flying fish for the officers.

"Must eat today, McCoull Sahib. Tomorrow fish no good."

He held his nose and grimaced.

Thoughts of Solene fishing took Chris back to the happiest four days of his life, spent with her in the forest cabin.

"Oh bébé , oh bébé ," Chris said to the headwind carrying his love to Canada.

In the galley Chris and the chef filleted the flying fish. Fernandez soaked the filets in diluted salted lime juice. The chef fetched breadcrumbs while Chris and Fernandez prepared a mix of three peppers: cayenne, white and black; paprika, dried basil and thyme.

The filets were dipped in egg batter, then breadcrumbs, and finally seasoned and quick fried. The Serangs handed round dishes of fried fish to officers and crew on watch, and day workers at lunch. Chris had Fernandez serve the fish to officers at lunch.

On deck, Chris divided the filets with a fork, enjoying the sweet herring taste, facing aft to Canada and Solene.

* * *

Some days at sea Chris could not hide his fluctuating spirits. One day out in the Atlantic heading for a position twenty miles off Recife. Wally Barnes sat in Chris's cabin, a cool breeze flowing through the cabin ports. They sipped their pegs: gin and tonics, a mix of Gordon's Export Gin and Schweppes tonic water over ice.

"You're fed-up, Chris."

"Just a wee bit. What did you think of the dinner?"

"Chris, you're not worried about the food. The Peliopadus is the best feeder in the Michas Lines fleet. You're worried about that lovely girl."

Chris shrugged.

"Maybe she won't write."

"Don't be daft, Chris. She's dead keen on you. You're a lucky man. We'll be in Montevideo in five days. There'll be a packet of letters waiting for you."

"Thanks, Wally. I'm glad I'd a toothache in Halifax."

Wally grinned and shook his head. "You write to her, son. Send the letters she's longing for; tell her how you feel. Don't let her slip away."

After leaving Halifax, in the evenings before turning in, Chris made several false starts attempting a daily letter. He'd never written letters to anyone, even Dante. In the years serving aboard the Peliopadus, Chris had sent some postcards to Dante. An awkward Chris described life aboard the ship.

Dear Solene,

The days at sea since we left Halifax have been quiet, the crew going about the ship's business...

"Christ, Solene'll hate me if she reads this. It's as dull as dishwater."

He tore the sheet from the writing pad and shredded it into small pieces.

When he met Solene he'd fought embarrassment and had sought words for their tender lovemaking, and with time learned to surrender to Solene's candid, whispered endearments. The thought of writing love letters to her stymied Chris, still influenced by Westburn conventions of bottling up tender affection.

Solene had taught Chris to say what he felt as she lay in his arms, responding to her sweet tenderness, time after time telling her in different ways how much he loved her.

And yet when he sat at his desk to write, Chris struggled to overcome crippling shyness.

Why the hell can't I write about how much I love her?

But Chris knew why his pen kept still: the long shadow of home held him back. Westburn mores encouraged coarse blowhards.

"Ah got it fuckin' up her; got the dirty water away. She's a great ride."

Chris shied away from it.

Doubt sapped his confidence in Solene. Chris imagined Solene's first letter breaking it off. She'd had enough of him. A cruel justification; an unwise love match of black woman and a white man. The thought shamed him.

He desired her word. Hankered after opening Solene's first letter, the envelope lined with fragile protective matching paper. His fingers unfolding reams of bond covered in a strong hand of royal blue ink written with a fountain pen, the paper redolent of her perfume.

He sat back in his chair and Solene's voice, softer than tropical waves, enveloped him. And in a brave moment he defeated embarrassment. Chris picked up the pen, and wrote to Solene in a rapid, conversational voice about the beauty of the iceberg, stinking to high heaven of rotting cucumbers, the excitement and brief sense of danger when fire broke out in the stokehold. He described an epiphany of the voyage, the beautiful flying fish skimming the waves. Frying the fish reminded him of their tranquil days spent in the cabin in the woods. And he told her how much he missed her, and loved her. That he longed for her letters.

There followed a sleepless night, a day before entering Montevideo, with Chris talking to himself through the small hours.

"Bébé, write the way you talk. Take me close to your voice. Tell me how you look and how you feel. Solene, Solene, you're the love of my life."

He slid into a dream murmuring Solene's charged whisperings when they'd made love.

* * *

The Peliopadus berthed in the general cargo dock, winches clattering as the crew hoisted wooden pallets of whiskey out of the holds to the dockside.

Late afternoon, Chris and Wally Barnes stood on the boat deck facing the sea. The chief trained binoculars on the superstructure of a wrecked warship sunk in thirty-six feet of water in the outer roads. He handed the glasses to Chris.

"That's Graf Spee. One up for the Navy in 1939 when they drove her into Montevideo. Her captain, Hans Langsdorf, scuttled her, then shot himself."

"I heard teachers talking about it."

Chris had Fernandez pick up the mail from the agent when he came on board to sort and distribute to deck and Engineering.

Fernandez had riffed through the mail sack and extracted a bundle secured with an elastic band. His face split in a warm grin as he handed the bundle to Chris.

"Thanks, Fernandez. You'll deliver the mail to the captain and the chief?"

"I do that, McCoull Sahib."

The chandler, no stranger to lovesick seafarers, smiled.

"I'm going to see the captain and the chief. There's a good bar by the dock gate. You'll have read your mail and we can finish the business and have lunch."

"Thanks. The chap sorting the mail, he's my Second Steward, from Goa. I'll bring him. He's keen to learn the ship's business."

"I welcome him."

Solene's letters made Chris so happy. The details of her work. The walks to places they'd visited; mention of Lindy's—all of it brought Solene closer. Chris listened to her. He heard her voice.

Solene loved him.

Darling Chris,

I bury myself in work. Since you left, the practice is so busy I'm taking on an assistant. If I did not have my work, I'd go mad missing you, and perish longing for you.

I count the days until the year is gone, when Peliopadus returns to home waters, and you come back to me.

My beloved patient, my roving sweetheart, my sailor. My true love; I'll never forget the joy of meeting you and the days we spent together. My thoughts are of you, my guiding star.
All my love,
Solene XX

They sipped Patricia lager while waiting for the food. Chris's heart was full of Solene, having read her letters twice, and looking forward to reading them again and again.

"Very happy, McCoull Sahib?"

"Over the moon, Fernandez."

Ignacio Delossanto, an observer of sailors' moods, guessed that Chris had read love letters from his girl.

"May we drink to the health of your girl, Señor McCoull?"

"Yes. Very kind of you. Let's toast Solene."

They raised their glasses.

"To Solene."

The food came and eager hands grabbed the sandwiches.

"Chavito, national dish of my country."

They feasted on excellent bread filled with thinly sliced filet mignon, mozzarella, tomatoes, mayonnaise, black and green olives, bacon, fried eggs and ham. They drank more Patricia lager.

"Thank you, Señor Ignacio," Fernandez said. "Number one food."

"Great," Chris said, brimming with love for Solene and satiated with food. "I'm full, but I'd like another beer. The Patricia's excellent."

* * *

The next evening the chandler sent a taxi for Captain Graham, Wally Barnes, Beastie Willie and Chris for a run ashore. Ignacio met them in the Café Bar Tabaré, one of the oldest and best bars in the city. They had a glass or two of the national drink, grappamiel, a blend of alcohol and honey.

Later, they dined in Tango Bar El Hacha.

"I recommend the asado—meats from the grill," Ignacio said. "The stone walls you see are over 200 years old. The place has a unique mood."

A huge dinner followed. While the meat cooked they sampled chorizos, blood sausage, chitterlings, sweetbreads, and provoleta, a grilled provolone cheese.

Then there was a respite, fortified by excellent wine, Tannat. A deep red, fruity and soft, leaving ripe flavours on the tongue.

"You like the wine, gentlemen?" Ignacio said.

"Superb," Wally Barnes said, refilling his glass.

They went at it again, devouring short ribs, flank steak, a taste of chicken, and kid, with bread and a simple salad of lettuce, tomato and onion seasoned with lemon, olive oil and salt. More wine.

One day when he got back to Halifax, Chris meant to go beyond words and show Solene the depth of his love for her; he'd cook her such a banquet.

Chris alone accepted the challenge of dessert. He chose arroz con leche, a rich creamy rice pudding.

"Where do you put it, Chris?" Captain Graham said. "You're Rab Haw, the Glesca Glutton."

Laughter; Chris blushed. They nursed shots of grappa lemoni.

* * *

A dark, pretty girl gave Chris the eye. Chris didn't rate himself a dancer. An occasional shuffle round the Palais de Danses of Westburn on his evening off, wasting time chatting up gum-chewing hairies, the flinty girls of the woollen mill, the canning factory and ropeworks. But on his first visit to Buenos Aires, Amanda, the mature owner of a small bar in La Boca, had taught him to tango.

"That lassie fancies you, Chris," Beastie Willie said.

"I'm ready. Just one dance."

"Away with you, Chris; dance with her," Wally said. "And behave yourself."

Captain Graham grinned.

"I will, I will. Don't worry about me."

Half-cut with wine and grappa limone, he thought about Solene.

"Solene loves me, but just one dance. I wish she was here."

He offered his hand and the girl accepted. They waited for the music.

"I am Magali. What is your name?"

"I'm Chris, from Scotland."

A violin led, and behind it an accordion and a cello. With Magali's hand on his shoulder, she caught his movement.

"El Choclo; a classic," Chris said.

"You know tango?"

"I learned to tango in Buenos Aires; like a Portena."

"To tango is to be free."

They swayed with no space between them. Chris melded with Magali, Portena fashion, executing the walk and turns.

"Oh, Cristo, you can dance," Amanda said. "Hold me, trust me, lead me."

And he did, throwing Magali into a feline arch, and she, bending her left knee, thrusting a shapely right leg from the slashed opening of her long skirt.

Chris hexed Magali. The band played more classics: La Cumparsita, La Bordona, and several more; a half hour of Magali, in free-form dance. Tango with Magali was heaven.

She was a lovely girl, but Chris ached for Solene to be in his arms.

He returned Magali to her table. The girlfriend gazed at him.

"I like you, Cristo," Magali said "You tango like Portena. You like to sit with us?"

"I have a girl."
"She is not here."
Chris touched his heart. "She is here."
"Ah; I am sorry. You are good man, Cristo."

* * *

Above all things, Chris wanted the ship to sail from Montevideo, the navigators and engineers coaxing the Peliopadus to her top speed of seventeen knots, to be underway at sea bringing him closer to the day when he would be with Solene. Through the Panama Canal to Vancouver and Australia, closer to year's end, then the ship in home waters, heralding his return to Halifax and Solene.

Chris posted his packet of letters to Solene the day before the Peliopadus put to sea for the Panama Canal. They carried the plain words of a sailor. He prayed that she'd hear his voice. The final letter, written with a Parker 51 fountain pen filled with turquoise ink, bought in Montevideo, said everything about his love for her.

Dearest Solene,

My true, my only love.

Remember, when this voyage is over, we will be together always to love one another. I needed love, and now that I've found you, I am lost without you.

I long to hear your voice, to laugh with you and to make you happy.

My darling, you're lovely and unique; graceful, tender, sexy. I want to kiss your beautiful eyes. I adore you.

The desolate days alone at sea. But I speak to her, and I ask the waves to carry my love to you.

I dream of you. Darling Solene, may our love be more beautiful than any other love.

I say these things to bring you to my side.

Love me forever.
Many, many kisses.
All my love,
Chris

* * *

Eight days sailing from Montevideo to the Panama Canal. Days of rising early, in fine weather, and watching the sunrise. And if bad weather and rough seas, going straight to the galley for coffee, and there meeting the chef and Fernandez to discuss work for the day.

Chris had established high standards for Catering. He listened to the chef and Fernandez, and delegated, allowing them to run the galley and saloon. And he checked with the deck and engine room Serangs that the crew were well fed.

Chris led Catering, and his men respected him.

With breakfast over, Chris looked in on preparations for lunch, and checked stocks and established requirements to replenish stores at the next port. And once a week, prior to Captain Graham's Sunday inspection, he checked housekeeping in officers' quarters and Catering.

There was a young Glaswegian, a Junior Engineer, socially out of his depth, hiding his embarrassment behind a screen of bluster and bad manners. Chris had a word with him.

"The Steward's not your flunkey, or aboard to clean up after you. You don't keep engine room shoes and boiler suits in your cabin. They stay in the changing room. Keep your cabin clean and treat the steward with respect."

"S'at a fact, mate?"

Chris heard all the contempt this stripling of twenty had for the men of Catering who served and looked after him.

"I'm not your mate. I'm Chief Steward. You're one of four Junior Engineers aboard. You know sweet fuck-all."

The Junior Engineer began squaring up to Chris. Chris shoved him against the bulkhead.

"Don't even think about it, son. You want sacked, a double DR in your discharge book? Behave like an officer, or the chief'll bounce you ashore at the next port."

Chris turned at the cabin door.

"Now listen, mister, at table don't chew your food with your mouth open; it's disgusting. You don't eat peas with your knife. You cut the food with the knife and use the fork to eat. Got that?"

The Junior Engineer's face turned brick red and he looked down at the cabin deck.

"And for Christ's sake, use the showers. Or you might find your shipmates'll work you over with a scrubbing brush."

Chris later mentioned the incident to Wally Barnes.

"He'll trap now, Wally. He'll behave himself."

"Thanks, Chris. I'll have a word with him."

* * *

"Twelve locks in the fifty-mile length of the Canal," Captain Graham said.

Chris had asked permission to come on the bridge, watched the captain, hands on his command. The ship was Captain Graham's responsibility, in spite of the Peliopadus being in the charge of a canal pilot.

"How long does it take, sir?" Chris asked.

"Between eight and ten hours till we get to the Pacific."

No mail came on board from Colón, the port at the Atlantic entry to the Canal.

"Stop worrying, Chris," Captain Graham said. "The agent'll bring the mail once we're through the Canal and bunkering in Balboa."

Solene's letters; a euphoric Chris was pierced with the lightning flashes of her love when he read and reread the pages of her letters. By the tenth reading, the blue bond writing paper was already rubbed thin by his caresses; potent words in blue ink from her fountain pen flowed across the page; Solene's strong hand, the lingering fragrance of her perfume. Chris felt the force of Solene's love.

"Chris is crazy about that girl," Wally Barnes said to Captain Graham.

"He's a happy man. I hope it lasts. A black woman and a white man together. They're on a hard road."

Shipboard life, the true and tested routines of life afloat, carried Chris through eighteen days steaming from Balboa to Vancouver.

The routine was broken by the deck Tindal, the Serang's assistant. He'd complained of a toothache three days out from Montevideo.

The First Mate came to see Chris. "Have a look at him, will you? He might be malingering."

The Tindal's jaw was swollen and he moaned when Chris touched a back tooth with a probe.

"Might be an abscess; hard to tell. I'm a first aid man, not a dentist."

Chris gave the Tindal oil of cloves to apply to the tooth. Captain Graham had Beastie Willie send a radio message asking for advice. The reply said, besides oil of cloves, to give him a course of penicillin to kill any infections. And he should see a dentist in Balboa.

The Tindal had several days off work, claiming sickness from lack of sleep and toothache. The Mate sent him ashore with the Third Mate in Balboa, where a dentist extracted the tooth and drained a small abscess. The Mate had the Tindal back at work that afternoon.

Two days later at sea, the Mate came to see Chris.

"He's at it again, Chris; malingering. Lazy bugger claims the dentist took out the wrong tooth. Says he can't sleep from the pain and wants off duty."

"Bring him to the office in an hour. I'll have a look at him, and if he is at it, I'll frighten the shite out of him."

Chris got out the medical kit and laid probe, forceps, scalpel, hypodermic syringe, and novocaine on a white tablecloth covering the desk.

The Mate propelled the Tindal through the cabin door.

"He says his mouth hurts."

"Ah, McCoull Sahib. Dentist; man of no account. Pull wrong tooth. Make number one pain. No sleep."

Chris pointed to the office chair.

"Sit down, Tindal."

Chris pushed him back into the chair until his head hung over the back. He showed the Tindal the tools.

"I'll probe around your teeth. If I have to pull the tooth, I'll stick this needle into your gum, and inject novocaine to reduce the pain." Chris picked up the scalpel and showed it to the Tindal.

"I might have to slit your gum."

He waved the forceps in front of the Tindal's face, now covered with a film of greasy sweat. "Then I'll pull out your tooth. It'll be over in no time."

Chris made a wrenching, twisting movement with the forceps.

The Tindal's eyes rolled back in his head; he moaned.

"Oh, McCoull Sahib, this bring more pain. I afraid."

The Mate stood grinning behind the chair.

Chris forced the Tindal's mouth wide open. He moved the probe round the empty socket where the Balboa dentist had removed the tooth.

"Does that hurt?"

"Oh, oh, is much better, McCoull Sahib."

"Close to three weeks until Vancouver. I'd better just pull the teeth on either side of the socket; just to be sure."

The Tindal shot out of the chair.

"McCoull Sahib, you number one damned fine fellow. Give Tindal aspirin. Much better. Leave teeth."

The Tindal went back to work clutching a bottle of aspirin.

"He'll be okay now," the Mate said. "He's a good man."

* * *

Mail came aboard at Vancouver, but there was nothing for Chris. He felt low, and dashed off letters seeking assurance that Solene was not ill, that she was alright.

At Vancouver they discharged frozen beef, and the Peliopadus loaded general cargo for Melbourne and Darwin, Australia. A distraught Chris was hoping, praying that a letter from Solene would arrive before the Peliopadus made her way across the Pacific.

Sailing north from Balboa to Vancouver, past Mexico, the wireless had picked up American radio stations. One song stuck in his mind: *You Send Me*, by Sam Cooke. The words were a mantra of hope and love for Chris. Every time he heard it he thought about Solene and it made him feel good.

Darling, you send me…
Honest you do…
At first I thought it was infatuation
But, woo, it's lasted so long…
Now I find myself wanting
To marry you and take you home…

By the time the Peliopadus sailed, and with no letters from Solene, the lyric had become a punishment, a curse, a scab on his heart.

Chris thought he kept his pain hidden, forgetting what he knew well: aboard the ship, much that one might want to remain private was visible to shipmates.

Captain Graham worried.

"The job runs as well as it ever did. But he's working too bloody hard. Wally, keep an eye on him."

One morning, while Chris was meeting the chef and Fernandez to discuss the day's work, the ship was heaving and twisting in heavy seas; creaking, screeching wood and metal; engine racing, then slowing as the governor cut in when the screw came out of the water. The Peliopadus dropped and shuddered into a trough between waves and threw Fernandez against Chris, sending him staggering, knocking coffee cup and saucer out of his hand, to shatter on the galley deck. Chris snapped.

"For fuck's sake, Fernandez, have you lost your fucking sea legs?"

A shocked Fernandez picked up a spotless dish cloth to dab dry Chris's fresh khaki uniform shirt and pants.

"So sorry, McCoull Sahib."

"Go to hell."

Chris left the galley, furious at himself, vexed that he'd cut Fernandez, who couldn't answer back. Fernandez, his right arm, a man he liked, and who liked and respected Chris; a good friend.

"I have to put this right. What a cunt I am. I'm getting like that bastard Wiggins. I was right out of line."

Chris phoned the galley.

"Fernandez, come on round to the office."

Moments later a knock came at the door.

"Come in."

Fernandez stood in front of Chris. His red eyes cut Chris to the quick. His friend needed a drink.

Chris got up and pulled out a chair.

"Fernandez, please sit down."

"I stand, McCoull Sahib," he said, voice thick with emotion.

Chris wrung his hands, on the verge of upset. *He* needed a bloody drink.

"I am sorry I said that to you. There's no excuse; none. Please accept my apology."

Fernandez nodded, fighting hard to contain his emotion. He wiped his eyes with the sleeve of his white serving jacket.

Chris handed him a clean handkerchief.

"I'm so, so sorry, my friend."

He laid his hand on Fernandez's shoulder, easing him into the chair. He got out the office bottle and poured two shots of Glen Fiddich.

"Fernandez, we both need a drink."

Chris raised his glass and waited. His heart was glad when Fernandez raised his glass and the glasses rang.

"We're still friends?"

Fernandez managed a smile and nodded.

"Fernandez, you are number one damned fine fellow."

They drank off the malt whisky. Chris didn't want anyone to see his friend upset; he was upset himself.

"Fernandez, take the morning off. I'll look after breakfast."

"I do lunch."

They rose and Chris extended his hand for a firm handshake.

"McCoull Sahib, you are good man, Atcha Walla; proper Pukka Sahib. I pray letters come for you in Australia."

"Thanks, my friend."

Chris went to the galley. He grabbed the chef and they went out on deck.

"Chef, I'm sorry about what happened in the galley. I've apologised to Fernandez. I'll fill in for breakfast."

"Thank you, McCoull Sahib."

Breakfast finished, Chris stood midships on deck, swaying with the movement of the ship. He felt hand on his shoulder.

"You all right Chris? Everything okay?" Wally Barnes asked.

"No, it's not all right. I made a right fucking mess of things this morning."

Chris told Wally what had happened with Fernandez.

"Oh, Chris, that is bad. I saw him down aft looking glum. He's a bloody good bloke, Fernandez."

"I know, and he's a friend, my right arm. I could kick myself."

"Chris, you're like a hen with a sore arse. Everyone's been dancing on eggshells around you since Vancouver. You know letters can go adrift, and miss the ship. Solene's letters will be waiting for you when we dock in Melbourne."

"I didn't realise it showed so much. Sorry, Wally."

"Look Chris, you've got friends on the Peliopadus who worry about you."

* * *

For Chris, the crossing of the Pacific was desolate. He attended to the ship's routine and kept sane. But at night, and when he was alone, the worry that something had happened to Solene ate into him. He didn't want to think that this lovely girl had thrown him over.

Captain Graham worried more about him.

"You're looking a bit gaunt, Chris. Everything okay?"

Chris shrugged. "I'm holding on, sir. I hope my mail catches up with me in Melbourne."

"It usually does, eventually. Probably just a hiccup. Think of all those hours reading her letters. You've been writing to Solene?"

"I hope you're right, sir. Yes, I've been writing every day. I sent off a packet of letters before we left Vancouver."

But there was no mail waiting for Chris in Melbourne.

By now, none of the shipmates mentioned mail to him. He went ashore a couple of times with Wally Barnes and Beastie Willie. He took in nothing of Melbourne. It could have been the dark side of the moon. At night, Black Dog haunted Chris.

Sailing north to Darwin was a jail sentence. He'd just about given up on ever hearing from Solene again. Going on without her, the creeping realisation that he might never see her again deepened his love for her—the out-of-reach perfect love.

More than anyone else on board, Fernandez worried about Chris. He could see his boss, his mentor, his most valued friend disintegrating: deep shadows under tired eyes from restless, sleepless nights. Chris's appetite failed; he skipped meals, lost weight, his uniform KDs hanging on a gaunt frame.

Chris worked harder than ever, but it was by super-human effort he overcame crippling lethargy.

Fernandez dared not cross that invisible but palpable barrier existing between the European officers and Indian and Goanese crew. Not that the officers treated the crew harshly. The men were looked after, treated fairly and with respect. Captain Graham, the Chief Engineer, Wally Barnes, and Chris set the highest standards of leadership and conduct.

The Peliopadus docked at Darwin, and Chris dreaded the delivery of the mail. He saw the agent mounting the brow to be met by Captain Graham. Chris sent Fernandez to pick up the mail bag, sort it by department and distribute the contents.

"One envelope for you, McCoull Sahib."

Fernandez handed Chris a large stiff brown envelope well bound with sellotape to keep it sealed. A bold ornate hand had printed several times on the envelope, "Do not bend: photographs."

The hand on the envelope was not Solene's. Chris's stomach hollowed out, a painful empty space. He struggled with pain, and the threat of loose bowels. His dick shrank.

The fan blew hot, humid air around the cabin. Cold sweat trickled down his torso, darkening the sides and back of his khaki uniform shirt. Chris picked up the large envelope and slit the seals with his pocket knife.

The envelope contained a dozen black and white photographs, and a letter from Hank Gill, the owner of Lindy's.

Solene and Chris had gone there several times. Chris glanced at the letter and followed Hank's guidance.

Dear Chris,

This is Hank Gill from Lindy's writing to tell you what has happened to Solene. I hadn't seen her for a few days and went to her apartment to see if she was okay.

There's a note from Solene in a blue envelope. Read my letter first. Look at the pictures, then read her note. She dashed it off before I left her apartment.

Her mother dropped dead in Martinique. Right after the funeral, her father came to Halifax demanding Solene give up her practice and return home to take care of him and the family home.

Solene refused and told him about you and your plans to marry and settle in Halifax. He raged, out of control because you're a white man, and beat his daughter. There's a picture showing Solene's injuries.

If Solene had gone on refusing to return to Martinique, he might have killed her.

They vanished after ten days, Solene's practice and her property put in the hands of lawyers to sell. He's a nasty old man; a monster.

I wanted to sort the bastard out, and for Solene to come away with me and stay with my wife and kids until he left. I reckoned he'd never find us, but Solene said I didn't know her father and it would just make things worse. She worried her father would come back, find me and punish her.

Solene didn't go to hospital. She treated herself. She worried about her younger sisters, for her elder brother lives in fear of the old devil and will do nothing. Her younger brother is away in the French Navy.

I wasn't sure about you when you came with her to Lindy's, Solene being black and you being white. There's nasty people around who'd hate you for just being together. Her father is a cruel example. I'm a black man; but I'm not like him.

I enclose two pictures of the band, a memento. The rest are of you and Solene. You didn't know I had you in the lens, so you're both natural. You and Solene are in love, and I caught the mood. Two people so right for each other.

If I hear from Martinique, I'll write. If I can help, contact me.
Best wishes,
Hank

Chris searched for the picture: the head and shoulders of his beloved; face punched and slapped. Right eye closed, the left eye half shut, bruised cheeks and brow, swollen nose and face. Rage and horror at Solene's father consumed Chris, a thick gorge coursing through his body, becoming a herculean desire to thrash a father who beat and injured his loving daughter. Then anger ebbed, and a whirlpool of despair sucked Chris down.

He turned to the blue envelope, clinging to a sliver of hope, running his fingers across Solene's handwriting, then sliding the small blade of his pocket knife under the seal.

Darling Chris,

What happened is terrible, my mother dead and my father drinking, grieving, in the grip of madness, dragging me home to God knows what. My father attacked me when I told him about us. I'm terrified if I refuse to return home he'll kill me.

My darling, I'll always love you, and long for you. I don't know what is going to happen in Martinique, or for how long I'll be tied there.

Close your eyes, my love, and I'll be with you. I am proud of my broken heart; proud of the pain I felt when you went away; proud of our love that no one can take away from us.

When I can, I'll come to you.
All my love, my dearest Chris,
Solene

He examined the pictures of Solene and himself, and then laid them out on his desk. Black and white photographs taken without a flash in low light. Hank had a good eye. He'd caught the moment when Solene said, "Ask me to dance." Chris's face was cast in shadowed profile. Using the dim light of Lindy's, Hank had caught Solene smiling at Chris. He'd also captured Solene kissing him, a brief, intense brushing of lips. There was a picture of them standing lit by a street light outside Lindy's, waiting for a cab—the few minutes when they'd acknowledged their newfound love. Chris heard his words and Solene's reply.

"I'll drop you, then he can run me to the ship."

"We have a bit more than a month, Chris. It's not long enough. Tonight, stay with me a while."

"It's okay if I stay? I mean, you're sure?"

"I'm sure, Chris. Stay with me."

He'd never known such desolation; could not ever have imagined how low he now felt. Black Dog made Chris feel sick.

"Oh Christ," he muttered.

Solene must be in agony, perhaps worse than himself, going through the emotional and spiritual horrors while she carried the pain and disfigurement of the beating given by her father. Chris sank lower still, powerless to struggle out from the vortex of despair.

He read her letter again and her words lifted him. She was strong, maybe stronger than him. He felt an overpowering urge to go to Solene, to give succour. He prayed that Solene might find a way. If she asked him, he would go to Martinique.

By early evening, word had leaked out to the ship: Chris had received a large envelope bringing bad news.

* * *

The engine room Serang liked Chris and worried about him. He took a chance and, dressed in his best camice, lungi and well-polished chapples, knocked on the office door.

"Come in," Chris called.

The Serang hovered in the door, grinning and waggling his head, anxious that he might upset a good man.

"Ah, McCoull Sahib. Good evening, sir."

"Come on in, Serang. Sit down."

Chris picked up the phone and asked Fernandez to send round a pot of coffee and currant cake. The Serang had a sweet tooth and he loved milky sweet coffee and cake. The pot of coffee and cake came in a trice. Chris played Mum, pouring and milking the Serang's cup. He added three teaspoonfuls of sugar and stirred it in.

"How's that, Serang?"

"Oh, one more sugar, sir."

They drank coffee and ate cake in silence. The Serang covered his mouth and coughed.

"Excuse me, McCoull Sahib, but I worry something wrong with food. Bhandari ask why you no have curry anymore."

"Oh, nothing's wrong with the curries. Best I've tasted; I say they're the best in the Michas Lines fleet."

"Thank you, thank you, McCoull Sahib. I tell Bhandari; make him very happy."

"I wasn't as hungry the last few weeks."

The Serang had come out of concern for Chris, who knew full well the courage it took for this kind man to visit and risk a dressing down. There were a few officers aboard who'd be affronted by an Indian crewman's concern; would have humiliated the Serang for daring to visit, and sent him packing.

Chris felt honoured and respected by this good man. He was proud to belong to the Peliopadus.

Chris offered the Serang more coffee and cake. The Serang moved in the chair. He wanted to say something, but found it difficult to begin.

"Ah, McCoull Sahib, today I go with Bhandari to fishing boat. We buy golden snapper. All fish." He extended his hands more than two feet. "Very good fish. I eat last time here."

The Serang explained that the Bhandari had bought prawns too.

"Tomorrow night I bring curried prawns, then curried golden snapper, chapatis, saffron rice."

Chris's eyes brightened. This kind seafarer made him feel human again.

"Serang, you honour me. Thank you. Can I invite the Chief Engineer?"

"Acha, Sahib. Chief Engineer and you: Acha Wallahs; Pukka Sahibs."

"Can I help with the expense?"

"Oh no, McCoull Sahib. Is from us to you. We serve here?"

"Yes."

"Fernandez make table and serve you and chief."

So Fernandez was in on this too. Chris felt better about the world.

* * *

Wally Barnes and Chris sipped gin and tonics while waiting for the curried prawns and fish.

"I'm not poking my nose in, Chris, but I gather you've had bad news."

"Yes; very bad. Solene's been dragged back to Martinique. Her father's made her a prisoner."

He handed the head-and-shoulders picture of Solene to Wally.

"Her old man did that."

"Jesus Christ, Chris, that's awful. Her father did that? He's off his head. A bad bastard."

The Peliopadus was in Darwin discharging general cargo from Melbourne, now loading frozen beef and dairy produce for the UK. It had been eight days since Chris received the package from Hank Gill, and Solene's letter, the only word from her since the ship had left Montevideo.

Chris felt bad, but had started picking himself up, recognising that he couldn't go on languishing in the Slough of Despond during the solitude of a long voyage home. Wallowing in Despond, he'd remain a pain in the arse to his friends and shipmates. Worse, he might be tempted to throw himself over the side.

"I've been brooding on it since we came alongside and I got the letters and the pictures. There's nothing I can do. I'm powerless. I've asked for leave. I thought about flying to Martinique once I paid off, but her father's a nutter. I might get Solene hurt again, or worse, killed. Time for home, Wally."

"You're right going home, son. Rest up; get well again."

Beastie Willie had made the voyage from Canada to the Antipodes some years before, had said after Darwin, the Peliopadus was bound for Japan. A year ago orders for Japan would have excited Chris. Everyone aboard who'd been to the Home Islands said the Japanese girls were special. But a year ago he hadn't met Solene.

Chris and Wally Barnes pushed chairs back from table. Chris poured two shots of Glen Fiddich to ease digestion. Wally had his pipe going well, the bowl glowing red as he puffed, sending up clusters of sweet-smelling smoke from the aromatic tobacco.

"What a meal, Chris. That Bhandari can make a curry. Delicious prawns, and the fish."

The chief shook his head in silent admiration.

"How about the presentation? The Serang was dead chuffed bringing in the serving dishes. And Fernandez; he's a brilliant waiter."

"You're feeling better, Chris. I can tell."

A butler would not replace Chris. As the ships in the Michas fleet changed crews, Chief Stewards came on board. On the job they'd be assisted by a Goanese Second Steward.

"I hope we get a good man, Chris. You're a hard act to follow."

No one on board wanted a skinflint eager to skim off the top, a return to the bad old days of Jangler Jim and the butler.

"I've sailed with some evil Chief Stewards," Wally said. "Bastards like Half-a-Kipper Turner, Bread-and-Butter Sammy, Sparing Waring, and Jack The Rat."

Chris had heard these stories several times from Wally—split a kipper between two men, and one sausage shared at breakfast.

"Captain Graham'll sit on him until he gets it right," Chris said.

* * *

For five years Chris had had little desire for leave. He would take a day or two off when the Peliopadus was in port for a week or more, but no more than that.

"How long, sir?"

"We'll be in London, Royal Docks, on the thirty-second day after leaving Darwin. Close to eleven thousand miles,

He handed Chris a note from the radio office in Beastie Willie's hand.

"Your leave has come through."

Chris had about five months' leave due. The route was imprinted on his brain after a few beers with Beastie Willie the previous evening. Out of Darwin and into the Timor Sea, on to the Indian Ocean and the Arabian Sea. Turn into the Gulf of Aden, through Bap el Mandib—the Gates of Hell, Willie called it. Chris was sure he'd have a sense of Europe in the Gulf of Suez for passage through the Suez Canal. Through the Med, the Straits of Gibraltar. Past the west coast of Spain and enter the Bay of Biscay.

"The Channels'll hit you then, Chris."

Chris laughed. "Got the Channels already, Willie. I suppose it'll get worse once we're in the Channel and sailing up the Thames."

Chris had no expectations of a better life in Westburn. He suffered heartache over Solene. It irked daily that he could do nothing for her. Going to Martinique might put both of them in danger. He and Solene, victims of her father's rage. Had Solene dumped him, thrown him over, it might have been easier to bear the pain by hating her.

Chris needed to see the Rinaldis; his real family. He hurt from losing Solene, suffered emotional scars he'd carry for the rest of his life. Chris realised that wherever he moved on to, Solene would be with him. He'd burdened his shipmates enough, and recognised that while it was right to feel sorrow, he had to pick himself up if he wanted to keep the respect of his shipmates.

When he arrived home he'd not want to burden Dante and Chiarina. He'd lick his wounds in solitude.

Chapter Eleven

"Taxi from Royal Docks to Euston Station, Caledonian Express, First Class, Chris, all the way," Captain Graham said. "The agent has booked your ticket and reserved a seat. Send your expenses to the London Office."

Chris's relief had come on board the previous day, a Second Steward out of Hungry Hogarth's lured to Michas Lines by better wages, improved conditions and promotion. He seemed to know his job and the handover went smoothly.

Chris found it hard to let go after five years aboard the ship. He prolonged the leavetaking.

"First time sailing with Indian and Goanese crew?" Chris said.

"Yes."

"The Chief Engineer can help you learn Urdu. There's a lot of goodwill from the crew if you master the basics. I asked about it and he said to come round to his day room once you're settled in."

"Thanks."

"Work with them. They won't mind you keeping your hand in. They're dead loyal. The engine room Serang is a good bloke. You'll be working with him when you buy Halal supplies. The chef is good; very reliable. Fernandez is an outstanding Second Steward."

Chris took his leave, and said farewell to the captain, Wally Barnes and Beastie Willie.

"Take it easy, Chris," Wally Barnes said. "I hope we'll be shipmates again."

"Amen to that," Willie said.

"We'll meet again, Chris," the captain said.

A farewell party of the crew gathered at the brow. Some of the men had shipped two and three times with Chris; they knew him well. In the lead were Fernandez and the engine room Serang. The deck Serang sent a couple of sailors to carry Chris's luggage off the ship to the waiting taxi taking him to Euston Station.

The engine room Serang came forward.

"Good bye-bye, McCoull Sahib. You are number one damned fine fellow."

They shook hands. He handed Chris a package: a hard object, something sewn into a thick cotton wrap.

"Open on train."

"Thank you, Serang."

The deck Serang shook hands with him, and then Fernandez, who broke with protocol and embraced Chris.

"Good bye-bye, McCoull Sahib. With the Blessing, I sail with you again."

In less than an hour Chris was in Euston Station. A porter took his luggage and stowed it in the racks of the first-class compartment. Chris, flush and feeling strange to be off the ship, gave him a generous tip and settled into his reserved seat.

The Caledonian chugged out of London gathering speed, shooting along the track, clattering across points, through signals, past the outskirts of the capital. The rhythmic clickety-clack of the wheels beat out *Solene Aimie, Solene Aimie*. Chris, depressed enough as it was, thought he might go mad. He pushed the beat of the wheels on the track to the back of his mind and fetched the crew's present from one of his soft folding bags.

He cast an admiring eye over the thin-bladed, smooth, golden brown teak letter knife, with an edge and point. He placed the knife in the shallow recess on the compact desk stand of matching wood with a slot for a couple of fountain pens and round holes at each end for ink bottles.

One of the Chippy's mates, a crewman, had carved it from a piece of solid teak, sanding the edges and surface to a fine smoothness. Letter knife and desk stand were both sealed with clear varnish, preserving the colours and grain for years to come. That the crew thought well enough of him to make this beautiful gift moved Chris. He felt his throat swelling, and swallowed hard.

"Maybe I should have stayed on the ship," he murmured.

He laughed, remembering the night when he'd had a few beers with Beastie Wille, and Willie had named him the Peliopadus's Ancient Mariner.

"Chris, you'll be on the ship forever, sailing the Seven Seas."

It was a quiet train. Chris travelled without company, the sole occupant of the first-class compartment all the way to Glasgow.

By the time the Caledonian had passed to the South Midlands, sadness at leaving the Peliopadus had given way to the euphoria of going home after five years away. To see Dante again, and all the Rinaldis who'd made his life worthwhile.

A late sitting at lunch lifted the gloom. He dined well. Silver service, liveried, white-coated waiters served excellent food. A gin and tonic sharpened his appetite for Scotch broth, roast leg of lamb, carrots and peas, and boiled new potatoes; a half bottle of claret followed, along with apple tart and custard, black coffee and a shot of brandy.

A full stomach brought contentment. The background clack of wheels on the track and the quiet comfort of the first-class compartment sent him to sleep and a bad dream. His father, a ghostly drunk risen from the grave, more resolute than he'd ever been in life. In step, the Good Mother's spirit, a wraith, weighed down by wine. Chris wondered if she had died. They beckoned him and he fought the temptation to join them.

He fell into space and felt he was leaving life. The dark held Chris and he struggled, opening his eyes, searching for a way out. He jerked awake, drenched in sweat.

Faraway an announcement: the train was approaching Glasgow Central. The spoor of sulphurous burning stone coated his tongue, fouled his mouth and polluted his nose. Chris bottled down fear and wiped cold sweat from his face with a disgusted glance at his creased, rumpled clothes.

Chris alighted the Caledonian at Platform One. An elderly porter placed his luggage on a barrow and hurried him across to Platform Fifteen.

"There's a train to Westburn in five minutes."

Luggage on board and in the racks, Chris handed him a ten-shilling note.

"Kind of you, sir; many thanks."

He moved in his seat, a restless twisting of his legs. Chris forced himself awake, shutting out the nightmare on the Caledonian. He made a hurried sign of the cross.

* * *

Saturday night, an hour after leaving Glasgow, the train slowed to a halt in Westburn. Little had changed at the West Station in the five years that Chris had been at sea. The last steam from the engine drifted skywards into the dark as the train rattled through the tunnel heading for Fort Matilda and Kempock. He saw the jungle of vivid green moss sprouting from the cracks and decayed cement pointing of the red sandstone retaining wall, water leaking, gathering in puddles and damp patches on the platform.

Outside the station doors, the first thing he noticed was the spare ground where a couple of shops had been demolished. A caravan was parked beside an ancient saloon car, a pole stuck in among the small stones, with a sign on top: Johnny's Taxis.

The West Station area was quiet, pubs shutting at nine o' clock. Chris recognised Fat O'Rourke; he'd been a couple of years ahead of Chris in school. A drunk Fat emptied his bladder, the piss steaming up from the glass of the phone box. His mate—Chris didn't recognise him—was bent double honking, puke splattering the pavement.

Chris's eye rested on the shop front of Roy's Gents' Hairdressers, the bright spot among the last of the shabby shops. He ruffled his reddish-fair hair. Monday, he'd go in for a haircut and enjoy the ill-natured ribbing from Wee Charlie, wielding scissors and comb, snipping close to his ears, daring him to answer back. Chris grinned, picking up his bags.

"It's Westburn."

He saw a middle-aged couple cross the road, staggering over rough ground towards the caravan, the woman collapsing in the man's arms. Her hoarse, maudlin voice drifted over the spare ground. He'd know that voice anywhere.

"Ah'm naebody's child. Ah'm naebody's child.

Naebody wants me; Ah'm naebody's child."

Chris leaned forward for a closer look. He didn't recognise the man—younger than the Good Mother, and drunk, but holding it well. A new man taking his father's place. Chris's movement caught her eye. She stopped and peered, her vision distorted by myopia and drink.

"That you, Chris?"

Chris remained silent.

The Good Mother turned to her consort.

"That's Chris, ma stepson hame tae see his Good Mother."

The couple re-crossed the road and stood in front of Chris; he weighed them up. The man was in his late forties, in a cheap dark suit, tie awry. Strong build but running to seed, a big gut preventing him closing his jacket. Drink had worn her down, but the Good Mother had not yet sunk as low as the wraith in his bad dream.

"This is ma new fella, Rab Cowan; jist call him Rab. Have ye no' got a wee present for yer Good Mother, Chris?"

He nodded and, wanting rid of them, decided to hand over a few quid.

"Ah'm no' stayin' long. Here's a fiver. Huv a drink on me."

"Thanks, son. Yer a good boy right enough. We're livin' oot on fourteen Auchmead Road. Ma name's on the door, as well as Rab's. Come and see us. We'll huv a wee party fur ye."

Chris shuddered at the thought of a visit to the pits of desolation where he'd be expected to pay for a cargo of booze.

"If there's time Ah'll mebbe come and see ye."

"Cheerio then, Chris. Be seein' ye."

"No' if Ah can help it," Chris murmured.

But he had not seen the last of her, and he knew it. Knowing that Chris had come home, the Good Mother would surface again, ferreting him out, begging for drinking money.

The Good Mother and Rab Cowan staggered back across the road to get a taxi.

"Four or five months of this. Christ, Ah'll never stick it," Chris muttered, thinking of Solene, light years from the sordidness he'd just encountered. Solene, so beautiful and tender, his lost love.

"Ah wish right now we were together."

Chris touched his two folding service bags; he'd gotten the luggage from an American Marine in Norfolk, Virginia, for a couple of bottles of whisky. He'd departed for sea with a beat up old case secured by a broad leather strap, but finished up giving it to Fernandez. He waited, unable to leave the shabbiness of the West Station, elbows resting on the railings at the edge of the pavement, looking across the streets. This was Chris's neighbourhood, where he'd grown up, passing through on his way to school. There was the La Scala cinema with the Saturday matinees he'd loved until the Good Mother came and stopped him going.

"Fuckin' old cow," he said.

Chris had hated when his old man married her, an Irish harridan meant to replace his mum. By his early teens his life was a cycle of beatings and bad food, in a squalid tenement flat, and mockery at school for his dirty, ragged clothes.

Chris spat, getting rid of the lump in his throat.

"Ah'm no fuckin' tramp now."

He looked down at his sturdy, expensive Australian boots, the khaki jeans.

He always felt good in the navy pea jacket bought in Norfolk, and the best quality Hathaway shirt underneath it—there were more than a dozen in his luggage and the quality clothing for going ashore, his tailored khakis for the ship, and the chef's clothing for the ship's galley.

Johnny's taxi crept out from the spare ground, and passed heading west to the housing schemes built on the frontiers of Westburn, his drunken Good Mother slumped in the back.

"Thank God Ah don't live out there," Chris whispered.

Sharp right turn, walk fifty yards up Newton Street, and Chris turned into Dante Rinaldi's chip shop.

Dante's head came up and he vaulted across the serving counter, white apron flying, and grabbed Chris by the shoulders.

"Jesus Christ, Chris. You could've written and let me know. Yer lookin' well, son."

But Dante saw behind the smart appearance the haggard inner Chris. Up close, the tired eyes were deeper set than he remembered. Chris looked lean, but to Dante's friendly, knowing eye, Chris could do with putting on a pound or two.

Dante had moved the fish fryer back to open out the front of the shop. Four new dining booths and five tables and chairs seating about thirty people filled the space. Fresh cream paint work.

"It's no' just a chipper. It's a fish restaurant, and doin' well. Hungry?"

"I'm hungry, Dante, for one of your fish teas."

Chris liked the changes Dante had made to the shop. He ate in silence as Dante wiped down, turned off the fryer, preparing to shut the shop for the night. He sat in the back of a booth, closed his knife and fork, ate the last slice of bread and butter and drained his tea cup.

"Dante, no doubt about it. Best fish tea anywhere."

"Thanks, son."

Dante hadn't changed much—a bit heavier perhaps, but he remained the same man Chris loved as an older brother and the sole person he'd sent postcards from abroad.

Chris, hidden in the booth, heard loud drunken voices breaking into a ragged chorus of The Sash. Four men in their thirties spilled through the shop door. Eighty thousand people in Westburn and four Blue Noses—Protestants who hadn't stopped hating Catholics, out looking for trouble—came into Dante's shop. Chris wrung his hands, then wiped the palms on a paper napkin. There would be a fight.

"Four fish suppers, big man," one said.

"Sorry, boys, shop's closing."

"Ye'd serve a Fenian," another one said.

"Ah serve anybody, an' if you're Fenian, Ah'm still closing. Good night, boys. Away home."

Chris murmured, "Here we go. Religion, Westburn's tablespoon of bile."

He meant to get in the first dig and finish it before the brawl got out of hand. He'd learned that working in The Old Hotel and at sea.

Gut shrinking, mouth dry, he reached into the fold of his soft case, grabbing the taped end with a sweaty palm, and withdrew a sawn-off wooden shaft brought from the Peliopadus.

Dante came from behind the counter.

"Go home."

"Fuckin' Eyetie-Tims," one Blue Nose said, loosening up to throw a punch.

Chris moved, driving the shaft end into the kidneys of the two men standing back; they collapsed on the floor. Dante head-butted the loudmouth and Chris cracked the skull of the other man. Blood ran down his shirt collar.

"Clear off," Chris said.

"Aye, do that," Dante said. "Big Lachie's due any minute."

Sergeant Lachlan Ponsonby, Westburn Constabulary, coming for his supper.

"Don't come back here," Chris said.

"Trouble, Dante?" Sergeant Ponsonby said later as he tucked into fish and chips saved for him. "Ah had a look at they four comin' out the shop. Not from this part of Westburn."

"Just noise."

"Didn't hit them, did you son?"

"No, sir," Chris said, the sawn-off wooden shaft hidden again in his luggage. "But a couple of them fell at the door."

"Good. Enjoyed the fish supper," Sergeant Ponsonby said, laying payment on the counter. "Goodnight, Dante; goodnight, Chris. Ah remember when you were a wee boy." He smiled and left.

"Big Lachie's all right; straight as a die; knows the score. He's got plenty of common sense. Where are you stayin', Chris?"

"How about callin' The Old Hotel"?

"How about stayin' with Chiarina and me? The weans'll love it. Ah told you about the wee girls?"

"You did, you sent me a couple of letters. Thanks. Ah'll find digs by Monday."

"No need, son. Sure ye know Chiarina likes you."

Chris was glad to hear it.

"I'll phone Chiarina and let her know you're here. Then Ah'll get the car."

Dante helped Chris carry his luggage into the house. They struggled with the weight of the bags until they reached the bedroom.

"You'll be fine in here," Dante said.

Chris looked around the bedroom. Plain white walls, a plaster rose cornice, twelve-foot ceilings, a double window facing the river, where the lights of anchored ships twinkled. Old, ample furniture: wardrobe, dressing table, two chairs at the double window. And a grand double bed with a white counterpane.

"You come into money, Dante?"

"Ah'm doin' okay, Chris. Come down to the livin' room when yer ready, an' we'll have a drink, an' ye'll sleep well.

* * *

"Jap whisky? You're kiddin' me, Chris," Dante said.

"Yamazaki; that's a twelve-year-old malt; light. Good tastes of dried fruits and honey. An' this is a fifteen-year-old malt; heavy body an' a taste of spicy cherries. Ah picked up the whisky when the Peliopadus bunkered in Aden."

While Dante poured two measures of the twelve-year-old Malt, Chiarina came downstairs in her robe and slippers, wakened by the voices and the opening and shutting of doors. Dante poured another measure, a small one.

"Oh, Chris, I wondered when you were due home. It's been five years. Come here."

Chiarina took Chris by the shoulders, looked up and kissed him on both cheeks. "I'm so glad you're safe and well."

Chris remembered when he met Chiarina for the first time. He'd brought the meat sauce from The Old Hotel for the evening meal. She'd been pretty and demure, sitting up straight in a fireside chair, in the Rinaldis' living room on Holmscroft Street. Hands folded on her lap, legs pressed together. Dante had introduced them. She'd had no English, smiled, blushed a little when she said, ciao. A country girl dressed for town, wearing simple, well-cared-for clothes. A plain dark blue woolen skirt, an off-white cotton blouse under a dark blue woolen jersey. Thick woollen stockings and sensible shoes.

Now Chris saw a beautiful woman in her twenties, and in wearing her night things had not yet removed her makeup. She had a flawless ivory complexion, dark brown hair bright and shiny. She'd filled out, being the mother of two daughters. Chiarina was sultry, attractive; a fulfilled wife and mother.

She sipped her whisky but didn't finish it.

"Don't keep Chris up late, Dante."

The friends lingered over the Yamazaki malt.

"Good stuff," Dante said.

The clock chimed midnight, and they had another, this time a shot of the fifteen-year-old malt.

"You're not married, Chris, are you? You don't have a wife in a foreign port somewhere?"

"I met a lovely girl in Halifax, Nova Scotia. Her name's Solene Aimie."

Chris explained that he'd met Solene when she treated him for toothache.

"She's black; from Martinique."

"A black girl; that's a stony road, Chris."

Chris's head came up.

"Does that bother you?"

"For Christ's sake, Chris. You know me better than that."

Chris showed Dante a picture of Solene taken aboard the ship.

"She's gorgeous."

"She's beautiful and she's smart. But it didn't work out."

"Want to talk about it?"

"All right."

Chris told Dante how he'd met Solene; he with an abscess, she a dentist.

"Christ, Dante, for me it was love at first sight. She was all business and kind of prim in her white coat. Beautiful eyes. She knocked me out. Later, Solene told me she knew from the start how I felt."

"That's what happened when I met Chiarina."

Dante remembered a young partisan, dressed in a medley of Italian Army uniform and shepherd's clothing.

"I thought she was a boy. But when she took off the bustina? Jesus, she was lovely. Wonderful dark brown hair. Gorgeous brown eyes and ivory complexion. I fell in love."

A few minutes of silence followed as the friends sipped the Yamazaki, each staying with memories.

"I knew the minute I met Solene she was someone very special. By the time the ship sailed for Montevideo, we were crazy about each other. In a year, the Peliopadus would be in home waters. I meant to pay off and fly to Halifax. We'd marry and settle there. I planned to open a restaurant."

"What happened?"

"Her mother died and her father made a lot of trouble. He came from Martinique to Halifax; just about half killed her because I'm white."

Chris held up his hand.

"It's hard admitting I'll never see her again. I say more right now and I won't sleep. Maybe chat about it tomorrow."

"That's hard, Chris. I'm so sorry."

Poor, lovesick, broken-hearted Chris, missing his girl, Dante thought. No wonder he looked tired and worn.

"I had a hellish dream on the train from London; a nightmare. My old man's ghost straight out of hell, the Good Mother hanging onto him. Waving me to join them in drunkenness. I had to fight the urge. Christ knows why, but I was tempted to leave my body and go to them. Horrible. I thought I'd snuffed it. Scared the life out of me. Then I ran into her with the boyfriend, Rab Cowan."

"The Good Mother is nasty. Cowan is a waster," Dante said. "Have a word with a priest; pray for protection."

"No priests, Dante, but I believe in protection. You believe in it?"

"Too right I believe in it. When I was in the partisans, my grandfather prayed to the Crusading Knight, Nicolo the Lombard, for my safe return. His tomb is in the church at Garbugliago."

Dante reached inside his shirt and withdrew a silver chain with a worn silver medal attached.

"Old Mario gave me this as well."

He held up the medal to Chris.

"It's Mithras, god of the Roman soldiers. My grandfather wanted to make sure one of the old gods watched over me. It's always with me. I never take it off. But I'm taking it off now."

Dante crossed the room to the sideboard and opened a drawer. He returned to his chair, clutching a silver medal with a silver chain attached.

"Here, put Mithras round your neck. The Soldier's God and The Lombard kept me alive when I was fighting up in the mountains. They'll protect you too."

"What about yourself?"

"I'll wear this one, Saint Maurice, Roman soldier of the Theban Legion, patron saint of the Alpini. I got it from one of the partisans, an old soldier, an Alpini. He gave it to me when we disbanded. Protection on the way home, he said. My dad served in the Alpini in the First War. The Pope made him Maurice Alpini, patron saint, in 1941."

"Thanks, Dante."

"Tonight and every night until the dreams go away, pray to Nicolo the Lombard and Mithras. Nothing fancy. Just ask for courage and protection from evil."

The friends sipped the last of their Yamazakis. Dante raised his hand to the window and the night sky.

"There's things we don't understand, Chris. Bad things. Let's turn in."

* * *

Chris rose before six, washed, made up the bed and sat at the double windows in the bedroom gazing at the ships anchored in the river. He was glad to see Dante and Chiarina, and to be staying in their beautiful house, but his home town made him uneasy: a burgh where shipyards and foundries ate men up; where drink and the tribal wars of religion ruined their souls; and it scared Chris that Westburn might devour him. Again, he considered cutting his leave to four or five weeks rather than take four or five months.

Dante knocked the door at seven.

"Good you're up. Sleep okay?"

"Ah slept well."

"Ah'm goin' to eight o' clock Mass in St. Patrick's. We've enough time to walk the back road and get to the church. Come with me?"

Chris preferred this lovely Victorian house, but he'd go because Dante asked.

"Okay, I'm ready. I'll keep you company."

"Ah'm fasting, Chris. You'd like tea and toast?"

"Ah'll wait."

"The old parish church," Dante said. "Made my First Communion an' Confirmation in St. Pat's."

"Me as well."

But Chris's faith had always been lax. His old man and the Good Mother, nominal Catholics given to drink, never forced him to Mass, though teachers did so. Those same teachers beat him for lying, saying that he'd been at church when he lay in his bed on a Sunday morning.

"I've packed in the church since goin' to sea. I gave missions and Catholic churches churches a wide berth."

"Hmm. I go to Mass, Chris, not because I'm good, but because I'm bad."

St. Patrick's, built of vivid red Lancashire brick, soared above Orangefield Place. The bas relief of Saint Patrick blessing a child rose between the two main doors. Chris saw the confident look on Dante's face, an expression of his faith.

Old Toner, now parish priest, said the Mass.

"I'll not be having a word with him," Chris murmured.

Toner's fat face had grown more belligerent with age. He wore slippers and shuffled about the altar.

"Sloppy old shit," Chris muttered.

Chris had never liked the priest, ever since the tongue-lashing given him by Toner at thirteen, for admitting that he'd not attended confession for six months. Toner had demanded Chris make his confession again, and for penance say two decats of the Rosary, the Sorrowful Mysteries. Chris had left the confessional, ignored his penance, and walked out of the church.

"Fuckin' old bastard," he'd said.

Toner busied himself at the altar transforming the bread and wine into the Body and Blood of Christ.

Six months after the bruising confession with Toner, the Mulligans, neighbours of Chris, had suffered Toner's arrogance. For a week the incident was the talk of Holmscroft Street.

The Mulligans were decent Scots-Irish—the hard-working father was employed in the abattoir, and Mrs Mulligan, unlike the slatternly Good Mother, kept her landing and stairs clean, and the house like a new pin. Their two children, older than Chris, grew up in time for the war. The boy, Gerald, was in the army, fighting in North Africa and Italy. The daughter, Erin, was employed in war work as a precision fitter making torpedoes.

Erin met a young sailor in the Canadian Navy, on convoy duty out of Westburn, a Yeoman aboard a corvette. He was a Protestant and they married outside the Catholic Church. In due course they had a child, a little girl.

One Saturday morning Toner made it his business to call at the Mulligans' flat. As was his habit, he opened the door of the flat and walked in. Toner, in black overcoat and matching fedora, fancying himself a cut above Bing Crosby in Going My Way, did not remove his hat.

The girl nursed her baby. Toner looked about the kitchen-cum-living room, appraising the situation. He pointed to the mother and child.

"That'll be the bastard of the infernal union. Time it was baptised, and yer marriage regularised. Ye'll need a canon lawyer."

When he heard about it, rage and hatred for Toner had filled Chris's heart.

After the consecration of the Host, two lines of men and women waited to receive Communion. Dante, among the first to go forward, returned from the altar, hands joined. The sunshine flooded through the dormer windows shining on Dante, and his face was beatific.

Chris frowned. *I hope Dante won't let religion get in the way of real life.*

While Dante prayed, Chris watched the receivers of the Eucharist return to their seats. He hadn't missed any of this, not once in five years at sea. Chris recognised some men from school, mid-twenties running to seed: Westburn had added its pounds of flesh.

I need to get back to sea. Can't see me spending my entire leave in Westburn.

At the stoup on the way out, dipping the right hand into the holy water and blessed themselves, making the sign of the cross.

"Your soul's safe this week," Dante said.

"That right enough?"

At the main door Toner, still wearing his vestments, spoke to the parishioners, shaking hands with them as they left the church.

"When did he start this?" Chris said.

"About a year ago; he's getting civilised," Dante said.

"Can't stand the old devil."

Toner shook hands with Dante.

"Good morning , Dante. How are the children and Chiarina? Coming to ten o' clock Mass?

For form's sake Chris shook hands with the priest and, grunting, turned to get away from him. But Toner held Chris's hand in a strong grip.

"You'll be the McCoull boy. Chris, isn't it?"

Chris stared at him. The priest's complacent face was split by a smug grin, expecting deference.

"Too bad about your father, a stalwart of the parish. Never missed Mass. I said his Requiem Mass."

Chris squeezed hard on Toner's hand, holding onto it.

"He was a drunk; a piss artist with his head wasted when he married that boozy old hag from Ireland."

He squeezed harder, and smiled when a wince replaced the indignation clouding Toner's face. Chris released Toner's hand and left the church by the front steps.

Dante caught up with Chris at the bottom of the church stairs.

"Did you have to be so short with him? He's an old man and he is the parish priest."

"I can't bloody well stand him. A pious old rogue."

Chris felt Dante was close to falling out with him. The friends walked home in silence.

"Dante, I'll be out of the house in an hour."

Dante stopped and grabbed Chris by the shoulder.

"You're home one day after five years away, and you're about to insult Chiarina and me and walk out of our house? Toner's difficult, but we're not falling out over him. Behave yourself."

"Sorry, Dante. I don't know what the hell is wrong with me this morning."

But Dante knew what was wrong. Chris had been frightened by the bad dream and was hurting over this girl, Solene.

"Let's get home and have a good breakfast. We'll talk later."

* * *

Chiarina brought the children back from ten o' clock Children's Mass.

"Girls, come and meet Uncle Chris," Dante said. "This is Lalia, and Bella."

"Hello, Lalia, Bella."

Blushing, they pressed Chris's hand. He sat the girls on either side, helping them with the late breakfast he'd made: cereals, fried eggs, bacon, Italian black pudding, tomatoes, fried potato scones, toast.

"Was that a good breakfast?"

"Yes; thank you, Uncle Chris."

"You weren't here when I went away. But I'm glad you're here when I got back."

Chris felt the chairs move as the girls, overcome with shyness, swung their legs and looked at the table, faces crimson.

"Good that you made the breakfast, Chris."

"No bother, Chiarina. I'm a cook; chef in The Old Hotel, along the road.

Chiarina laughed. "You can make pasta; lasagna, rigatoni arrabbiata?"

"Try me; I can make anything: Italian, Greek, French. And on the ship, a great Bhandari taught me to cook Punjabi dishes.

Chris poured more tea for Chiarina, Dante and himself.

"Chiarina, Dante, thanks for the room. I appreciate it. I'd like to put in something for the housekeeping."

"Oh no, Chris," Chiarina said. "We're glad to have you stay."

"Make yourself useful. Take the girls to play."

"Would you like that, Lalia, Bella?"

"Oh, yes, Uncle Chris," they said, recovered from embarrassment.

"Tell me about your names."

The girls giggled.

"Eulalia's my Sunday name. It means well-spoken, but I like Lalia."

The younger one blushed and twisted her fingers. "Orabella is my Sunday name, and my mum says it means golden and beautiful. I like Bella."

"Well, I think you're both lovely."

Chris reached into his pocket and withdrew two half crowns and gave one to each of the girls.

Dante, Chris and the girls went into the south-facing walled garden. Chris capered with the children, throwing them up and catching them. They shrieked and laughed, tugging at his denim leg for another throw.

"Lalia, Bella, mind your good Sunday dresses, an' let Uncle Chris have peace."

The girls went to play at the edge of a flower bed.

"Some place."

Dante smiled and gazed at the family home, an early Victorian villa built in the late 1830s.

"Solid, eh?" Dante jerked his head. "Five bedrooms on the top, an' a bathroom; kitchen, livin' room, another bathroom, a study an' a good room on the level."

"Snooty neighbours, but not bad for a Jock-Eyetie."

"It's terrific."

Expanding the chip shop had brought in more income, and Dante's share of his uncle's estate had given him the confidence to buy the house.

"I'm payin' the mortgage, but I've got a couple of things going. The bedrooms; my mother is gettin' on, and she might need a place. And Anselmo—you remember him—he comes over from Italy. He's like a father to Chiarina."

Chris and Dante sat down on garden chairs shaded by an ancient Japanese cherry tree. The girls dashed about the garden, performing childish capers.

"Lalia, Bella, be careful now."

The two friends sat quietly. A bee hovered, gathering pollen at the stamen of a fading red tulip. A pair of white butterflies, waltzing above the border of snow in summer, fled across the hedge into a neighbour's garden.

"Flowers here, Chris. I like flowers. Chiarina takes care of it."

"Peaceful."

Lalia and Bella chased the white butterflies that fluttered back over the hedge. Five years since they'd talked. Infrequent postcards from around the globe, but Chris had not written a letter to Dante.

"We've done okay, Chris. You're a chef and a Chief Steward, a four-ringer. I'm Scots-Italian; born here, but to some people in Westburn, I'm just an Eyetie."

The new fish restaurant and the elegant Victorian house had established Dante, a successful businessman; his reputation glistered.

"Give it time; we'll show them. We've arrived, son, and we'll keep going."

* * *

"Last year Ah was in Bone, a big port in Algeria. The ship discharged general cargo. Ah ran into a bloke from Westburn. He was in the Foreign Legion."

Chris had gone ashore knowing there was curfew, but confident he'd find his way back to the ship in good time. He'd got lost, missed curfew and was picked up by a Legion patrol near the docks. They slammed him against a wall and gave him a rough frisking.

"This young soldier in charge questioned me. He was about nineteen; hard as nails."

Chris convinced him that he didn't speak French and that he was a seafarer.

"They were after someone. Next thing I was on the ground and kicked under the Jeep. I heard shouting in French, then a shot. 'Got him,' this boy soldier said. Then a lot of French on a radio and another Jeep skidded to a halt beside me."

"Was his name Tim Ronsard?"

"How'd you know that, Dante?"

"Ah know the boy's father. Bit of a scandal at the time. The boy had an affair with his music teacher. Older. Not old; like twenty-four and lovely. She went away and the young fella was heartbroken. He took off when he was eighteen. His mother was mad with grief and jealousy."

"Poor kid. I know how he felt."

"Solene; it was that serious?"

"That, and a lot more. Anyway, I liked these those legionnaires. I entertained them."

Next day Chris had the four men aboard the ship for food and drink.

"They were armed. A German sergeant came. Ronsard called him Dieter. Big man, was a POW near Westburn. First-class types, all of them. Hard men. Tim Ronsard, he loved the Legion."

"Thinking about joining?"

"Not on your life. Anyway, I failed the army medical here because Ah'd rheumatic fever when Ah was a kid."

The girls came to stand in front of Dante.

"I'm takin' yer Uncle Chris to the allotment, and Mum is taking you two to Aunt Graziella's cafe for ice cream. Is that good?"

Lalia and Bella.

"Oh yes, Daddy!"

Dante bent over and kissed his daughters.

* * *

Dante handed Chris an old Italian army knapsack, a relic from his days in the Fiamme Verde.

"Bring some pictures. I want to hear about life on the ocean wave."

Chris and Dante turned left at the house, walked up Forsyth Street, turned left onto tree-lined Union Street, and passed The Little Sisters of The Poor—a Catholic home for the aged.

"Good people, the Little Sisters," Dante said. "Been here a long time, the Holy Rosary Residence."

They passed six churches, a medley of Protestant sects, Episcopal, United Presbyterian, Church of Scotland, Union Church, and St. George's with the Shankland Bells. But the friends, Catholics, had no interest in the beliefs of the congregations, or the various styles of construction, from square-built Gothic to late Mediaeval.

At the The Old Hotel, they stopped, and Chris gazed at the familiar facade.

"I learned my trade in there."

Chris had come to appreciate the fine features of The Old Hotel. His life before he worked there had afforded little that was handsome. Living in the basic staff quarters had been an uplift compared to the squalor of home. John Turner, the long long-serving manager, had shared his love of the Hotel with him, and Chris had discovered beauty for the first time.

"Ah couldn't believe ma luck when you got me the job," Chris said.

They looked on the glazed square porch, the hewn stone quadrants linking single-storey pavilion wings.

"Ah like the mouldings round the windows," Dante said.

"Lovely," Chris said. "An' look at the Greek fret frieze at the top."

The friends gazed over the beautiful, ornate cast iron fence surrounding Ardgowan Bowling Green and Tennis Courts opposite The Old Hotel.

"Ardgowan Square is lovely," Chris said.

"We'd never get into the bowling," Dante said. "Catholics not welcome."

"Westburn. Anyway, I couldn't care less. Tennis and bowls; pure rubbish."

At the corner of Union Street and Patrick Street, they stopped at the Mansion House, once a grand town residence for local nobility, but now a collection of offices.

St. Mary's Parish Church lay three hundred yards to their left, the one Catholic church in the West End.

Chris pointed to the tall, square red sandstone building diagonally opposite the church.

"Ah got dragged there to the church when Ah went to St. Mary's School."

"Ah got some schooling in Italy during the War," Dante said.

Nelson Street, the frontier dividing the affluent West End from the working-class East End, the Sheriff Court, and opposite, the red brick of the Eye Infirmary. McCulloch's Clock; midway up the West Kirk steeple. It rang out two o'clock. Another minute and they'd pass the EU Congregational Church.

"The churchgoers, they like my fish and chips."

They turned into Newton Street and passed the restaurant, shuttered on Sunday.

"Ah look forward to ma day off."

They started up steep Mount Pleasant Street, stopping to glance along Holmscroft Street, a cobbled, gloomy canyon of tall and sooty tenements, a rash of shabby shops and a solitary pub, the Clachan Bar. Chris and Dante had grown up on Holmscroft Street.

"Mah mum still lives in the family house opposite St. Pat's. But Forsyth Street's better, eh, Chris?"

"You're dead right."

Halfway up Mount Pleasant Street Dante was panting, a clapped-out steam engine, his weight telling on him. Chris took long, easy strides.

"Jesus Christ, Chris, how'd you manage it, stuck on a boat? You look like a rebel in them denims and boots."

"R.M. Williams boots; Australian. I stay in shape."

They walked in silence, Dante's sweat glistening on his forehead. Left on Prospect Hill Street, right on Dunn Street.

"This jacket and corduroys. Too heavy for a day like this."

On level Cornhaddock Street, Dante's breath purred again. Up Lemon Street, over the railway bridge, and Dante spread his arms.

"The Orto; a vegetable garden. And a few flowers."

"It's good to see the place again."

Dante's blooms: wild lemon Icelandic poppies that he'd let root on borders; late tulips, red, yellow and purple heads swaying and nodding in the westerly breeze; fading daffodils from early spring. The greenhouse, glass on an aluminium frame, warmed by the sun, the glass magnifying the heat, held Dante's treasures: Roma tomatoes.

"I'm bringing on a wee peach tree and a fig tree. I might try a couple of vines."

"Dante, it's great."

"I like workin' the ground and growin' things. Fresh stuff for the kitchen and good for the table. But no work the day."

* * *

Dante came out of the hut where he kept tools. The door faced south, to catch the sun. He placed a bowl of olive oil and a plate of crusty bread on the bench between them.

"Dip the bread in the oil."

"Tasty."

Dante filled two half-pint tumblers with red wine from a half-full flagon, handing one to Chris.

"Montepulciano. Ah like to drink wine more than I used to. Salute."

"Good health."

"You've been away, what, five years, Chris? How was it?"

"A good five years; a long time. Mr Stavros Michas lifted me out of a rut when I signed on the Peliopadus; gave me the chance to shine. I ran Catering. After a few months, Old Man Michas had me rated Chief Steward. Indian and Goanese crew, British officers. Bit of resentment at first, but that passed when I gave them great food. The first time for them."

Chris explained the tense situation with the butler, and the burning 'accident.'

"I worked him over, Dante. It was him or me. The bastard could've killed me. I saw him off. He choked to death in his own puke."

"Tough it was at the start?"

"A bit, but I fixed things."

Dante wanted more from Chris. He'd missed his young friend and had worried about him. The postcards Chris'd sent hadn't told him enough.

"Did you have to stay five years?"

"No; I stayed because the Peliopadus was a great ship. I'd liked The Old Hotel, but the ship was better. Old Man Michas gave me responsibility. I stepped up to it. I made Catering my own. The Good Ship Peliopadus is the best feeder in the Michas Lines fleet."

Passing through the Suez Canal had been a unique experience for Chris.

"First time I sailed through the Suez Canal was an eye-opener. Crafty characters, always on the bum. Officials who never left the ship without begging a carton of cigarettes and a bottle of whisky."

"Really?"

"The ship was moored in the Bitter Lakes. This big Nubian cop, part of the security squad put on board by the Egyptians, said to me, 'Oh sir, give me one pound, I be your friend for life.'

I hunted him. And you needed eyes in the back of your head for the boatmen who moored the ship."

A pair of them sold Fernandez a toy leather camel, stuffed with used surgical dressings.

Chris found them by the scow at the number two hatch, a pair of unshaven affable rogues, dressed in a medley of shabby Egyptian and European clothes, wide grins, and decaying teeth below big noses. But behind the cordiality they observed and listened from the moment they came aboard, sizing up the crew for opportunities to relieve them of money. The charming devious boatmen.

One of the boatmen faked a Scots accent, heard from Scots soldiers of the British Garrison in the Canal Zone.

"He just about floored me. 'Good afternoon, Mr McCoull. Yer a Jock just like me. Ma name's Robbie McGregor fae Govan.' He laughed so hard at the look on my face. Then he said, 'Us Jocks huv tae stick the gither.' I got Fernandez's money back when I said we'd have a look at his 'feelthy postcards'."

"Ah, Mr McCoull, You like feelthy postcards? I make good price."

Chris and Fernandez examined a collection of worn Victorian and Edwardian photographs of scantily clad plump women.

"I don't like this rubbish," Chris said.

"Ah McCoull, sir, you are man of taste."

The boatman handed Chris another packet.

"Very cheap, very beautiful feelthy postcards."

Well-thumbed revolting pictures; women of the fin de siècle fondling dogs and humping small donkeys. Chris fanned the postcards, boxed them and sprayed them across the hatch cover. Several cards went into the Bitter Lakes.

"You are one dirty bastard," Chris said.

"Give me money, give me money. I am poor man."

"Ah got rid of the pair of them. Operators making a living. But Ah found it hard not to like them."

In his five years aboard the Peliopadus, Chris had passed through the Suez Canal many times, north and south. On the long passage from Darwin, bunkering in Aden notwithstanding, domestic water had to be managed. But he knew that by the time they'd passed through the Canal, Port Said would be at hand.

The ship might bunker again, depending on orders, but she always took on sweet water, and the excellent fruit and vegetables.

Knowing he was going on leave, Chris had bought a generous amount of fruit and green stuff for the voyage into the Med.

"You had to be up early to catch them."

"How's that?" Dante asked.

"Deception; sleight of hand."

He'd ordered eggs and they came in large baskets. A beautiful presentation. Gorgeous, large brown and white eggs on top. By the time the chef reached the bottom of the basket he found small poulet eggs.

"You could buy white goatskin shoes; comfortable. I've two or three new pairs in my kit. I'll give you a pair. They'll fit. Good for the shop."

"Thanks, Chris."

Chris liked the impermanence of roving, sailing on a tramp steamer, never certain where the next cargo was to be picked up from and delivered to, as Old Man Michas worked his trading magic; and the excitement of a run ashore in an unknown port.

But while he loved the roving life, he valued the security of employment with Michas Lines, a great company to work for. And he loved, too, the ordered life at sea, the comforting routine: watch-keepers changing, regular patterns of day workers.

When the Peliopadus dry-docked in Halifax, life was sweet. He met Solene Aimie.

"Goin' back to sea when your leave's up?"

"I'm not sure. Mr Michas is buyin' another ship. A Clan Line ship that's for sale. Ah could sail on her, once she's ready, or go back to the Peliopadus. But for less than five years. A year or two at sea maybe. Ah've four or five months to think about it."

Westburn men home from sea spent hard-earned money on gambling, drink and women. Preying relatives leeching cash off them until the money was gone. The men went back to sea broke. What was left of Chris's family, the Good Mother, a stepbrother and -sister, was a bad lot. Dante didn't want them mooching off Chris.

"Did you ever write to your old man?"

"No; and I never left an address. No word in five years."

"Your dad died a couple of years ago. I wrote to you about it. I went to the Requiem Mass and to the cemetery. I had a cord."

"I remember. I appreciate that. Thanks, Dante."

Chris stared over the allotment, not seeing, remembering the good years before his mother died. Then the bad years, after his mother's death, when his old man took up with the Good Mother.

Chris was not stricken by grief hearing again his father was dead; there had been too many beatings, too much hunger, and the wrecking of a modest, hard-working, respectable home by the Good Mother. Chris had hated watching his father become a hapless boozer inhabiting a squalid den of drunkenness. He loathed the Good Mother for the ruination brought on them. Chris regretted his father's death, but he could not mourn him.

"I'll maybe go to the cemetery; see his grave."

"Right enough. What about the Good Mother?"

"Ah wouldn't give her the time of day. Not a penny after that carry-on last night. Just before I came into the shop."

"You save your money?"

"Bankroll's back in your house. Plus savings in the bank."

"Forget the bank. Ma adviser can help. Ah've a safe in the house. Put the bankroll in when we get back. Ah'll help with your money."

"That'd be good, Dante."

"Remember when we brought the place on just after the war when I came home from Italy?"

"How can I forget? The army boots, the woollen jumper and trousers that smelled of sheep."

Dante led Chris around the allotment. He'd brought the allotment on more in the five years Chris had been away.

"Spuds, carrots, Calabrese, broccoli, swedes, peas and Borlotti and Cannellini beans, this summer."

Carrots from the storage pyramid, oregano and mint from the herb garden, and two dry garlic bulbs went into an old basket.

"For the dinner. Chiarina's roasting a leg of lamb. Oh, Graziella and Fred are comin' for dinner, the kids too. They're lookin' forward to seeing you."

"Great. It'll be good to see them again."

Dante made a few practice swings with a long-handled grape hoe, tapping the eight-inch blade with a reaper file.

Chris reached for the hoe, and gave it a razor edge.

They sat outside the hut enjoying the late afternoon sun, sipping the last of their wine.

"Ah could use some help, Chris. Nothing too strenuous. A bit like the old days. There's money; some through the books, the rest straight in your pocket."

"You're no' kidding me?"

"I'm serious. Some digging and weeding up here. Tidying round the shop. Help with the girls. Come to the fish market with me. You'll meet Jimmy Adams, my partner. You remember him?"

"I'd like that; he's a good man. Just like old times when I was growing up. Thanks a lot, Dante."

Dante filled the glasses close to the brim.

"I like this wine."

"Me, too."

The friends spent half an hour looking at highlights of Chris's pictures of the ship, people and places, and he commented on time and place, identifying his friends and colleagues among officers and crew.

"A good bunch, mostly. I made a few good friends on board. An outstanding captain, Rodney Graham, half Burmese, and the Chief Engineer, Wally Barnes. The radio operator too, Beastie Willie; a great bloke from Aberdeen. My Second Steward Fernandez, an exceptional bloke."

"Tell me more about Solene."

Chris showed Dante the less intimate pictures of the evenings in Lindy's taken by Hank Gill, the owner. Snaps too of the weekend spent in the cabin and the time Solene visited the Peliopadus.

"You both look so happy; and I have to say it, Chris: so much in love."

Chris handed Dante the head-and-shoulders picture of Solene.

"Her old man did that when he found out about me."

"Jesus Christ. God help the poor girl. That man is evil; right off his head."

"I thought love was for mugs until I met Solene. And now I can't help her. You can see that if I went to Martinique the swine would beat her again. He might kill her."

"It's awful. I'm so, so sorry. I just wish I could do something to help both of you."

Dante rose and took the last of the wine into the hut. Chris picked up the hoe, and followed Dante. They came out and Dante locked the door.

"It's gettin' chilly. Let's get home."

* * *

The weeks of leave passed quietly. Chris was glad of the work. He didn't need the money and said to Dante he didn't want paid.

"Nothing doin', Chris," Dante said. "You'll get paid. Anyway, I like it this way. Just like the old days when I came back from the war and you were growin' up."

Working the chipper, driving to the fish market, meeting Jimmy Adams again, looking after the allotment; so different from life aboard the Peliopadus. Chris liked it this way—staying with the Rinaldis, sharing their life and work, and he felt he belonged. The Rinaldis had made him part of their family.

Chris had fried fourteen stone of haddock for hungry customers celebrating the two weeks free from work. The coming weekend would be quiet, for much of Westburn had departed to the Clyde Coast, Ireland and the resorts of Northern England, the annual two-week break, the Fair Fortnight when the shipyards, the engine foundries, and sugar refineries closed; the slaves freed.

The friends relaxed by the fryer, dressed in crisp white tunics, trousers, and long aprons that Chris had suggested they wear. Chris wore his blue neckerchief.

"Let's look the part," he'd said.

"Yer a dab hand at this, Chris. How about stayin'? Never mind the sea. You and me, partners; we could open a restaurant!"

Chris smiled, thinking of good days on the Peliopadus.

"Yer flatterin' me, Dante. It's crossed my mind to stay, but sure ye know Ah'm a rover."

"If Solene was here you'd stay?"

"Chance would be a fine thing. I doubt I'll ever see her again."

"Don't give up hope, Chris." Dante pointed to the sky. "Him up there, and Mithras and The Lombard, they work in quiet ways. Doing things we don't understand."

"Ah'll put on a dozen fish and fresh chips," Chris said. "Catch the picture-goers goin' home."

Chris sprinkled water from his fingertips into the hot frying pans; when the fat spat the water back to him it was ready for the fish and the chips. He cooked it to perfection: the chip pan fat bubbling and smoking, chips emerging on the cradle pale, sharp on the bite, and inside tender as new baked bread. The haddock, golden crispy batter protecting sweet, flaky white flesh. Fish and chips; delicious with tea and slices of buttered bread, or to take away wrapped in paper to be eaten at home, or devoured on the hoof.

After eight o' clock, a few customers expected: some drunks, a handful of women from Thursday evening service at St. Patrick's. Chris turned over the frying potatoes—a few more minutes; then he moved to the fish fryer, bringing battered haddock filets to the surface. Dante peeled potatoes in the back shop. The friends were content.

* * *

The following Sunday, a warm afternoon in early July, Chris and Dante sat by the door of the allotment hut, having arrived there after attending Mass in St. Mary's. They cooled down after four hours of work, the vegetable garden well-dug, and the flowerbeds hoed.

Chris removed tight-fitting leather working gloves bought in Houston, Texas, undid a red workman's neckerchief and wiped his brow.

"It's no' exactly Italy, but the place is lookin' well," Dante said.

"Yer right. Not bad, not bad at all."

Pleased at what he saw, Chris gazed across the allotment to the hoed rows of vegetables, and the flowers, the mottled purple and yellow petals of pansy flocks, the raspberry petals of sweet-scented Paeonia and clusters of mecanopis, the blue poppies with delicate stamens.

Dante pointed in the direction of the frame for sweet peas and the clumps of freesia.

"Nice, eh?"

"Hmmm."

Chris gathered greens for the evening meal: lettuce, rocket, turnip leaves, tomatoes from the greenhouse, basil from the herb garden, a garlic bulb, a couple of red onions, and about a pound of fine green beans. He brought it all back to the hut, packing it in a canvas shopping bag.

He entered the hut for a sharp knife, went to the flowerbeds, cut sweet peas and orange freesia. Drawn by yellow petals fluttering in the breeze, Chris cut Icelandic poppies and tied the blooms in a fragrant bouquet, laying them by the canvas bag of greens.

Chiarina adored flowers, loved to stuff untidy bunches into vases, filling the kitchen and the living rooms with colourful, sweet perfumed blooms.

He imagined that Solene was near, that he'd just cut flowers for her. Chris longed for her to see the things he'd grown.

Working in the allotment made Chris happy, the satisfying ache of hard physical labour taking him back to the happy days when he first met Dante.

Dante brought a flagon of red wine from the hut and two half-pint tumblers.

"I'll get the weeds away," Chris said.

He pulled on the work gloves and gathered up weeds, taking them to the compost heap at the west corner of the allotment.

"Primitivo, from Puglia," Dante said. "It's good wine."

"The sandwiches are delicious."

"Chiarina's a dab hand," Dante said, sprawled on the bench. "Tonight she's making a salad, then spaghetti and meatballs for dinner."

Dante refilled the half-pint tumblers. He held the glass to the sun, admiring the vinuous red and purple hues; he waved the tumbler beneath his nose.

"Puglia vino; Ah love the fumes. It's good stuff, Chris."

Chris took another swallow and smiled. "Lovely; goin' to ma head."

Dante refilled the tumblers with the Puglia wine.

"Ah'll tidy up here," Dante said. "Back to sea when your leave is up, Chris?"

"Maybe; I'm thinking about it. But I won't go for five years. It's too long. A couple of years, that would be okay. I hear Mr Michas is buying more ships. He gave me a start; he's a good man. I wouldn't mind going back to my old ship, the Peliopadus. She's a duchess of the sea. Great shipmates, too. I loved her. We all did. I got so close to her."

"Loved only the ship?"

"What do you think?

Only Solene could lead him out from the dark places.

After five years at sea, Chris believed he was free of his dead father, hadn't imagined his old man would haunt him from beyond the grave. But the Good Mother was very much alive. Seeing her his first evening home made him realise that he'd have to deal with her begging and troublemaking.

"The pair of them haven't come again in the night. But the odd time I'm scared to go to sleep. Could I handle another round of it?"

"You'll handle it. The Lombard and Mithras; and I'm not kidding, they're protecting you."

* * *

The Good Mother, a malicious snooper, established that Chris worked in Dante's chipper. They'd seen him there late mornings and early afternoons preparing for opening at five o'clock.

In a rare lucid moment, she figured Chris was living with the Rinaldis in their 'Big Hoose doon the West End.' One day, almost sober, she found the Rinaldis' address in the phone book. Her vixen instincts meant putting the hard word on Chris. An ambush would yield a handful of the readies. A smile exposed her disgusting false teeth, and she lit her smoke of choice, a Woodbine, her great wee cigarette. She inhaled, rotting her lungs, anticipating the crisp texture of a wad of pound notes in her leathery hand; funds for days of serious bevvying.

The Good Mother meant to surprise Chris, attacking him at his most vulnerable, when her importuning would yield big takings. She meant to raise her demands above a tenner.

Rab Cowan would go with her, the heavy physical threat, persuading Chris to hand over money.

They drank tumblerfuls of nameless red gut rot from an unlabelled bottle. One Woodbine smoked down to the last quarter inch of nicotine, saliva saturating shag and paper, and they lit another one.

"He's back at the fuckin' chapel," the Good Mother said.

"Aye, an' no' jist chapel wi' the punters," Rab Cowan said. "Fuckin' hingin' aboot wi' swanky fuckin' Tims. Goes tae the Little Sisters. Wu'll fuckin' nail him there on Sunday. Ambush the cunt."

The Good Mother cackled, her laughter smothered by throaty mucus and coughing. She hawked and spat a gob of green-yellow filth into a bucket kept by her side.

"Get him fur at least a tenner. Naw, wu'll squeeze twenty oot o' him. He's a fuckin' saft mark."

* * *

On Sundays when Dante and Chiarina, and Celestina and the children went to the Holy Rosary Mass, Chris liked to go with them. Being with the family, he felt he belonged.

"It won't do you any harm," Dante said. "Keep your hand in."

And Lalia and Bella loved walking into the chapel each holding a hand of their Uncle Chris; and with the Mass over, they loved it when they left the chapel, Chris's hands on their shoulders, ushering them out the doors.

The priest who said Mass at the Little Sisters, a young curate from the nearby St. Mary's, jaloused Chris would not welcome his attention and left contact at a polite grin and a handshake.

Chris saw them waiting at the gates to the Chapel of the Holy Rosary.

"Trouble, Dante."

Chris nodded in the direction of the Good Mother and her consort.

"I'll get rid of them."

"Take it easy, Chris."

When he got to a few feet of them, Chris caught the reek of booze. Last night's session was still on them.

"Hey, how's it goin', Chris?" Rab Cowan asked.

Chris ignored him, and addressed the Good Mother.

"What do you want?"

"Don't you fuckin' talk tae yer Good Mother like that. She brought ye up. Yer ain mother did fuck-all fur ye."

"How much this time?"

" 'Aw, jist a wee handout, Chris. Enough tae keep us goin'."

Chris dug into his pocket and peeled off three fivers.

"Fifteen quid. Clear off and don't come back."

"Ya miserable cunt," Rab Cowan said. "Gie us twinty quid an' well go."

Shame enveloped Chris, that the Rinaldis had to see his humiliation after Mass. He moved close to the consort.

"Raise my mother again and I'll send you to the Royal Infirmary for six months."

Dante watched and could see that Chris was preparing to flatten Rab Cowan. He moved with rapid strides, got between Chris and Cowan and walked him out the gate. Hidden from the worshippers, Dante put him against the wall.

"Ya fuckin' Tally bastard."

"Scram, or I'll have you lifted. A word to Sergeant Ponsonby and you'll be lookin' at thirty days in the Barlinnie Gaol."

Dante pushed him well away from the gate to the corner of Campbell Street. The Good Mother shuffled past, clutching her three fivers.

"If he comes back," Chris said, "I'll hammer him."

"No, you won't. I'll see Big Lachie. He'll put a stop to it."

A week later on the Monday night late, Sergeant Ponsonby, his shift finished, came in for his fish supper.

He sat in a booth, hat off, and tucked in. With the food finished, he asked Chris for a refill of tea.

"Sit down, Chris. How are you?"

"Pretty good. How about yourself?"

"Not bad at all."

"Mrs McCoull, the Good Mother? I had a word with her on Friday. She was well on. You'll no' have any more bother. I gave her a lift to Auchmead Road in the squad car, but I told her any more bother and she was looking at a night in the cells."

"What about that clown she's hanging about with?"

"I put the frighteners on him. He was drunk and incapable on Friday night. A public nuisance, pissing in the street. I lifted Cowan. Locked him up in the cells for the weekend. He appeared in the police court this morning. Got off with a warning from the JP. He'll not bother you again, Chris."

"Thanks very much."

"No need to thank me for getting on with the job. You're doing well, son. I'm proud of you and Dante."

* * *

Dante explained to Chris that he'd never confessed anything he'd done in Italy: as a Fiamme Verde partisan, he'd fought evil serving in a just war.

"When we disbanded, Ah made a good Act of Contrition for possible misdeeds and sins of omission."

Chris, feeling low, had gone into greater detail about unexpected difficulties the first few months aboard the Peliopadus, and Dante, a good practicing Catholic, had fallen back on doctrine and orthodoxy to help his friend.

"Confession? It's not bloody well on," Chris said. "I'm not sorry for what I did. It was the right thing to do. The butler would have killed me for burial at sea. He was a bad bastard. *Ah* buried *him* at sea. Maybe he'd have crippled me. Had me put ashore in some shithole. Sent home as a distressed British seaman. There was a big sigh of relief from the officers and crew when the corpse went over the side and splashed into the drink."

"Maybe confession would make you feel better. Lighten things if you feel a burden."

"What fucking burden? I had bad dreams and worried more about finishing up like my old man, but I'm through that, thanks to Nicolo the Lombard and Mithras. A great idea of yours, Dante, asking them for help."

"You killed a man; that's what you said."

"I injured him. I wrecked his right hand to get him off the ship. And Ah'd do it again. He passed out and choked on his own puke. It was him or me. The bastard tried to burn me, and Ah mean bad. But Ah was lucky, Ah got off with a burnt face and hands. I couldn't let that go. He would have tried to kill me. Toner could never get his head round that. He'd tell me Ah should've turned the other cheek, just like Jesus said. Toner's too fucking slow. Might have gone to the police."

"He wouldn't do that. Priests take an oath. The confession's sacred. What you say in confession is never told to anyone else. Anyway, there's nothing to tell."

"Ah've heard that one. Ah'll take it with a pinch of salt. They should never have let him out of Ireland."

"Chris, you're losing the plot."

"Like fuck. You think I'm going into the dark box with a shitbag like Toner? He's a fucking creep. He'd want to poke his nose in about Solene."

"Another priest then?"

"No priests. Do you confess?"

"Once in a while. But Ah always make ma Easter duties."

"You go into Toner's black box?"

"Not on yer nelly. When Ah go to confession, Ah go to St. Ninian's down in Kempock. There's a Scots curate; a civilised wee fella. We've never met. He doesn't know me."

Dante believed issues of right and wrong were a matter of conscience.

"Chris, I'd have done the same thing as you. If you feel the need, make an Act of Contrition."

"Okay, Dante. Ah'll think about it."

* * *

Loud knocking at the main door of Dante's house. Chris heard voices, couldn't think why anyone might want him at such an unearthly hour, and rolled over and fell asleep.

A hand on his shoulder woke him, a gentle rocking. He opened his eyes, gone to slits against the sun shining on the blinds.

"Better get up, Chris," Dante said. "It's the police. Big Lachie and a constable. Wouldn't say what's up."

"I'll be right down."

"In the kitchen, Chris."

Chris entered the kitchen in slippers, robe wrapped around him. Sergeant Ponsonby and the constable, hats off, sat at table with Dante drinking tea. Chris poured himself a cup.

"Something wrong?"

"Your Good Mother's dead. A couple found her body in Waverley Lane. She'd been drinking in the Gunner's Club. We need formal identification."

"She's nothing to me. What about her son and daughter?"

"The daughter's emigrated to Canada. Son's overseas in the army."

"Smart moves, getting away from her."

A few moments of embarrassed silence.

"Will you identify the body, Chris?" Sergeant Ponsonby asked.

"Okay."

The Police Mortuary was across Dalrymple Street from the police station, next to the Sailor's Rest. A bleak and forbidding place: the Inn of the Troublesome Dead.

The Good Mother's remains lay on a slab covered by a rubber sheet. The mortuary assistant uncovered her head and shoulders.

"What about the rest?"

He looked to Sergeant Ponsonby, who nodded.

He uncovered her torso.

"All of her."

The attendant uncovered the Good Mother's remains.

Chris looked at the corpse. Her mouth gaping, showing her cheap, stained false teeth; the nicotine-tanned fingers, dirt crescents crowning her nails; the greasy hair dyed black, grey roots showing; the flattened, shrunken tits, empty wine sacks, folds of skin at the waist, scrawny legs. Dirty feet, and horny talons topped her toes. Chris swallowed hard, suppressing an urge to boak. He let his eyes rest on her black bush. A grubby drunken vixen who'd lived by her wits, bumming money for drink, wrecking lives.

Chris felt like venting all the loathing he felt for this wretched woman; to shout, "Can ye imagine shagging that?" But he held his tongue.

"Cover her; get her out of my sight."

He wondered what his father ever saw in her. She'd been too much for him and he'd surrendered to her influence, taking to the red biddy.

"A fucking hopeless case. She'd have sucked cheap wine through a shitty clout," Chris said. "That's her alright. She liked a good bucket."

"The pathologist'll conduct a post-mortem this afternoon," Big Lachie said. "He'll give her a wash; open her to find the cause of death."

"He puts her back together?"

"Bare-handed; he'll stuff her organs inside her gut and stitch her up. Why are you asking me?

"She's bad news. Brought grief to my father."

"I know."

They left the mortuary and walked to the police station.

"We should release the body by tomorrow. What arrangements are you making?"

"She's nothing to me. Westburn can bury her."

They left the police station. Dante held Chris back outside the door.

"Get a grip, Chris. You can't condemn her to a pauper's funeral. I know what she was like, but for Christ's sake, show some respect for the dead."

"She was trouble from start to finish. Fuck her."

"It's not on, son. I never told you this, but I paid for your dad's funeral. She had no money to pay for it. I might as well arrange for her funeral."

Dante had shut Chris up. They walked in silence.

"You're right, Dante. I have to take care of it. What about… my father's funeral?"

"You don't owe me anything."

Chris decided on a quiet funeral, the body to go to P. B. Wright for preparation and interment.

"I'm not going near Toner. She wouldn't have given a shit about a Requiem Mass. I'll ask the undertaker to say say a few words at the grave. Put a notice in the Westburn Gazette. Get the stonemason to add her name to the grave stone."

"He'll do that, I'm sure."

Chris and Dante went to the impoverished house in Auchmead Road. Rab Cowan had vanished. A bed with soiled sheets, a few sticks of furniture, a reeking bathroom. In the kitchen the soles of their shoes stuck to the floor. There was nothing of value in the house. Rummaging through drawers they found a rent book, the payments in arrears. Hidden under the mattress they found a title deed for a lair where she'd buried her first husband.

"I'll take care of the rent money. We'll put her in the old lair beside him. I'm not having her buried beside my father and mother."

They walked to the car.

"Need to clear the place out."

"You know Jake that comes into the chipper?"

"Sure."

"He'll do it for a few quid. I'll speak to him."

"Thanks, Dante."

Later that day Chris called Sergeant Ponsonby and let him know.

"The pathologist's finished. She'd been drinking a lot. On a bender; died of liver failure."

A day later the undertaker phoned Chris to say that the Good Mother's remains were ready for viewing.

"No thanks. Screw her down. Close the coffin."

* * *

A still morning, light dimmed by a curtain of fine rain. A cortege: the hearse containing the Good Mother's body sealed in a pale oak coffin with a wreath of white roses on top, followed by the mourner's car with Chris and Dante inside. The convoy navigated Grey Place, turned left onto Patrick Street, left on Union Street, and right onto Nelson Street, straight to the cemetery gate.

Chris and Dante followed the undertaker's men carrying the coffin resting on two wooden battens, but they stopped short of the open lair. Gravediggers leaning on shovels waited a few yards back. A dozen people, men and women, stood nearby; drinking friends of the Good Mother.

"Call for eight volunteers to lower her away," Chris said.

Chris felt no emotion as they lifted the coffin and lowered it into the hole. A bump, and her boozing cronies dropped the cords to clatter on the coffin lid.

The undertaker recited the Lord's Prayer. The drinking companions, heads bowed, hands joined, mumbled along with him.

"May the souls of the faithful departed rest in peace, Amen," the undertaker intoned.

The cordholders stepped off the planks and back from the grave.

"They'll be expecting food and a drink for coming," Dante said. "I'll let them know."

Dante called to Junior McHugh.

"Junior, take the boys to the Black Cat. Chris has set it up. Big Eddie is layin' on purvey, shell pies and bridies; there's a bevvy goin'."

Chris eschewed the shaking of hands, confining himself to a nod of acknowledgement as the Good Mother's drinking friends passed.

Ten o'clock, and the mourners who'd come to the cemetery would be slugging shots of Bell's and half-pint beer chasers, munching on hot pies stuffed with mince and flaky bridie, pastry parcels of forced meat.

A chilled Dante and Chris sat round Dante's kitchen table. Dante poured two shots of grappa.

"Heat you up."

Chris swallowed the grappa in one go, left the table, and fried eggs, bacon, and potato scones. He made a pile of buttered toast and a pot of strong black coffee. He set two places and laid dishes of jam and marmalade on the table. Dante sipped grappa.

"Great breakfast," Dante said.

Chris felt a burden lifted, but he refused hypocrisy pretending grief. He was glad to see the back of the Good Mother, a poison in his life, the cause of his father's early death.

"I'm glad that's over. Ah was always afraid I'd finish up like them. You and Chiarina, your mum and Graziella, kept me from that. Thanks. I'm grateful."

"No bother, Chris. You're one of my family."

They finished their grappa.

"You've been here a while, Chris. Have you thought any more about going back to sea?"

"Not directly. Mr Michas wants me to relieve Chief Stewards and audit Catering when ships dock in UK or Europe. Maximum two-week trips. Full pay while waiting here for the next ship. I've said yes. It's a good offer."

"Then what?"

"Not sure. Mr Michas is buying ships for the fleet. There could be ten ships to audit. But I reckon I'll have a good picture of what's going on after I check out four or five vessels. Then I'll think about the future."

"What about opening the restaurant?"

The friends had talked about it. An Italian restaurant; the first in Westburn. It might be hard work attracting customers.

"Me in the front shop," Dante said. "You in the kitchen. I'll bring waiters over from Italy. But you being away is a wee problem."

Chris thought they could manage the problem. Bring in a young chef with experience of Scotland. Train him and work with him while waiting on the calls from Mr Michas.

"We can do it, Dante."

"How's that? Might be short of cash if you're out of the business," Dante said. "I don't want to get in deep with the bank."

Chris had barely touched his bankroll brought with him when he came on leave. Dante paid him well for his work, and he'd tucked a good part of Chris's cash with his financial adviser, and the bankroll had grown. He'd kept a small fund in the safe for Chris. Dante, a shrewd backer of horses, had bet Chris's money and his own, and added steady, modest winnings. At the start, he'd kept quiet; a couple of early he'd made good from his own funds. Now a flush Chris let Dante place bets on his behalf.

Chris meant to do something to allay Dante's fears. Dante filled the grappa glasses.

"I'll be helping with the cash to get up and running."

"But you'll be sailing away."

They sipped grappa. Chris rose from table, made coffee in the espresso pot. Dante uncorked the grappa and topped up their glasses.

"I see it this way," Chris said. "Mr Michas pays well. I'll be back on full pay. Might have some to spare. The bankroll and the winnings; all my cash goin' into the business. I'm a partner. It'll take a few months to audit the fleet. Ah'll be around; run the kitchen; train the kitchen staff, waiters an' all."

Dante rose and embraced his friend.

"You're the brother I never had."

"Things are pretty good, Dante. The bad dreams are gone. The prayers to the Crusader Knight, Nicolo the Lombard, and to Mithras worked; the medal protected me. I'll give it back to you."

"How are you feeling? I mean about Solene?"

Chris shrugged.

"I don't think that'll ever be right."

"Keep the medal, Chris. Miracles happen."

Chapter Twelve

Solene had gone to the hospital in Martinique and the surgeon had done his best, but her injured nose healed with an ugly, disfiguring twist and a stretched left eyebrow, hooding the eye.

Solene's father couldn't hide his guilt from himself. His Catholic conscience tortured him by day, and brought nightmares when he slept. Shame for what he'd done to his daughter crushed him. The ignominy became as hard to bear as the grief suffered at losing his wife. He went to Father Andre, preferring to confess to an old-fashioned pastor, supportive of fathers over daughters.

Confessing his sins to Father Andre did not lift the burden of guilt. Fabien's whispered, guilty Act of Contrition and his conscience gave him hell. The priest's perfunctory forgiveness of his sins—the meagre penance, a trivial few decats of the Rosary—stoked Fabien's remorse.

Solene managed the household and made sure her three younger sisters behaved and attended school. Only Solene could make Fabien whole again, and he looked for her forgiveness. She rejected her father's attempts at warmth. Solene ignored his compliments about meals she cooked. If he tried to kiss her cheek or touch her shoulders, Solene turned away. Her rejection of his attempts at reconciliation added to Fabien's guilt, and he could not bear it. Feeling hard done by, he often drank rum till he passed out.

Solene refused to attend church with her her damaged face. Father Andre agreed to visit Solene to turn her to her father. Her injuries appalled Father Andre. With an uneasy conscience, he pleaded the father's case for love and forgiveness.

"But Solene, come to Mass and Communion. Receive His love. Jesus our Saviour said to turn the other cheek. Forgive those who wrong us. Fabien loves you."

"Why didn't he ask me to come home? Chris would have understood and come to me. But my father thought only of himself and ordered me home. I refused and he beat me and sold my practice. He took me from the man I love because he's white. Let him suffer. I'll not turn my other cheek."

"Try, my child. Jesus loves you. Through me, He has absolved your father of sin. Solene, child, forgive your father. Make your home here with your family."

"No, Father Andre. Damn you, damn Jesus, and the Church. I've done nothing that needs forgiving. You can all go to hell. Drink rum with my father; rot your souls together. One day I'll get away from here."

The weeks passed and the father, grief-stricken for his dead wife, often lay stupefied with rum and belligerent remorse. Guilt overwhelmed him, and as he weakened, Solene's resistance strengthened.

She spent nine months of hell in Martinique. She found the father dead on the bathroom floor one Sunday morning, killed by a massive stroke. The God of the Old Testament had handed out rough justice and released her from bondage.

A private funeral, and they buried their troubled father. Yann, stationed with the fleet in Toulon, did not attend the interment. Her elder brother and younger sisters wept and mourned, but Solene, dry-eyed, stood aside from the grave, filled with regret at what had happened to her and the family. She looked in her heart to forgive her father, but she found no charity there.

The father's will left Solene her share of the estate, and the monies from the disposal of her property in Canada. Matthieu mortgaged the family home and released her one-sixth share of its value. Solene paid for a flight to Paris via New York, traveling with light luggage.

Her teenage sisters, busy growing up, would recover soon enough from Fabien's death. Sure, she could have stayed and sacrificed her future to look after them, but—not without stabs of guilt—she left that responsibility to her weak elder brother, free from the dark paternal shadow, now head of the family, owner and chairman of the law practice established by Fabien. Solene expected spineless Matthieu to act like a man, and find the guts to carry out his duty to his sisters until they married or left home.

She examined her face in the mirror in the toilet of the Air France Super Constellation due to land at Orly. Solene shuddered, and though still good-looking, she felt tarnished and cursed. She repaired her makeup. The physical injuries meted out by her father had mended. No marks or bruises remained on her face, and her battered torso had recovered from the slaps and punches rained on it, but her broken nose and hooded eye were physical clues to the emotional pain she felt in her heart.

Solene had been unsure about going directly to Scotland to find Chris. She did not want her beloved to see her wounded face. She'd written to Yann, a Navy Corpsman, after sea duty on a destroyer, posted to the Naval Hospital in Toulon. She prayed he'd find a surgeon capable of straightening her eyebrow and restoring the true shape of her nose. Solene sought, too, her brother's love and support. If Yann failed her, she'd be alone.

She traveled by taxi from Orly to the train station. In a quiet compartment on the train she slept most of the way from Paris to Toulon.

* * *

She looked for a sailor when she got off the train and wasn't disappointed when Yann, smart in dress blues, white hat with the red pom-pom, met her in the station foyer. Brother and sister embraced and he held her at arm's length. Yann tried to hide his shock at Solene's hooded eye and broken nose, and Solene knew it.

"You look well, Solene."

"Yes; apart from father's legacy to my face."

"I'm so sorry. But listen, Solene. After I got your letter, I spoke to my commanding officer. He got in touch with a good ENT and rhinoplasty surgeon. She was a naval nurse and went on to study medicine. You'll see her the day after tomorrow."

"Thank you. You found me a hotel?"

"No. You're staying with me. I have enough room."

Yann rented an apartment high up in an ancient tenement in the old town, a small place with charm. He would sleep in a cabinet bed in the living room, and Solene would have the bedroom.

"Oh, Yann, I can't do that."

"Yes, you can, and you're going to do it."

Solene stayed in hospital two days. She looked rough after the operation: swelling and bruising spread out on either side from her nose, and her eyes were reduced to slits. Yann came to sit with her in the evenings. On the first evening after the operation, Solene wept.

"Look at my face. I've seen it in the mirror."

Yann held her hand.

"It's temporary bruising and swelling. I asked the surgeon. You'll see, in a few days you'll be as good as new."

Yann asked for four days leave and brought her to his apartment. When she left hospital, the dressings had been removed and her nose had returned to its pert, beautiful shape, the hooded eyelid repaired. She hid her still swollen eyelids behind dark glasses. The wavy irregular hues of yellow, blue and black on her face melded, vanishing into her complexion. Yann came home each evening and tried to share the household chores.

"No, Yann. I want to do it."

She kept to the apartment, and went out in the neighbourhood to buy food and household items. She kept house and cooked for her brother. Her confidence returned, but not yet to the level of her life in Halifax. Solene stayed a month in Toulon.

She yearned for Chris. The longer they were apart, the more her yearning to be with him strengthened. The assumption that Chris loved her had kept Solene sane in the grim periods on Martinique. Her father's death had liberated her from a house that had become a prison.

Solene decided to visit Westburn worried that Chris might have changed, and no longer cared for her. If Chris was not home, or had gone back to sea, or, God forbid, sent her away, she'd move back to France, and settle in Toulon to be near her brother.

When Solene felt low, she doubted Chris's love. But she meant to go to him and dreamt of an ecstatic hug from Chris, followed by nights of tenderness—dreams that turned Solene warm with love and lust.

Ten days before her flight from Paris, she added elegant French clothing and accessories to her baggage.

"Solene, you're sure about this?"

"Very sure."

Solene had shown Yann snaps of Chris. He said Chris looked like a decent man. He liked the fact that Chris, like himself, followed the sea, and practiced first aid.

"It's a big step, Solene. I mean, Scotland. It's Presbyterian. Wet and cold and bleak."

"No worse than a Halifax winter. I had Scots Presbyterian patients. They were fine. Until I met Chris—and he's Catholic, but detached like me after putting up with Father Andre—I'd made up my mind to stay on in Halifax. I liked the four seasons."

"I like that about Toulon. The summers are wonderful and the winters mild."

"One thing is certain. I'm not going home, and I won't go to Halifax after what happened there."

"If it turns out bad, come back here."

Solene hugged Yann. She had his understanding and sympathy. He'd had his own difficulties with their father over his desire to serve in the French Navy. Yann was in love with Anna, a beautiful Creole girl from the island of La Réunion, in the Indian Ocean. Anna's mother was Creole and her father French.

"I'm sorry I won't meet Anna."

"It's too bad. She's gone home for three or four months."

"Are you bothered that Chris is a white man?"

"Not at all. But I worry that you might have a hard time in Scotland. There are prejudiced people everywhere; black and white."

"I know; just like our father. If he'd just asked me to come home. I never expected the violence. I mean, he was strict, but I loved him; he was always a good father. He really set about me. It was horrible. I managed to get a note sent to Chris telling him what happened and not to come to Martinique. I was afraid Father would kill me, and something terrible would happen to Chris if he came. Yann, our father died a drunk."

"The old man had that dark flinty face for the world. But it failed when our mother died, and he fell apart. I'm glad I left home. I like the Navy."

"Chris asked me to marry. I said yes. I went to to see his ship leave Halifax for Montevideo. He gave me this cross and swore he's he'd come back to me."

Solene fingered the gold Celtic Cross cross inlaid with agate.

"Lovely piece. I wondered if someone gave it you."

"I still feel the same about Chris. I love him. I hope he feels the same way about me. I have to find out."

* * *

She found Dante Rinaldi's address and number in the telephone book, but was uneasy about appearing at his door unannounced. He might dislike her for leaving Chris.

Solene discussed allotments located near a woollen mill above the town with the manager of The Old Hotel. She liked John Turner, from the County Down; loved his Ulster accent.

"Now why would you want to be going up there?"

There was nothing for Solene to hide.

"I'm looking for a friend, Chris McCoull."

"Sure, Chris was chef here before he went away to the Merchant Navy. He's a grand lad."

"Is he here?"

"Chris is home. Most Sundays he's at the allotment. Dante might be there, too."

Solene decided she'd cope with Dante.

Chris had visited the hotel several times since coming home on leave, and often John Turner would find him in low spirits. Dante must know what ailed Chris, but ever the discreet Ulsterman, John would never ask. If Chris wanted him to know what was wrong, he'd tell him.

He liked Solene Aimie for her striking looks, her poise, and quiet good manners. She was his first guest from Martinique. He knew that Chris lived with the Rinaldis, their house not a ten-minute walk from The Old Hotel. John Turner considered telling Solene and giving her the address, but decided against it. Had she wanted to, she'd have found it in the phone book. Miss Amie must have her reasons for going to the allotment.

"Would you call me a taxi?"

"It's Sunday, Miss; you'll not find one in Westburn."

"Could you give me directions, and I'll walk?"

John Turner figured he could aid two good people.

"You could get a bus, but they're few today. Tell you what, I'll drive you. It's no trouble."

"Thank you so much, Mr Turner."

* * *

Solene watched Chris tying two bird-feeders to a six-and-a-half-foot stake dug in near the door of the allotment hut. Chris worked, confident movements of his ungloved hands knotting heavy twine. She was glad when he pulled on protective tight-fitting leather work gloves. She did not want his fine hands toughened and coarsened. He moved to the south-west side of the vegetable plot, a slim, lissome, graceful figure in dark woollen pullover, faded jeans, and sturdy work boots. A weak fire of weeds, beyond composting, smouldered, sending gossamer lattices of wan blue smoke to the pale winter sun. Chris raked and piled old tough weeds close to the dying fire for later burning. She gazed across the allotment to the hard-pruned roses, and the turned black soil where Chris had planted spring-flowering bulbs. Solene saw the work of a man hiding deep in routines.

Seeing Chris again, Solene knew that she'd been right to make the journey to Scotland. Her beloved was so near and her heart soared. Just to see him made the pain of having her face remedied worthwhile. Surely he would radiate the love for her that she felt for him.

He ignored the sound of footsteps on the gravel path, assuming a local had come for a bag of winter vegetables. But then he recognised the oddity in the muted footsteps; a woman's shoes.

He turned and saw Solene.

"Hello, Chris."

He looked at his hands and found them clean, but he rubbed them on the legs of his jeans. She held her hand to stay him, palm out.

"I want to come to you."

Chris grabbed her gloved hands, and felt her warmth through the fine leather. He took her in his arms and held her.

"Jesus, it's you. Oh, Solene. Bébé, oh, bébé."

"Darling Chris. My love, my life. I've missed you."

They sat on the bench outside the allotment hut. His eyes lingered on her: face framed by a pretty grey cloche hat. She was lovely, demure, in an azure check plaid dress, grey wool jacket, a red silk scarf at her throat, sheer stockings, elegant black shoes. They were silenced by happiness at seeing each other, but each wondering if the other cared in the same way.

"Solene, you came; I wanted to go to you. I worried about you. I was going crazy without you."

"I asked you not to come. It was safer for both of us. My father was out of his mind."

"You feel the same about me?"

He heard tears in her voice, and gazed at her shining eyes.

"Bébé, bébé, I feel the same. Seeing you, I know, it's only you."

Solene kissed Chris.

"Darling Chris; love of my life."

"What about you, how have you been since Halifax?"

Solene described her nine months living in Martinique.

"Before Halifax, I loved my father. He was old-fashioned, but a good father."

She cried. Chris held her and she turned into him.

"When he died, I couldn't mourn him. Not after what he did."

"It's all right."

"Am I bad, Chris? Really bad?"

"No."

"And the priest, Father Andre. He tried to persuade me to stay, to turn the other cheek. I told him to go to hell."

Solene dried her eyes and blew her nose. She explained that she went to Toulon to stay with Yann, her brother, a Corpsman in the French Navy. After sea duty on a destroyer, Yann posted to the Naval Hospital, and had rooms ashore.

"My father broke my nose and twisted my eyelid when he beat me, and they did not heal well. I looked terrible, I felt awful, and couldn't come to you. Yann found a surgeon. I'm glad I had the operation. What do you think?"

"It's beautiful. Just like before. I love it."

He kissed the tip of Solene's nose.

Solene leaned back and crossed her legs. Chris touched her knees, getting a jolt from the texture of her sheer stockings. His hand slipped under the hem of her skirt. Solene smiled.

"Chris, I can't wait. I'm nothing without you."

Chris glanced at the door of the hut.

"We can go inside."

The hut contained gardening tools put by, a couple of old easy chairs where Chris and Dante sat on days of bad weather, and squeezed in, an ancient, sturdy chaise longue, covered with a clean, worn bedspread. On warm days Chris or Dante might nap on it.

"Jesus, Solene, I'm afraid to touch you, you look so wonderful and beautiful. Christ, how I missed you."

"Trust me, my darling."

Solene touched Chris's shoulders, and had him sit down. She undid his belt.

"Are you ready?"

"I'm ready."

Solene raised her skirt, they made love.

* * *

"We can catch the Cornhaddock bus to the town and walk along Union Street," Chris said.

Solene had arranged her clothing and tidied her hair and makeup. She'd become quite dishevelled from their time in the hut.

"Is it so far that we can't walk?"

"No, not that far. All right, we'll walk."

They stood on Murdieston Street by the iron railings above the sloping retaining banks looking down at the compensation loch built in the nineteenth century. Diminutive model racing yachts, driven by the western breeze, raced across the surface of sun-dappled waters, bows digging into a gentle chop. Fathers who'd hand-built these boats, perfect in every detail, sent sons sprinting along the path to where the products of their craft and artistry would touch bottom.

"Turn her round, son, turn her round!" a father shouted. "Send her back to me."

"I always fancied a wee boat when I was a boy. I could never scare up enough money."

Solene smiled and tightened her grip on Chris's hand.

"The proper name," Chris said, gesturing to the water, "is the Cowdenknowes Dam, but everybody calls it the Murdieston Dam. I used to come here for peace and quiet."

Memories of his old life flooded in. Chris shuddered thinking about the Good Mother, a bad bastard, and his father rancid as old piss.

He put his arm round Solene's shoulder.

"I'm just so glad you're here."

"How's your leave been?"

"Good. In Westburn, it would've been grim without the Rinaldis. I worked with Dante and went back on Michas Lines's payroll in July. I join ships in ports between the Elbe and Brest;UK ports too. I stay on board for up to two weeks to let the Chief Stewards go on leave, and I join the ship to audit Catering. At home I stay on full pay. I think Mr Michas is up to something."

He told Solene about working with Dante, and his troubles with the Good Mother, but spared Solene the gruesome details of her demise. Chris shook at the thought of her.

"Chris, you're trembling; are you all right?"

"I just imagined the Good Mother escaping the grave to make trouble. She's well away on the other side. I'm okay."

Chris steered Solene into Holmscroft Street. They passed St. Patrick's church.

"It's beautiful," Solene said.

"Yes, it is. I went there with Dante."

Solene smiled and pressed Chris's hand.

He'd show her the beautiful parts of the town, but now he wanted her to see where he'd come from. She had to know everything about him. Better to find out if she'd be put off by his origins. Chris meant to keep no secrets from Solene. They passed the respectable part of the street where Dante had been raised. They crossed Mount Pleasant Street, entering the canyon of sooty tenements, its line broken by a cluster of shops and the Clachan Bar, stretching all the way to Duncan Street and the badlands of the Avenues.

"This is where I was born, where I grew up," Chris said.

"Was it hard?"

Chris knew he risked frightening Solene that she'd come among a bad lot. He had to be honest with her. Take care of the issues now.

"Hard enough. Some rough customers. Once my old man got in tow with the Good Mother, life changed for the worse. She was a rascal, a filthy drunk."

A lacerating memory assailed Chris. The Headmaster of St. Mary's School sent a letter to his father telling him and the Good Mother to look after Chris and clean him up, or he'd be taken into care by the court. He was too ashamed to tell Solene.

"Decent folk live here, but it is shabby."

They stopped at the Salvation Army Hall opposite the chipper opened by Dante's father, Luigi. Dante still owned the shop but let it to a young man from Garbugliagio.

He'd mentioned the Rinaldis to Solene, but felt compelled to tell her again that Mrs Rinaldi, Celestina, and Graziella had helped him survive childhood. And Dante, home from the war in Italy, had made him a man.

"I'd be in the gutter without the Rinaldis."

"No, you wouldn't. I know you love the family and I'm dying to meet them. But you'd have found a way."

They turned and ran into Mrs Mulligan, Chris's old neighbour, returning home with shopping.

"Chris McCoull, you're a sight for sore eyes."

Mrs Mulligan shook Chris's hand.

"And who is this lovely girl you're with?"

Chris introduced Solene and Mrs Mulligan.

Nothing would do but they accept Mrs Mulligan's invitation to come up to the flat for a cup of tea. Chris knew the apartment would be spotless, but he worried that Solene might have to use the outside jakes. They passed the door of the flat where he grew up, occupied now by a young married couple. They sat in Mrs Mulligan's front room, the good room, dust-free, furniture gleaming, seldom used, the air suffused with the aroma of superior beeswax furniture polish.

They sat round a low table in front of the window overlooking Holmscroft Street, with a view of the Rinaldi chipper. They spent a pleasant hour taking tea and digestive biscuits. The Mulligan daughter had moved to Canada with her husband and the son had married, flitted to one of the new housing estates built on the frontiers of Westburn.

"How did you meet?"

"I'm from Martinique. I'm a dentist. I studied in Canada. I had a practice in Halifax. Chris was my patient.

Chris grinned. "I had an abscess, a toothache. Solene looked after me. My ship was in dry dock for a month."

"Chris asked me out and I said yes. We met often after that."

"And you came here?"

"We were apart for almost a year. I had to go home. Yes, I came to Scotland to find Chris again."

Mrs Mulligan, removed a handkerchief folded inside the slim silver bangle on her left wrist, and dabbed her eyes. She laughed.

"Och, sure I am an old fool, but it's such a lovely story."

Finished drying her eyes, Mrs Mulligan reminisced about the old days.

"I remember your mum and dad before the war. Such a handsome couple. I used to see them at the dancin'. Your Dad dad was a great dancer. Your mum was a lovely Irish lady."

Mrs Mulligan smothered a grin with her right hand.

"Chris was such a serious wee chap. His mum brought him round at Halloween. He was great wee Galoshan."

"What's that?"

"Like trick or treat."

Chris felt hot blushing spread up his neck to his face. What the hell would Mrs Mulligan say next?

"His dad was a great one for Ireland. Dressed Chris as a leprechaun." Mrs Mulligan looked at Solene. "You know, the wee folk."

Chris's face, a red beacon for a dark night, turned to Solene.

"A leprechaun, like an elf."

Solene smiled.

"He'd sing the Wearin' of The Green. Chris was a great wee singer. I'd give him an apple and an orange. If I was flush, I'd give him a few coppers, as well."

Happy days; his dad working Sunday overtime, Chris's mum dressed for Mass in her Sunday best. Bobbed auburn hair framing her sweet face; not a fashionable hairstyle in the late thirties and during the war, but the style suited his mum. She looked well in the grey wool fitted coat, black leather gloves and shoes, dressed for church. She'd cover her head before entering St. Patrick's Church, but Chris thought she looked better bare-headed.

"Yes, my mum was good-looking, and good-natured, too."

"It's a shame about the baffle wall falling on her. The bloody war."

Chris remembered the walls of corrugated sheeting, seven feet high, two feet thick and seven feet wide, stretching across the entrance to the tenements, the cavity filled with sand and brick stretching across the entrance to the tenements, forming a protective barrier against bomb blast.

A day after the Blitz his mother had walked down Provident Street, passing east on Cathcart Street, well clear, she thought, of the debris. A baffle wall, tottering by the rubble of a bombed-out tenement, collapsed on top of her. She was dead when the firemen dug her out.

Chris's sadness was overwhelming at his mum's funeral, taking her remains to the church the evening before burial. His father and seven neighbours carried the coffin on their shoulders down the centre isle of the church, and Chris shed bitter tears at the Requiem Mass. He remembered fondly the dignified way his father behaved during those terrible days.

Chris wanted Mrs Mullgan to stop. He knew she meant well, but she was making him sad and terrified she'd say something dreadful about life after his dad married the Good Mother.

Mrs Mulligan got up and went to the sideboard. She withdrew a bottle of Johnny Walker Red Label and three glasses. She poured three halfs.

"I meant to give you a drink earlier."

Mrs Mulligan talked about the hard war years, and what the chipper meant to the people of the neighbourhood.

"Mrs Rinaldi and Graziella always cheered us up. And them grieving for husbands killed in the war, and worried sick about Dante stuck in Italy. And Chris working in the back shop, looking out the door grinning at the customers."

"Chris told me about it."

"But I'll tell you this, Solene," and she gestured to Chris. "I was glad for Chris when Dante came back from the war in Italy, and him and Chris good pals. The pair of them, just a couple of lads, made that chipper great again. Just like before the war. You should have seen the pair of them in white aprons serving the best fish suppers in Westburn."

Chris looked at the floor, embarrassed, but proud, too.

"You've done well, Chris. You've come through hard times. You're a credit to your mum. She'd be proud of you, son."

Mrs Mulligan's mentioning his mum pleased Chris. They finished their whisky.

"Solene, Chris, come back and see me. Chris, you're a lucky chap. You look after Solene. She's a lovely lassie."

They shook hands and said farewell to Mrs Mulligan.

"Mrs Mulligan's alright," Chris said.

"I like Mrs Mulligan; she was so kind."

"Now you know everything about me."

"Oh, I want to know all about you. And I'll tell you everything about me in the coming days."

They walked the length of Nelson Street, turned left at George Square onto Union Street, heading for Forsyth Street.

"Your friends won't mind you bringing me to the house?"

"I'd be in trouble from Dante and Chiarina if I *didn't* bring you home."

* * *

The doorbell rang twice, piercing the quiet Sunday midafternoon. Lalia and Bella sprinted out of the kitchen from helping Chiarina set table for the family dinner in the early evening. They opened the front door.

Solene on Chris's arm, striking in her French clothes, looked down.

Lalia and Bella smiled, looking up at Solene.

"Uncle Chris," Lalia said, "is this lady Solene?"

"Yes, she is."

"Please come in," Bella said. "Mum, mum, come quick! Uncle Chris has brought Solene. She's a lovely black lady."

When Chiarina came from the kitchen, she found her daughters looking up to Solene's face, grinning like mad, each holding a gloved hand, having tugged her away from Chris and across the doorstep.

"Mum, Solene is here," Lalia said. "She's even nicer than in the pictures in Uncle Chris's room."

"She's lovely," Bella said.

"Lalia, Bella, let go of the young lady. Say you're sorry."

"Oh, it's all right. Lalia and Bella have been so nice to me."

Chiarina smiled. She too recognised Solene from her pictures.

"Solene, so nice to meet you. I'm Chiarina Rinaldi. Come right in. Lalia, Bella. Go up the stairs to your room, and play."

The girls dragged their feet away from the main door.

"Cheerio, Solene and Uncle Chris. Can we come and say goodbye when you leave?"

Solene smiled. "Of course, I'd like that; as long as your mum says yes."

That night nothing would do but Solene coming to stay with the Rinaldis in one of the spare bedrooms. While Chris cleaned up after the allotment, Dante went with Solene to The Old Hotel to settle the bill and pick up her luggage.

Chiarina put Solene in the room next to Chris. It had adjoining doors usually kept locked. Later, Dante gave the key to Chris.

"I know how you're both feeling. I talked to Chiarina, and it's okay. But take care, Chris, and not every night. Okay? I don't want Lalia and Bella asking awkward questions."

An embarrassed Chris took the key and whispered thanks.

"I asked Solene in Halifax if she'd marry me. She said yes. I'm going to ask again. I hope she'll say yes."

"She'll say yes. She didn't stand up for you and come here for fun. She looks at you the way you look at her."

Chris went to Solene. He dropped his robe. She raised the covers and he lay beside her.

"Oh, Chris, should we? What about Bella and Lalia?"

"It's all right. Dante and Chiarina know how we feel. Dante gave me the key. He just asked that we be careful; and not every night."

Solene held him.

"You are everything. It's wonderful that you love me."

"You're as crazy about me as I am crazy about you."

"You know everything about me."

They held each other and they stayed together for some hours, making love, sleeping and making love again.

Chris kissed Solene and left her bed before sunrise.

"Forget the shop for the next few days," Dante told Chris over breakfast. "Let Solene see the town that shaped you."

Chris had told Solene about his upbringing. Had taken Solene to where he'd grown up. Now, he'd show her the best of Westburn. He wanted Solene to be happy.

That Monday, fine early winter weather blessed the lovers: clear blue skies, pale sun shining from the south-west, giving warmth to sheltered spots. They walked up South Street to the vantage point on Lyle Hill and the Cross of Lorraine, the memorial to the sailors of the Free French Navy who died in the Battle of the Atlantic.

"Westburn was the headquarters of the Free French Navy during the war," Chris said.

"I didn't know that."

"France sends a warship every year. Sailors parade and lay a wreath."

"My brother Yann would like this."

They gazed at the Cowal Peninsula and the Argyll Hills, the peaks and edges sharp on the skyline. A few cargo ships lay at anchor in the blue waters of the Tail o' the Bank, waiting on berths.

"Cold?"

"Oh no. I'm used to freezing Halifax winters."

Chris pointed to the wild quarter below the hill. "Dante and me, we used to hunt rabbits down there. At the end of the war there was rationing; hardly any meat."

"It's beautiful. All of it," Solene said. She swept her arm to the horizon.

"Yes, it is," Chris said.

They walked down Lyle Road to Eldon Street and on to The Esplanade, the river on their left, past the Royal West Rowing Club, and strolled the mile and a quarter length admiring the fine Victorian houses. They walked up Campbell Street, past the bombed-out West End Baths, turned onto Union Street, and made for The Old Hotel.

John Turner made a great fuss, and said they were his guests for lunch. Chris accepted the gift with good grace, but would leave a generous tip for the staff who'd looked after them.

"You order for me," Solene said.

She looked around the quiet, well-proportioned oak-panelled room. They had the place to themselves.

"Mondays are quiet," Chris said.

"It's a dining room for intimacy," Solene said. "A haven for lovers."

They dined on plain Scots fare: a full-flavoured mushroom soup, roast point of the rump, served rare. Mashed potatoes, finely chopped cabbage. A glass or two of red wine. Duff and custard. Coffee.

But Chris had a nagging worry. Where would they live? He had to know how Solene felt. He refilled her coffee cup.

"Solene, you have to tell me. Do you think you'd be okay living here? Would you be happy in Westburn? If you're worried about anything, I'll come with you to France or to Martinique."

Solene, wiser than Chris, knew that she could make the leap to Westburn much easier than Chris could move to France or

Martinique. He had more to give up. And she, with a Canadian degree in dentistry, was confident of finding work, and longer-term, setting up practice.

"I want to live here as long as you're with me."

"I'm not going back to sea. I'm still working for Mr Michas, but no more deep sea."

"Oh, Chris, I wanted so much to hear you say that."

Chris caught Solene's hand under the table and she laid it on her stockinged leg.

"Jesus, Solene; I couldn't stand being away from you."

"What will you do?"

"Well, Dante and me, we talked about opening a restaurant. I'd be a partner. I've put up some cash. There's work going on in the premises, getting the place ready."

After lunch they walked back to the Rinaldis' house on Forsyth Street. It was Monday afternoon, so Dante was at the chipper preparing for the evening opening. Chiarina and the children were visiting Graziella.

They went to Solene's room and made love.

"We can't keep doing this," Solene said, lying in Chris's embrace.

"You're right. Let's marry. Have our own place. You'd like that?"

"Above all things. Bébé, bébé, I love you. Everything is going so fast, just as I hoped."

* * *

Two weeks passed since the lovers had decided to make things permanent and get married. They decided that they wanted nothing to do with priests. Both of them had been put off their faith by contact with stupid, malevolent clergy: in Solene's case, Father Andre, her parish priest in Martinique, and for Chris, the spectre of Toner, the detested parish priest of St. Patrick's. Father Andre was far away, but Toner would jump at the opportunity to humiliate with rude, awkward questions. Dante, anxious to help, suggested one of the younger curates in St. Mary's.

"Dante, it's kind of you to offer help. But I'm wary of priests after what happened to me."

"That was bad, Solene. I didn't mean to interfere."

"Don't be daft, Dante," Chris said. "You're not interfering. But no priests."

And they needed a place of their own. To be together. In censorious Westburn it would never do for them, unmarried, to set up house and live in sin.

Solene was anxious to return to work. Dante, with many friends and associates in the Italian community and among Westburnians, made enquiries. A local dentist wanted to hire a locum. Dante made contact and he interviewed Solene. He was delighted and she would start work in a week. It was a good first step.

Longer term, Solene meant to open her own practice. She had the capital.

* * *

Saturday mid-morning. A thin rain falling. Trees dripping, a curtain of fine drizzle enveloping the garden, too wet for the children to play outside. Bella and Lalia roamed the house, but always returned after a few minutes to the kitchen where Dante, Chiarina, Chris and Solene sat round the table drinking coffee. Lalia and Bella loved to listen to the adults; they had taken a particular liking to Solene. And Chiarina had given up chasing her daughters into another room to play.

The doorbell rang twice.

"I wonder who that is at this time in the morning," Dante said.

Before he could rise from the table the girls had rushed out the kitchen to open the door. The adults paused in conversation, expecting to hear a voice or voices in the hall.

Silence.

"I'll go," Chris said.

Chris found Lalia and Bella fixed to the spot, holding hands, surprised at seeing their first black man waiting in the doorway.

"Uncle Chris, he says he's your friend," Lalia said.

"And so he is. He's my good friend Fernandez Xavier from my ship, the Peliopadus. Ask him to come in. Tell Solene and your mum and dad we have a visitor."

Fernandez, wet from walking from the James Watt Dock where the Peliopadus berthed, wiped his feet.

"Ah, good morning, McCoull Sahib. Very glad to see you again."

Chris helped him remove his pea jacket. The old shipmates shook hands and Chris embraced Fernandez.

The Peliopadus, with a cargo of sugar bound for the Thames and Surrey Docks, had a change of orders to discharge in Westburn. Mr Michas had taken the opportunity to have minor repairs carried out by the Outside Squad from Reid's Foundry.

Chris grabbed Fernandez's shoulder and steered him towards the bathroom. He took a fresh towel from the linen basket.

"Here, my friend, your head is soaking."

Chris ushered Fernandez into the kitchen.

"Oh, Fernandez, what a lovely surprise," Solene said.

Solene held Fernandez's hand and kissed him on the cheeks. Poor Fernandez blushed, glad but overcome at the intimacy.

"Oh, Memsahib, I pleased to see you again."

Chris introduced Fernandez to Chiarina and Dante. Dante pulled a chair back from the table.

"Sit down, beside Chris and Solene."

"Welcome, welcome, Fernandez," Chiarina said. "Chris has told us so many good things about you."

"Thank you, thank you, Memsahib."

"I'll drink to that," Dante said.

Fernandez, sent by Captain Graham, had an invitation for Chris. Dinner tomorrow evening aboard the Peliopadus; bring any friend he chose. Mr Michas would be aboard, staying in the owner's suite, arriving Saturday evening. It was his personal invitation to Chris.

"Captain Graham and Chief Barnes on board," Fernandez said. "But new Captain and new chief coming. Mr Michas, he make big changes to Michas Lines.

* * *

Dante gave Chris and Solene a lift to the Peliopadus at the sugar berth in the James Watt Dock. Fernandez, in white liveried jacket and dark trousers, waited for them at the brow.

"Welcome, McCoull Sahib and Good Missus. Mr Michas waiting for you."

They followed Fernandez to the owner's suite on the boat deck.

"Does Fernandez think we're married?" Solene said.

"No; he likes you, Solene. He's being very polite."

Chris had been in the suite many times during his five years aboard the Peliopadus. It comprised a sleeping cabin with ample storage, and a day room with light stained oak panelling on the bulkheads. Plain, good quality furniture: a settee, four matching easy chairs, a low, ornate mahogany table from India. On the inboard side stood a light oak dining table and six matching chairs. Fernandez had laid table for six with the ship's best silver and china.

Solene took to Mr Michas, an avuncular man of sixty, tall at six feet, and a trim figure. He carried himself straight and erect.

"Trade is good. I'm going to order two new ships, here in Westburn, at the Dockyard," Mr Michas said. "Klondike, the locals call the yard. They build ships for Clan Line. I'll buy four

Liberty ships to start Michas Lines's expansion. Reid's Foundry and Klondike will get them up to Michas Lines standards."

Mr Michas managed company business from offices in London and Piraeus: finding cargoes, crewing and arranging repairs. Growth meant delegation, and movement. He would continue to register his ships in Panama.

"I've offered Captain Graham the job of Marine Superintendent, and Chief Wally Barnes the Engineering Superintendent's job.

"Good men," Chris said.

"You're a good man, Chris. Both have accepted. I'm moving the head office to Glasgow, rubbing shoulders with Clan Line, Anchor Line, Ellerman's, Lyle Shipping, Andrew Weir's. But I'll have a presence in London and Piraeus.

There's a new position in the company: Catering Superintendent."

He described the job: based in the Glasgow office with some travel to European and UK ports, and India. A small staff reporting to the superintendent. A handsome salary.

"How would you like the job?"

Chris glanced at Solene, anxious to know how she felt about the offer. Their eyes locked. Solene raised her eyebrows as she inclined her head.

"Yes, delighted to accept, Mr Michas. Thank you. I'm honoured."

"Oh, Mr Michas, Chris, that's wonderful," Solene said.

And Solene, filled with happiness knowing the job meant they could be together in Westburn and Chris could build on his successful years in Michas Lines.

"Well, I know two people who'll be pleased you've accepted," Mr Michas said.

He rang for Fernandez to invite Captain Graham and Chief Wally Barnes to dine.

"Chris, Solene," Captain Graham said. "Wonderful to see you again."

"I had a hunch we'd be working together, Chris," Wally said.

He grabbed Solene by her hands and raised her to her feet. "Miss Aimie. You're a sight for sore eyes. And you're with Chris. My heart is glad."

He kissed Solene on both cheeks. Solene blushed but was pleased by the warmth of Wally's greeting.

"I'd hoped for Greek food," Mr Michas said. "But you are on leave, Chris. Your successor and Fernandez have prepared something special."

They dined on a lightly spiced Goanese prawn soup with oysters added. The main course was salmon en croute—delicious crisp pastry layers, spinach, soft cream cheese and prime Scotch salmon, served with roasted asparagus spears, tomatoes, and small roast potatoes. A perfect dish for this special evening. They drank white wine from Mr Michas's stock, Biblia Chora Areti.

"Good wine from the island of Santorini," Mr Michas said. He smiled. "Not too expensive; perfect with seafood and fish."

"Great food," Chris said. "My successor is doing a good job."

"That he is," Captain Graham said.

"There's been improvements in Catering throughout the fleet," Mr Michas said.

"Word of your work aboard the Peliopadus spread," Wally Barnes said.

"A couple of ships are lagging. Catering stuck in the old ways," Mr Michas added. "But I'll leave that to you to put right, Chris."

Solene couldn't suppress the smile, the euphoria. She glanced at Chris, evidently proud of him.

For dessert they had Golub Jamun, Punjabi donuts deep fried and covered in sweet syrup, served hot in creamy yogurt.

"Delicious with yogurt," Captain Graham said. "Sweet and sour flavours."

Chris whispered to Solene, "I bet Fernadez made the Golub Jamun. He's a dab hand."

Dinner finished, the company relaxed at table. They sipped good Madras coffee. Mr Michas poured Metaxa Five Star Greek Brandy to celebrate their new venture. He refilled their glasses.

"To Chris and Solene: may you be happy all your lives."

"We're not married yet, but we're going to marry soon," Chris said.

Neither Chris nor Solene wanted to discuss their difficulties with priests. But Wally Barnes, an old Merseyside Tim, knew the curse of the Irish priesthood. Often at sea he and Chris had swapped yarns, and he'd jaloused that despite knocking hell out of his daughter, Solene's father would have the support of a priest in Martinique. He looked at Captain Graham, who nodded.

"There's a relieving skipper coming on board in a couple of days. He's an old Union Castle man."

"Correct, Wally," Mr Michas said. "When I interviewed him he mentioned on Union Castle passenger ships captains had a licence to marry couples. He has one."

Mr Michas glanced at Captain Graham.

"Well, Chris, Solene. You could get married aboard the Peliopadus. She'll be in port for a couple of weeks."

"Solene, Chris," Mr Michas said. "You'd honour the ship and the company if you said yes."

About the Author

I'm from the West of Scotland. I served five years as an apprentice engineer, followed by three years as a sea-going engineer. Then, a year as a tool setter in a canning factory.

I worked in IBM Manufacturing for almost three decades, managing production planning and personnel.

I followed IBM with ten years lecturing at Glasgow Caledonian University, teaching my research interests, and supervising undergraduate and postgraduate research. I have a BA (Hons.), History and Literature, and an MSc, by research. I studied organisational behaviour and the history of management ideas.

I've been writing for some time.

When I'm not writing, I'm reading.

I listen to Jazz and enjoy travelling the world with my wife.

Books by the Author

One Summer
The Last Hundred
The Music Room
Westburn Blues

Lightning Source UK Ltd.
Milton Keynes UK
UKHW050152120521
383500UK00010BA/597/J

9 781034 372912